# THE LAST NURSE

## Dani King

Front cover image by Rbkka.

Lastnurse.com

Print ISBN: 978-1-66783-605-8

eBook ISBN: 978-1-66783-606-5

Printed in the United States of America on SFI Certified paper.

First Edition

Valerie, this one's for you.

# ACKNOWLEDGEMENTS

I would like to start by saying that even though I've loosely based some aspects of this story on my real-life experiences, knowledge, and emotions, this is a completely fictional work and in no way represents my past or current employers, my family, or my friends. All names, characters, places and occurrences are a product of my imagination, fictional in nature. Any resemblance to actual events, people, places, or business establishments is purely coincidental.

I would also like to further clarify that this novel does not portray either a likeness to my mother's character or my personal relationship with my mother. She has voiced her fears that people will read this novel and throw tomatoes at her if they see her in public. I kindly ask if you see my mom, please don't throw produce at her. She's my best friend.

On that note, I would like to thank my parents, David (Smitty) and Toni Smith for their undying support over the years and for raising me to reach for the stars.

Thank you to my loving husband, Joshua King, for his support during this entire process including, most importantly, allowing me to lock myself inside my office for days on end to write this novel.

Thank you to John Juadines for not only convincing me to sign up for that self-publishing class, but for taking it along with me. It was in that class, on pen and paper, that I wrote the first few pages of this story. Also, thank you for convincing me I couldn't write a novel by hand, motivating me to buy a working laptop.

A huge thank you to my fearless editors, Molly McBride and Anthony Cabrera. The two of them helped me take a rough draft of ideas and turn it into a story—a story I'm proud of. None of this would be possible without both of you.

Thank you to Rbkka for creating such a breathtaking cover. You took the picture inside my head and brought it to life.

Thank you to my very first readers, Kaylee King, Robert Bezotte, Denise King, Melany Laughter and Ijana Loss. (Robert explicitly refused to be called a "beta reader.")

Thank you to Alexander Torres, Chase White, Jaymi Letchworth, Andrea Collins, Penny Pukall and Ijana. In one way or another, all of you shared parts of your own stories with me (be it professional or personal) to help create this story.

I have to thank my three best friends growing up, Brittny Sanchez, Lydia Favela and Jennifer Roberts, for standing by me all these years. Being friends with the three of you has undoubtedly made me a better person.

I would like to thank my real-life Sober Squad. Finding all of you helped remind me that I wasn't alone in a world that can feel so lonely.

A special thank you to my friend Neshelle Infantino for teaching me the ways of technology (or at least trying to) and convincing me that I could do this—that I could actually write a book.

Last but certainly not least, I would like to thank all of the amazing people I've had the opportunity to work beside in my decade of nursing. Thank you for the constant sacrifices you continue to make in your own lives to be able to care for those who desperately need you. As much as I wrote this story for me, I also wrote it for all of you. It's time the world truly knew what it means to dedicate your life to the service of others.

# PROLOGUE:

At some point during childhood, most every child wishes they could be a superhero. Of course, there's the kid who wants to be a ballerina with a sparkling pink tutu and a perfect pirouette, or the kid who longs to be an astronaut who rockets into space and dances on the moon. But the epitome of any awesome childhood fantasy career has to be the superhero.

Superheroes are undeniably appealing. They're strong. They're fast. Some of them can even fly. (I know, right? Who doesn't want to be able to fly?)

Admit it. Whether you wished to morph into a badass Power Ranger, to respond to a personalized signal and slide into your tricked out Batmobile, or even to flawlessly wield a truth-revealing lasso, you have indeed wished to be a superhero at one point in your youth. But besides all the cool gadgets and rad powers, what is it that's truly the most admirable quality of a superhero? I think all us fanatics can agree, it's the fact that they save people. Superheroes swoop in at the direst of times, when all hope is lost and they save the day, they save lives.

As the little girl in the Superman shirt is led down the long, cold corridor of the building where "the sick people go," she wishes she could just fly away like Superman. She thinks of all the comic books she has read, all the cartoons she has watched, and wishes she, herself, was a real-life superhero. She wishes she could be the one to save him. The one to swoop in and save the day since they now know that all hope is lost.

She grasps her tiny hand around her father's strong one and obediently places one foot in front of the other; she must keep moving. She gazes up at her father, tears welling in her eyes. Until today she could have sworn her dad was a real-life superhero. He always made everything better. When there were monsters hiding in her closet, he would be the one to slay them. When she fell off her bike and skinned her knee, he was there within seconds to carry her to safety. She knew this wasn't his fault, she wasn't mad at her father. She knew that if her dad could save him—if he could take all the hurt away—he would. But this monster was just too big. This hurt was just too bad. Their family had finally met their match.

She continued clutching her father's hand as they floated down the long hallway. She didn't even feel like she was walking anymore. She no longer felt like she was intentionally moving her feet, yet she somehow continued moving forward. She was drifting away on what felt like a stream of tears. As she looked up once more toward her father, she saw tears mirroring her own rolling down his face. He forcefully brushed the tears from his cheek with his opposite hand.

As they continued floating on their tears to his room, a lady in pajamas with a big, shiny necklace draped across her neck rushed by them. The lady softly smiled at her as she passed. It was a knowing smile, a sad smile. Her dad informed her that the lady was not in fact wearing pajamas and a gaudy necklace, but she was wearing something called scrubs and a stethoscope. Her father told her that the nice lady was a nurse, and a nurse's job was to help sick people. She timidly glanced back over her shoulder at the lady that passed, thinking to herself that maybe nurses were kind of like superheroes but in outfits that looked like pajamas.

When they neared his room, she could hear guttural sobs, the cries of which were undeniably her mother's. She had heard her mother make such sounds before, late at night locked away in her bedroom over the last few months. However, this was the first time she had heard her make these noises in the light of day rather than behind the safety of her bedroom door where she thought no one could hear her despair. The little girl knew that for her mother to allow herself to be seen and heard so uncomposed in public, her brother's situation had to have moved from bad to worse.

The little girl's mother was the definition of perfection. Or at least that is how she portrayed herself to the outside world. She was always impeccably groomed, her clothes always so lovely, fitting her slender frame perfectly. Her hair was always styled into flawless curls that seemed to effortlessly cascade down her back, unlike the little girl's own hair that often resembled a frizzy nest where birds would reside. Her mother always seemed to carry herself with such grace and poise. The outside world could have easily mistaken her for a real-life princess, but the little girl knew better. Her mother was hurting more than she would ever let the world see and, over the years to come, the hidden pain her mother concealed would slowly start to destroy them all. Unbeknownst to the little girl, this would be the last day in a very long time where she felt she had a mother who truly cared for her, a mother who could look into her daughter's dark blue eyes and not be reminded of what she lost on that cold December day.

As the little girl and her father reached the doorway to Matthew's hospital room, their silent stream of tears met with her mother's ocean of violent cries. No longer did the girl feel like she was mindlessly floating in her sadness; now she was drowning in the sorrow that filled the small room located at the Summit Valley Pediatric ICU. The little girl felt like she could no longer breathe. Her chest was heavy, and her reddened cheeks were soaked with tears. She could not do this. She was not strong enough. The t-shirt she adorned was just a lie. She was no Superman. She was simply a scared, seven-year-old girl who was about to lose her brother.

As she attempted to run out of the hospital room that held a little boy who no longer resembled the older brother she once knew, she collided into the legs of a different nurse lady in a pair of bright yellow scrub pajamas. After collecting herself, the little girl hurled her small body around the new nurse lady and slid to the cold, shiny floor of the hallway. Her tiny body aggressively shook with every sob that escaped her.

Suddenly, she felt a kind hand rest upon her shoulder. She expected to look up and see the face of her father waiting to console her. Her mother had recoiled so enormously from her role within the family over the last few months that the girl would have been astounded if she managed to pull herself away from her son's bedside to console her daughter. The girl doubted her mother even noticed her existence anymore, let alone her sudden and obvious distress. As the little girl peered up through her pool of tears, she realized it was neither her mother nor her father but the new nurse lady she had just passed.

The nurse, in scrubs that looked like sunshine, slowly kneeled until she was seated beside her. The lady spoke softly, "Hi sweetheart. My name is Emma and I'm going to be your brother's new nurse. I brought you an apple juice. Are you thirsty?"

The little girl slowly nodded, timidly reaching for the small carton of juice. While the little girl cautiously sipped, the nurse's smile grew as she asked, "Do you like Superman? I'm a big fan of superheroes too. My favorite is Wonder Woman."

The girl's face immediately lit up, "I love Superman! Wonder Woman is cool too, but not as cool as Superman. Sorry, it's the truth. When I grow up, I want to be a superhero."

Emma let out a loud laugh that took the girl by surprise. The girl never heard anyone laugh at this place where all the sick people go.

Once the girl took the last sip of her apple juice, she moved her gaze from the shiny, white hospital floor to Emma's friendly smile. "Is it okay if I ask you a question?" the little girl inquired.

Emma's smile widened, "Of course, sweetie. Shoot!" The little girl's brows furrowed as she pondered over Emma's reply. "What am I supposed to shoot?" the girl questioned.

Once more, the joyous sounds of Emma's unconfined laughter echoed throughout the gloomy halls of the hospital floor. "Oh, honey!" Emma chuckled. "I forget that I'm talkin' to a tiny human. It's what we call a figure of speech. It means 'go ahead and ask all the questions your lil' heart desires."

The girl grinned, "I know you don't have a cape or anything, but my dad told me that nurses help people just like superheroes do. I was wondering...are you a superhero?"

Emma's smile somehow became even bigger. "Well, that's a really good question," she thoughtfully replied. "I'd like to think that, in a way, us nurses are kind of unsung heroes. We go to work each day and before anything else, even ourselves, we put our patients first. We make their needs and comfort our primary focus for twelve hours a day. We are healers by nature and when we're unable to heal, we try our best to ease the pain and to take away the fear. That's the type of nurse I am." Emma paused briefly, her smile appearing sadder as she softly placed her hand atop one of the little girl's hands. "I am a nurse that comes to help a person be comfortable when a sickness can't be healed. I help take the pain away, so they don't hurt anymore. Do you understand, honey?" Emma asked.

The little girl slowly nodded once more as she lifted her gaze from the nurse's hand resting atop her own. Her dark blue eyes locked with Emma's honey-colored eyes, and she confidently proclaimed, "I want to be a nurse when I grow up, just like you!"

Once again, Emma's grin grew wide. "Well, sweetheart. I think you would make an excellent nurse one day, but you have lots of time to decide. In the meantime, my dear, there's something we gotta do," Emma replied. She slowly stood, still holding the little girl's hand within her own. The girl followed Emma's lead. She lifted her body from the unforgiving hospital floor, and the pair somberly walked into Matthew's room hand in hand.

When they reached the threshold of her brother's room, the girl immediately felt the climate change. The artificial air pumping from the ceiling vent felt icy and bitter; the atmosphere of the room felt cruel and ruthless. Her parents sat on either side of the narrow hospital bed that was positioned in the middle of the small room. Her father was tightly grasping Matthew's frail hand with both of his own. Upon hearing them enter the room, her father swiftly rotated his body in the small chair to face his little girl. His eyes were full of tears as he smiled at her. The little girl thought she had never seen eyes that looked so sad.

"Come here pumpkin. Come sit with me," he sweetly coaxed. The girl released Nurse Emma's hand and raced into her father's awaiting arms, the only place where she truly felt safe. She buried her face into her father's shirt as the sobs returned for what felt like the hundredth time that day. He gently rocked her back and forth on his lap as, once more, their separate tears united to become a single stream of anguish.

When the girl regained her breath and her tears momentarily ceased, she raised her head from the comfort of her father's chest. She rested her gaze upon her mother, sitting on the opposite side of Matthew's bed. She silently noted to herself that her mother hadn't once acknowledged her presence since returning to the hospital with her father today. It's rare her mother sees her at all these days. If she does see her, it means she sees him, the child she can't save, the child she is losing. Her mother's upper body was splayed over Matthew's as she wept into his chest.

Her mom repeatedly whined, "My baby, not my baby! Don't leave me, not yet!" Suddenly, the girl felt pure anger towards her mother. She wasn't the only one losing him. The little girl was losing her big brother, her best friend in the entire world.

Matty was the one who told her about Superman, her absolute favorite superhero. Matty's favorite was Batman, but she always thought Batman was too flashy. Matty was who taught her how to read comic books, because there is a certain way they are supposed to be read. "Any true comic book fan knows that!" Matty would tell her.

The little girl almost forgot her new friend Nurse Emma was in the room. She was always told by her parents to be cautious around strangers, but even though she only knew Nurse Emma for a short time, she felt as though she could trust her. She felt as if she was already her friend.

Nurse Emma carefully walked around Matthew's bed and placed her hand lightly upon the mother's shoulder. "Mrs. Carter, my name is Emma. I am one of the registered nurses from the hospice floor. I have already spoken with your husband but wanted to be sure you were in agreement with Matthew's new plan of care."

Emma gazed down at the mother's hunched, shaking form, patiently waiting for a reply. Without lifting her body from where it rested on Matthew's chest most of the afternoon, the mother forcefully snapped, "I am aware that we have no other options now. Do what you must."

The girl's father spoke hurriedly, with an apologetic tone, "Thank you again for coming to us, Emma. We truly do appreciate it."

Emma slowly removed her hand from the mother's shoulder and walked toward the girl's father. She quietly spoke, "With Matthew's sudden change in condition, it would just be too traumatic to try to transfer him to our unit now. We want to make him as comfortable as possible at this time."

As the little girl absorbed what Nurse Emma said, for the first time all afternoon, she turned her gaze onto her brother's face. He looked like a shell of the Matty she knew. His cheeks were sunken, dark purple circles rested beneath his eyes, his lips had begun to take on a bluish tint, and the skin on his face appeared abnormally pale and waxy. She knew Matty was really sick. She knew that the monster he had been fighting for so long was finally declaring victory, and the monster's prize would be her nine-year-old brother. Her parents thought she was merely a baby, that she didn't understand, that her seven-year-old brain couldn't possibly comprehend what was happening. They were so incredibly wrong. She knew exactly what was going on. The little girl even knew the monster's name. She heard her parents whisper it many times when they didn't think she could hear. This was the worst monster of all time, much worse than the monsters in any of her comic books at home. Even her beloved Superman was no match for this evil, brother-stealing monster named Cancer.

The little girl climbed down from her father's lap as Emma continued speaking to her father in a hushed way. The girl suspected this was so her mother couldn't hear them. She tiptoed to the head of her brother's bed, peeking her head over the side rail. Matty was sleeping now. Earlier, she heard a man in a white coat tell her parents Matty wasn't going to wake up or talk to them anymore. Suddenly, the girl had visions of watching *Sleeping Beauty* on their VCR at home, curled in her mother's lap, the two of them sharing a bowl of salty, buttery microwave popcorn.

If Matty could hear her next thought, she knew he would cringe: what if all he needed was true love's kiss to wake him up and make everything better? I mean, it also worked for Snow White so there must be something to it, right? But once again, tears came to the little girl's eyes as she remembered her brother was only nine years old. From what she knew, nine-year-old kids usually didn't have true loves yet. And in her brother's case, "not yet" actually meant "never," because Matty would forever be nine years old, frozen in this moment for all of time. Although the little girl would continue getting older and growing bigger, the brother she once knew would eternally remain the young boy that fell asleep and couldn't wake up again, not even to say goodbye to his sister.

As the little girl inched her small hand through the bed's side rail to rest it on her brother's cold arm, she noticed he was breathing differently than she had seen him breathe before. He almost looked like he was snoring but without sound. She noticed his breathing was more spaced than normal, as if he was trying to hold his breath but then decided he needed a few short, small breaths every so often. She was reminded of last summer, swimming at the community center with Matty, and how awful he had been at holding his breath under-water. She always could beat him by at least ten seconds.

The girl turned to look toward her parents. Her mother remained hunched over, completely removed from the world. Her father contin-ued to be in what looked like a very important conversation with Nurse Emma. The little girl wanted to ask why Matty's breathing suddenly looked different, but she was always scolded for interrupting adults talking. She didn't want to have to sit in timeout and leave Matty's side. She had been notorious for her stints in timeout lately.

The last timeout she was unfairly given, she ended up propelling her tiny chair over her head, hurling it to the ground where it subse-quently splintered into pieces. She hadn't broken the chair to be an "ungrateful brat" like her mother had called her. She had broken the chair simply so her mother would speak to her at all. She indeed got her wish when her mother began to uncontrollably scream at her. At least in that very moment she felt like her mother remembered she existed. Her mother eventually locked herself away in her bedroom, summoning the girl's father to pick up the pieces of their daughter's newest tantrum. The little girl's father guided her to stand in the corner of the room facing the cream-colored wall for the remainder of her timeout as he picked up the pieces of the chair she had ruined.

This time, the girl decided interrupting was worth the possibility of a timeout. At least the walls on this floor, where the kids went that were sick like Matty, had paintings of animals on them which were much more interesting for staring purposes than cream-colored walls.

She gathered up her last ounce of courage and squeaked, "Daddy, why is Matty breathing like when our goldfish fell out of the water when I accidentally knocked his bowl over?"

As the girl spoke the last word of her question, she heard the deafening sound of her mother's scream. Her father and Nurse Emma rushed to where the little girl was standing. The girl watched as Emma took the stethoscope she wore around her neck and fit one end of it into her ears, placing the other end onto her brother's chest.

Emma looked to the girl's father and said, "He is transitioning now, Mr. Carter. This is what we call agonal breathing. It's just a sign that he is very close to passing. It doesn't mean he is distressful, even though it sometimes can appear that way. The Morphine drip he is on should hopefully keep him from feeling any pain."

The words Nurse Emma spoke made no sense to the little girl, but her father must have understood because he solemnly nodded his head as he lifted the little girl into his strong arms. On most days, she felt she was too old to be carried like she was a baby; today, she felt as if she never wanted her father to let her go.

"Don't let me go Daddy," the girl whispered into her father's ear. "Never, pumpkin. Never," he whispered back into his daughter's wavy brown hair. Her father continued holding her tightly as he turned to his wife. As her father spoke, the girl could feel him shaking. She could feel his pain.

"Caroline, I don't think Samantha should be here for this. This is too much. She's too young. I'm going to take her to the cafeteria to sit with the rest of the family." The girl's mother swiftly nodded towards her husband, then returned her attention to her son lying in the narrow hospital bed, taking the last few breaths this world would allow him.

The girl immediately reacted to her father's attempt to remove her from her brother's side, "Daddy, no! Don't take me away from Matty, he needs me. I'm the Robin to his Batman." She sobbed, "Batman needs Robin!"

Her father cried into her mess of brown waves tied in a haphazard ponytail atop her head. "You will understand all of this one-day pumpkin, but today you need to go with your Aunt Cindy."

As the girl's father began carrying her out of the hospital room and into her aunt's waiting arms, the girl screamed for her father to stop. "Wait, Daddy! Wait! I have to give Matty something!"

The girl's memory drifted back to the many lazy Sunday afternoons she and Matty spent playing their favorite game together on their Nintendo, Super Mario Brothers. Matty had taught her how to play when she turned six. She was so excited to finally be able to play with him and religiously listened to every word as he instructed her on which buttons to press. Matty said he taught her how to play so he could have help fighting all the big bosses. Being that she was only six then, she was pretty scared of these monsters he called "the big bosses." He confidently told her, "Sam, you just can't try to fight a big boss alone. You have to help each other, that way it's not so scary. You'll see!"

After her father gently let her down out of his protective hold, she scurried over to her brother's bedside where her friend, Nurse Emma, stood checking machines that she knew gave Matty the medicine he needed. The girl's dark blue eyes expectantly looked up at the closest thing to a real-life superhero she had ever seen, besides her own dad of course. She timidly asked, "Can Matty still hear me?"

Emma kneeled and brought both of the girl's petite hands into her own. "I truly believe he can, sweetie. Matthew knows his sister is here with him. You go ahead and talk to your Matty. Don't be scared. Even though he looks a little different now, he's still your brother."

The little girl turned on her heels to face her brother's bed and dove her small hand into her coat pocket. She pulled out her favorite Superman action figure. She carried him with her everywhere. She gave Superman a swift kiss (for luck, of course) and gently placed her most valuable possession on Matty's pillow beside his head. Her hand then found its rightful place upon her brother's slender arm. She whispered to him, "You have to face the big boss now, Matty. But don't be scared. You won't have to fight him alone, now."

She turned around and walked back into the safety net of her father's arms. As she waved goodbye to her new friend Emma, she realized the nurse looked like she was crying now, too. *Tears must be contagious when the monster named Cancer is involved*, she thought.

The girl's father lifted her back into his arms as Emma walked over to them. Emma smiled at the little girl and softly said, "Matthew is lucky to have such a strong and brave sister. You are my hero, Miss Samantha."

The girl shyly smiled at Nurse Emma as her father carried her back out into the hallway. Waiting outside the room was her Aunt Cindy with arms wide open for her to climb into.

"It's time Cindy," her father breathed. "Thanks for taking Samantha. She shouldn't have to see this." Cindy replied to her brother through her own tears, "Of course, Mark. I'm always here. Whatever you need, I'm here."

Once the girl was safely nestled into her aunt's arms, her father kissed her on the top of her head and quickly rushed back into Matthew's room. The girl knew her Aunt Cindy was her father's little sister, just like she was Matthew's little sister. She mourned the fact that she would never be granted the same future with her big brother.

As the girl's aunt cradled her in her loving embrace, she began the long descent down the cold hospital corridor to the cafeteria where the rest of her family waited for news that they prayed wouldn't be the news they were about to receive. The little girl gazed once more upon the room that concealed her Matty within it. She knew in that moment that, although, she would never see her brother again, she would never forget a single thing about him.

As Matty's hospital room faded into a blur of fluorescent lights and tears, she thought about something that often consumed her waking thoughts—superheroes. She knew that superheroes were people with special powers that saved those who needed help. The world needs superheroes to protect us from all the scary bad guys, from all the big bosses, and especially from the monsters they call Cancer. The little girl thought of people like Matty and of the monsters that were just too bad and too strong to conquer. She asked herself, "Don't the people who can't be saved need heroes, too?"

As her eyes began feeling heavy from what seemed like the gallons upon gallons of tears she shed on that cold December day, she finally allowed herself to fall into a dreamless sleep in the comfort of her favorite aunt's arms. The last thought that came to Samantha Carter's mind at 3:57 PM on December 9th, 1997, was that, just maybe, she could grow up to be a superhero like her new friend Nurse Emma. Sam didn't hear the wail that escaped from deep within her mother's soul or the loud thud of her father's knees crashing to the unforgiving hospital floor.

At the very same moment Sam had drifted off to sleep, her brother Matty had drifted away.

# CHAPTER ONE

## (November 2011):

Alarms. Alarms sounding everywhere. I stand frozen in place as people rush back and forth in front of me. Everyone is moving quickly but with calculated purpose. The ICU, or intensive care unit operates efficiently, like a buzzing beehive. And, of course every hive has its queen bee. This hive's queen bee yells my name, snapping me back to reality. To make matters worse, she yells my *full* name, which I have reminded her time and again that I despise. But now is not the time for logistics.

I hear the hospital intercom system roar above me, "Code Blue, room 252. All available personnel. Code Blue, room 252."

Margo Hatcher, said queen bee of Summit Valley Hospital ICU, calls detailed instructions to me as I attempt to thrust a crash cart with a lopsided wheel across the hospital floor. I'm immediately regretting not going to the gym more last semester, because I'm now aware that my struggle to maneuver this cart is wildly apparent.

Margo Hatcher momentarily pauses her delegating to glare at me. My God, she's terrifying. "Samantha, if you cannot handle steering a simple cart, maybe I should have you sit back down and continue needlessly color-coordinating your insignificant flashcards," she spits in my direction.

If I could say what I wish I could, I would coolly reply that this crash cart is absolutely ancient. But probably not quite as ancient as my bitchy preceptor. And this cheap ass hospital should at least invest in some WD-40 if they won't cough up enough money for new carts.

Unfortunately, because this is real life, I would most likely be kicked out of this clinical rotation for speaking anything that nearly resembled the truth. I'm also not ashamed to admit that I'm deathly afraid of my preceptor. So, I make the intelligent decision to keep my mouth shut.

I try to calm my rapid breathing and attempt to gain some control of the crash cart I'm uncontrollably hurling down the corridor toward room 252. Now is not the time for another anxiety attack. I'm so exhausted with trying to battle my increasing feelings of anxiety. Why can't I just get my shit together? As my mother lovingly tells me whenever I'm battling these feelings, "Stop acting like such a fragile, little flower, Samantha. You have to grow a backbone or life will just swallow you whole!"

Well, isn't that just the pot calling the kettle black? My mother, or Caroline as I refer to her now, is literally the most fragile person I've ever met. Caroline Carter couldn't even take her own trash can to the curb without a Prozac, a side of Xanax, a fucking pep talk beforehand, and a round of applause for the finale. I personally know raccoons that are more emotionally equipped to handle trash disposal than Caroline.

Caroline's hypocritical attitude is just one of the many reasons I've chosen to work full-time at a movie theatre snack bar throughout nursing school. I wanted to prove I could scrounge up enough money to move into an apartment with my best friend. All the long days of work, school, clinicals, and not to forget the many sleepless nights spent studying, have all been worth not having to coexist in the same residence as Caroline Carter. She and I are now solely on a first-name basis. If she could stop acting like a mom to me when I was only seven, why the hell should she deserve the title now?

If I truly wanted to, I could have asked to live with my father for the remainder of my nursing program, but I know that if I would've asked him, he would've felt obligated to say yes. I love my dad too much to put him out like that. Besides, he has a new family now and he deserves a little happiness. God knows Caroline drained him of it for all those years.

Now, don't get the wrong idea. I'm in no way the bitter daughter who despises her father's new family because I'm jealous of all the love and attention he pours into Family 2.0 and feel like he withholds the same from me. My dad is a damn good dad. I also happen to love my half-sister Taylor more than anything on this planet. I even like my stepmom, Amanda. If I'm being honest with myself, I'd have to admit that Amanda has been more of a mother to me than Caroline has been these last eight years. I know my father's family would happily take me in if I asked, but I just don't want to be the wrench thrown into their well-oiled family machine. If anything, my father's family machine is so well-oiled, they could spare a bit of that oil for this pathetic hospital crash cart I'm currently forcing to continue its torturous crawl down this hallway.

Once again, I'm back to thinking about how lazy I've physically become during nursing school. I wonder if I could even find my gym anymore without typing it into my GPS. I've never been the type of person to lose their appetite when stressed and effortlessly shed pounds. Stress does not look fantastic on me; unlike some people I know. Jill, my roommate and best friend, is one of those annoyingly perfect people who looks flawless even under dire stress. She's currently a student in the same local college that I'm attending, but she's in the respiratory therapy program. She's doing her clinical rotation here at Summit Valley as well, just a few floors above where I'm standing. Jill is such a nice and caring person that it's impossible to hate her, even if she's damn near perfect. I often refer to her as Mary Poppins. She also just so happens to have an affinity for large bags that tend to hold anything anyone could ever need or want.

I hear my preceptor's voice bellow down the hall, "Samantha, would it be possible for you to move like someone's life is on the line and not like you're enjoying a leisurely day at the farmer's market?"

And just like that, we're back to Margo Hatcher, the terrifying, semi-ancient preceptor. Margo has been a registered nurse for over thirty-six years, and my goodness it shows. She enjoys reminding all her co-workers about her longevity in the field of nursing whenever she's questioned. If I'm being honest though, only new-grad nurses, brand new residents, and plain ol' dumbasses questioned Margo. She was hands-down the most intelligent, experienced, and well-rounded nurse to grace the floors of this hospital. Margo has been the charge nurse on the Summit Valley Hospital ICU floor for just over twenty years, and she runs a tight ship. Who am I to question her when she's been charge nurse for about as long as I've been alive? Seeing as I'm not yet a new-grad nurse or a resident, I didn't want to be filed away in the category of plain ol' dumbasses, so I keep my mouth shut once again and continue to push.

Margo is the type of nurse that the new residents, or the "fresh meat" as she likes to call them, are visibly afraid of. She gives them the orders she wants for her patients. If they're smart, they'll listen and write the orders as she requests. If they're not too smart, they become noticeably offended and retaliate by disregarding Margo's well-informed requests and write completely opposite orders.

For example, last week Margo reported to one of the new residents, a tall, handsome man who looked like he was in his late twenties, that a patient had become increasingly uncomfortable throughout the night. The patient was a fifty-two-year-old male who had suffered multiple fractures throughout his body after a motor vehicle accident. The man had also suffered swelling to his brain. He was placed in an induced coma and intubated. At this point, the man had been on the ICU floor for three days. Margo was appalled by the lack of medication orders in place to control the man's pain, and trust me, as the nursing student who administered the man's bed bath, I can assure you he was in absolute agony if he was moved at all.

I reported the man's non-verbal signs of pain throughout the bathing process. Afterward, Margo said to me, "The man broke half his damn body, and this jackass wants me to give him two milligrams of Morphine every eight hours! Might as well just give him a Tylenol and a bit of pixie dust, for God's sake!" I truly admire Margo's passion and how she's never afraid to advocate for her patients. She has an innate need to be their voice when they're unable to speak for themselves.

As Margo reported her patient's symptoms of pain and her worry that the patient was suffering, Dr. Jackass gave no sign that he was listening. He even pulled out his cell phone from the pocket of his lab coat and began texting. At that moment, every staff member sitting at the nurses' station darted their eyes from Dr. Jackass's speedy fingers tapping away at his screen, back to Margo who was visibly seething by this point.

Dr. Jackass swears the text he just "had to" reply to at that very moment was completely work-related, but at least one CNA and one RN swore they saw his fingers send quite a few emojis in said text. After the incident, rumors even swirled across the unit that the infamous eggplant emoji was involved. Doesn't seem very work-related to me now, does it Dr. Connors? Oh, did you think Dr. Jackass was his actual name? It would be fitting, but no. Sadly, it's much more boring...

but we do all refer to him as Dr. Jackass. Not to his face, of course—we aren't plain ol' dumbasses, now.

Margo says physicians like Dr. Connors are the worst type of residents because they often evolve into arrogant, narrow-minded doctors who always think *they* know best. These are the doctors who think nurses are beneath them and so often appear to be working against the floor staff instead of with them. In reply, I reminded Margo of the fact that, as a nurse, our title is technically below a doctor's.

In that moment, I thought she was going to aggressively hurl her hemostat straight into my eye. This is one of the many reasons I refuse to get Lasik and only wear my glasses to work, never my contacts. Not only do my glasses help me see, but they are also protection from crazy, pissed off preceptors. *And* patients' bodily fluids. Besides, I think they're cute. My large, black, cat-eye frames have kind of become my staple. I'm in rare form if anyone sees me wearing my contacts. That's usually only reserved for weddings or other special occasions where photos are sure to be taken and people are bound to complain about the glare my glasses create in the pictures. A struggling nursing student doesn't have an extra hundred dollars laying around to upgrade to the anti-glare lenses.

After Margo calmed down from my "ridiculous comment," she proceeded to inform me that good nurses were a doctor's eyes and ears. If the doctors listened to the nurses, they'd have a direct look into the patient's entire picture. The nurses and nursing assistants were at a patient's bedside for twelve or more hours a day; typically, doctors spent about ten minutes with a single patient before they were on to the next one. Of course, this doesn't hold true for all doctors, and it isn't always their fault that they can't spend more time at a patient's bedside. Here, our doctors are too often pulled in a million different directions.

This very moment was a prime example. As I turn the corner at the end of the hall, I witness multiple MDs race through the corridor in opposite directions. The overhead intercom system alerts of a code white in the emergency department, which in turn pulls half of the rapid response team members that were actively barreling through the ICU floor toward room 252 back down to the emergency room. When I hear the announcement, I scramble to flip over my student ID badge and quickly scan the back of it, where I had taped a cheat sheet of all the hospital codes. Code white is a possible stroke, I silently recite to myself as the rickety crash cart I had been pushing comes to an abrupt halt at the threshold of room 252.

Now, I'm starting to panic. This is the first code I have participated in, and so far, I feel like I've been hindering the operation more than I've been helping it. For the thousandth time in the last two years, I wonder if I'm really cut out for this. Will I really make a half-decent nurse?

I turn to look over my shoulder as the queen bee comes running into room 252. She comes to a sudden stop, directly in front of the crash cart I'm still unconsciously grasping. The hive around me is buzzing; every team member knows their role and executes it flawlessly.

I watch as one of the floor RNs, Tim, continues to perform chest compressions at a perfectly even depth on the frail, older man's chest as he lay lifeless. Another RN continues to administer respirations to the man via an Ambu bag in precisely measured increments of time. Dr. Connors stands in the middle of the commotion, confidently relaying orders to the staff whirring around him. He has been forced to run this code alone due to all the personnel being summoned down to the ED by the code white. Most residents would probably be shaking in their Nike's at the thought of having to operate solo in this situation, but he looks like a well-seasoned veteran out there rather than a "fresh meat" resident, as Margo claimed. Even though he kind of acts like an arrogant jackass, and he possibly uses the eggplant emoji in a "business conversation," he might become a pretty good doctor after all.

I steady myself for Margo's inevitable verbal assault as I stand motionless, continuing to clutch the crash cart as the floor nurses around me rifle through it for the medications and supplies necessary to run the code.

I feel like a failure. This was the time I was supposed to step up and show that I wasn't some unmotivated, worthless twenty-one-year-old who enrolled in nursing school to appease her mommy and daddy. I truly want this. I want to help people. I want to become a nurse to change people's lives, just like a kind nurse had changed mine all those years ago. I was supposed to be trusting my instincts, diving into the fire and fighting the flames in crucial moments such as this.

Instead, I am frozen. My bones have become ice. My thoughts have turned into flakes of snow. If I attempt to move, I feel as if I will simply shatter. If I lunge into the fire, it will inevitably cause me to melt. And if I attempt to control my consciousness now, the flurries of my thoughts will blow away, dissipating before my very eyes. I feel the embarrassment of tears I didn't want to shed invading my vision. I can no longer breathe; my lungs are on fire now. The noises around me have become deafening, and the room I stand in is beginning to slowly shrink around me. I feel as if I've walked into a maniacal funhouse, where I am the main attraction. I feel an unshakeable sense of impending doom. I know I have to run, because if I can't escape in this very moment, I'm positive I will implode. I know that walking out of this room will solidify all my fears: I am not cut out to be a nurse.

But I'm suddenly hurled back to reality, pulled out of the waves of anxiety that have been crashing over me. Margo grasps both of my shoulders, turning my body to face hers. My eyes lock with my preceptor's stare.

"Sam, just breathe. I know this is scary, but you can do this. You just follow my lead, and I won't steer you wrong. We are all in this together. You are not alone, okay?" Margo speaks to me in a hushed voice as she gives an encouraging squeeze to both of my shoulders.

Why is she being so nice to me? I could've sworn she hated me.

I take a deep breath, silence my dread, and follow my preceptor's lead. Margo immediately turns on her heels and races to the patient's bedside. I follow suit and force my body to move forward. At that exact moment, a memory I had long since hidden deep in my subconscious forcefully digs its way to the surface.

I think of lazy Sunday afternoons, slamming my small fingers onto a rectangular game controller, hoping to push the right buttons. To be honest, I never knew what the hell I was doing. I never wanted to disappoint him. He needed me to help beat the big boss. We had to beat him together. The memory of when I wasn't alone floods back to me. I'm reminded in this moment that I'm not alone either.

As I listen closely to Margo's instructions, I slide between two nurses to assume the responsibility of chest compressions. As I repeatedly thrust my palms into the elderly man's chest, I feel as if his bone has snapped beneath my hands. I immediately flinch, my movements falter, and I pause.

Margo senses my distress and places her hand on my shoulder as she whispers into my ear, "If you're feeling ribs crack, then you know you're doing CPR correctly. Keep going," she ushers.

I silently start to sing "Stayin' Alive" to myself as I work to keep the rhythm of the compressions. Last semester, when my medical surgical instructor told the class about this trick to keep pace while administering CPR, the entire class burst into a roar of laughter, myself included. I thought it was incredibly dumb and there was no way I'd ever be caught dead (no pun intended) singing a disco song. Not even to myself. I guess trauma makes you do crazy things. This by no means suggests that I am becoming a disco fan. It's not like I'm completely uncultured, though. I love oldies and classic rock. I'm always thankful that my dad passed his love of good music down to me. But disco is where I draw a hard line, the only exception now being CPR administration.

After about four minutes of chest compressions, Tim taps me on my shoulder and proceeds to relieve me from my post. I will admit, four minutes of chest compressions feels like forty. I dare you to try doing tricep dips for four minutes unbroken; it's not as easy as you would think. I'm immediately embarrassed by how much my arms are shaking. This marks the third time today I've been mad at myself for evolving into a human sloth this semester. Nursing school kind of consumes your entire existence. I mentally vow to take my ass back to the gym this weekend.

Margo guides me to the head of the patient's bed to assume the role of administering breaths. I confidently take hold of the Ambu bag from one of the members of the rapid response team and ensure the face mask is well-fitted over the patient's nose and mouth. For a split second, I almost feel like I actually know what I'm doing. While Margo takes a verbal order from Dr. Connors to administer another dose of medication via IV push, she nods at me as if to reassure me that I'm not totally jacking everything up.

As I lift my head to gaze across the small hospital room for the first time, I notice that the patient's son is standing in the corner of the room. He is visibly shaking, yelling to someone on his cellphone, tears running down his face. I wish I could tell this man that everything was going to be okay, that his dad would be fine. As I stare down at the lifeless form below me, I fear this man's son won't receive the news he is praying for. I know Mr. Gomez is gone.

The man lying in the middle of all this chaos is seventy-nine-year-old Hector Gomez. Mr. Gomez has a diagnosis of stage-four lung cancer that, unfortunately, has metastasized, or spread, to his bones and brain. From reading his chart earlier in the day, I also know that he has multiple comorbidities, meaning multiple other diseases effecting his overall health, including congestive heart failure and chronic kidney failure. Mr. Gomez has been receiving dialysis three times a week to keep him alive. Dialysis works in the place of the kidneys when they fail to filter the blood of toxins. You never realize how much you need your kidneys until they're no longer working as they should.

If I'm to be blunt, Mr. Gomez's quality of life was poor. This afternoon, one of the hospital's hospice and palliative care physicians was in to speak with the patient's son Jose and provide a consult for the hospital's hospice program. Since I told Margo that hospice and palliative care is what I would like to specialize in when I graduate, she asked the physician and the son if I could sit in to observe the consultation. Since they both agreed to my presence, I timidly took a seat in the corner of the room as they started. Just this afternoon, I sat in the same corner as Jose stands now and listened to Dr. Lee tell him about what hospice care was and how his father would "benefit" from it.

Mr. Gomez had become deeply lethargic at that point and was no longer able to make medical decisions for himself. In turn, Jose chose for his father. His dad was to keep fighting. Hospice care was just not in the cards for Hector Gomez, even after Dr. Lee, Summit Valley's lead hospice and palliative care physician, thoroughly explained to Jose how bleak the outlook was for his father's survival and how the hospice team would be able to administer different medication than the ICU could to help to make him more comfortable. Dr. Lee continued to explain that the hospice team could help to control his father's pain and increasing shortness of breath, that aggressive treatment was no longer recommended with his father's status.

Following the consult, Dr. Lee and I exited the hospital room side-by-side. He mentioned to me that if Mr. Gomez had created an advance directive prior to his change in mental status, none of these tough decisions would have fallen on his son's shoulders. Dr. Lee spoke about how tough a decision like this was to make for a loved one and how much guilt was often involved in making such crucial decisions as these.

After hearing Dr. Lee's words, I immediately thought about a cold December day, back when I was still just a little girl who didn't yet have a clue how cruel this world could be. I was standing behind my father, grasping fiercely onto his pant leg as he had a similarly painful conversation with a different physician adorned in an identical white coat. The doctor gazed down to my small form, as I held onto my father for dear life with regretful eyes. Even then, I could tell the doctor felt uncomfortable with a child so young being witness to such a sorrowful conversation. But during the dreadful months leading up to that day, my dad had become my human security blanket. I refused to leave his side without inflicting a tantrum from Hell on anyone who tried to pull me away from him. I still remember the sound of my father's voice as he choked back tears, forcing himself to make the decision he and Caroline had dreaded more than anything. That was the moment he was forced to accept the inescapable truth, the moment that demanded he undertake the heartbreaking process of saying goodbye to his boy.

I quickly pulled my thoughts away from the past to focus on Dr. Lee's voice. I was simply astonished at how eloquent he was when he spoke to the man's son. He was more kind and patient than any physician I had seen thus far in my nursing school clinical rotations. He had a way of appearing tremendously caring yet completely realistic. Per Dr. Lee's own words, not administering false hope to the patient's son was imperative. He stated that if he was to sugarcoat Mr. Gomez's prognosis with the intention of sparing his son undue emotional pain now, it would only end up crushing him more in the end. Dr. Lee told me one last thing before he returned to his busy workday, "It is my duty to tell people the truth, be it patients themselves or their family members. People deserve to know the truth, even if it's the last thing in the world they want to hear."

After that declaration he promptly stuck his hand out towards mine. I immediately scrambled to meet his grasp with my own and shook his hand. He smiled at me and said, "It was nice to meet you Samantha, I look forward to hopefully working with you one day."

I had never met a celebrity or ever felt starstruck, but this feeling must have been a close equivalent. I stumbled over my words in reply, "Uh, yeah. Um, thank you. Me too." It was the only thing I could manage to say.

He nodded at me, then quickly turned and walked down the hallway to the elevators. I contemplated his words as I gazed after him, walking swiftly towards the end of the unit. I knew then and there that I would do just about anything to be able to work with that man one day.

Now, I rip my vision away from the corner of the room where Mr. Gomez's son still stands, yelling more desperately now into his cell phone. I search for Margo to relay to me what I'm supposed to do next. A nurse from the rapid response team assumes my current position to administer breaths. My eyes find Margo's as she rushes back to the patient's bedside holding another syringe of medication. I feel like I'm surrounded by blaring sound, as machines continue their monotonous beeping and alarms continue projecting their piercing alert.

Suddenly, Dr. Connors's voice bellows above all the noise, instantly commanding the room. "I have to call it," he mournfully announces, removing his stethoscope from the man's chest and pulling his fingers away from the man's neck where a carotid pulse no longer existed. "Time of death: 17:09," he speaks, turning to solemnly face Jose, who simultaneously slides his back down the wall and collapses to the hospital floor.

"No! He can't be gone," Jose cries. "My sister is running up here now from the cafeteria. She was only gone twenty minutes," he sobs. "She went to get me something to eat." Jose's hands cover his face, and his body starts to heave with every sob expelled.

In the middle of all the commotion, I take a few unnoticed steps to the patient's bedside and place a gloved hand upon his cold, unmoving one. I allow myself a moment to think, a moment to process having seen life leave someone's body.

Mr. Gomez, I'm sorry you had to die in pain. I'm sorry you had to feel the pressure of my hands needlessly breaking your ribs as you struggled to let go. I'm sorry that everything had to be so loud, so hectic. That we were unable to grant you well-deserved peace in a time when you so needed it. I truly apologize that you had to feel strangers' hands upon your body in your final moments rather than the hands of your family, your son. The same son who stood terrified in the corner of this room, watching all of this unfold with tear-filled eyes, wondering if he made the wrong decision after all.

# CHAPTER TWO:

# HECTOR GOMEZ

## November 18, 2011, 17:09

feel like I'm sinking, falling deeper and deeper within myself. The only thing that snaps me out of my fall is the pain. I feel it in my lower back, like daggers repeatedly stabbing me. The pain starts radiating throughout my entire body. I don't know how much time has passed since I first fell within these depths, but it seems like an eternity.

As each eternity passes, the pain amplifies; but this pain is nothing compared to the feeling of my breath being slowly stolen from my lungs. My body struggles to inhale the oxygen it took for granted all these years, feeling daggers again. The breath I exhale feels like shards of glass ripping through me as my lungs collapse into themselves. My body is tired. Exhaustion consumes me, but I can't let go. I cannot leave them.

I hear my son's cries as his hand holds mine. Jose sounds so far away, but I know the hand holding mine is his. My Amelia is here, my daughter. I'd know her voice anywhere. The despair I hear in her *sweet voice when she speaks overtakes me. I know I must hold onto whatever life I have left as I hear my children's voices telling me to fight, begging me not to give up.*

*But I miss you more than anything, Laura. My beautiful bride. It's been twelve years since I was last captivated by the beauty of your eyes, twelve years since you've been gone. I can sense you here now, Laura. I know you're close. As I begin to slip deeper within myself, the fluorescent lighting fades and all I see is your face. The beeping of the machinery I've been tethered to for far too long diminishes. All I can hear is your voice. As your presence hovers above me, I feel a sense of calm knowing I will be reunited with you again soon.*

*Suddenly, I feel an indescribable jolt of pain as the pressure of the world comes crashing down onto my chest. Again and again, I'm pummeled by an immense force. Your face is stolen from my vision as bright lights blind me once again. The soft warmth of my love's soothing voice is ripped away. Now, all I hear are shrieking alarms and unfamiliar voices. I try searching for Jose's or Amelia's voice through the noise, but nothing is recognizable. I can no longer feel my children's presence.*

*I'm in agony as the steady blows to my chest continue. Abruptly, something foreign is placed over my face and I feel as if I'm suffocating. I don't think I can survive another moment of this torture. Immense fear begins to consume me. Where are my children? Please, Lord. I beg you to make this stop.*

*Then all at once, the pain dissipates. You've come to my aid again, Laura, as you did loyally for forty-seven years. The best years of my life. I can see you clearly now. You're here to save me. I reach for you again, only this time I can finally feel you. Relief washes over me. I'm finally home and with my hand in yours, I allow myself to let go.*

# CHAPTER THREE:

After the events in room 252, Margo and I walk side by side in silence back to the nurses' station. I notice this is the first time she has walked beside me rather than in front of me. I'm feeling disappointed in myself, as if I had just been tested and somehow failed miserably. My eyes focus on my feet and the clunky, white Sketchers Shape-ups I'm wearing. When we reach the nurses' station, I gain the courage to steal a glance at Margo, expecting her to be scowling at me in disapproval. To my surprise, she has a small smile on her face and, if I'm not mistaken, it's directed at me.

"Ya did good in there, kid," she whispers to me, nudging me with her elbow in a loving way.

I am so damn confused! For one, I could have sworn this woman despised me. Second, I feel like I totally dropped the ball in there. I was the definition of a hot mess.

"I'm confused," I say, holding her gaze. "I froze. I feel like I messed up everything."

Margo sighs, "Samantha, it was your first code. You need to stop being so hard on yourself. You show me any nurse that didn't practically shit themselves during their first code, and I'll fall over dead right where I stand."

I immediately burst into laughter, slapping my hand over my mouth in a failed attempt to stifle it. "So, you're telling me that you were as terrified as I just was during your first code?" I chuckle. Now, it's Margo's turn to laugh.

"Of course I was! If I recall, I may have *literally* shit myself," she snickers. "But that was almost a hundred years ago, so who the hell knows? Even when you become a geriatric nurse like me, you still won't always know everything. There will always be more to learn. You're going to make mistakes and feel like, at times, you mess everything up. Remember, you're human, Sam."

I stand speechless, staring at Margo as she places her arm around me and gives my shoulder an encouraging squeeze. I'm realizing how much I secretly like my preceptor. I never thought I'd see the day when Margo Hatcher would be giving me a pep talk. And an Oscar worthy one at that. She may be hard on me, sometimes, and I may be deathly afraid of her wrath, all the time, but I'm now acutely aware of how great a mentor she has been.

"Thank you. I needed that," I say, smiling down at my Shape-ups.

"I know you did. We all need a little encouragement after pushing that piece of shit crash cart," Margo laughs as she turns back to the nursing station to grab a chart from the counter. "Now for the worst part of my job—charting. Don't forget, Samantha. If you didn't chart it, then it didn't happen. Cover your ass and document well."

I quickly nod my head in agreement and make a mental note to myself. Margo takes a seat behind her computer and pats her hand gently on the chair next to her, motioning for me to sit. "Now, let me show you how we handle a patient expiration," Margo says.

When the clock hits 7:00, I hustle to shove my textbooks and notebook (or my "brain" as I like to refer to it) into my Superman backpack and swiftly swing it over my shoulder. I don't start work until 7:30 at The Cinedome tonight, but if I want to make a pit stop at the hospital cafeteria for a much-needed cup of coffee before my shift, I need to pick up the pace.

I take the elevator to the ground floor, racing into the hospital lobby as soon as the doors of the metal death trap release me. I've never been a fan of elevators, or any other confined space, for that matter. Spending most of my time in hospitals that are quite frankly never just one floor has forced me to overcome my elevator phobia.

As I rush into the cafeteria, I'm surprised at how crowded it is at this hour. That's change of shift for you, I guess. Walking toward the highly coveted coffee machine, I notice two paramedics who appear to be about my age eating dinner at a table to my right. Or maybe it's their lunch? Could even be their breakfast! Who knows with the hours paramedics have to work?

One of the men looks to be your typical pretty boy: impeccably styled blonde hair, sparkling blue eyes, perfectly proportioned facial features, and overly muscular arms straining at the fabric of his uniform. Why couldn't he request a bigger uniform? That just seems wildly uncomfortable. I can't deny he's attractive, but he's not my type whatsoever. He's not a man I would even give a second look. Now if you asked my friend Jill, she would probably be gushing that this was her ideal dream guy.

My gaze wanders to the partner sitting beside him, who takes a huge bite of his hamburger right as I unintentionally lock eyes with him. Unlike the pretty boy, this guy has an unconventional charm about him. He has a mess of thick, brown, curly hair that lays in such a lovely way, I subconsciously wonder if he styled it to look like that on purpose. At a brief glance, his eyes appear to be a true hazel. In my opinion, people claim to have hazel eyes but tend to actually have an eye color that either leans more toward light brown or green. It's rare to see true hazel eyes.

I notice a small, faint scar just atop his upper lip. Realizing I'm now staring at this man's lips, I hurriedly lift my gaze to meet his eyes once again. I catch myself wondering whether that scar was acquired from a childhood injury or maybe from a more recent fist to the face. Is this the type of guy that did something for which a punch to the face was deserved? Why the hell am I thinking so much about a scar on a stranger's face?

He holds my stare, setting his hamburger back onto his plate as a small, sideways smirk forms on his face. I return his smile with my own and my attention draws to the small smear of ketchup on the corner of his handsome smile. *His handsome smile? What the hell is wrong with me?*

Heat instantly travels to both of my cheeks, and I know I've turned the color of a damn tomato. I break our awkward staring contest and fix my vision back onto my destination—the coffee maker. Just a few more steps.

I can feel his gaze on my back as I reach the coffee maker and grab a Styrofoam cup off of the stack by the machine. Why do I feel so nervous? It's just another random guy with an oddly adorable smile.

I pour piping hot coffee into my cup and smack a travel lid on top, no cream for me. Becoming a nursing student has taught me to prefer my coffee black. No need for any frilly foam or snooty syrups, just straight to the point.

As I scurry over to the cashier, I check my watch. Shit. I've wasted ten minutes getting a coffee and daydreaming about a boy I don't even know. I've got to go. I reach the cashier and attempt to hand her two dollars. The older woman smiles sweetly at me, "Oh, honey. You look like you've had a hard day."

She catches me by surprise, and I falter, still holding out my hand grasping the bills. Her smile widens and she whispers to me, "This one's on me, honey. Hope your day gets better."

I return her smile with my own, "Um, thank you. I really appreciate it!"

She nods toward me, reassuring me that it's okay to take my coffee and run. I shove my two dollars into one of my scrub pockets as I wave at the kind, older woman and speed walk towards the hospital exit.

I quickly pass by the table where the two paramedics are still seated, purposefully keeping my head down. No time for awkward stare-offs now. I'm almost to the hospital lobby when I hear a voice call, "Nice backpack!"

I tell myself to just keep walking. I don't have time to deal with these assholes. But the voice calls to me again, louder this time, "Those shoes are even better!"

And I officially lose all self-control. I abruptly turn and charge in the opposite direction. I've almost reached the men's table when the pretty boy speaks once again, "You know, they say those are the stripper shoes of nurses."

The frat boy wannabe turns to his friend with the hazel eyes and curly brown hair. "And by the height of this girl's shoes, I assume that must be how she's paying for school," the frat boy asshole laughs.

I'm already simmering, but when the frat boy's friend starts to join in on this grand ol' laugh at my expense, I boil over. I yank back the empty chair at the table and throw my body into the seat. Both men look surprised as I slam both of my hands onto their table. The pretty boy's soda immediately knocks over and spills into his lap from the force of my hands meeting the table.

He jolts up to a standing position and yells, "What the fuck!"

I mentally pat myself on the back. That was in no way purposeful, on my part. I'll just chalk it up to a happy accident.

The other man remains completely silent in his seat beside the Justin Timberlake knock-off. The man standing in front of me, now attempting to tower over me, is visibly seething with rage. Little does this piece of shit know that when crossed—and I'm not saying I'm proud of this—I'm a crazy bitch.

I take a deep breath, then begin. "I suggest you sit your soggy crotch back down and shut the fuck up," I spit at the frat boy. I hear a choking sound from the man who's seated as he tries to stifle his laughter.

Meanwhile, the asshole who was just attempting to intimidate me with his size now slowly shrinks back, his mouth agape. I get the feeling this guy is used to dishing out the insults, not receiving them.

I continue my rant, scooting my chair closer to the table, "What didn't you understand? Sit down!" I roar. Pretty boy promptly returns his ass to his chair, soggy crotch and all.

I exhale and proceed, "I had a pretty hard day today. Now I have to go to my *actual* job and work all night. Which isn't at a strip club but even if it was, that's none of your business. And the last thing I need right now is some frat boy wannabe heckling me about my choice of footwear."

I pause from yelling at this man and stare at his hair, "Now that I'm closer, I cannot believe that this Backstreet Boy over here actually has frosted tips!" I start laughing uncontrollably as I conclude my spiel, "I can't even fathom how you have the audacity to mock my backpack and shoes when you look like a bootleg, reject-member of 98 Degrees. And for your information, these shoes are very comfortable and have superb arch support!"

I'm practically panting as I finish screaming at this douchebag. The only person who's allowed to mock my shoes is me. I know part of me is projecting; what's truly upsetting me more than anything is having seen a person die in front of me just over two hours ago. Nonetheless, this guy deserves to be knocked down a few pegs.

Frat boy responds with the cleverest insult of all time. He calls me a bitch. To my surprise, his companion speaks up, "Hey, bro. That's too far. Don't talk to her like that."

I steal a glance at the frat boy's friend and meet his hazel eyes once again. Why is this guy always staring at me? And why do I suddenly feel nervous again?

Pretty boy turns to his friend and whines, "But she called me a Backstreet Boy!"

Suddenly the boy with the hazel eyes and I break into a chorus of laughter. I'm laughing so hard I can feel tears spring to my eyes. My eyes definitely haven't been a stranger to tears today, but tears of laughter are a pleasant change.

I look down at my watch. 7:20. Shit, I'm going to be late! I pull myself out of my borrowed chair and sprint toward the parking lot.

Do I chance one glance back at the boy with the hazel eyes and sideways smirk? Probably not a good idea in these three-inch high tennis shoes. Better to just keep running.

As I reach my car in the parking lot, I unlock the door and hurl my Superman backpack into the back seat of my hunter green 2001 Chevy Blazer. My "Old Faithful" as I like to call her. Even though she's ten years old, she runs like a dream. Jill always talks about the different fancy cars she's going to buy once she graduates school and gets a better paying job. I'd personally prefer to drive Old Faithful until she explodes.

I slide into the driver's seat and jam my key in the ignition as my eyes dart to the clock on the stereo. 7:23. SHIT! I pull my Blazer out of the hospital parking lot and onto Main Street.

Summit Valley Hospital is located smack in the middle of Bristol, the town where I've lived my entire twenty-one years. I was born and raised in Bristol, Virginia just like my friend Jill. And as our welcome sign boasts, it's "A Good Place to Live." It's also the twin city to Bristol, Tennessee; the line that divides the states runs right down the middle of Main Street.

As I speed down Main Street, I'm thankful The Cinedome is only five minutes away from the hospital. That leaves me only two minutes to park, rush into the theatre, and barrel into the restroom to change from my scrubs into my godawful uniform. Tonight is a big movie premiere, so we're offering a rare, late night showing that won't finish until about 2:00 AM. I'm predicting that once my head finally hits my pillow, I'll have been awake for at least twenty-four hours.

I'm crossing my fingers that I don't get stuck cleaning the kettle corn popper again tonight. That machine is always absolutely disgusting.

I smile as I remember Veronica picked up the premiere shift tonight as well. At least I have one thing to look forward to. Veronica is my second closest friend, Jill being the first of course.

I've worked at The Cinedome for a little over four years now. I started working there after I graduated from high school. Since my birthday falls in the beginning of September, I graduated at seventeen. So, I graduated early not because I'm some sort of genius or anything, but because of a well-placed date of birth and the opportunity to start school at the age of four.

About six months after I started working at The Cinedome, Veronica joined our team of movie loving nerds. She and I were instant friends. She's only a year older than me and moved to Bristol with her mom in 2008 after her parents divorced. Our initial bond ignited from our mutual bitching about being children of divorce. While I love Jill and can talk to her about anything, her parents are still happily married. I feel like it's hard for someone to truly relate if they haven't had to witness the marriage of the two most important people in their life disintegrate in front of them.

Shortly after I started bringing Veronica around outside of work, she and Jill quickly hit it off as well. Thus, the three musketeers were born!

Veronica is wild and carefree. She doesn't care what anyone thinks of her and lives life by her own rules. She's a fiercely loyal friend and has become Jill's and my protector.

A couple months ago, the three of us were at a bar downtown enjoying a few beers when a man about our age came up behind me. He lightly placed his hand on my shoulder, asking if he could borrow my cell phone to make a quick call because his was dead. Before I could even process what happened, Veronica had punched the unsuspecting patron in the face. The man was in shock and was at a loss for words. I tried to explain to Veronica that the man simply asked to borrow my cell phone, but she wasn't buying it. She said no man should touch a woman without her consent and forced the bleeding man to apologize. Jill and I are Veronica's "Sammie Bear" and "Jilly Bean" and that means no one dares to mess with us if she's in the general vicinity.

All at once, my sour mood floats away and a smile overtakes my face at the excitement of seeing my friend. Veronica always knows how to cheer me up.

# CHAPTER FOUR:

I screech into the parking lot of The Cinedome and swerve into an empty space in the back of the lot. This place is officially a zoo, but that's no surprise to me. The fourth *Twilight* movie is premiering tonight, *Breaking Dawn: Part One*.

Veronica gives us shit, but Jill and I have religiously read all the books and loved them. We both agree that the movies are nowhere near as good as the books, but to be honest, movies are rarely able to rival their book predecessors. That still doesn't stop Jill and me from quoting scenes of the movies to annoy Veronica.

A prime example of Jill's and my ridicule was last weekend when the three of us decided to have dinner at Applebee's. In the middle of the conversation, we were having about the newest guy Veronica was dating, Jill belted out, "I know what you are."

Without a single prompt, I assumed my role and growled, "Say it. Out loud. Say it!"

In unison, Jill and I screamed, "Vampire!" We burst into fits of laughter and successfully got everyone in the bar area to stare at us.

Veronica groaned in embarrassment and covered her face with her menu as she whispered, "I hate you guys." Jill and I confidently responded, "You know you love us!"

I jump out of my car and start racing toward the theatre, maneuvering around customers who are leisurely walking in the same direction as me. I'm not a fan of any form of cardio, but desperate times call for desperate measures. I fling open the door to the theatre and dash past the ticket booth, offering a quick wave to my coworkers sitting behind the booth. I'm running too quickly to register whether any of them waved back at me.

Continuing my sprint towards the women's bathroom to change into my uniform, I spot our shift supervisor, Zach, lugging a crate of nachos to the snack bar. He drops the crate onto the counter and stares after me as he yells, "You have one minute, Sam!"

Wow, one minute! I'm making excellent time. I sweetly yell back, "That's all I need, Zachary." He hates being called by his full name almost as much as I do.

Zach is three years older than me and has been the object of my affection since he started working here two years ago. Meaning he actually has no clue how I feel about him and that I secretly pine after him. I tell Veronica daily how cute he is, to which she usually replies, "Yeah, I mean, he'd totally be fuckable if he cut off that dumb ponytail, man-bun thing." I then counter her insult by telling her it makes him look like a modern-day Kurt Cobain, except Zach's way less angsty and disheveled.

Veronica has been encouraging me to tell Zach how I feel about him, but I adamantly refuse. She says he's constantly flirting with me and it's so apparent our feelings are mutual. Only a major idiot wouldn't realize it. She always winks at me as she says the last part, inferring that I am the major idiot.

I'm just so petrified of rejection that, in my mind, it's safer to carry along as I have been and never truly know if my feelings for Zach are one-sided.

And it's easy for Veronica to give me such advice; it's as if confidence seeps from her pores. Veronica is a force of nature with her fiery red hair and bright green eyes. She has a perfect number of freckles dotted across her button nose and a pout that people pay for. She stands five-foot-six with a stunning figure and boobs that people would also pay for. At one point, there was a rumor circulating at work that Veronica had breast implants. She was so offended by the false accusations, she made everyone feel them to ensure they were in fact real.

Veronica has about three inches on me in height and if she was considered more top-heavy, I would be considered the opposite. I barely fill out a B-cup bra but am considerably curvy in my hips and bottom. I may not be slender like Jill, but I've been blessed with a small waist and flat stomach. Caroline loves to remind me that if I continue to snack like I do and slack on my gym regimen, I'll blow up like a hot air balloon by the time I'm twenty-five—just another one of my mother's infamous rants that I try to tune out. Besides, it's impossible not to snack when you're surrounded by an endless sea of buttery popcorn every day at work. At least I've never been caught drinking the butter straight from the spout like my coworker Craig.

After I rip off my scrubs, I'm now donning my black slacks and burgundy button-up shirt with The Cinedome logo plastered over the breast pocket, I swing the bathroom stall door open and rush to the full-length mirror. I rapidly tuck my button-up into my slacks. We're often reminded that it's company policy to have our shirts tucked in. Veronica simply refuses and has been written up twice for it over the years. "I'm not going to look like some huge dweeb! If it's that big of a deal to these tools in upper management, they can personally come down here and fire my happy ass," she belted loud enough for the entire theatre to hear after being served her second dress code write-up.

After Veronica's last outburst on the matter, upper management must've decided it wasn't worth it to fight with her anymore because for the last year they've decided to turn the other cheek to the situation.

I attempt to smooth the frizz out of my wavy medium brown hair that falls in a tangled mess just below my shoulders. No use, I sigh to myself and pull it back haphazardly into a ponytail. I briefly remove my thick, black cat-eye frames and quickly pull a jet-black eyeliner pencil out of my backpack. I dab the tip of the pencil to my tongue before carelessly lining my dark blue eyes. Eh, good enough. I gaze at my reflection and note how pale my ivory complexion appears under the bathroom's fluorescent lighting. I brush a stroke of soft pink blush to both of my cheekbones, at least now I don't look like a total zombie.

When I was still living with my mother, she would constantly drag me along to go spray tanning with her. She swore it made me look "healthier." I think Caroline's favorite motto is, "If you can't tone it, tan it!" After I decided to move out on my own, the luxury of spray tanning was no longer in my budget.

Lastly, I pull out a tube of hot pink lip gloss from my backpack, swipe the gloss across my lips, and instinctively smack them together. My pout may not be as perfect as Veronica's, but it isn't half bad. I silently thank Jill for convincing me it's necessary to always carry an emergency supply of cosmetics.

Eyeing myself in the bathroom mirror one final time, I pop an orange Tic Tac in my mouth to get rid of the coffee taste. I think of the sweet older woman who insisted I not pay for my coffee tonight and smile into the mirror. At least some people out there are still friendly, unlike those asshole paramedics.

As I dart out of the women's bathroom, Superman backpack slung over my shoulder, I finagle my way through the crowd of patrons impatiently waiting for their overpriced snacks. I gracefully slide my body under the snack bar countertop because I'm in too much of a hurry to lift the folding counter to walk through it. I dramatically twirl into a well-rehearsed pirouette in front of the hot dog cooker to alert my coworkers of my arrival before gliding into the backroom to put my bag in my locker.

"Nice of you to join us, princess!" I hear Craig call to me as he chuckles at my performance.

All those years of ballet class my mother forced me to endure paid off for something—a flawless grand entrance. As I shut my locker, I hear someone approach behind me. "You're five minutes late, SAMAN-THA!" Zach draws out my full name as he says it.

I spin around to sweetly smile at him and say, "Five extra minutes is a small price to pay for me to look this adorable." I can tell that he's trying hard not to smile at me. Trying and failing.

"You may be adorable, but you're also incredibly annoying and a tad infuriating," he states as his grin begins to widen.

"All I heard was that you think I'm adorable," I reply to him in a sing-song voice as I lift both my hands to rest under my chin and flash him a cheeky grin.

His smile now reaches ear to ear. "Get out there, Sam," he chuckles. "We're drowning and need all hands-on deck." I nod to him in understanding and skip out to the snack bar to join my crew in what's bound to be a long shift.

"Hey, Sam! How are you?" Craig asks as I join his side by the popcorn bin.

Craig is the epitome of a sweet, Southern gentleman and has become one of my great friends at The Cinedome. That's after we got over the awkwardness of him insistently asking me to set him up with Veronica. I repeatedly reminded him that she doesn't date younger men. In turn, he repeatedly reminded me that he's very mature for his age. Secretly, I do think they'd make an adorable couple.

Craig is undeniably cute, but Veronica, unfortunately, says she sees him more as a little brother than a potential match. He's a couple inches taller than her with a muscular build, a huge, pearly white smile, and dark brown hair that he always keeps cut short. Our coworkers at The Cinedome and his mama (as he calls her) might be the only people that actually know what Craig's hair looks like because when he isn't at work, he religiously wears his cowboy hat.

A year or so ago, Craig had a passionate debate with Zach about how it wasn't fair that he couldn't wear his cowboy hat to work when Veronica was allowed to flaunt her untucked shirt in front of him.

"This is downright sexism!" Craig pouted as we all snickered. "What?" he shouted. "Y'all don't think sexism goes both ways? Just 'cause Veronica is pretty; she gets to do whatever her lil' heart desires. And ugly blokes like me are stuck wearin' high-water knickers with shirts tucked into our damn belly buttons and forced to have cold, lonely heads!"

Veronica giggled and sauntered over to Craig, promptly pecking him on his cheek, "Oh Craig, but I happen to think you're real purty, too," she purred, mocking his accent. Craig instantly turned ten shades of red and fell silent, obviously at a complete loss for words.

"Okay, let's get to work," the sound of Zach's voice pulls my thoughts back to the present and I realize I never answered Craig's question. I smile back at Craig as his pale blue eyes meet mine, "I had a rough day at the hospital," I sigh. "Tell you about it later."

He lightly pats me on the back, then pulls me into a subtle side hug. "Keep your head up, girly. You're gonna make a great nurse one day," he reassures me as he ushers the next customer to approach the counter.

How is it that everyone in my life but me is so confident I'm going to be an excellent nurse? How could they even be so sure?

I wave to the next customer to let them know I'm ready to take their order and sweetly greet them when they approach the counter. As I hand the patron her fresh popcorn, I feel a swift smack to my shoulder. "Hey, bitch!" the voice addresses me.

I swivel around and am immediately greeted by one of my best friend's embraces. I love her hugs so much. "Howdy bitch!" I reply.

"Oh God, you've been hanging around Craig too much. You're starting to sound like a certified hick," Veronica gripes.

"I feel personally victimized," Craig shouts over to us as Veronica and I start to laugh.

"So, get this," Veronica starts, "I convinced Zach to allow us to do a private showing of the movie for the staff after we close. I know you've been working at the hospital all day, but I also know how coo-coo bananas you are for this *Twilight* stuff."

I clasp my hands together, a huge smile forming on my face. "You love me, you really love me," I declare.

"Yeah, yeah. Whatever. But here's the best part," she continues, "I convinced Zach to allow me to sneak Jilly Bean in to join us for our private showing!"

Now I'm squealing as I proceed to jump up and down with excitement. I look like a small child who's just received the news that she's going to Disney World for the first time. I propel myself into my friend's arms as I shriek, "Has anyone ever told you that you're the best?"

Veronica wraps her arms around me as she starts to laugh, "Mmm hmm," she smirks, "...of course they have." I step out of her arms to give her a well-deserved eye-roll. She's truly one of a kind.

Veronica puts her finger in the air and begins to lecture, "But don't think I'm doing all this for you, Sammie Bear. I'm doing this purely because I find it entertaining how obsessed the two of you are with a bunch of fictional characters."

I silently think how it will actually be Jill and me who will be entertained with our new arsenal of movie quotes to publicly embarrass Veronica with, but I keep that thought to myself. I know deep down Veronica is full of crap. She would happily do just about anything for Jill and me.

As Veronica and I continue conversing about our plans for the movie tonight, I see Zach start stomping over to us in my peripheral vision. "Ladies, come on," he groans. "We have a line of over fifteen customers and you two have been chit-chatting for the last five minutes while Craig runs his ass off!"

At the same time, Veronica and I glance to where Craig is standing and watch as he dramatically slaps the back of his hand to his forehead, pretending he's about to faint from pure exhaustion. I shake my head at him as I mouth, "Drama queen."

He proceeds to wink at me as he points his trademark "finger guns" in my direction. "Hey! You best holster those bad boys, cowboy!" Veronica shouts to him over the sound of the popcorn popper blasting out a new batch of golden goodness.

If you can't tell, I have an unrequited love for popcorn. I say that because the love between me and popcorn is completely one-sided. I worship every delicious piece of the to-go bag of popcorn I take home nightly, even after the popper has relentlessly assaulted me by pelting scalding hot kernels at my defenseless face and arms throughout my workday. I subconsciously rub my arms, feeling the small, scattered burn marks I have littered across them from those kernels, and think about how tumultuous our relationship truly is. Maybe I need an intervention? Or maybe I enjoy the abuse?

I pull my gaze away from Craig's theatrics and give Zach an apologetic look. "We're sorry, Zach," I say, "We just got momentarily distracted. Don't worry, it won't happen again."

He tilts his head to the side as he stares at me, knowing damn well that's a blatant lie. He sighs, "Okay. Just try to talk a little less and work a little more, yeah?" he requests as he turns to walk back to the storage room for another case of nachos. I guess *Twilight* fans are also big nacho fans because we're already out of supply.

As Veronica mopes back to her station to fill cups with ice and soda, she mutters, "If you want to kiss his ass so badly, maybe the two of you should just get a room...or maybe utilize the back of theatre twelve. I hear it's empty, tonight."

I respond to her badgering by forcefully stomping my foot onto hers. Veronica yelps, "Damn, Sam! You didn't have to accost me with your fucking platform tennis shoes!"

My vision immediately darts down to my feet, and I realize I'm still wearing my Shape-ups. I forgot to change into my dress code-approved black, non-slip shoes. Oh well. No time to trudge back out to my Blazer to shuffle through my messy backseat to search for my work shoes.

"You deserved it!" I playfully hiss at her as I stick my tongue out and turn around to serve another Twihard a bucket of buttery bliss.

"Whatever, dress code offender," she yells at me over her shoulder.

I glance back at my best friend, who has tied her burgundy Cinedome shirt into a cute little knot to bare her well-toned midriff and reveal her sparkly, heart-shaped belly button ring. I dramatically roll my eyes. That's Veronica for you.

# CHAPTER FIVE:

As we prepare for the last rush of customers before the final showing of the night, Veronica starts passing around cups of coffee. Zach has just gone to open the back door of the theatre to allow Jill in. He has always been a fan of Jill and says she's the "good influence" Veronica and I need in our lives.

Jill and Zach stroll towards the snack bar area together. Veronica starts hollering as she ends her coffee catering by handing a steaming cup to Craig. "Wake up, sleepy heads!" she shouts. "Start drinking your coffees, losers. We're going to be awake until dawn...watching *Breaking Dawn!*" She cackles as we all roll our eyes at her lame joke.

"Your jokes are about as bad as your barista skills, girly!" Craig shouts back as he takes a sip of his coffee and gags in another one of his over-the-top performances. I swear this kid should be an actor. Veronica proceeds to stare daggers at him while I continue to mind my own business and sip my awful coffee in silence.

As Jill reaches the cafe area of the snack bar, she daintily sets her enormous tote on one of the tables. She decided she'd rather come early to sit and study in the snack bar's cafe area as Veronica and I finish working than sit alone at home in the apartment until 2:00 AM. Jill is convinced our apartment is haunted and hates to be there alone if she doesn't have to. I've told Jill that I don't think ghosts haunt apartment complexes—they prefer more spacious places like old, Victorian mansions.

A few weeks ago, after I got home from a day at the hospital, Jill began divulging to me her deep, dark worries about me becoming a hospice nurse. Her fear was that the spirits of the patients I care for will attach themselves to my soul and follow me throughout my life. My mouth fell open as I stared at my best friend in disbelief. I quickly ripped the remote control out of her grasp and powered off the television in the middle of her *Ghost Adventures* marathon.

"No more scary television programming for you, Jillian. You're on restriction," I snapped. She instantly folded her arms across her body, threw herself back into the sofa like a petulant child, and pouted. "You know you get nightmares when you watch this stuff anyway, Jill," I reminded her.

"No, I don't!" she whined as she threw the blanket that lay on the back of our hand-me-down sofa over her head.

At 3:15 AM that morning I woke to a soft knocking at my bedroom door. I groaned as I dragged myself out of my bed and shuffled my way to the bedroom door while the knocking continued. I cracked open the door and peered out with bleary eyes. My vision slowly focused on my best friend huddled against the wall, clasping her blanket tightly around her, her hand still raised in mid-knock.

"Yes?" I slowly asked, then noticed her cheeks were red and tear stained.

"I had this awful nightmare," she whispered, "It woke me up. It even made me bolt upright in bed! Then I looked over at my alarm clock and saw it was the witching hour!" She shivered as she finished.

"Why are you whispering? And what the hell is a witching hour?" I asked.

She looked at me, stunned that I didn't know what she was referring to. "The witching hour," she continued whispering for no apparent reason, "Everyone knows the witching hour is 3:00 AM!"

I was too exhausted to have that conversation. I sighed, "Come on." I waved her into my room. She immediately scurried past me and dove under my covers. I chuckled as I slid into bed next to her, "I told you that you'd have nightmares watching that," I teased.

"Shush," she replied, "I'm sleeping."

The squeak of a metal cafe chair pulls my attention back to Jill, who is now sitting comfortably in the cafe. Veronica and I abruptly abandon our posts to rush over and greet Jill as she starts unloading her textbooks from her tote bag. She jumps out of her chair to engulf us in a group hug. I love Jill's solo hugs too, but what I love most of all is having one arm around both of them.

"Thanks for coming over, Jill," I say as we release each other from our mutual embrace.

"It's just because she didn't want to be taken advantage of by a horny poltergeist," Veronica blurts, teasing her about her well-known fear of ghosts.

Jill's mouth falls open in shock as her hands bolt to her hips in a defensive stance. "Veronica Mae, you really should clean up your vocabulary!" she scolds in a hushed voice. Veronica hates her middle name, but Jill loves to use it whenever something outrageous comes barreling out of her mouth.

"Calm down, Jilly Bean!" Veronica laughs, "Horny isn't even a bad word!"

"It's not the word itself but the context that you used it in," Jill asserts, "And I'm never telling you anything personal again if you're going to just throw it in my face!"

"Okay children, that's enough!" I interrupt as I give Veronica a disapproving glare.

Veronica dramatically shrugs her shoulders and sighs. "I'm sorry for being a bitch, Jill. You know I love you," she mutters.

In response, Jill warmly smiles at her and wraps her in a big hug once more. That's better, I think to myself.

Suddenly Zach calls over to me, annoyance dripping from his voice, "Samantha, what happened to more working, less talking?" he asks.

I look to where he's standing as I see him motion for me to return to my place behind the snack bar. "You have a customer!" he bellows at me like I'm a football field's length away instead of six feet.

I irritatedly note that Zach only demands *my* presence back behind the counter. He acts as if he doesn't see Veronica now sitting with Jill at the cafe table leisurely chatting. I have to admit, I'm totally team Craig on this one. She always gets whatever her lil' heart desires. Poor Craig and I are the ones left with cold, lonely heads.

"Coming, Zachary," I call sweetly, in a purposeful attempt to mask how pissed off I feel.

As I trudge towards the snack bar, I see an extremely tall man standing at the counter with his back facing me. He must be at least 6'4". As I round the counter, I discreetly eye him up and down. The man has a lean but athletic build, just the right amount of muscle. I'm not a fan of those beefed-up jughead types.

As I approach the other side of the counter, I glance down at my shirt and realize I've somehow squirted butter all down the front of it. I unsuccessfully rub at the butter stain on my shirt as I reach the snack bar counter and hear the man awkwardly clear his throat. If this man is trying to get my attention, I'm obviously already aware he's standing there.

Feeling extremely irked but doing an excellent job of hiding it, my gaze lifts from my shirt to the man standing before me as I pleasantly begin greeting him.

"Hello, what may I get you to..." And I'm suddenly at a loss for words. Well, except for the words I utter next. "...What the fuck," I whisper as hazel eyes lock with mine and I'm greeted with a familiar sideways smile.

"Hey, it's you. I didn't know you worked here," the paramedic greets me with a huge grin.

"Well of course you didn't know I worked here!" I snap at him. "Because you don't even know who I am, so why on earth would you know where a stranger works?" His hazel eyes widen as both of his hands shoot up defensively.

"Whoa! Well, aren't you just full of piss and vinegar this evening?" he blurts. At this point, I'm ready to throw my body over this counter and choke him out.

"Hey look," he continues. "I'm really sorry for how Brett acted earlier tonight. He can be a total dick sometimes." So, the frat boy has a name, Brett, which just so happens to sound like the name of a complete frat boy douchebag. Fitting.

I interrupt the man to ponder aloud, "Do you think his mother named him Brett in the hope he'd live up to the name and meet his full douchebag potential? Or do you think it was in the hope that he'd beat all the odds, overcome the douchery of his birth-given name, and become a halfway-decent human being?" I stare at him blankly once I finish my thought.

The man erupts into laughter so loud it not only catches the attention of Jill and Veronica, but Zach and Craig turn to stare at us as well. He has a wonderful laugh, almost contagious.

"I like you," the man declares. "Is douchery even a word?" he then asks.

"I created it for your guy Brett," I reply, starting to snicker now myself. "He should feel so special."

The man points a finger at me as he continues chuckling. "Hey, no one said I claim him," he corrects me. "Seriously though, Brett's used to girls just falling all over him. But not you. You really put him in his place tonight and it was fantastic to watch. So, thank you, Samantha."

He says my name softer than the rest of his sentence, almost as if he's testing how it tastes on his tongue. How the hell does this guy know my name? I then realize that I'm wearing a name tag.

I decide at this moment I need to attempt to re-tuck my shirt into my slacks. This shirt is so ugly. I'm also acutely aware of how frizzy my hair has become over the last couple of hours. I softly tuck a strand of hair that has fallen loose from my ponytail behind my ear as my vision falls to my shoes. Why do I suddenly feel so nervous? I slowly lift my gaze back up from my feet to find hazel eyes staring at me.

"I go by Sam," I quietly tell him.

"Hello, Sam. I go by Miles," he falters. "Well, I mean... I'm Miles. Miles is my name. So, um yeah, that's what people call me," he stutters.

Why does he suddenly seem to be nervous too? I see a faint blush rise to his cheeks as he grants me another one of his adorable sideways smirks. My gaze travels down from his eyes to rest upon his lips and the small, faint scar above his upper lip. For some reason, that scar is wildly sexy, and he really does have nice lips. My breath catches as I watch his lips slightly part as he exhales. I wonder what his lips would feel like on mine.

And here I go again being extremely creepy and thinking embarrassing thoughts about a complete stranger. I pull myself out of my trance and drop my vision to my feet again. I am one hundred percent positive he caught me staring at his mouth. Luckily, he doesn't call me out on it.

"Hey bro, what's taking so long? I thought you were just getting popcorn! They said they're running late, and we should save them seats." My head immediately snaps up and I lock eyes with Brett. He momentarily seems to be caught off guard at seeing me in front of him, but he quickly recovers and gives me a devilish grin.

"Well, well, well. Look who we have here, Miles," Brett purrs at me, "It's my girl from the cafeteria."

"I'm not your girl and I never will be," I spit at him as Miles appears to look increasingly uncomfortable. I expect a smart-ass reply from Brett, but he's fallen silent.

Brett's vision narrows as his eyes bore into me. His composure appears to have snapped and his posture stiffens. He noticeably scowls as the right side of his mouth lifts into a snarl. If I didn't know better, I would've sworn this man had just suffered a small stroke. I've said way worse things to him just tonight. I mean, I called him a Backstreet Boy and ridiculed his frosted tips. I even spilled an entire large soda on his crotch, and he didn't look this angry. I wonder what caused his drastic mood change this time?

"Why don't you just get us a tub of popcorn and stop wasting my time? Extra butter," he barks at me. The sooner I get this man what he wants the sooner he will get the hell away from me. How did I get so lucky to have to endure two encounters with Brett in a single evening?

I start layering popcorn into a bucket with a metal scoop, intermittently drizzling butter into the tub and keeping my eyes down the whole time. The bucket is almost full, thank goodness. Then I can shove it into his hands and this ridiculously tense ordeal can be over.

As I finish filling the tub of popcorn, I look back up to the men and see that once again Brett is grinning at me. How can a smile so perfect somehow look so evil? Miles stands awkwardly next to him, looking as if he wished he could crawl out of his skin. As Brett continues to mockingly grin down at me, I'm all at once very aware this is what people refer to as "the calm before the storm."

Brett turns his body to Miles, suddenly pretending that I am no longer there, and slaps him on the back. "You know, Miles," Brett chuckles, "This chick might not be as hideous if she learned how to shut her fucking mouth."

I drop the metal scoop I was grasping, and it falls to the floor with a loud clank. Tears spring to my eyes as every insecurity I've buried inside me over the years claws its way to the surface. I've never felt beautiful, never thought I was pretty, not in comparison to my two drop-dead gorgeous best friends. These are thoughts I've never said aloud, but I've always felt like the ugly duckling while Jill and Veronica are the swans. This day has been downright awful. I don't have an ounce of energy left to continue fighting with Brett. As my tears begin to roll down my cheeks, I know he has won. He's gotten me to react exactly how he hoped I would.

"That's enough, Brett!" Miles bellows. My vision darts up to the two men as I watch Miles throw his palms into Brett's chest, propelling him backward. Brett falls back a few steps before catching himself. He yells back to Miles, "What the hell dude? Why are you defending her?"

"Because you crossed the line, Brett," Miles replies frankly.

Through my tears I find myself smiling at Miles as he gives Brett his best death stare. Brett sighs as he turns back to the counter to face me, and I continue beaming at Miles. Although I know I'm staring now, I can't help but admire him. Watching him defend my honor was pretty damn attractive. I hear Brett forcefully inhale. I turn my attention to his shaking form as I notice him balling his fists at his sides. Suddenly the frat boy wannabe has gone from looking considerably pissed to looking undeniably irate. I stand alone, unable to pull my stare away from Brett's icy blue eyes, preparing myself for the attack I know is coming.

I suddenly sense Veronica approach behind me at the snack bar. She comes to stand at my side, her arms defensively crossed over her chest. I hear her breathing quicken as she clicks her tongue against the roof of her mouth. If you know Veronica, you know this is one of her tells, a sign that she's about to pounce. In my peripheral vision, I catch Jill standing as she lifts her huge bag onto her shoulder and saunters to the outskirts of the snack bar near where Miles and Brett stand. Jill may be the definition of a lady, but she's absolutely fearless when it comes to defending the people she loves.

I notice Craig, now. He sets down the plastic bucket he was using to fill the ice machine and casually walks around to the end of the snack bar, silently lifting the countertop so he can walk through it. The whole time his stare never breaks from the two men standing at the other end of the counter. The final *Twilight* showing has already started, so no other patrons remain in the theatre lobby at this point.

Last but not least, I turn my head slightly to the left to see Zach walking out of the backroom, clipboard in hand. He appears to immediately sense the change in atmosphere, the tension is almost palpable. Zach looks to Craig's tense posture as he stands on the opposite side of the counter, then his eyes dart to meet mine. Somehow, he's able to instantly sense my distress. He tosses his clipboard onto the counter and starts walking towards where Veronica and I stand.

For the second time today, I'm comforted by the realization that I'm not alone. This group of misfits are the closest friends I've ever had. I've found my pack. Or maybe they found me? Nevertheless, I now have the family I felt was cruelly ripped away from me fourteen years ago.

Superman was remarkable, but some would argue he was truly nothing without his Justice League.

# CHAPTER SIX:

I pull my vision from Zach's to settle on Brett's devious glower once more. I lift the tub of warm popcorn I've been clutching, timidly offering it to Brett. In my head, I beg him to please just take the tub and walk away. Maybe he'll notice the presence of my four friends who all have begun moving closer to where he stands, all simultaneously giving him a warning glare. Maybe he'll just take the tub of popcorn and leave—he's already late for the movie. I won't even charge him for it if that means he'll disappear from my life and never return. I'll just tell Zach to take it out of my check. Money well spent.

As Brett calmly takes the tub from my hands, I let out a sigh of relief. The box office staff has already left for the night and all but two patrons have taken their seats inside the theatre. The lobby is so eerily quiet that I swear I can hear the crickets chirping outside; however, that silence doesn't remain.

The next sound I hear is Brett hissing my name. "Samantha. Let me make myself clear," he snarls, "The next time you spill something on my dick, I'm going to make you lick it off!" As he finishes his verbal assault, he hurls the tub of popcorn at Veronica and me. My mouth falls to the floor and from that point, everything happens rather quickly.

Veronica slams her hands onto the glass countertop, catapulting herself over it like a deranged spider monkey. Her body collides into Brett's, the force of her attack knocking him back into the glass case that houses the soft pretzels. The case tips over and pretzels rain down onto the floor around the two of them. Veronica, now sitting atop Brett's chest, attempts to use both of her knees to pin down his arms. She then proceeds to grab a pretzel off the floor and smack him across the face with it hard enough that I see beads of salt sail through the air. If Brett thought I was a crazy bitch, he had never met Miss Veronica Sanders.

All attention is abruptly drawn to Craig standing at the opposite end of the counter as he roars a quote from his favorite comic book, catching us all off guard. Craig is more of a Marvel Comics fan while I, of course, am the ultimate DC Comics fan. We have constant heated arguments over which universe is better. He suddenly starts charging toward the commotion like a human freight train. What would a physical fight in a movie theatre be without a battle call of cinematic proportions? I stand frozen behind the counter as I watch Craig pummel Miles, forcefully knocking his tall figure to the floor. Miles looks momentarily dazed as he tries to regain his footing. He's just a second too late as Craig lands a right hook square to his jaw. This cannot be happening.

I seriously think Miles might be dead as I watch his body lie motionless on the hideous theatre carpet, but I'm unexpectedly stunned to see his long body rotate and sweep Craig's legs out from under him. I think Craig is just about as stunned as I am. I watch wide-eyed as Craig instinctively throws both of his hands forward in an attempt to catch his falling body. As Craig plummets to the ground, Miles lands a solid jab to the middle of his nose and blood instantly begins to spray.

Holy shit, I think Miles just broke Craig's nose.

Craig reacts without pause, throwing his entire body weight into Miles and forcing his body to slam back onto the floor. I cringe as I hear the sound of Miles's head smacking into the ground.

Holy shit, I think Craig just gave Miles a concussion.

As I continue watching the two men roll around on the floor in a tangle of punches and kicks, I decide this has officially gone too far. This has been a more evenly matched fight than I originally predicted it would be. Miles may have almost eight inches on Craig, but Craig is built like a bulldog. Compact and all muscle. I now recall Craig telling me he used to wrestle in high school as I watch him put Miles into a half nelson. Even though part of me would love to see how this pans out, I know I can't continue to stand by and let these two beat the shit out of each other.

I run around the back of the counter and can see Brett lift Veronica off of him and gently set her thrashing body onto the floor beside him. He starts to crawl away from her as she continues her bread assault, hurling soft pretzels at his retreating form. When he moves to stand, I see Jill sashay over to him, fearless and utterly fabulous. I watch as she wallops him across the back of his head with her industrial-sized purse.

And now we have a possible second concussion on our hands.

Jill shrieks, "No one talks to my best friend like that you jerk!" Even when Jillian Moore is enraged, she still keeps her vocabulary squeaky clean.

Brett grabs the back of his head with one hand and throws his other hand out to protect his face when Jill revs up to swing her weapon again. I round the corner at the end of the snack bar counter just as Zach catches my arm, pulling my vision to his.

"Sam, are you okay? What the hell is happening?" he asks as his breathing quickens. He appears to be equally, if not more, stunned than I am.

"I'm fine and I'm not really sure, but we have to stop this. This is insane," I respond to him breathlessly. For the second time today, I can feel the start of a panic attack encroaching into the space of my normally rational thoughts. Why does anxiety always pick the worst time to rear its ugly, inconvenient head?

Zach nods to me. We both turn in unison and run towards the chaos. As I move forward, I watch Veronica and Jill circle around where Brett is still kneeling, like a frenzy of sharks about to rip their defenseless prey piece by piece. I'm not saying he doesn't deserve it, but he has already been pretty roughed up tonight by overpriced movie theatre snacks. When I am about to reach the three of them, I hear a loud clank as Miles and Craig roll into one of the metal cafe tables and knock it to the floor. Has everyone here lost all common sense except for Zach and me?

I finally reach Veronica's side and rip a pretzel out of her death grip. "STOP! Please, just stop!" I scream at the same time my three-inch-high tennis shoe slips on a stray piece of popcorn and sends me spinning backward onto the tiled area of the snack bar. Death by popcorn. Somehow, I always knew this is how it would end for me.

As I'm falling, I can see Zach reach out to try and help me. But, alas, he is too far for me to catch his grasp. I'm starting to realize this is why upper management is such a stickler about us wearing non-slip shoes.

That's when *he* catches me. Yes, Brett. Instinctively reacting to my horrified screaming, he spins around on his knees to face my direction. As my body goes flying to the ground, he catches me in his open arms and eases me onto his lap, one of his arms under both my knees and the other resting across my upper back. He looks down at my face and we lock eyes. His eyes are the same hue of blue as before, but they somehow seem less cold now.

This is how the whole ordeal ends, with this man cradling me on his lap, only five minutes after he indirectly told me to give him a blow job. Then my fiercely loyal, yet semi-insane, friends attacked with such vengeance that even I was left flabbergasted.

You may ask what I do next, like whether I in fact give this disrespectful man-child the earful he deserves for acting like an unforgivable asshole. Well, what I actually do is I start to laugh hysterically. And as my laughter continues, everyone stops to stare at me. They have to see how funny this all is—how ridiculous.

Instead, Veronica, Jill, and Zach collectively look down at me from where they stand, still as statues, all three of them appearing completely confused by my sudden humor. Miles and Craig finally stop rolling around on the floor like children and sit up to stare at me. Both are bloodied and battered. As my vision finds them now, sitting side by side in silence on the hideous carpet, I laugh even louder. They both look absolutely horrendous and somehow that makes this moment even more hysterical to me.

Suddenly, I feel Brett's body start subtly shaking under me. I look up to him as he joins me in unrestrained laughter, still holding me in his arms. Why is he still holding me like I'm an infant? By then, we are all laughing, the sound echoing across the almost-empty theatre lobby.

I snicker to Brett, "She slapped you in the face with a pretzel!"

"I know she did. I can still taste the salt!" he chuckles, "She pitched more than a few stray pretzels at my head." He turns his head to look up at Veronica. "Did you play softball in high school?" he laughs.

"You wanna see my fastball?" Veronica asks as she reaches down, grabbing another pretzel off the ground. Zach immediately slaps it out of her hand, and it falls back to the floor.

"That's a perfectly good waste of a delicious pretzel, if you ask me," Veronica smirks. "And no, I won't be licking any salt off your face, dick-wad!" she declares.

We all laugh even harder at how utterly ridiculous seven adults have just behaved. Brett starts to stand, and he lifts me to my feet. Once he knows I'm steady and won't take another tumble to the floor, he removes his arms from around my waist and shoves his hands into his pockets. It almost looks like a precaution to prevent himself from touching my body again.

"See, I told you that you were asking for it in those shoes," he laughs. "I tried to warn you they were dangerous, but no, you didn't listen. You even wore them to work," he says with a wide grin.

"That's definitely not what you meant," I gripe. It's strange how quickly the dynamic has changed between him and me. He's gone from tearing me apart to almost flirting with me.

Miles and Craig both begin lifting themselves off the floor, not without a few grunts and moans. They turn to look at each other and laugh once more as they shake each other's hands in what appears to be a peace offering. I've always found it strange how men can be attempting to kill each other one second, then bros the next. And they complain women are confusing.

Miles has a pretty gnarly busted lip, and I can already see a bruise forming on his jaw from Craig's fist. I'm more concerned with the blow he took to the back of his head, though. Craig doesn't look to be in much better shape either. His nose is still oozing blood down his face and onto his Cinedome button-up. I wonder if we have any hydrogen peroxide in the backroom to get that blood out of his shirt.

After I'm done worrying about the potential survival outcome of his hideous uniform, I'm instantly concerned that his nose may be broken. I walk over to examine the two men as my nursing student instincts take the wheel.

"Hey there, cowboy. Let me see that nose of yours," I approach Craig first, giving him my best drawl in an attempt to imitate his own southern accent. Maybe if I lighten the mood, this will all be a little less awkward.

He grins at me, then throws his trademark finger-guns my way as he replies, "It'd be my pleasure to have the best darn nurse in all of Bristol give me the once-over."

"Almost-nurse," I correct him as I eye his nose. Good, it doesn't look broken.

"It's not broken," I hear Miles interrupt my assessment.

I shoot him a glare because I can obviously see that.

"Just trying to help," he says as his hands shoot up defensively. That seems to be Miles's trademark move. "You know I do have a bit of medical training myself," he winks at me. At this moment, he's no longer endearing—he's just annoying.

"Since you're the one who punched him in the face, you don't get to be the one to decide if it's broken or not!" I stomp my shoe on the ground as I give Miles my most intimidating glare. I'm annoyed because I feel like he's trying to undermine my own medical knowledge and weasel in his own two cents.

He narrows his eyes at me and smirks as he replies, "Alright, then. Please give us your diagnosis, nurse."

"First off, nurses can't diagnose. It's not within our scope of practice. And, like I just said, almost-nurse," I mutter. Does this guy even listen? I turn back to Craig and simply say, "It's not broken."

I hear Miles laugh and whisper, "Told ya."

Craig nods, eyeing Miles before joining in on the laughter. Now they're both annoying me. "You two don't need to be fighting over me, now. There's enough to go around," Craig says as he winks at me and does a little twirl, putting himself on display for us. How dare he try to steal my signature pirouette entrance! I roll my eyes at both of them, then take a step towards Miles.

"Let me see your head," I demand.

"Whoa, at least take me to dinner first," Miles laughs. I scoff and roll my eyes even more dramatically at this infuriating man.

"The one on your shoulders. The one that might have a concussion," I snap at him.

He runs his hand through his wild, curly hair and smiles a sideways grin at me, "I'm okay, Sam. I've hit my head way harder than that before. Don't worry," he replies. I'm instantly distracted at hearing my name float from his lips. I like how it sounds when he says it. And now I'm staring at his lips again. I blush, then focus on the scar above his lip. I think to myself that he's probably being truthful; he probably has hit his head much harder than this before.

"How did you get that scar above your lip?" I hastily slap my hand over my mouth. I can't believe I just asked him that out loud. He seems a bit surprised, as well. I don't blame him. This nosy girl just randomly asked him something fairly personal. It naturally takes him a few seconds to formulate an answer.

"I was in an accident," he replies simply.

"I'm sorry," I breathe, "Sometimes words fall from my lips before my brain can catch up and tell me to shut my mouth." He laughs, then runs his hand through his hair once more.

"We'll call it even if I get to ask you a question now," he says as he smiles at me. Little does he know, there's nothing interesting about me. No questions worth asking.

"That would only be fair," I nod at him. He glances down at his shoes, takes a deep breath, and slowly lifts his vision to meet mine again.

"Will you get coffee with me?" he almost whispers.

I'm completely caught off-guard by this. I'm at a loss for words. Is he asking me on a date? "Are you asking me on a date?" I finally manage to reply.

"What? No!" he answers a bit too forcefully if you ask me. "I'm not asking you to marry me or anything, Sam. I'm asking you to coffee. As a friend. Only a friend," he defends.

Jesus, Miles. I get it. No need to embarrass me any further for thinking such an apparently ludicrous thought.

"I get it," I try to say as disinterested as possible before turning to walk back to the others, now chatting amongst themselves. Civilly, I might add. Let me just pick my destroyed self-esteem up off the floor first. Then I can run away and hide in the women's bathroom until he leaves. I'm already planning ways I can avoid ever having to see this man again when I feel him grab my hand.

"Sam, wait. I didn't mean to hurt your feelings," he apologizes.

"I don't have feelings," I growl at him, "and if I did, you surely couldn't hurt them!" What the hell am I even saying? Who cares? He hurt my feelings.

"I'm sorry," he says, running his hand through his wild hair once again. "I didn't mean it like that. I didn't mean to sound like a jerk. I just moved here a couple months ago and Brett's really my only friend. I'm just looking for more friends and you seem like a cool person," he confesses. "I also know you drink coffee since you got one in the cafeteria tonight," he tells me as if I forgot about the fact that I drink coffee.

"You don't really have quantity *or* quality going for you in the friend department, do you?" I laugh. I glance over to Brett who appears to be invested in a pretty serious conversation with Jill. She must've just said something funny because he laughs and smiles at her. I notice how her eyes light up when he flashes her that hundred-watt smile of his. I guess he really isn't all that bad.

As if reading my mind, Miles laughs and explains, "He isn't all that bad. He can be an asshole, but he really does have a good heart. We've been friends since we were kids. Brett moved out here for a job first, then I followed him."

"He has succeeded at being an asshole to me during every encounter we've ever had," I state.

"For some reason, you seem to get under his skin more than anyone I've ever seen. Even me," he chuckles.

"Do I get under your skin, too?" I question him.

He smirks at me and replies, "Not yet, but hopefully, we have plenty of time."

"Fine, friend," I respond. "I will drink a cup of coffee in your presence when it best suits my schedule."

Miles chuckles as his smile widens, "I'm looking forward to it. That is if I can remember this conversation with the concussion I probably just suffered. You really should've assessed me," he teases. I swiftly smack him in the arm and he grunts. "Ouch," he whispers.

I turn to walk back towards the other side of the snack bar. As the seven of us now stand in the tiled area of the snack bar, which now resembles a carbohydrate graveyard, I feel Brett lightly tap my shoulder. I look up to meet his gaze and suddenly feel nervous. Why do I feel nervous? He wouldn't say something horrendous to me again now, would he?

"Um, I guess I should probably apologize," he mumbles. He's apologizing? Someone pinch me, I must be dreaming.

"You guess you should apologize? You should be groveling at her feet and kissing her ugly shoes, asshole!" Veronica interrupts, scolding him.

Brett softly chuckles and points at Veronica, "Please don't sic this terrifying creature on me again." Veronica proceeds to make a hissing sound and scratch at the air in front of where he's standing like a pissed-off house cat.

"The next person to make a comment about my shoes is getting kicked in the ass by one!" I threaten. I'm so fed up with this unnecessary abuse about my choice of footwear.

Brett then looks my way and gives me an over-exaggerated wink. Without thinking, I step toward him and playfully swat him on the arm like we're old friends—not like we were just at war with one another fifteen minutes ago. He catches my hand in his, momentarily holding onto it before releasing me. He offers me the first genuine smile I've seen him give me, and I can't help but return it with my own. He really does have the potential to be charming if he didn't behave like such a dick-wad, as Veronica so eloquently put it.

"I don't think you should be complaining over there," Miles calls to Brett. "You got to wrestle with two pretty girls while I got violently tackled by Captain Cowboy." Miles lovingly smacks Craig on the back after he walks over to us. "Obviously, I drew the short straw here." We all break out into another chorus of laughter.

Out loud I'm laughing, but subconsciously I find myself feeling a slight pang of jealousy. I'm aware of how Miles just referred to my two best friends as pretty, but only minutes ago, he insisted that he just wants to be friends with me. I hate how insecure I feel about this. I thought that he and I possibly had a moment earlier this evening, maybe the hint of something to come. Then again, I'm the girl who has pined after my boss for two years without even an inkling that he feels the same. Maybe I'm not the best judge of potentially romantic encounters. It doesn't seem far-fetched that I'd be a bit delusional about the two brief encounters between Miles and me. It's not like I have time for any of this anyway. I'm in a very committed relationship with nursing school and only have about thirty thousand dollars worth of school loans riding on the hopes that this works out for me. So, I guess you could say I'm already taken.

Zach pulls me out of my internal battle over whether I care if Miles thinks I'm pretty or not when he addresses Brett and Miles.

"So, you guys have missed a pretty good amount of the movie by now," he informs them. "If you both keep your mouths shut about what happened here tonight and help us clean this all up, you can tag along for our private viewing once this last showing gets out."

I'm shocked Zach just invited them to watch the movie with us. This was just supposed to be our friend group. Our pack. I don't know how I feel about two strangers barging in on our private showing. Not to mention we also just had a full-out brawl with them in front of the snack bar counter. Suddenly, I'm a bit pissed-off. Do they deserve to join us? It was supposed to be just the five of us tonight. I don't want Miles and Brett somehow ruining this movie for me.

"Well, we were actually meeting some, um, girls at this movie," Miles stutters. "They're probably going to be pretty pissed if we stand them up," he finishes.

Of course, they were meeting girls. This doesn't seem much like a "bro date" movie. I thought Miles was just looking for friends, though. Or maybe he was just looking to be friends with me...

"Oh, no way!" Veronica gushes. "You mean you two boys weren't going to see a *Twilight* movie, just the two of you?" She smiles deviously and continues, "Wait? Are you two not together? Silly me, I could've sworn you were lovers."

Brett glares at her, while Miles is left speechless. Oh, Veronica Mae. There's always something outrageous falling from your lips.

"I think that's awesome if y'all are lovers," Craig declares. "Stop sounding so judgmental, Veronica," he scolds. I snicker as Miles's mouth falls open. I'm reminded how much I love Craig. He has such a loving soul. That is when he isn't beating up Miles.

Miles finally remembers how to speak, "We're just friends. But if that was the case, you'd be more of my type anyway, Craig," he says with a straight face. Then, for what feels like the hundredth time this evening, we all start to laugh.

"You're pretty funny," Veronica tells Miles, "I like this one," she declares.

"I like them both," Jill chimes in. "I say you two join us. There's no better way to watch a movie than with the whole theatre to yourself," she states.

"Would it be okay if we joined you guys, Sam?" Brett asks me unexpectedly, pulling my attention to him once more. I find him and Miles both staring at me, now. Then I realize that everyone seems to be staring at me, waiting for my answer.

I point at Brett and muster up my most threatening voice, "Not another smart remark from you, mister. Or I'll personally beat your ass with one of these Nathan's hotdogs. They aren't nearly as soft as those pretzels," I tell him.

"Yes, ma'am," he nods as he grants me another smile.

"Then you both may join us," I announce as Veronica, Jill, and Craig start to cheer. Oh, how the tables have turned.

Brett looks toward Miles, shrugging his shoulders. "Well, I can tell you for a fact that Ashleigh and Madison are already pissed at us," he laughs. "I have four texts from Madison. And the last one called us some explicit names, Miles."

Miles glances at Zach, then looks to me as he asks, "Is there somewhere you can hide us when that movie gets out? I don't think Brett and I can handle another beating."

Brett dramatically shudders and murmurs, "I'll never look at a pretzel the same way again."

# CHAPTER SEVEN:

As the last *Breaking Dawn* showing finally releases, Veronica and I usher out the late-night moviegoers and formulate our plan. To make a spur-of-the-moment private showing a hit, a well-formulated plan must be in order. If you couldn't tell, these are the exact words of one Miss Jillian Moore, the plan-master extraordinaire.

Jill, Brett, and Miles are currently hiding out in the stock room while the last stragglers exit the theatre. As Veronica and I stand outside the entrance to theatre number three, we notice two blonde women about our age walking out of the theatre with scowls plastered on their faces. Needless to say, they both look extremely pissed-off.

"I guess they didn't like the movie," Veronica whispers to me while eyeing the two women.

"Um, I don't think that's why they're pissed-off," I snicker back to her.

"I can't believe those assholes just stood us up," one woman complains to the other. "He said that they were here getting popcorn. Do you think he was lying?"

I give Veronica a look that says don't get involved, but I know my best friend better than that. I sigh as I watch her take a few steps towards them.

"All men are liars," Veronica announces. "It's just best to keep your expectations low. Like I mean bottom of the barrel low. With the male gender as a whole. But I warn you, they'll still manage to disappoint you even with the lowest of standards," she finishes, gazing at both women with a sweet smile on her face—the fakest damn smile, I've ever seen.

"Excuse me?" one of the women questions, sassily placing a hand on her hip. "No one was talking to you. I suggest you mind your own business," she spits at Veronica.

Here we go, again. Thankfully there are no soft pretzels in our general vicinity.

"Well, I suggest you—" Veronica starts to hiss before I forcefully grab her arm and pull her behind me. I'm way too exhausted for another tumultuous event tonight.

"—We suggest you two have a great night," I speak through gritted teeth to the women.

They both respond by giving me a nasty look, turning simultaneously with dramatic hair flips like bitchy synchronized swimmers, and walking off.

"Ew! They are absolutely awful!" Veronica remarks. I laugh and give her a light shove with my shoulder.

"Down, girl. You've pounced on enough people this evening," I chuckle to her.

"All for you, Sammie Bear," she smiles at me.

As the final patrons exit the theatre, Veronica and I rush inside. I'm pushing a huge trash can while Veronica is in tow with a broom and dustpan.

Whenever Zach allows us to do private showings after-hours, it's always Veronica's and my job to hurriedly clean the last theatre while Craig is on snack duty. Craig always pops a ton of fresh popcorn and shovels it into a huge trash bag—a clean one, of course—then proceeds to pour a boatload of butter into the bag. If you've never eaten buttered popcorn out of a giant garbage bag you've never truly lived.

Zach learned how to operate the projector from one of his friends who usually works the late shift, so it's his job to start the film once we're ready. I believe his friend's name is Todd, but I've never really talked with him because he's always locked up in the projection booth. Zach invited Todd to our private showing, but since he's already had to watch this same movie multiple times today, he politely declined. As he always does.

Lastly, Jill's job is to supervise the operation. All well-functioning machines have many moving parts.

Veronica and I return to the snack bar after cleaning the theatre to find Craig taking a gulp of butter-flavored oil, straight from the nozzle. I hate to be a party pooper, but the "butter" used at movie theaters is in fact not real butter. Real butter would make the popcorn too soggy.

"Craig Corey!" I bellow at him. I've always thought he had a name that sounded like he should be famous. Who knows? Maybe one day he'll surprise us all. "You get your filthy mouth away from that nozzle," I reprimand him as Jill, Brett, and Miles join us at the snack bar.

"Sam, relax," Craig sighs. "You know I waterfall. No mouth-to-mouth on that bad boy," he says defensively.

"It's a nozzle. You can't give a nozzle mouth-to-mouth, Craig. It doesn't have a mouth," I say exasperatedly as Craig laughs at me.

"Thanks for clarifying that, almost-nurse," Miles teases, bending down to nudge my shoulder. The man is just over a foot taller than me, so even with my Shape-ups, the top of my head only reaches his chest.

I scowl up at him. "Since you may or may not have a concussion, I'll let that one slide," I warn as he throws his hands up in defense.

I feel my phone vibrate in the pocket of my slacks and pull it out to see a text from Zach. "Okay, guys. Zach's ready for us," I announce.

"You all really have this down to a science, don't you?" Brett laughs.

"Y'all bet we do," Craig drawls, shooting Brett his good ol' finger guns. "I got the popcorn," he announces as he hoists the garbage bag over his shoulder. "But if y'all want some pop, you'll have to handle that yourself," he points to the soda fountain.

I nod towards Craig and ask him, "Do you want me to grab you a soda?"

"No, I always keep this bottle full of that red stuff," he says, pointing to the water bottle under his arm. "You know, I try not to drink too much water. It bloats me."

"That red stuff is called fruit punch," I remind him with a laugh. Only Craig. The man that runs on comic book quotes, fruit punch, and butter-flavored oil.

I watch as Brett and Miles pour themselves drinks, then follow Craig's lead into theatre twelve. Veronica, Jill, and I are the only ones left at the snack bar. Jill proceeds to pour herself a Diet Coke. It's not like she needs to drink diet, but she's one of those weird people who claim Diet Coke just tastes better.

"Alright, ladies," Veronica pulls our attention to her. "I got us a little treat for the movie. I went and picked it up on my break." She pulls a bottle of Smirnoff Vodka out of the tote bag that's resting on her shoulder. "I sprung for the good stuff, too. No rubbing alcohol for us tonight," she proclaims.

Usually, we all drink cheap liquor and even cheaper beer. The three of us are financially struggling college students. I've found that the faster you drink, the less you notice how awful it tastes.

Jill gasps. "Veronica Mae, you know we can't drink here. Are you trying to get Sam and you fired?" she scolds Veronica in a hushed voice.

"I might have to agree with Jill on this one," I say. "You know Zach is cool, but I think he'll draw the line with this."

"That's why we're not going to tell him, duh!" she responds, obviously annoyed at us questioning her.

"I want no part of this," Jill pouts. "You two can do whatever you want. They're *your* jobs. I'm going to go find a good seat," she chastises and stomps off.

I refrain from mentioning that all the seats are good since we have the entire theatre to ourselves.

"God, she's so uptight sometimes," Veronica moans. "Well, Sam, do you want some? I know you need something to help you deal with this shitty day."

I think back to all that has happened today. Well technically it's 2:20 AM, but since I haven't slept yet I still consider it the same day. Today, a man died before my eyes. That was the first time in my life I'd seen someone die. My brother died when I was seven, but my parents wouldn't let me stay in the room with them when he passed.

I think once more of Mr. Gomez, the man who lost his life. I felt his ribs break beneath my palms. I watched him struggle and writhe in pain earlier that day as his son made the decision that he would remain a full code. I was neither able to save him nor help him pass away peacefully, free from the agony I can only imagine he endured. I felt completely helpless. Like I failed him.

I grab a disposable cup off of the stack by the counter, fill it with ice, and thrust the cup at Veronica. I just want to feel numb to all of this. I don't want to think about Mr. Gomez anymore tonight. I want to enjoy this movie and have a good time with my friends. A couple drinks in my system not only helps take the edge off my anxiousness, but it always seems to help me have a better time overall.

"Fill it," I command. She grabs the cup from me and obediently fills it with vodka, a sinful smile playing on her face.

"You and I are cut from the same cloth, Sammie Bear," she smiles. "We know how to have a good time, unlike our Little Goody Two-Shoes," she says with an eye roll.

Jill is fun, she's just not as reckless as Veronica and I have proven to be time and again. Whatever cloth Veronica and I are cut from isn't necessarily a good piece of cloth. She and I are a quilt made up of long nights, one too many drinks, and regretful mornings.

"Leave a little room for some of that red stuff," I laugh. I can't drink it on the rocks the way she can. I still need a little bit of a mixer in mine.

"Okay, Craig. Would you like a little butter-flavored oil in here as well?" she mocks, "One day you can join the big kid's club and learn to drink your liquor straight up, Sam." I avoid telling her that she doesn't technically drink her liquor straight up either, because she drinks it with ice.

Veronica fills the last quarter of my cup with fruit punch, smacks a lid on it, and hands it back to me. Thank God we don't have cameras in this place, or we all would've been fired ten times over tonight.

"Alright bitch. Let's roll out," she exclaims once she's finished pouring vodka over her cup of ice. We begin walking towards theatre twelve side by side. As I take the first sip from my straw, the vodka instantly burns my throat while simultaneously making my entire body warm. I can already feel my body relaxing after I take my second sip.

"Okay, maybe this was a pretty good idea," I say to her with a smirk.

Veronica takes a huge gulp from her cup before we enter theatre twelve. "All my ideas are good, Sam. I thought you would've come to this realization by now," she grins at me and bumps my hip with hers in a loving way.

As Veronica and I enter the theatre, I take in the self-appointed seating chart. To my surprise, I can see Jill has saved Veronica and my seats. I thought for sure she'd still be pissed at us. To Jill's left sits Brett, Miles, and Craig, who all appear to be deep in conversation. I see Craig's hands fly into the air as he yells something about Captain America.

To Jill's right are two empty seats and at the other end of the empty seats is Zach who has already started the movie's previews. I always make him play the previews for us. It's honestly my favorite part of watching a movie in the theaters. It's exciting to get a glimpse of what movies are to come, what my next escape from reality will be.

"You better sit your ass next to Zach," Veronica whispers. "You can totally tell he wants you to."

"And how exactly can you tell that?" I scoff.

"Don't question me, Samantha," she snips while shoving me into the chair next to Zach. She gracefully sits in the open chair between Jill and me. I feel her hand subtly slip a few Tic Tacs into mine. She thinks of everything. If I'm going to sit by Zach for two hours sipping on my spiked fruit punch, I need to be careful.

Zach turns and grins at me. "You're late again," he jokes.

I playfully stick my tongue out at him. "Only by five minutes," I reply.

"A small price to pay for you to look this adorable," he says in a lower voice than before, his smile softening.

Suddenly, I feel nervous, and my normal snarky comebacks have escaped me. Why would I feel nervous? I've known Zach for years.

We are friends after all. Our normal banter seems different at this moment. My cheeks feel warm, and I know I'm blushing now. But what the hell do I know? Earlier, I thought Miles was asking me on a date and it turned out he was definitely not doing that. Some might even say he appeared mildly disgusted that I'd contemplated such an idea.

After a second too long, I'm finally able to smile back at Zach, then I quickly turn my body to face the screen. I grab my disposable cup from the drink holder and take a long sip from the straw. I instantly feel less nervous and let out a long sigh. This day hasn't been kind to my nerves, but vodka is fixing that.

As the final credits of the movie roll, I look over to find both Brett and Miles sleeping. Brett's head is resting on Miles's shoulder. They're both much cuter when they're asleep and not irritating me.

Craig looks at the two men, then to me as he chuckles, "Guess it's past these boys' bedtimes." Craig lightly shakes Miles's shoulder. "Wake up, buds. Movie's over. Time to pack it up," he says.

Miles jumps in his seat and scans the theatre with wide eyes. It takes him a second to remember where he is. Brett lazily yawns and stretches his arms, begrudgingly lifting his head from Miles's shoulder.

Jill stands and hoists her enormous bag over her shoulder. "I just love how much Edward loves Bella, he'd do anything for her," she gushes.

"Except refrain from knocking her up with a half-monster child that technically kills her," Zach complains.

"The baby is half-vampire, Zach—not monster! Did you even watch the movie?" Jill yells.

"I really tried not to," Zach laughs.

"He doesn't understand, Jill." I give her a reassuring smile. "Their love is beautiful."

"Let's blow this pop stand, bitches," Veronica announces, interrupting Jill and I praising the movie. She stands and saunters out of the theatre.

I'm still a bit buzzed, but I'm mostly exhausted. I stand slowly and grasp the hand railing as I maneuver my body down the stairs to exit the theatre. Vodka, lack of sleep, stairs, and platform tennis shoes are not a safe combination. I've decided if I fall again, I'm just going to take a nap on the floor. It's called multi-tasking.

With my Superman backpack slung over my shoulder, I step outside the theatre and admire how beautiful the sunrise is. I silently thank the universe I don't have work, class, or clinical today. While I'd been pushing that awful crash cart, I made a promise to myself that I'd go back to the gym today, but today's forecast for physical activity is starting to look extremely bleak.

I know Veronica takes a class on Saturday mornings. I wonder if she's going to make it. She has a higher tolerance than I do, but I know she's still at least a little buzzed.

Veronica's taking her prerequisites at the same community college Jill and I attend. She plans on eventually getting her master's degree and becoming a social worker. I know she'll be an amazing social worker one day. Even though she's downright crazy sometimes, she has the biggest heart of anyone I know.

I feel a hand lightly rest on my shoulder and look up to see hazel eyes gazing down at me. Miles's hair is a mess of curls but still looks great. At least I know this time that he didn't intentionally style it that way.

"Can you fit that cup of coffee into your schedule now?" he asks me with a sideways smirk.

"Right now?" I question. "It's like...early as hell!" I say shocked.

He chuckles, "People drink coffee early, Sam. It's kind of like a common thing."

"Wait, where are you two going?" Jill asks us. She was obviously eavesdropping. We unfortunately now have everyone's attention.

"I'll get coffee with you, but I warn you, we're all kind of a package deal," I proclaim, pointing behind me to where Jill, Veronica, Craig, and Zach are standing.

"Well, that's perfect," Miles responds. "I have my own package that comes with me," he says as he grabs Brett's arm and pulls him over to stand next to him.

Brett appears to be in a sleep-induced fog. He's totally lost, staring blankly at us with bloodshot eyes. "What's going on?" he asks mid-yawn.

"We're going for coffee," Miles notifies him.

"Great, the more the merrier!" Jill proclaims while Veronica lets out a loud groan.

"I think Jill's more interested in Brett's package than she is a cup of coffee," Veronica mutters. Jill gasps and swats Veronica on the arm. I have to agree with Veronica, though. I'm starting to see the beginnings of one of Jill's many crushes. But I have no room to talk. I've had a crush on Zach for over two years now and have done nothing about it.

The seven of us walk together to the McDonald's around the corner from The Cinedome, most of us half-asleep. Two of us half-drunk.

That morning, seven cups of McCafé coffee turned into three hours of conversation, an endless string of laughter, and what looked like the beginning of a few new friendships.

# CHAPTER EIGHT

## (December 2012):

Today is my first day working as a graduate nurse at Summit Valley Hospital on their hospice and palliative care floor—the first day I've run back and forth across these hospital floors and actually gotten paid for it. It's a glorious thing! Tonight, is also my last shift at The Cinedome. While I'm excited to be starting my career as a registered nurse, I'm also a bit somber about leaving a job where I get to work with all my friends and watch free movies.

Zach has planned a special, private viewing in my honor after we close tonight. Thankfully it's not a big premiere weekend, so we won't all be up 'til the crack of dawn this time. Our theatre has digital projectors now, making it easier for Zach to obtain digital copies of movies rather than film reels.

Somehow, Zach got his hands on a copy of the 1978 film *Superman*, with Christopher Reeve and Marlon Brando. Veronica groaned about the "boring" selection but has primarily kept her comments to herself. Today is my day, and I'm so excited to have the opportunity to see one of my favorite movies on the big screen with my best friends.

I gave my notice to The Cinedome about a month ago. I know a month's notice is ridiculously generous, but after years of working there, I felt like I owed them more than two weeks. It was much harder than I imagined resigning from the theatre, but once I landed a graduate nurse position, I knew it was time to close that chapter of my life.

Being a graduate nurse means that I've graduated from nursing school but have not yet taken my boards to become a full-fledged registered nurse. It's extremely rare to be offered a position as a graduate nurse straight out of school. But when you have Margo Hatcher singing your praises throughout Summit Valley Hospital, amazing things happen. Over the last year, Margo has become like a second mother to me. Well, more like a *first* mother since I'm not speaking with my *actual* mother at the moment.

If I'm being honest, Margo has become the mother hen to our entire pack. She insists on religiously hosting Sunday dinner for all of us every week. Although we aren't all able to make it every Sunday due to half of us being shift workers, we all try to make it a priority if we aren't working. Margo repeatedly tells us that we all, Jill, Veronica, Zach, Craig, Miles, Brett, Tony, and me, always have a place at her table. Obviously, her table has a leaf expansion option. That's a lot of hungry mouths to feed!

Tony is the newest addition to our pack. He's a paramedic and Miles's new partner. Brett successfully graduated from the fire academy at the beginning of this year and is the newest firefighter to join the ranks of the Bristol County Fire Department. Brett may act like an arrogant jackass sometimes, but he and I have actually grown to be great friends and I'm extremely proud of him and his recent accomplishments.

Our entire group instantly fell in love with Tony, or "Tony Cakes" as Veronica nicknamed him, once Miles started bringing him around. It is a true honor to be gifted a nickname by the great Veronica

Sanders. It's a well-known fact that she only gives her favorite people nicknames.

Tony is Zach's age and just celebrated his twenty-fifth birthday. Or I should say we all celebrated *for* him. We partied all night long at The Barn Door, our favorite local bar. Tony is over a year sober, so he enjoyed plain Cokes while the rest of us enjoyed ours with a side of Jack Daniels. Or, more accurately, our Jack with a side of Coke. Tony hasn't gone into great length on why he decided to stop drinking, but we all respect his decision, and we never pressure him to drink with us.

Once again, back to Zach—the day I put in my notice at The Cinedome, Zach asked me if I wanted to get something to eat with him after our shift ended. I didn't think twice about it. Zach and I had gone to eat together many times over the years. Zach let me choose the restaurant that night, and of course, I chose Applebee's.

As soon as we were seated by the hostess, I ordered a margarita with a salt rim. Putting in my resignation had caused me a mass amount of anxiety and I needed a drink, STAT! When the waitress returned with my STAT margarita, Zach ordered a Bud Light along with chips and salsa for us to share.

"Sam, I wanted to ask you if I could pay for your dinner tonight?" Zach stared at me as he awaited my answer. Zach and I usually go Dutch, as I do with all my friends.

Miles and I have made it a point over the last year to maintain our weekly coffee, um... "get-togethers" I'll call them. They are absolutely *not* coffee dates. I'm sure my dear friend Miles would have a coronary infarction at the idea of being on a date with me, so coffee "get-togethers" they shall be coined. He always offers to pay for my coffee, and I always adamantly refuse. I can definitely pay for my own coffee.

I had just licked the salt remnants off my lip from my last sip of margarita when I gazed up at him. "If you're offering to pay in honor of my graduation, remember I said that we aren't celebrating until my pinning next month," I naively responded.

"I don't want to pay for your dinner because you graduated..." he replied simply.

I looked up from the salsa-covered chip I was holding, briefly studying him. I noted at that moment, how he looked especially handsome tonight, his long, sandy-brown hair tied back into one of those man-bun ponytail things. I don't care what Veronica says, I still think he looks totally hot with long hair. His dark brown eyes were boring into me, waiting for me to speak, and suddenly I felt anxious.

I didn't know what to say to him. I didn't want to ask him if dinner was supposed to be a date, because the last time I asked a man that, I ended up completely humiliated.

"I don't understand. Why do you want to pay for my dinner?" I finally questioned.

He let out a long sigh and reached across the table to grab my hand, thankfully the hand that *wasn't* holding the chip loaded with salsa.

"Sam, I've kinda had a thing for you for awhile now but didn't want anything to become awkward with us working together. Since you're leaving The Cinedome now, I decided this was probably the right time to tell you how I feel," Zach divulged.

I stared at him, stunned. After all these years, he had finally uttered the words I had always secretly hoped he'd say to me. I was indeed happy to hear them leave his lips; I just wasn't as elated as I always thought I'd be. I chalked up my sudden hesitation to my all too familiar recent battle with anxiety. Unfortunately, my anxiety has gotten worse instead of better over the last year, the mental aftermath of a brutal nursing program I suppose.

"How do you feel about me?" I quietly asked as he still held my hand. I finally sat the tortilla chip I was holding back onto the plate.

"I want to be more than just friends, Sam," he professed. I couldn't help but give him the hugest grin. It was endearing to see him so nervous. When he saw me smile, I instantly saw his posture relax.

"I've always wanted that, Zach," I confessed. As the words fell out of my mouth, I oddly felt a pit forming in my stomach. Hadn't I always wanted that? Yes, I convinced myself, as I lightly squeezed Zach's hand.

The last month has honestly been amazing. I'm waiting for someone to pinch me and wake me up from what feels like a dream. Not only did I finally graduate nursing school, but the boy I have secretly crushed on for the last three years is now my boyfriend. I almost feel like I'm holding my breath as I wait for the other shoe to drop. It's almost too good to be true.

The only issue now is that Zach and I are currently dating in secret. Of course, Jill and Veronica know. How could I not tell my two best friends and roommates? The three of us do not keep secrets from each other, period.

Veronica has been crashing on Jill's and my hand-me-down sofa for the last few months after she and the guy she was dating suddenly broke up. None of our pack had really liked the guy—he was kind of a chauvinistic pig—but Veronica did what she wanted and made no apologies for it. Brett bluntly told Veronica once that her boyfriend was an asshole and that she should break up with him. If Brett, who is a self-proclaimed asshole, calls someone *else* an asshole you know that the person is, indeed, a major asshole. Jill and I were especially concerned when Veronica decided to move out of her mom's house and into the guy's apartment after just two months of dating.

Veronica doesn't like to talk about their break-up. Sometimes that girl is an emotional vault. I do know that things ended badly between them and he promptly kicked her butt to the curb. She felt like it would be an absolute failure to move back in with her mom, so she asked Jill and me if we would take her in for a while. Veronica has been accepted into Belview University and is planning a big move to Nashville next spring. I'm sure she would have eventually broken up with that asshole anyway before she moved away from Bristol. If anything, he did her a favor.

Jill and I were devastated when we discovered that Veronica was planning to move out of Bristol soon, but we are both so proud of her. We are also very excited to visit her in Nashville one day and party our asses off on Lower Broadway.

As for my relationship with Zach, I've sworn Jill and Veronica to secrecy. They both think we should reveal to the rest of our friends that we're dating but, to be honest, I'm nervous about telling everyone. I don't want this to drive a wedge right down the middle of our group. Everything is perfect right now.

Zach says he could care less about what anyone says, and if they aren't supportive of our relationship, then they're not really our friends. While I know he's right, I just can't risk losing any of them. Besides my dad's family, my friends are all I have.

I do plan to bring it up to Miles first at our next "coffee get-to-gether" in a few days; I've accepted I can't keep Zach and me a secret forever. I'd rather just get through my pinning ceremony before things potentially get extremely awkward is all.

A pinning ceremony is a rite of passage for a brand-new nurse like me. As nurses, we couldn't care less about our graduation ceremony with the cap and gown nonsense. It's all about the pinning ceremony, and mine is tomorrow.

Per tradition, graduates ask a current nurse to welcome them into the nursing field by placing a pin on their lab coats in front of their family and friends. I swear I saw Margo shed a tear when I asked her to pin me. She repeatedly told me how honored she was that I had asked her. In my mind, it was a given. How could she not expect me to ask her? Margo did surprise me though by asking if she could have an extra ticket to bring a plus-one to the ceremony. I had no clue she was even dating anyone. Of course, I obliged. Then I made a mental note to grill her later about the details of her dating life.

My thoughts are immediately pulled back to the present as Tanya calls my name. Tanya is the registered nurse who will be training me for the next eleven weeks of my hospital orientation. If I had to guess, I would say she's probably in her early forties and I'm almost positive she has children because her coffee mug has "Mom Life" plastered across it. She seems to be extremely kind but also not one to take shit from anyone. Or at least that is my initial impression. Since today is my first day working on the unit, I only just met the woman a few hours ago. So, my first impression could, in fact, be completely wrong.

"Sam, I think Mr. Williams is transitioning. On my last rounds I noticed he is starting to have periods of apnea," Tanya says as she reaches the nurses' station and leans against the counter, speaking in a hushed tone.

Apnea is a change in a person's breathing that occurs when they are coming closer to death. Tanya had said that she heard nurses dub it "guppy breathing" because it looks like how a fish would breathe out of water. When she told me that, I instantly thought of Matty and how his breathing had looked the last time I saw him, all those years ago.

I stare up at her in disbelief. I had just assessed this patient less than an hour ago and he was responsive and breathing evenly. "I don't understand, I just assessed him," I respond.

"Sometimes it can happen that quickly," Tanya informs me. "I've seen patients go from talking and walking, to actively dying within an hour."

My mouth falls to the floor, I have so much to learn. "Does the apnea mean he's in distress? Is he short of breath?" I ask her.

"As the body begins shutting down, the agonal breathing and periods of apnea are kind of like the body's autopilot mode. This type of breathing may appear strange, but it doesn't necessarily mean the patient is distressful," she educates me. "Mr. Williams's Dilaudid dosing appears to be keeping him comfortable. To me, he looks peaceful," she finishes.

I stand from my chair behind the nurses' station and grab my school-assigned stethoscope off the desk. I've already decided that with my first real nurse paycheck, I'm buying a Littmann stethoscope. My current stethoscope, the one given to me in nursing school, is absolute garbage. Not only does the Littmann stethoscope have better sound quality, but it's lighter weight as well.

Tanya nods to me to follow her, and we walk side-by-side to room 542. The hospice and palliative care unit is on the fifth floor of Summit Valley Hospital, only three floors above where Margo Hatcher currently orchestrates the operations of the ICU.

"His family is still at bedside and appears to understand his transition. They seem to be very accepting. He's had such a long battle with this disease," Tanya somberly voices.

When Tanya first approached the nurses' station, I had already been reading through George Williams's chart. He is eighty-two years old and has a hospice diagnosis of end-stage Alzheimer's disease. He was unfortunately diagnosed with Alzheimer's over ten years ago. When his disease progressed to the point that he was bed-bound, and no longer able to eat or drink orally, his family elected to admit him into hospice. His wife had informed me earlier today that they had followed George's wishes and enrolled him into hospice services when his disease had progressed past a certain point. His wife had also informed me that before George's confusion started setting in, he created a medical advance directive so that his wishes for the remainder of his life would be known without a question or a doubt.

Specializing in hospice care has led me to learn an awful lot about medical advance directives. They're not something most people think of creating until they're faced with a potentially life-altering situation, but they're truly something we should all have in place. I've decided that even at the ripe old age of twenty-two, I would create my own advance directive. If something were to happen to me, I don't want to leave my father with another heart-shattering decision. As far as I'm concerned, my mother is out of my life for good, so what she would or would not want for me in a dire situation is not a factor. As I mentally start forming my own advance directive, I can't help but think of Hector Gomez, the first patient I performed CPR on over a year ago.

If Mr. Gomez would have created his own advance directive, his son would not have been left to make such difficult decisions about the path in which his father's medical care would proceed. If Mr. Gomez would have made his wishes known, his final moments could have been different. If Mr. Gomez would have passed away peacefully, I wouldn't still be agonizing over his death a year later.

As Tanya and I reach the entrance to room 542, she turns to me and softly places her hand on my shoulder. "If Mr. Williams is to pass now, I want you to be the one to pronounce him. You're ready, Sam. You know what to do," she reassures me.

My stomach drops. I suddenly feel like both my lungs are attempting to oxygenate themselves through a silly straw. No, I can't have a panic attack right now! Why would she think I'm ready? She barely knows me!

Inside, I'm screaming. On the outside, I try to remain as calm as possible. I slowly nod my head to her in agreement, harshly swallowing as I continue to feel a burn in my chest. I feel like I'm having heart palpitations. Am I having a heart attack? Maybe making an advance directive at twenty-two isn't such an absurd idea after all.

With my garbage stethoscope around my neck and my hands discreetly trembling in my scrub pockets, I stifle my fears, lift my chin, and force my feet to steer my petrified body into my patient's room.

# CHAPTER NINE:

As I enter room 542, I see Mr. Williams lying in the hospital bed. The only motions I see within that bed are his short, shallow breaths every twenty seconds or so. His face appears slack. His body appears somehow relieved of all the struggle it has endured over the last ten years. He is not currently attached to any tubing. His Dilaudid is given every four hours via IV push to keep his pain and shortness of breath under control. His hands remain free, unencumbered by wires and tubing, so they may be easily held by those that love him.

On the right side of Mr. Williams's bed sits his wife, Anne. She holds his large hand within her two petite ones as I hear her softly speak to her husband. "It's okay, George. You can rest now. You did good, honey. The girls and I will be okay," she whispers.

On the opposite side of his bed sit his two adult daughters, tears streaming down both their faces as they each rest a hand delicately upon their father's left one. "We love you always, Dad," one of George's daughters murmurs to him.

I now notice there is soft jazz music playing in Mr. Williams's room. My gaze then falls to the essential oil diffuser on the bedside table which is intermittently dispersing a faint scent of lavender throughout the room. I was beyond impressed when I discovered the hospice unit had its own aromatherapy department, not to mention a pet therapy and massage therapy department as well.

Suddenly my doubt and anxiety vanish and my instincts kick in. I walk around the hospital bed and stand next to George's wife. I then lightly place my hand atop her shoulder in support. I may not know everything there is to know about being a hospice nurse yet, but I do know people and I do know sorrow. All too well. I have endured this same sorrow. The gut-wrenching, earth-shattering sorrow of having to say goodbye to one of the most important people in your world.

Anne looks up to me and sweetly smiles through her tears. "It's Miles Davis," she says, pointing to her phone which sits on the side of the bed, continuing to play beautiful music. "He was George's favorite."

I instantly think of my friend Miles and what he would tell me at this moment, something he reminds me of often. Whenever I over-analyze a mistake I've made, overthink something I've said, or worry that I'm just not good enough, he simply says to me, "Sam, if you could only see yourself as I see you, then you'd never have to doubt yourself again."

Now that I think about it, Miles really is a damn good friend. I probably should be the one buying him a coffee at our next "get-together."

I proceed to walk around the chair in which Anne is sitting, moving towards the head of Mr. Williams's bed. As I walk, I begin removing my garbage stethoscope from around my neck, dreaming once again of the beautiful Littmann stethoscope I will soon be the owner of.

"Am I in your way at all, Sam?" Anne asks me.

"Not at all Mrs. Williams," I politely respond.

"I've told you, Sam, please call me Anne," she says with another sweet smile that I return with a smile of my own.

I was calling her Anne in my head this entire time but alas, my mouth did not comply. I give her a slight nod as if to tell her I will respect her request. As someone who hates being called by my full name, I try making it a point to address people how they request.

As I turn my vision towards Mr. Williams lying in the bed below me, I realize his respirations have ceased. My eyes shoot up to the corner of the room where Tanya is standing. I know she's purposefully stepping back to allow me to take the reins. Tanya nods at me to proceed and I hesitantly inch toward the edge of Mr. Williams's bed. I place the tips of my stethoscope in each ear, then gently place the diaphragm of the stethoscope over Mr. Williams's heart. I listen to the lack of a heartbeat, simultaneously placing two of my fingers to his carotid artery in search of a pulse. My fingers are met with utter stillness as I continue listening to the silence within his chest, where his heart once proudly pounded. As the diaphragm of my stethoscope gradually moves over Mr. Williams's lungs, searching for the faintest sign of breath, I am met once more with deafening silence. Gradually, my fingers leave his neck to gently lift his eyelid. There, I find his pupils appear fixed, completely immobile, and dilated.

I quickly comprehend everything I've just assessed as I lift the diaphragm of my stethoscope off Mr. Williams's chest. I remove the tips of the stethoscope from my ears, then slowly place my garbage stethoscope back around my neck. Though my current stethoscope is far from excellent, it's still fully capable of pronouncing a man deceased.

I steadily lift my head to find both of George's daughters staring at me in silence, tears pooling in their dark brown eyes. From where I'm standing, I can't see Anne, who is standing to my right. But I'm acutely aware of her presence. I hear her breath catch in her throat when I lift my gaze from her husband to focus on her daughters.

I swallow the fear I feel engulfing me, the dread of delivering the most horrific news. I'm the Courier of Catastrophe. "I'm so sorry. He's gone," I say softly, with tears filling my own eyes. I look down to my watch which encases my right wrist, solemnly noting the time: 15:37.

George's daughters cry in unison, immediately turning to hug each other. They appear to be close in age and, I assume, have kept a close relationship with one another throughout their lives. I wonder what it would have been like to have had more time with my own brother...

Hearing Anne's sniffles pulls me from my brief daydream. I instinctively turn to console her. As my body turns to face her, I'm quickly pulled into her arms. She hugs me fiercely as she attempts to stifle her sobs. After about a minute, she releases me from her embrace. Tanya is now standing beside us. She offers Anne a tissue from the box she's holding.

"I'm so very sorry for your loss," Tanya says in a hushed tone.

Anne nods towards Tanya, proceeding to blow her nose with the tissue she was given. "He's not suffering anymore. That's what's most important. He battled this awful disease for so long. He was such a strong man, it was so awful to see him in that state," Anne divulges.

She directs her attention solely at me and begins to speak again, "Throughout these last ten years, he's had many nurses care for him. I'll tell you that, mostly, they've all been great."

She sighs deeply as she wipes a tear from her cheek. She continues to speak and locks her gaze with mine. "Of all the nurses who have cared for my darling George throughout his terrible illness...it is you, Sam—the last nurse—that I will always remember." Despite her tears, she sweetly smiles at me once more. "You were his angel," she whispers.

And in this moment, it all makes sense. There is no doubt, this is what I was meant to do.

# CHAPTER TEN:

# GEORGE WILLIAMS

### December 13, 2012, 15:37

hear voices. Many different voices surround me. Three of those voices, though, hold some obscure sense of familiarity. The kind of familiarity that was once yours but is no longer. The type of comprehension that belongs in another life.

I've forgotten. Forgotten everything now. For so long, my body continued to feel strong as my mind continued to forget, continued to grow weak. It began by forgetting simple things: items at the store, where I placed my keys. Then I began forgetting where I was supposed to be going until I couldn't remember where I was at all.

My mind eventually convinced my legs that they could no longer walk. Then, to my horror, my bladder and bowels no longer released themselves on my command but rather when they saw fit.

As time passed—how much time I haven't a clue—I started forgetting words, until my mind persuaded my mouth that it no longer knew how to speak at all. That's when I became trapped, locked away *within the prison of my mind. I felt fear. I felt alone. I wanted to scream for help. Couldn't they see how I was suffering? No, they couldn't. Because on the outside, my body lay still. I could not make a sound. The war raging within me was my burden and my burden alone.*

*Towards the end of my war, my mind finally coerced my body into losing its ability to swallow. They continued trying to cajole me into drinking liquids of a thick, abnormal consistency; then, pureed foods that resembled something a baby would eat. Alas, it was to no avail. My body succumbed to my mind as I coughed and choked on anything I tried to consume.*

*At that point, I no longer felt hunger. The only feeling I still remembered was sadness. The final blow my body was able to endure was when my mental prison conquered all, robbing me of the one thing that meant more to me than life itself. My mind stole them away, leaving three strangers in their place.*

*As I lay here now, I feel my body finally succumbing to the devastation which my mind has inflicted. I may no longer know much of anything, but I do know that my war is almost over. I wave the infamous white flag. I finally surrender.*

*I hear music playing. I can't remember where I've heard it before, but it's beautiful. As the soft sounds emanate around my body, my fear begins to dissipate.*

*Of the three voices which have continually surrounded me, one feels the most familiar. I hear this recognizable voice speak to me. The sound is somehow sweeter than the music playing. The voice calls me George. That must be my name, but I have no way to be sure. I simply cannot remember.*

*The voice tells me that I have done well. That it's okay. That now I can rest.*

*I'm tired now. I no longer wish to fight this battle. Even though this is my surrender, I don't feel like I've lost.*

*As the sweet voice which I can no longer remember continues, I release my final tether to this body that is no longer mine. My mind begins to become quiet, the sweet voice becoming faint. I'm unsure whose voice it is that speaks so sweetly, yet I know I will deeply miss it.*

*My body expels its concluding breath. I begin to leave the world that is no longer my home. My mind allows me one final thought before I depart, a glorious parting gift.*

*The sweet voice speaks the last words my ears will ever hear and, all at once, familiarity consumes me. My lungs exhale their final supply of air as every thought stolen from me, every memory I was robbed of, is brought barreling back with one final moment of recollection:*

**Anne.**

# CHAPTER ELEVEN:

I walk out of room 542 with Tanya by my side. Once we've both exited the room, I slowly shut the door behind us to allow Anne and her daughters some privacy. My mind is still racing with everything that just occurred. Only moments ago, I pronounced my first patient expiration as a graduate nurse.

As Tanya and I walk back to the nurses' station to begin the charting process for a patient expiration, I gradually come to a stop in the middle of the hallway and look at her expectantly. Straight away, she senses my hesitation and turns to face me. I'm expecting her to critique me, now. I just hope that she isn't too hard on me. I don't know if I can take it, at the moment.

"Did I...um...do okay?" I ask her nervously.

"Oh, girl! You did fabulously! You're definitely a natural at this," she praises me.

I instantly feel a weight lift off my shoulders. I was terrified that I screwed everything up. I can't help but shyly grin at her as I respond, "I just wasn't sure what to say. I felt like I was so awkward. I just felt nervous with his entire family staring at me."

"It will always feel awkward because, honestly, it is an awkward situation. You are about to give someone the worst news they may ever hear. I still get nervous when I have to give a patient's family members news like that," Tanya sighs. "But remember, Sam, we may kind of be like superheroes with stethoscopes, but we're still human. We're still allowed to feel nervous," she finishes.

I beam at her; I love that she just referred to nurses as superheroes. Ever since I was a little girl, I was convinced that a nurse was the closest thing to a real-life superhero. It's honestly why I became a nurse. Or "almost nurse." It's nice to know I'm not the only one who thinks that way.

Tanya snaps me out of my daydream when she speaks again, "Didn't you say you wanted to go to lunch around this time?"

Crap, I forgot I was supposed to meet Margo in the hospital cafeteria for lunch today in honor of my first day. My vision darts to my watch and I'm relieved to find that I'm only five minutes late. Margo is an extremely prompt person, and I'm positive she's already waiting impatiently for me, her foot rapidly tapping the floor like it always does when she's forced to wait for anything.

"I totally forgot! Thank you for reminding me," I tell Tanya. "Are you sure you don't mind if I leave the floor and have lunch in the cafeteria today?" I ask.

"I don't mind one bit," she smiles. "Plus, you better take advantage of the luxury of lunch breaks when you're still in training. Unfortunately, you won't always get them when you're on your own," she finishes with a slight frown.

I know she hasn't been able to take a break yet today because of how busy we have been, and I instantly feel selfish for abandoning her.

"Can I bring you back anything, Tanya?" I ask.

"Oh no, you don't have to do that," she mutters in response.

"I think I'm going to have to insist," I reply with a huge grin on my face.

"Well, if you insist," she chuckles. "Cheeseburger with tater tots, please."

I laugh as I nod to her, then I turn to sprint to the time clock, then down the hallway towards the elevators. Seven minutes late now. I hold my breath as the elevator sends me down to the ground floor. I will never be a fan of these metal death traps.

As soon as the elevator doors open, I shoot my body out of the small space, directly into a man who's standing and waiting for the elevator to open. I try to steady myself after the collision but lose my footing when my nursing clog causes my ankle to roll. Yes, I've swapped my Sketchers Shape-ups for the preferred clog of the nursing profession. These clogs may be somewhat more attractive than the Shape-ups, but obviously, they're still wildly dangerous. Or maybe they're just dangerous for someone who's extremely clumsy, like myself. I could probably take a tumble in *any* type of footwear. Subsequently, I fall (very hard I might add) to the hospital floor.

"Oh shit! Are you okay?"

I look up to meet none other than Dr. Connors's gaze. I immediately recognize him, but I'm confident there's no way he would remember who I am. There are so many nursing students regularly rotating through the floors of Summit Valley Hospital.

"Hey, weren't you a nursing student on the ICU floor last year? Remind me of your name," he says.

I'm proven wrong, once more. It's a running theme for me.

He bends down and gently examines my ankle. Again, I feel anxious. This is also a running theme for me.

"My name is Sam," I finally say as I remember how to speak.

"Well, Nurse Sam. I think your ankle will be fine. Let me help you up," Dr. Connors offers.

"Almost nurse," I instinctively correct him. "I take my boards exam in two weeks."

He smiles at me politely, nodding as he helps lift me off the floor. Suddenly, I hear a voice call my name from what sounds like the hospital lobby. Dr. Connors and I both turn toward the lobby to see Miles jogging to us in full uniform.

"Sam," he repeats as he reaches us, "We've been waiting for you. Tony and I only have like twenty more minutes before we have to get back. Margo is gonna go ballistic if you make her wait any longer."

"I would get moving if I were you. We all know how terrifying she can be," Dr. Connors chuckles.

Miles briefly glares at him, then looks back at me. "Who's this guy?" he asks.

I can't help but laugh. "This is Dr. Connors," I respond to him. "I fell on the ground. He helped me up. Don't worry, I'm okay."

"Jesus, again?" Miles blurts out. "You really need to stop wearing those damn platform shoes, Sam."

"They're super comfortable and have great arch support." I instinctively defend my choice of footwear.

Dr. Connors lets out a loud laugh. "Does this happen often?" he asks, pointing to the floor where my body was just splayed out.

"Yes," Miles and I reply in unison.

"Well, try to be more careful, Sam," Dr. Connors says as he gives me a wink. "You two have a good day." He then steps into the elevator that just opened.

I turn towards Miles and we both begin walking to the hospital cafeteria.

"I don't like that guy," Miles announces. "Who winks at people? It's creepy."

I laugh and give him a light shove. When he turns to glare at me, I give him a dramatic wink.

"Creep," he mouths.

# CHAPTER TWELVE:

Miles and I rush to the hospital cafeteria and my eyes immediately dart to Margo, standing by a table where Tony is currently sitting. I notice her foot is tapping a mile a minute. Meanwhile, Tony is staring longingly at the cheeseburger sitting before him as he politely waits for what I can only assume is my arrival.

When Miles and I arrive at the table, Margo glares at me, her arms crossed in front of her chest. "Samantha, you are almost fifteen minutes late," she scolds me. I know she's irritated when she uses my full name. "I know they allowed you to go to lunch at 4:00 because I called the charge nurse on your floor, and she said you had already left."

My mouth gapes open. "You did what?" I question.

Margo ignores me and my obvious horror at her calling my charge nurse to continue scolding me, "Poor Anthony is famished, and he has been forced to let his food become cold waiting for you."

Wow, Margo is really on a full name-calling kick now. "Look at him," she bellows. "He's practically wasting away!"

I stare at Tony who smirks back at me. He then gives me an exaggerated pout before looking back down at his cheeseburger. Tony is far from wasting away. Even though he may be a bit shorter than

Craig at about 5'6", he has an extremely muscular build. I'm almost positive he could kick Miles's ass, even though he's nearly ten inches shorter than him. But Tony is far too sweet to get into any type of physical altercation.

"Hola, Señorita Sam," Tony grins at me. Tony has slowly but surely been teaching me Spanish. He makes it a point to try to speak to me in Spanish as often as he can. At the moment though, I'm not in the mood to struggle to pronounce a sentence in Spanish.

"Hey, Tony," I mutter as he narrows his vision at me, obviously unimpressed at my English response.

"Sam rolled her ankle and fell outside of the elevators by the lobby. Super embarrassing. But that's probably why she's late," Miles somewhat defends me. Keyword "somewhat."

"Your face is embarrassing," I snipe at him in annoyance. Miles and Tony both burst into laughter as Miles gives me his infamous sideways smirk.

"Alright, that's enough children!" Margo reprimands. Margo always refers to us as children; she once revealed to me that although she always wanted to be a mother, she was unable to have children. She was married for almost eighteen years to a man named Peter, but she and Peter finalized their divorce about a decade ago. Even though half of the time we all drive her bat shit crazy (her words not mine), she says we're the eight asshole kids she never had.

For some of us, Margo is the mother figure we've been desperately missing in our lives. This year, I had a huge falling out with Caroline, and we are no longer on speaking terms.

At the beginning of the year, Caroline decided she was going to stop drinking alcohol. The typical "new year, new me" bullshit. Now she suddenly thinks she's better than everyone else. On the evening of our fight, she had the audacity to inform me that I am "just like her." That I need to stop drinking before I ruin my own life. This coming from the person who ruined the majority of my childhood and completely tore apart our family. I was appalled she would dare compare herself to me. I'm absolutely nothing like that woman. I would have to be clinically insane to take life advice from Caroline Carter.

After our fight, I told her to never speak to me again. In the eight months since then, she hasn't tried to contact me once. If I would have known it would be that easy, I would have requested this from her years ago. Good riddance.

Another member of our pack who cherishes Margo's motherly love more than anything is Miles. Miles's mother tragically passed away when he was just fifteen years old. Miles revealed to me over one of our many coffee "get-togethers" that the faint scar above his lip was from being involved in a terrible car accident when he was a teenager. He said he was the lucky one that day. He walked away with only minor cuts and bruises; his mom, on the other hand, wasn't so lucky.

He came to tell me that it was an ordinary Saturday afternoon. His mother picked him up from baseball practice like she always did. He asked her if they could stop to get something to eat before they headed back home. At first, she insisted they didn't have time; she had promised Miles's older sister, Kylie, that she could borrow the family car to go to the movies with her friends. However, Miles's mother would always cave in when it came to him and, without much of a fight, she agreed to take him to the Arby's drive-thru.

To reach Arby's, she had to turn the car around and drive back in the opposite direction. Once they changed direction, she and Miles began chatting about how he'd like to celebrate his upcoming birthday. Of course, when you're fifteen you think turning sixteen is the biggest thing in the world. That is until sixty seconds later when the car you're riding in—on the way to Arby's to get the roast beef sandwich you begged your mom for—is slammed into by a drunk driver. The truck had run a red light in the middle of an intersection and then collided into the driver's side of his mom's sedan. Bettie Streelman was killed instantly; the twenty-two-year-old man who was drunk at 3:00 PM on that ordinary Saturday and decided to get behind the wheel of his truck was uninjured. After all was said and done, the young man responsible for taking Miles's mother's life only served eight months in jail before he was released on parole. How you ask? As Miles tells it, it helps to have ridiculously rich parents.

The more Miles opened up to me about the topic, the more I sensed how much he blamed himself for his mother's death. He claimed he was selfish for making her turn the car around. That it should have been *him* to lose his life that day—not her. I think he's been suffering from something called survivor's guilt. I have repeatedly reassured him that it was not his fault. He wasn't the one who decided to drive a vehicle while severely intoxicated. He always gives me a simple, sad nod and says, "I know that." Yet sometimes I feel he might not.

Lastly, there's Craig. Our Captain Cowboy. Miles gave Craig the nickname after he pummeled him to the floor in the great movie theatre brawl last year and, ever since, Craig has insisted we all refer to him as such. He loves the nickname so much he even had Jill make him a shirt that says "Captain Cowboy" on her Cricut t-shirt press. He probably wears that thing every other day.

Craig hasn't lost his mother. He hasn't had a huge falling out with her. His situation is much different but equally as hard. Over the last year, he has become one of the primary caregivers for his mom as she battles an aggressive form of multiple sclerosis. Craig's father has had to get a second job to make up for the fact that his mother is no longer able to work. This means Craig has been mostly at his mom's bedside, trying to assist her however he can.

Craig recently revealed to the group his secret dream of moving to Nashville to pursue his country music career. I felt like an awful friend for having no idea he could sing or play the guitar as well as he can, but then again, Craig is surprisingly shy when it comes to sharing personal things. From his boisterous and friendly demeanor, you would have no idea there was actually a modest guy hiding underneath.

Margo has been Craig's sounding board for the trials and tribulations he has discovered come with being a caregiver for an ill family member. Although all of us have offered to help in any way possible, Margo has given him a type of emotional support none of us are capable of. Craig started referring to her as "Mama Margo" and it eventually stuck.

To a lot of our pack, she was like a second mother. To a couple of us, she was the only mother we had.

Margo starts to speak again pulling our attention back to her. "Are you two done bickering?" She glares at us as she asks. Miles and I both nod silently.

"Great! Now I only have fifteen minutes of my break left," Margo mutters, more to herself than to the three of us. "Sam, Miles ordered you a turkey burger," she informs me as I sit at the table beside Tony.

I smile up at my annoying friend. He drives me crazy sometimes, but he does know what I like.

"Thanks, butthead," I say with a smirk. Miles rolls his eyes at me.

"Anything for you," he replies as he slides me a paper plate holding a ginormous turkey burger.

I watch Miles collapse into the chair next to Margo. He quickly takes a huge bite of his cheeseburger, ketchup smearing on the side of his mouth. Over the last year, I've discovered Miles is a chronically messy eater.

At this point, Tony has already almost finished his entire burger and is starting to steal Miles's fries. I grab a handful of my own fries and plop them onto Tony's empty plate. His eyes immediately light up, and he proceeds to blow me a kiss to show his gratitude.

"Are you coming tonight, Mama Margo?" Tony asks with a mouthful of my fries.

"Oh no," she says, daintily poking her fork around her chef salad. "I think it's just meant to be for the young folks tonight."

I give her an exaggerated sigh. "Margo, I told you a million times we all want you there. Especially me. And it's my night, so you have to come."

"Why does *every* night feel like it's your night?" Miles gripes. I shoot him a quick glare.

"Plus," Tony starts, "that Christopher Reeve guy is in this movie, and you've repeatedly said how much of a total hottie he is."

"I do not think I've ever uttered the words 'total hottie' in my life," Margo corrects him. "But he sure was a handsome fellow."

"Then it's settled," I state. "You're coming. Do you want a plus-one for tonight, too?" I give her a sly smile.

"Plus-one?" Miles questions. "Wait. Are you dating someone Margo?" He abruptly drops his french fry back onto his paper plate.

"She totally is," I answer for her. "She asked for a plus-one for my pinning ceremony tomorrow." Margo audibly groans.

"Mama, we need details. All the deets! ASAP!" Tony practically shouts as he claps his hands together in front of him. If there was one thing Tony loves more than french fries, it's a tidbit of juicy gossip.

"Fine. I will attend the movie tonight, but there will be no more talk of my plus-one. End of story," Margo forcibly jabs her plastic fork into a leaf of iceberg lettuce.

I reach over and wrap Margo in an awkward sideways hug, feeling her body noticeably relax as she sighs. "You know I can never say no to you Sam," she whispers.

"I love you," I tell her, releasing her from my embrace and giving her a huge grin.

"I love you more, Mama Margo," Tony professes as he throws a french fry in my direction. One of my french fries, that I so graciously donated to him, to be specific.

"I will always love her the most," Miles claims as he takes a sip from his soda.

Margo looks up from her chef salad and gazes at Miles. She slightly tilts her head to the side, as if she's assessing him. "Were you talking about me or Sam?" Margo asks Miles. Her lips form a soft smile.

Miles instantly starts coughing, possibly choking, on the sip of soda he has just taken. His cheeks turn a bright shade of red while he tries and fails to compose himself.

"Whoa, buddy," Tony says as he slaps Miles on the back. "You alright there?"

Miles coughs once more but is finally able to clear his throat and speak. "Yeah, I'm fine. Just went down the wrong pipe," he explains. "We better get back to work, Tony."

Tony nods at him and stands as Miles hastily grabs their plates and walks them over to the trash can.

"I'll see you both tonight," Tony says with a smile, giving Margo and me a quick hug. Miles avoids walking back over to us, instead, he gives us a wave goodbye from where he stands at the trash can.

Margo and I watch Tony jog to catch up with Miles's long strides as he leaves the cafeteria. I pick up my empty paper plate preparing to throw it away and return to work myself.

"You made him feel super awkward just now," I inform Margo.

"I didn't mean to. I was just confused," she sarcastically says. "I just wasn't sure who he was talking about."

I chuckle. She is such a shit-stirrer sometimes.

"You know Miles has a girlfriend, and I have..." I stop myself before I accidentally say too much.

"What is it that you have Sam?" Margo quizzically tilts her head to me.

"I, um, have to go," I stutter. "See you tonight!" I yell over my shoulder as I speed-walk towards the elevators.

"Try not to roll your other ankle!" I hear Margo yell back to me.

I glance down at my clogs as I hurriedly exit the cafeteria. I think I'd much rather chance a second rolled ankle than endure a Margo Hatcher interrogation.

# CHAPTER THIRTEEN:

To avoid Margo's questioning, I bolted out of the cafeteria without ordering Tanya's cheeseburger and tater tots. I couldn't leave my preceptor starving, so I immediately scurried back down to the cafeteria. Without injury, I might add.

I now watch Tanya finish charting the last patient we cared for today. I glance down at my watch for the tenth time in the last five minutes. Time is such a jerk. When you want it to go by quickly, it drags on at a snail's pace. When you want a moment to last forever, it somehow flies by in the blink of an eye.

"Do you have plans tonight?" Tanya asks me as she continues typing, obviously aware of my impatience.

"My last shift at The Cinedome is tonight at 7:30," I respond, looking up from my watch.

She stops typing to turn and glance at me. "Cutting it rather close, aren't you?"

"I'll have thirty minutes. Plenty of time to drive there and change out of my scrubs," I answer defensively.

Tanya snickers. "I forget how young you are. Young people do everything fast. My old bones just don't move that fast anymore," she finishes with a giggle.

"You are *not* old!" I laugh.

"If you asked my children, they would tell you I'm practically prehistoric," she says with an eye roll.

My watch reads 7:15 PM when I grab my things, shove them into my Superman backpack, and sling it over my shoulder. My dad bought me a legitimate nursing bag as a graduation present, but I'm partial to my backpack. I don't want to hurt his feelings though, so maybe I can use the nursing bag as a carry-on suitcase or something.

I wave to Tanya as I rush towards the elevators. Once I reach the exit of the hospital, I start speed-walking towards my Blazer. I'm one of those people who only do cardio by accident, like when I'm late for something. It's never a conscious decision, and if I do go to the gym, it's never to do cardio. I'm the opposite of Jill who, for one, is never late to anything and, secondly, is one of those nauseating people that consider running fun. I, however, consider running to be cruel torture and only do it under dire circumstances. So, if you ever see me running down the street, you better start running as well because it's probably the beginning of a zombie apocalypse.

I fumble to unlock my car door, dropping my keys to the asphalt. Okay, maybe giving myself only thirty minutes between jobs was cutting it a little close. I kneel down and grab my keys, then swiftly unlock my door. I hurl my body into the driver's seat, tossing my backpack into the back. Luckily, The Cinedome is only five minutes away from Summit Valley. I screech out of the hospital parking lot and begin racing down Main Street.

I dart through the doors of The Cinedome shortly after I park and run towards the women's bathroom. Yes, I'm currently running. Desperate times call for desperate measures. I really don't want to be late for my last shift. Solemnly, I think to myself that this will be the last time I change clothes in a Cinedome bathroom stall. I presume in the future, as a simple moviegoer, wardrobe changes will be unnecessary. I dash around a group of giggling teenage girls as I pass the snack bar en route to the bathroom. Shit, I only have five minutes. I should have predicted the change-of-shift report would run over. According to Tanya, it always does.

My run instinctively slows as my eyes find Zach standing outside of the snack bar counter. He looks like a "total hottie," leisurely leaning on the snack bar countertop. I note he subtly bites his bottom lip as he stares at me. Just last night, it was *my* bottom lip he was biting. I sigh. He's my very own Christopher Reeve with a man bun.

Suddenly I realize I've completely stopped. Now I'm standing still as stone, staring at Zach. He smiles at me and shouts, "You have four minutes Samantha!"

I grin at him and yell back, "That's plenty of time Zachary!"

I remind my feet to move, lurching myself forward toward the bathroom as I continue daydreaming about my boyfriend.

"Someone's smitten." I look up to see Veronica standing at the entrance of the women's bathroom.

"Shut up, Ronnie," I snip.

Over the last year, the Nickname Queen was finally given her own nickname by none other than Brett. One day Brett started randomly calling Veronica "Ronnie" and it's stuck ever since. The two of them have become fairly close friends over the last year, often hanging out solo like Miles and I do.

Jill grills Ronnie about her relationship with Brett and whether they are actually secretly dating. To Ronnie and me, it's obvious that Jill has a major crush on Brett, but she refuses to admit it. Ronnie is constantly reassuring Jill that she and Brett are just good friends, bonded over the fact that one of them slapped the other with a soft pretzel.

Ronnie and Brett are so alike it's almost scary. They're both outspoken, refuse to take crap from anyone, and are, most importantly, extremely loyal friends. I never thought I'd be referring to Brett Bowen as a loyal friend but sometimes the universe works in mysterious ways.

On multiple occasions, Brett has apologized for how he acted towards me the first day we met. On each occasion, I assure him that I've forgiven him, but from time to time he still likes to get too drunk and beg me again for forgiveness.

"Don't be so sensitive, Sammie Bear," Ronnie urges. "No one heard me."

"I'm going to tell Miles first when we go to coffee on Sunday morning," I inform her. "I just don't want things to be awkward for my pinning tomorrow."

"It's *totally* going to be awkward," she assures me. Ugh, deep down I know she's right.

"No, it's not," I lie. "Everyone is going to be totally cool with it. They'll probably even be happy for us."

"Okay, Sam. Give me a call when you leave Fantasy Land and rejoin us all in the real world."

"Wow, someone sure woke up on the wrong side of my couch this morning," I mumble as I look down at my watch. Just as I had suspected, I'm officially late.

Ronnie nudges my shoulder to get my attention. "Hey, I'm sorry I'm being a bitch," she apologizes. "I'm just super hungover and my head is killing me."

I figured she might be due to the fact that she didn't even get home from her night out at The Barn Door 'til I was getting ready for work this morning. I could barely sleep last night worrying about her. She decided to meet a random guy she'd been casually talking to from one of the many dating sites she's on. Ronnie made me swear not to tell Jill about her late-night rendezvous because she knew she would have a total conniption. So, I had to worry all night alone. I tossed and turned in bed imagining my friend ending up on an episode of *Forensic Files*.

"I thought you were murdered," I say, meeting her gaze.

"I know, I know," she sighs, "I'm sorry. I should have texted you."

"Yes, you should have," I scold her. "I don't know what I'd do if anything happened to you, Veronica."

"I promise I'm not going anywhere, Sam. Now get in there and change before you get fired on your last day," she says with a hearty laugh. I love the sound of my best friend's laugh. It makes me feel the same way that sunshine does on a beautiful summer day; warm.

A few minutes later, I rush out of the women's bathroom wearing my Cinedome button-up for the last time. My backpack is slung haphazardly over my shoulder. I glance down at my watch and note the time: 7:35. Luckily, I only work a half-shift. The last movie showing releases around 11:30 tonight.

Still staring at my watch, I run behind the counter of the snack bar and directly into Craig's chest. "Whoa there, lil' lady," Craig says, steadying me so I don't fall. All my friends are highly attuned to my ability to fall when confronted by even the slightest obstacle.

"Sorry, Craig." I regain my footing. Thankfully I'm actually wearing my non-slip shoes tonight.

"I can't believe it's your last day," he says suddenly. "I sure am gonna miss ya girly."

"Craig, we're friends! You're still going to see me all the time," I comfort him.

"But I ain't gonna get paid to see you anymore. You can't convince me there's anything better than getting paid to hang out with your best buds," he says on a sigh. Well, that's something I can't argue with. It isn't really the theatre I'll miss working at. It's working with these people—my best friends—that I'll truly miss.

"You're late." I look up to find Zach standing behind Craig with his arms crossed in front of his chest. I can tell he's attempting to look irritated, but he fails miserably when he smirks at me.

I decide this is the perfect moment to execute my final performance. I twirl my body into a perfect pirouette. My final dramatic work entrance. I have surprisingly good balance when I'm dancing, considering I can barely walk without falling on my face. Craig and Zach both laugh.

"That's our girl," Craig says as he pumps his fist into the air. He then strolls to the other end of the snack bar to help a customer that has just walked up.

Zach takes a few steps towards me, discreetly grabs my hand, and softly smiles at me. His gaze falls to our hands as he interlaces his fingers with mine.

"*My* girl," he whispers.

# CHAPTER FOURTEEN:

As the last showing lets out, Zach sneaks Jill, Tony, Miles, and Brett into the theatre through the back door. Margo arrived over an hour ago. She has been silently reading one of her historical romance novels at a cafe table while Craig, Ronnie, and I clean the popcorn makers. Craig has already popped an entire garbage bag full of popcorn covered in butter-flavored oil for our private viewing tonight.

"Hey Mama Margo," Brett calls as he, Tony, Miles, and Jill walk towards the snack bar from the back of the theatre. "You reading '*Little House on the Prairie* Porn' again?" He asks with a laugh.

"Watch your mouth, Brett," Margo scolds. She points a finger at him. "And I'll have you know; these novels are extremely tasteful *and* historically accurate."

Brett throws his hands up in defense and continues to laugh. "I'm only messing with you, Margo. Please don't hurt me," he pleads. Margo playfully swats him on the arm with her paperback book.

Ronnie and Craig have just gone to clean the final theatre. Meanwhile, I finish ushering out the remaining moviegoers. Usually, cleaning the theaters is Ronnie's and my job. However, Craig said that since it's my last day, I shouldn't have to clean. This is something I sincerely appreciate considering I already worked a twelve-hour day at the hospital before my shift at The Cinedome.

Zach's friend, Todd, operates the projectors and has finally agreed to stay for one of our private viewings in honor of my last shift. Todd was excited we were watching an older movie, not one he had been forced to watch multiple times in a day.

I feel my cell phone vibrate in the pocket of my slacks and pull it out to see a text from Zach. He went to meet Todd in theatre twelve to set up the projector.

**It's showtime, babe.**

I can't help but allow a huge smile to form on my face as I read Zach's text.

"Why are you smiling so weird?"

Feeling caught, I quickly shove my cell phone back into my slacks pocket. When I look up, I find Brett staring down at me.

"You think I have a weird smile?" I ask with a laugh, trying to act as though I'm not hiding anything from him.

"I don't think all of your smiles are weird. Just that one," Brett says with a smirk.

His comment catches me off-guard. "I have more than one smile?" I question, curiosity etched on my face.

"You definitely do. And that one's mine." He points down to me. "That's the smile you always give me, naturally it's your best smile," Brett explains before shoving his hands into the front pockets of his dark wash jeans.

Suddenly, I feel nervous again. Heat starts rushing to my cheeks. I know I'm visibly blushing. My vision darts down to my non-slip shoes as I try to control my anxiety. Why is almost every pair of shoes I own outrageously unattractive? Do I give Brett a different smile? Or is he purposely just trying to embarrass me?

"Do you know if we can go into the theatre yet, Sam?" Jill's voice pulls me from my panic.

"Um, yeah. They're ready for us."

"I like that shirt on you," Jill's attention has turned to Brett.

"Thanks, Jill. And you look as pretty as ever tonight," he says with a charming smile. Jill immediately blushes, twirling a strand of her long blonde hair around her dainty finger.

I audibly let out a sigh of relief. This is just how Brett interacts with women, even his friends. He's infamous for being overly flirtatious. There's no need for me to start spiraling about an off-handed comment he made about my smile. Or multiple smiles, I guess. Both Jill and Brett turn to look at me. I give the two of them a smile, not sure which one, then begin walking confidently towards theatre twelve. Jill and Brett easily catch up to me with their long legs and even longer strides. I forget how fast tall people walk. I can only assume that Margo, Tony, and Miles have gotten up to follow us when I hear metal chairs scraping across the tile.

Our group walks into the theatre together, and I spot Craig standing in front of the screen. He's already changed out of his Cinedome button-up and into his "Captain Cowboy" t-shirt. My eyes then find Zach sitting up a few rows next to Todd. Instinctively, I walk towards the empty seat on his right.

As I approach, Ronnie scoots in front of Miles who was following me up the stairs. She shoves a full cup of soda into my hand.

"I made you a drink. Just how you like it!" She shoots me a wink, then hops over the row below us to sit between her Jilly Bean and Tony Cakes. She gracefully slides into the middle seat, resting an arm over each of her friend's shoulders.

I take my seat next to Zach with Miles slipping into the seat on my right. Brett and Margo are seated to the right of Miles. I can hear Margo ask Brett about his new job with the fire department.

I lean down to take a long sip of the drink Ronnie handed me. The familiar burn of vodka hits my throat with a light aftertaste of fruit punch. Just how I like it. I enjoy the warmth throughout my body from the first swallow of vodka.

Earlier today, I pronounced my first patient deceased. I witnessed the cruel aftermath of the war Alzheimer's waged on George Williams's body. I've inadvertently internalized the despair projected by his family. As I take another sip of my spiked punch, my worries begin to dissipate. Suddenly, I feel lighter. Veronica always knows what I need.

I grab my tin of mints from my slacks pocket, then pop one into my mouth. Ever since our private viewing of *Breaking Dawn* over a year ago, Ronnie and I have made it a point to get a little buzzed with every movie we watch. Needless to say, I'm no longer a rookie when it comes to concealing my movie theatre alcohol consumption. Jill is well aware of Ronnie's and my antics, but she pretends to be oblivious and turns the other cheek.

The warmth of vodka consumes me while the flavor of mint masks the taste of alcohol in my mouth. I slowly glance at each person that sits around me. These very people happen to be some of the people I love more than anything. This moment could not be any more perfect.

"Alright, y'all. I'd like to say a few words in Sam's honor before we start the flick." Craig announces to the theatre, still standing in front of the screen.

"Speech!" Tony shouts.

I watch Brett stick two of his fingers into his mouth and let out a loud whistle.

I turn and see that Zach looks visibly nervous, fidgeting in his seat next to me. I wonder if he thinks he's going to have to make a speech now, too...

"I just want you to know how proud I am of you, Sam," Craig starts. "I hope that you and I are lifelong friends. I feel real blessed to have met you."

I can't help but beam at him as he speaks. I know how shy he can be and how hard public speaking is for him, even if it is just in front of our pack.

"I know things might've gotten a bit awkward there for a bit. You know. With me having that major crush on Veronica and asking you to put in a good word for me twenty times a day," he chuckles.

My mouth falls open. Craig hasn't uttered a word about his "major crush" on Ronnie in over a year. To my knowledge, this is intel that only Jill, Zach, Ronnie, and myself had. Well, until now that is.

Ronnie starts coughing on the sip of her drink she just took. I watch her try to clear her throat from the aisle below me. It isn't often that Ronnie is caught off guard.

I scan the rest of the aisle to see that Margo and Brett both have wide smiles plastered on their faces. Brett playfully kicks the back of Ronnie's seat, and she immediately spins her body around to glare up at him.

Craig begins to speak again, and I realize his speech isn't quite finished. To my left I see Zach moving his hands wildly in what looks like an attempt to signal Craig. What on earth is he doing? If I didn't have nursing school under my belt, I would've sworn Zach was having a seizure.

"I just want you to know that I'm happy for you, Sam. The two of you give a guy like me hope."

Oh, no.

"I think you and Zach are perfect for each other! Y'all are the perfect example that sometimes friends make the best lovers," Craig finishes. He gives Ronnie a huge smile.

I gasp as I slap my hand over my mouth. Now there isn't a doubt in my mind that things are about to get extremely awkward. Suddenly, a million things seem to happen at once. In my peripheral vision, I see Zach's head fall into his hands. I hear Jill shriek inaudibly while Ronnie yells at Craig for telling everyone my personal business. Zach abruptly stands and starts moving towards Craig in what, I can only assume, is an attempt to protect him from Veronica's wrath.

I'm positive Craig didn't announce Zach's and my news out of malice. He just isn't that type of person. If anything, I think his speech was driven by the renewed hope that one day Ronnie would actually give him a chance.

Zach makes it halfway down the aisle before he's confronted by Brett blocking his path.

"Dude, what the hell?" Brett exclaims.

"Get out of my way, Brett," Zach cautions.

Oh no, this can't be happening.

Suddenly, I feel a large hand atop my own. I instinctively turn my body to the right at this unexpected touch. Unbeknownst to me, however, Miles has leaned his body into mine in an attempt to whisper something into my ear. When I turn, mine and Miles's heads collide with such force that I finally think I understand the expression "seeing stars."

In the chaos, no one pays Miles and me any attention. The two of us slumped over, clutching our heads. They all continue screaming at each other. Todd has even left his seat to stand between Brett and Zach, their shouts growing louder.

"What the hell, Sam?" Miles groans.

"That was your fault!" I snap. "You're the one who invaded my personal space!"

"Oh, get over yourself," he snorts as he rubs his forehead.

"Excuse me?"

"Did you not hear me?" Miles sarcastically asks.

"Shut up!" He's really starting to piss me off.

"Okay," he calmly replies as he rolls his eyes at me.

And now I'm extremely pissed off.

"Stop being an asshole and apologize for head butting the shit out of me!" I demand.

"Stop being crazy and maybe I will!" He barks back at me.

I'm not sure why being called crazy triggers me as severely as it does, but before I know what's happening, I'm flying off the handle. Like a crazy person.

"FUCK YOU, MILES!" I scream at the top of my lungs. I watch as his mouth falls open, his eyes widening in shock. To be fair, I'm pretty shocked myself at this unplanned outburst.

As I recover from my anger, I become acutely aware that the entire theatre has fallen dead silent. When I turn, I see all our friends staring at us. It appears that everyone else is as shocked as I am.

"Yeah, fuck you, Miles!" Ronnie shouts.

Miles is still staring at me as I try to conceal the small smile forming on my face. That's Veronica Mae Sanders for you—the most loyal of friends.

Miles then turns to look down at where Ronnie now stands next to Craig at the front of the theatre. Ronnie has taken a short intermission from going after Craig to put Miles in his place.

"What the hell did I do to you, Ronnie?" Miles yells down to her.

"Whatever you did to Sam you did to me, asshole!"

"Watch out, bro. She sure knows how to wield a pretzel," Brett warns with a laugh.

Suddenly, I hear Jill shriek from where she stands beside Brett and Zach. I assume she was attempting to keep the peace between the two as she so often does.

"Yeah, screw you, Miles," Jill screams. Okay, not quite the response of a peacekeeper, but Jill does once more refrain from using a curse word.

"Jesus, why am I being attacked?" Miles agitatedly runs his hand through his wild hair. Over the last year, I've come to notice this is one of his nervous quirks.

Brett is now hysterically laughing, probably finding humor in the fact that Jill and Ronnie aren't going after *him* this time. "Miles, you just better run. This one's got the biggest purse I've ever seen," he chuckles, pointing at Jill. A vivid memory of Jill smacking Brett in the back of the head with her oversized handbag comes to my mind. At the thought, I can't help but start laughing out loud.

In reaction to what I can only imagine is the sound of my laughter, Miles whips his body around, glaring at me with angry hazel eyes. I can't help but smile at him. He's kind of adorable when he's sulking. With a dramatic exhale, he throws his body back into the seat below him and slouches his long form into the chair, visibly pouting. He looks like a petulant child, exaggeratedly crossing his arms in front of his chest and sticking out his lower lip.

I know he's playing the part, now. He secretly finds this just as amusing as the rest of us. He can't fool me—I know him too well by now.

"How is this fair? I did absolutely nothing, yet I'm about to be jumped by the damn Powerpuff Girls," Miles whines.

At that, none of us can keep our composure. The entire theatre bursts into a chorus of uncontrollable laughter. Well, everyone but Margo that is, who is also standing beside Brett and Zach now, looking extremely confused.

"What's a 'Powder Poof Girl'?" I hear Margo ask Brett. Brett is now laughing so hard he has tears running down his face.

I turn to look at Miles and am relieved to find him chuckling softly. Maybe things don't have to be awkward after all.

"Can I be Blossom?" Ronnie squeals, shooting her hand up into the air. Naturally, Veronica would be Blossom. She is our sassy, red-headed leader, after all.

"Jill is totally Bubbles," Brett softly nudges Jill with his shoulder. Jill immediately blushes at his touch. Why won't she just admit she's madly in love with him?

"But I want to be Wonder Woman," Jill sulks. One of the many things she and I have in common is our mutual love of comic books and superheroes. And *Twilight* quotes, of course.

"That's a completely different universe," Craig shouts up to her. "Not possible."

Miles tilts his head to look up to me from where he's sitting. All of us are now out of our seats, besides him. He gives me his best sideways smirk.

"I guess that makes you Buttercup," he chuckles.

"Well, then I guess that makes you that demented monkey thing." I stick my tongue out at him.

"Mojo Jojo."

"What?"

"That's the demented monkey thing's name," he informs me.

I raise my eyebrow at him as if to question how the hell he knows this information.

"I have a sister, okay?" He adds defensively, throwing both his hands in the air. We both laugh, and everything suddenly feels normal again. Everything feels right.

I turn to walk toward where Zach is standing, shaking Brett's hand in a truce. Before I move a step, I feel Miles grab my hand. I turn around, carefully I might add, and gaze down at him.

"I'm sorry," he mouths to me.

"I'm sorry, too."

"All I want is for you to be happy and if Zach makes you happy, then I'm glad the two of you are together now." I notice him slowly exhale before letting his gaze fall down to his hand still clasping mine.

"So, you're actually happy about Zach and me dating?"

"Whatever makes you happy makes me happy, Sam," he answers softly.

Without thinking, I throw myself into his arms and hug him. He wraps his arms around me and stands, lifting me up with him.

God, I love him, I think to myself. This thought has me instantly panicked.

I mean, I love Miles as a friend...that's what I meant.

I quickly step away from Miles, suddenly feeling guilty for hugging him the way I just did. I search the room for Zach, hoping I didn't just offend him by hurling myself into Miles's arms. I am relieved when I spot Zach chatting with Todd totally unfazed.

My vision shifts left and I'm met with an icy blue stare. Brett is standing completely still beside Todd and Zach. He isn't talking with them. Instead, he appears to be glaring at Miles and me. Why does he seem so perturbed by Miles and me hugging? Why would he even care?

"Alright children. And Todd. Settle down," Margo summons our attention. Since Todd is in his early thirties with a wife and a one-year-old son, he has officially graduated from child to adult in Margo's eyes.

"Brett and I have decided on a civil way to end this kerfuffle," Margo announces, lightly placing her hand on Brett's shoulder. Did she really just say "kerfuffle?" Now it's Brett's turn to speak. Oh geez. Here we go...

He steps forward before addressing all of us. "I believe we should implement a new rule within our group." Great. We are totally starting to sound like a cult. I didn't even know we had rules, let alone needed a new one. I walk over to stand beside Zach as I brace myself for Brett's "new rule."

"If any people within our group of friends wish to start a romantic relationship with one another, the rest of the group has a right to vote on the subject. Our 'pack' should have the opportunity to decide if the two parties becoming romantically involved is in the best interest of the 'pack' as a whole." He emphasizes the word pack with dramatic air quotes. He has never been quiet about his opinion that calling our group of friends a pack was absurd.

But in *my* honest opinion, this new rule he's proposing is what's absurd. I'll admit though if I wasn't so annoyed with Brett's ludicrous suggestion, I would actually be pretty impressed with how articulately he just spoke.

"What's next? We vote each other off of the island?" Ronnie sneers, her voice dripping with sarcasm. At least I'm not the only one who thinks Brett is insane.

"This is ridiculous," Zach mutters.

"If it prevents all of you from the behavior I just witnessed, then maybe it isn't such a bad idea," Margo chimes in.

She can't be serious. I've had enough. "My love life is not a democracy!" I bellow.

"Agreed," Tony adds. Thank you, Tony. Finally, someone is speaking some sense. "I really feel like dating Sam would be more comparable to a dictatorship."

Anthony Hernandez, you have failed me. I shoot daggers at Tony with my glare, all while he laughs and dramatically blows me a kiss.

"Ha-ha, so funny," I snap back sarcastically. Hearing Zach's muffled laughter, I abruptly turn and grant him my worst scowl. He immediately senses my anger, then quickly tries to stifle his laughter. I decide to give him a swift punch to his left arm—he deserves it.

"Yeah, Tony. Not funny," Zach says, now cradling the arm I just punched.

"Dang, girly," Craig hollers. "Those kickboxing classes sure are paying off. Nice right hook!"

"Thank you." I give Craig a quick smile and curtsy. I recently started going to a kickboxing gym in an attempt to be less of a human sloth. I can't use the nursing school excuse for my lack of physical activity anymore.

I feel Zach put his arm around my waist, pulling me into his side. I look up to his dark brown eyes as he leans down, softly kissing my lips. My ears are suddenly filled with the sound of simultaneous groans.

"Get a room!" Ronnie yells. I giggle and rest my head on Zach's chest. All of a sudden, I'm no longer annoyed at him.

"Alright, let's get this voting thing over with so we can watch the movie," Miles proclaims.

"Wait, we're actually going to do this?" asks Zach.

"Yes, this is happening," Brett declares. Then, all at once, he pushes his way between Zach and me. Zach shakes his head in disbelief while I look up at Brett with wide eyes, the shock apparent on my face. Has he lost his mind?

"You two aren't allowed to touch until after the voting is over," he orders.

Yes, he has indeed lost his damn mind.

"Sam and Zach don't get to vote since they're obviously biased," Craig calls up to us.

"Craig!" Zach yells. "Whose side are you on?"

"I'm on the side of justice," Craig pronounces, pounding his chest with his fist. "But don't worry, I'm totally voting for you two to stay together."

"Well, I'm voting that you and Sam break up," Brett mentions to Zach. Big surprise there.

"Of course you are, Brett," Zach snaps. Here we go again.

I stomp on Brett's foot in an attempt to shut him up before he has the chance to respond to Zach. Brett is wearing steel-toe boots, so I doubt he even feels the weight of my foot, but that doesn't stop him from acting as if I've fatally wounded him.

He narrows his eyes at me. "I don't appreciate all this violence, Sammie."

"No more smiles for you," I hiss back.

"We'll see about that." He gives me his own perfect smile to prove his point.

"I think they're so cute together! I vote they keep dating," Jill chimes in. Thank you, Jillian.

"I'm gonna have to side with my boy, Brett," Tony adds. "If things go badly between you two, it's going to get weird for all of us. Maybe you can date someone at your new job Sam."

"Seriously, Tony?" I'm dumbfounded.

"It'll be less messy that way," Tony says with a cheeky grin.

"You're nuts," I laugh. "Besides, everyone I work with is either married or a woman."

"Have you ever considered playing for the other team? I highly recommend it," Tony chuckles and gives me a wink. I can't help but giggle with him.

Margo clears her throat, drawing our attention to her. She has a way of effortlessly commanding a room.

"Sam." She turns her body to address me directly. "You need to be focusing on passing your boards exam. And Zach is trying to get accepted to law school. I think the two of you would be better off focusing on your futures right now."

I'm stunned. How could Margo not support me? The feeling of betrayal is instantaneous.

"What if Sam is my future, Margo?" Zach mumbles.

Margo releases a soft sigh. "You're all still so young. All of you have so much life left to live, so much you've yet to experience. None of you will be the same people in ten years that you are today."

I love Margo, but what does she know?

She pauses, quickly scanning the theatre. Her gaze then rests on Zach and me.

"I would just hate to see the two of you potentially harm a beautiful friendship by jumping into a relationship you may not be ready for." Her final words are nearly a whisper as she stares solely at me.

Beside me, I hear Zach's sharp intake of breath and am suddenly consumed by anxiety. I meet Zach's gaze. Is he having second thoughts about us?

He gives me a smile and a reassuring nod. I release a loud exhale. I hadn't realized I was holding my breath. Looking down, I notice my hands are trembling. I quickly shove my hands into my pockets to hide my anxiousness.

God, I need another drink of my spiked fruit punch.

"Well, I am totally shipping them," Ronnie blurts out. My head snaps up to look at her.

"What're ya shipping to them?" Craig asks in all seriousness.

"For crying out loud! It's an expression, Craig," Ronnie tells him, obviously exasperated. "It means I want them to be in a relationship. Plus, Sam has had this huge crush on Zach for like three years now. Am I right Jill?" She turns to Jill for support.

"It's true," Jill confirms. She then slaps her well-manicured hand over her mouth. "Oh no! Were we not supposed to say anything, Sam?"

I shake my head in disbelief. This must be Embarrass-the-Hell-out-of-Sam Day.

Zach turns to me and whispers, "You have?"

"I thought it was kind of obvious," I reply. I feel myself begin to blush and quickly glance down at my ugly, non-slip shoes.

"Not to me," Brett mutters under his breath.

"If it's alright with all of you, I'm going to pass on this whole voting thing. I'll be in the projection booth. Let me know when I can start the movie," Todd calls to us as he exits the theatre. I feel awful for him. The one time he decides to stay and watch a movie with us, it turns into an absolute shit show.

"I do believe the vote is tied," Jill announces. "That means Miles's vote will be the tiebreaker." Her gaze drifts to where Miles is sitting. And now all of us are staring at him.

After a few moments of silence, Miles begins to speak. "I think if Sam and Zach are happy together, then why can't the rest of us be happy for them? Let's just agree that no matter what happens we all stay friends, okay?"

"Finally, something we can all agree on," Ronnie says as she wraps her arms around Craig and gives him a peck on the cheek. He instantly turns the color of a tomato. Ronnie is probably the only person who can render Craig Corey speechless.

Altogether, we verbalize our agreement to uphold our vow of everlasting friendship. I know it sounds insanely corny. At this moment, though, they're the words I needed to hear.

"Should we all write this in blood or something?" Ronnie jokes as we all laugh.

Even though it felt great to hear my friends confirm their dedication to our friendship, there has never been a doubt in my mind that all of us would be life-long friends. We were meant to be, meant to find each other.

Everything feels right again as we settle in to watch a handsome Christopher Reeve on the big screen. One last post-shift private viewing.

I can't help but allow a ginormous grin to overtake my face. I don't know why I had been so nervous to tell everyone about Zach and me. I know that the nine of us might not always agree, but there is absolutely nothing in this world that could tear us apart.

# CHAPTER FIFTEEN:

I would be lying to myself if I said I wasn't hungover this morning. I think the anxiety of Zach's and my relationship being exposed caused me to drink a bit more spiked fruit punch than I normally do at our movie viewings. But it was my last shift at The Cinedome last night. I think I deserved to have a little fun.

Ronnie and I spent this morning sipping extra-strong Bloody Marys while Jill was at the salon getting her hair done for tonight.

A little hair of the dog was just what the doctor ordered. Thankfully, I no longer feel hungover.

Jill, Ronnie, and I are currently getting ready for my pinning ceremony in an hour and a half. Again, I'd be lying to myself if I said I wasn't a little tipsy at the moment. Ronnie drank just as much—if not more than me—and seems to be perfectly fine. I have to admit, that girl can hold her liquor.

I assume by the time the ceremony starts I'll have sobered up, but just in case, I set the curling iron down and walk to the kitchen to put something in my stomach.

I hear Jill saunter into the kitchen behind me. "It's your day, Sam. You should relax. I'll make you a sandwich."

I'm currently too tipsy to argue with her. I give her a small nod and take a seat on a bar stool.

After a few minutes pass, Jill slides a plate across the counter to me with a tuna sandwich on it. I greedily start to inhale it. I had no idea how hungry I actually was. Now that I think about it, I really haven't eaten anything today besides some Honey Nut Cheerios this morning. Oh...and about five Bloody Marys.

"You better sober up, Sammie Bear. Don't want you passing out before your own party," Ronnie softly nudges me with her elbow as she takes a seat beside me. After my pinning ceremony this evening, we all plan to celebrate at The Barn Door, our favorite bar.

"How are you not even remotely buzzed?" I ask with a mouthful of tuna fish sandwich.

Ronnie laughs as she leans down and steals a bite of the sandwich in my hand. She gives me a huge grin before swallowing. "It's because I'm a professional."

Jill calls from our laundry closet, "Sam, I'm ironing your dress." I've coined it a closet because the laundry room in our apartment can't possibly be considered an actual room.

"You don't have to do that, Jill," I call back to her as I finish my sandwich.

Jill walks into our living room holding up the white knee-length dress I purchased for tonight. I thought the white dress would go perfect with my blindingly white lab coat.

"If I don't iron it, who will?" She sassily places her hand on her hip. I give her a blank stare. She knows damn well that neither Ronnie nor I will be doing any ironing today.

"Exactly," Jill exclaims before turning back to the laundry closet. She abruptly stops, turning to face Ronnie as she points to our old hand-me-down sofa and scolds, "Make your bed, Veronica Mae."

"Yes, mother," Ronnie groans.

Meanwhile, Jill walks around the corner to return to one of her favorite pastimes—ironing.

I stand backstage at the Hartman Theatre, donning my crisply ironed white dress and stark white lab coat, surrounded by my fellow class-mates. Just as I predicted, the tuna fish sandwich combined with my nervousness has promptly sobered my ass right up.

I can tell the president of our nursing program has taken the stage when I hear the applause. I can't believe this moment is finally here. All of the sleepless nights studying, and long days filled with hospital clinicals, labs, and classes have finally paid off.

"We did it, guys!" one of my classmates loudly announces, pump-ing his fist into the air. We all cheer and hug one another as we prepare to take the stage to be pinned as registered nurses. This is our moment.

As I hear my name called by the announcer, I step onto the stage and am met with a firm handshake from the president of our program. He is such a kind man. I think I may actually miss his impromptu pep talks and intimidatingly firm handshakes.

As I continue walking under the bright theatre lights, I spot Margo walking up the stairs on the opposite side of the stage. She looks lovely in a navy-blue pantsuit. When I meet Margo at center stage, I'm warmed by the proud smile she gives me. It's almost as comforting as the warmth I felt from the first sip of vodka I took this morning. ...Almost.

My eyes briefly scan the audience. I immediately find my pack. In the second row of the theatre sit my dad, his wife Amanda with my two-year-old half-sister Taylor on her lap, and my Aunt Cindy. In the row behind them sit Jill, Ronnie, Brett, Miles, Tony, Craig, and Zach.

Zach looks incredibly handsome in a button-up shirt, his hair tied back into his trademark man-bun ponytail thing. It's not lost on me that he's clutching a bouquet of sunflowers. My favorite.

I turn back to face Margo as the announcer hands her my pin. Her proud smile remains plastered on her face as she delicately places the pin onto the collar of my lab coat. I beam at her as the sound of applause and cheering surrounds me. I still can't believe it. I made it.

After the ceremony comes to a close, I descend the stairs and head into the audience in search of my family and friends. As soon as I see my dad, I sprint into his arms. He has been, and always will be, my safety net.

"I'm so proud of you, Sam," he says, still locked in our embrace.

"Thanks, Dad."

As I step away from my dad's arms, I'm suddenly engulfed in a group hug by Jill and Ronnie. When they release me I turn to face Zach. He smiles sweetly at me as he hands me the beautiful bouquet of sunflowers.

"Congrats, babe," he whispers into my hair, pulling me into his arms.

"Thanks, babe." I feel the heat rise to my cheeks. I know I'm visibly blushing, but I don't care.

"Where's Margo?" I ask no one in particular.

"I think I saw her walk toward the back of the theatre," Brett replies.

I nod to him before heading toward the rear of the theatre to find Margo. Before I move more than a step, I feel Brett lightly touch my arm to gain my attention. I gaze up at him.

"I have something for you." He pulls a small box out of the back pocket of his jeans and hands it to me. "In honor of you becoming a nurse and all."

"Technically, I'm still an almost-nurse until I pass my boards," I correct him.

He laughs. "Just open it already."

The small white box is wrapped in a red ribbon. I untie the ribbon and pull off the lid. Inside the box lies a charm bracelet. Carefully lifting the bracelet out, I examine the delicate charms that dangle from the chain: a stethoscope, a nurse's hat, a tub of movie theatre popcorn, and the Superman emblem.

"I love it, Brett," I whisper. This may be the most thoughtful gift anyone has ever given me. And it's from Brett of all people.

"Oh, it's nothing. Just something I had lying around," he dismisses me with a wave of his hand and a chuckle.

"No, it's everything." My mouth forms into a huge smile. I think back to Brett's teasing last night and wonder if I just gave him some sort of personalized smile, like he claimed I do. I immediately stop smiling. "Would you help me put it on?"

He grins, then clasps the bracelet around my outstretched wrist. I twist my arm from side to side as I gaze adoringly at my new bracelet.

"I'm never taking it off."

"That clasp is pretty tricky. You may never be able to *get* it off."

I quickly turn around upon hearing Margo's voice, and I'm stunned at what I see. Standing beside Margo is the last person in the world that I want here—my mother.

"Why is she here?" I hiss at Margo as I point to the woman standing beside her.

"She's here as my plus-one," Margo responds calmly.

"How could you do this to me?"

"Sam, I did this *for* you. One day, you'd regret not having your mother at your pinning ceremony."

"That wasn't your decision to make." My hands are bunched into fists at my sides, anger coursing through my veins. I feel hands lightly rest themselves on both my shoulders in what I can only assume is an attempt to calm the storm raging inside of me. Looking up, I see Brett standing behind me. In my furious state, I had forgotten he was standing beside me when Margo and my mother first approached.

"I'm very proud of you, Samantha," Caroline voices. "This must be your new boyfriend. He's quite handsome."

She's delusional if she thinks I'm about to carry on a casual conversation with her. And how does she even know I have a boyfriend?

"You are unbelievable! You also weren't invited, Caroline." My mother is clearly wounded by my words and the use of her first name.

"Sam," Brett cautions.

I abruptly whip my body around to face him and angrily point my finger up at him. "Don't you defend her, Brett Bowen! You do not know this woman."

Brett decides at this moment to stay silent. Smart man.

I realize it's best to rein in my temper. The last thing I want is to let Caroline inadvertently ruin one of the best nights of my life. She has ruined enough of my life as it is.

"I know you had good intentions, Margo. I just wish you would have talked to me about this first. But thank you for pinning me." I'm still in utter disbelief that she brought my mother to my pinning ceremony as her date. Without my permission.

"See you at the bar," I mutter to Brett before turning and walking away from the three of them. I refuse to acknowledge Caroline any further. I won't waste another ounce of my energy on that woman. She's already stolen enough from me.

# CHAPTER SIXTEEN:

The Barn Door is packed tonight, but that's typical for a Friday night. As I swing open the heavy wooden doors and enter the bar, I recognize a lot of the usual weekend crowd. Zach is beside me with his arm around my waist, while Jill and Veronica are just behind us.

My eyes take a moment to adjust to the dark ambience inside the bar. Once they do, I spot Van, the owner and head bartender. He's behind the bar pouring a row of bourbon shots. I give him a friendly wave as I walk past the bustling bar top that's located smack dab in the middle of the room.

"Congrats, Sam!" Van shouts above the noise.

"Hell yeah! Let's party!" Ronnie yells from behind me, pumping her small fist into the air.

"Sam, come take a shot. On the house!" Van hollers. Well, you don't have to ask me twice.

I scurry back over to the bar and slide onto an empty barstool as if I'm a baseball player sliding into home plate. Van smiles at me as he slips a double shot of bourbon across the bar top in my direction.

Usually, I'm more of a vodka girl but beggars can't be choosers. Free is free.

Without hesitation, I throw back the shot and immediately feel the familiar intense burn as I swallow the cheap bourbon. The drink is absolutely disgusting, but the warm sensation coursing through my body is pure heaven.

"Alright, now I'm ready to party!" I yell, throwing both my hands in the air. Zach, Ronnie, Jill, and a few other patrons in our general vicinity start cheering. I know tonight will be one to remember. ...That's if the booze leaves me with any memory of tonight at all.

After departing from the bar top, I see Tony, Craig, Miles, and Brett already seated at our usual table toward the back of the building. I rode with Zach to the bar from the theatre. Jill and Ronnie followed behind us in Jill's Corolla. Jill never drinks much. I've only actually seen her drunk on a few occasions throughout our friendship. So, naturally, she's often one of our designated drivers. Since Tony is sober, he's also a self-appointed DD for the crew.

If Jill and Tony weren't in attendance tonight—or at any of our many nights at The Barn Door, for that matter—Miles would be staying sober. Miles has a zero-tolerance policy when it comes to any of us driving with alcohol in our systems. Even after just one drink. No exceptions. After losing his mother to a drunk driver, he knows better than anyone how a single, albeit small, lapse in judgment can inexorably impact many lives.

"Sammmmm!" Tony squeals when he sees me. He runs to greet me as I approach our table, wrapping me into a giant hug and planting a swift kiss on my cheek. "Take this godawful coat off so I can see that dress of yours up close."

"The coat was necessary, Tony. It's like thirty degrees out." Chuckling, I slough the huge winter coat off my shoulders and drape it over the back of an empty chair.

Tony looks me up and down then nods his approval. "This dress is hot, and you look super sexy in it! And you know that means a lot coming from a gay man." He gives me a dramatic wink. I adore him so much.

"That's quite a compliment coming from you," I joke, playfully smacking him on the arm.

"You know I just don't throw out compliments willy nilly. If you look jacked up, you better believe I'm gonna tell you."

"Oh, don't worry Tony Cakes. *We know*," Ronnie snidely chimes in.

"Girl, half the time *you* are a hot mess," Tony laughs and raises his eyebrow pointedly at Ronnie. "Those corset top things you always wear? That's a no for me. Straight-up looks like you're wearing lingerie." He gestures animatedly at Ronnie's top.

"Shut up, Anthony! These tops make my boobs look fantastic and you know it!" She glares at him playfully.

"I love your face, not so much your boobs," Tony says as he blows her a kiss. Ronnie's angry facade quickly fades and she's now all smiles.

Abruptly, Ronnie turns to Craig and gives him a playful smirk. "Are you staring at my boobs, Craig Corey?"

Craig instantly turns the exact shade of a tomato. It seems Ronnie often has this effect on him. "I...uh...was looking at your shirt thing," he stammers. "We were all just talking about your shirt thing!"

"Sure you were," Ronnie responds before giving him a quick smack on the ass.

I didn't know humans could turn this shade of scarlet without it being from a dire medical episode. Craig looks unmistakably mortified and Ronnie is enjoying every second of it.

Just then, Brett, Miles, and Zach return from the bar with a round of drinks for everyone. Zach places a cranberry vodka in my hand, and I immediately take a huge gulp of it.

"Pace yourself, Sam," Zach warns with a laugh. "I don't want to have to carry you out of here later tonight."

Just as I'm about to tell Zach to stop acting like my father, Craig starts tapping on the side of his beer glass with his pocketknife catching all of our attention. A true redneck intro to a toast.

"I'd like to talk about..." Craig begins before he's immediately met with a loud chorus of groans. The last time Craig made a speech it turned into a full-blown war amongst all of us. Which reminds me of something. As Craig begins to assure us that he has no intention of causing another ruckus (his words not mine), I turn to Zach.

"How did Craig know we were dating? You promised you wouldn't say anything," I whisper to Zach as I take another sip of my vodka cranberry. I'm suddenly very annoyed with my boyfriend.

Zach bites his lower lip and appears to think for a moment before replying in a hushed tone, "He knew how I felt about you before I even asked you out."

"What?"

"He's my best friend, Sam. We tell each other everything."

"I guess I can relate." After all, I did immediately run home and tell Jill and Ronnie everything that Zach confessed to me that night at Applebee's.

"I should have known better though," Zach chuckles. "Craig is many things but discrete isn't one of them."

"I think he may discreetly have a thing for Ronnie," I say sarcastically.

Zach laughs. "What on earth would make you think that?"

"I don't know. Just a hunch." I grin as my gaze falls over Craig and Ronnie who are currently standing beside each other.

Craig suddenly gets up on one of the chairs surrounding our table in an attempt to regain our attention.

"Get off the chair, Craig!" Van yells across the noisy bar. Craig immediately hops down.

"Sorry, brother. Just tryin' to get the attention of these rascals," Craig shouts back, motioning toward us said rascals. Van laughs and nods his head in understanding. All is immediately forgiven. It's impossible to stay upset with Craig.

"I wanted to start by saying congrats, Sam! I am so darn proud of you, girly," he exclaims.

"Thanks, Craig," I beam at him from where I'm sitting at the other side of our table. He's such a genuine person and a wonderful friend. I feel the warmth radiating throughout my body. This is partially due to the vodka I just consumed, but it's mostly due to my gratitude for this man's friendship.

Craig continues, "But more importantly, I wanted to talk to y'all about if we're doing this Secret Santa thing for Christmas or not."

My gratitude-induced warmth promptly fades away, yet I can't help but chuckle to myself. Craig's immense concern for organizing our Secret Santa gift exchange is hysterical. He has probably asked me about it three times this week alone.

"Really, Craig?" Ronnie scoffs. "It's Sam's night!"

"I thought last night was Sam's night. Like I said, seems like every night's her night," Miles laughs.

I give him a glare. He automatically throws his hands up in defense as he continues to laugh. He thinks he's so funny. Well, I strongly disagree.

"Craig has a point. Christmas is in like a week and a half. I need time to shop!" Jill blurts out.

"Fine," Brett sighs. "Give me your hat, Craig."

Craig reluctantly removes his cowboy hat and hands it over to Brett. He looks visibly uncomfortable without his beloved hat atop his head.

"Let's make this quick. We can't leave Craig with a cold, lonely head for long," Zach says with a grin.

Although Ronnie and I instantly burst into laughter, the rest of our group looks completely confused. Craig shakes his head in disapproval as if to relay that this is, in fact, not a laughing matter.

"It's a Cinedome inside joke," I snicker.

"Nah, you mean it's a prime example of Cinedome discrimination," Craig complains.

Zach, Ronnie, and I laugh even harder. I'm reminded once more of how I will truly miss working with my best friends.

"Alright, tear off a piece of napkin and write your name on it," Brett instructs us as he tosses a stack of napkins across the table. "Jill, I know you have a pen somewhere in that duffle bag of yours." He points to the giant purse resting on Jill's lap.

"I actually have an entire pocket full of pens," our very own Mary Poppins responds, removing a fistful of pens from her gigantic purse.

Jill begins passing out the pens as I rip off individual pieces of napkin and distribute them around the table. Brett places Craig's hat upside-down in the middle of our table. I write my name on a small piece of napkin, then toss it into Craig's hat. The rest of our pack follows suit and soon we have a hat full of names.

"If you pull your own name, obviously put it back and draw again," Brett informs us. He begins walking around to each of us, holding out Craig's hat.

Craig does the honors and draws out a ripped piece of napkin first. He opens the folded piece, smiling as soon as he reads the name written on it.

"Hot damn, I got Zach. Whatcha want buddy?" he asks.

"Craig, what the hell?" Ronnie shouts. "It's called *Secret* Santa, not Open-Your-Big-Ass-Mouth Santa!"

"Oh, shoot! My bad y'all."

He obviously had no clue what a Secret Santa gift exchange actually was. We all start to laugh once more. Like I said, it's impossible to stay upset with Craig.

I was hoping to get Zach but now that's obviously not a possibility. Now I just hope I either draw Ronnie or Jill. I know those two like the back of my hand. They will be a piece of cake to shop for.

Brett finally makes his way over to me. I thrust my hand into the cowboy hat and pull out a piece of folded napkin. While Brett hands the hat to Zach to draw a name, I carefully open my napkin to ensure no one else can see the name scribbled on it. I read the name sloppily scrawled on the napkin in my hand.

*Miles.*

Shit! His name is probably the last one I wanted to draw. I have no idea what to buy him. He's undoubtedly the most difficult to shop for of all my friends.

After the name drawing is complete, Brett sets Craig's cowboy hat back onto his head and gives him a loving pat on the back.

"Thanks, bro. Alright! Keep the names you drew to yourselves." Brett turns a teasing glance toward Craig.

"It was an honest mistake! I thought it was called Secret Santa because it's a secret that Santa isn't a real-life fella."

"Oh my gosh...Santa isn't real!?!" Ronnie squeals before pretending to sob hysterically.

"She's yankin' my leg, right?" Craig asks genuinely concerned as he points to the spectacle Ronnie is currently making. We all begin to laugh for what feels like the hundredth time tonight.

"I betcha wish it wasn't your leg she was yanking." Tony smirks as he throws his arm over Craig's shoulder. "Don't let these Scrooges get to you, Craig," he reassures.

Ignoring Tony's sexual innuendo and Craig's blatant embarrassment, Jill asks, "We agreed on a fifty-dollar limit, correct?" Mentally balancing her checkbook, I'm sure.

"Yes, ma'am," Miles answers.

"I'm going shopping tomorrow!" Jill claps her hands excitedly. Maybe Jill, shopper extraordinaire, can help me figure out what to get Miles. She always gives the best gifts.

Now that we have this whole Secret Santa ordeal out of the way, I'm ready to celebrate. I smile to myself as I finish my first cranberry vodka of the evening. No matter what Miles says, this is my night and nothing's going to ruin it.

I glance up from my empty glass just in time to spot Ashleigh and Madison, or the asshole Olsen twins as I like to refer to them, strut into the bar.

Well, shit. There goes my night.

# CHAPTER SEVENTEEN:

"Oh, great. Who invited *them*?" Ronnie snarls.

"Ashleigh is Miles's girlfriend. You can't really blame him for inviting her," Jill replies.

"Really, Jill?" Ronnie snaps.

"Okay, ladies. Let's not rip each other's hair out over this," Tony interrupts, trying to defuse the situation.

We all watch as Miles runs to where Ashleigh and her insufferable sidekick Madison are now sitting at the bar. Ronnie and I first had the pleasure of meeting these two at last year's late-night premiere of *Twilight Breaking Dawn: Part One*.

Remember the two lovely ladies Miles and Brett inadvertently stood up last November due to our movie theater brawl? Yes, this is them.

Ronnie's and my first encounter with Ashleigh and Madison was far from pleasant, but I've tried to play nice with them since Ashleigh officially became Miles's girlfriend.

Madison and Brett had a fling for about a month, but in true Brett fashion, he got bored and broke things off with her. Needless to say, now there's quite a bit of tension between Brett and Madison.

Naturally, Brett doesn't care and wouldn't have an issue being around Madison if she wasn't so rude to him. To put it simply though, Madison despises Brett with a passion that consumes her little black soul. And she doesn't bother hiding it. Every time Madison is in the same vicinity as Brett, she constantly takes small jabs at him. For Miles's sake, Brett usually ignores her.

It always feels incredibly awkward when the two women are around. Awkward is definitely not the vibe I'm shooting for tonight. It's also wildly apparent that Ashleigh and Madison are not huge fans of Ronnie, Jill, and me. They seem to be the type of women that feel as though any other woman they encounter is a threat and should be treated like it.

To sum it up, they aren't very nice to the three of us. They do seem to be a bit terrified of Ronnie though. They've heard the tales of what the infamous Veronica Sanders can do with a soft pretzel. Personally, I'd be scared too. They mostly remain cordial around us but are never too friendly.

The feeling is obviously mutual. We don't want to be their friends either. If I wanted to associate with prickly bitches, I'd plant a cactus garden. No, thank you.

"Oh, God. He's bringing them over here," Ronnie whines.

"There goes my night," Brett mutters under his breath. He verbalizes what I've been thinking from the moment the two women walked in.

"They're not that bad now, y'all," Craig cuts in.

"Not that bad to look at isn't the same as not that bad to be around," I inform Craig with a laugh.

"Those two are darn pretty now, aren't they?" Craig says to himself, obviously lost in some fantasy I want no part of.

Indeed, they're both undeniably pretty, but sometimes beauty is a lot deeper than what's on the exterior. In my humble opinion, Ashleigh and Madison would be drop-dead gorgeous if they were simply nice people.

"You could do better, Craig," Ronnie reassures him, catching us all off guard.

Craig turns his body toward Ronnie, a small smile forming on his face. He tips his hat at her. "That means a heap coming from a beauty like yourself."

Ronnie slightly blushes, nervously twirling a strand of her auburn hair around her index finger. I don't think I've ever seen Ronnie look so nervous. What's even more shocking? She's at a loss for words. What is happening right now?

Ronnie quickly changes the subject, whispering, "Here they come."

Tony lets out a loud fake laugh and the rest of us follow suit in an attempt to make it look like we haven't been talking about them for the last two minutes.

Miles strides towards us, his arm around Ashleigh. Madison follows a few paces behind them, sipping her bright blue drink through a tiny red straw as she saunters over.

"Hey, guys! Let's make room for Ashleigh and Madison." Miles motions to our table.

At Miles's request, Tony and Craig each swipe an extra chair for the two women. Brett remains in his seat, taking a long drink from his Budweiser and completely ignoring their arrival. Zach and I scoot our chairs over to make room for the girls to join us at the table.

"Hi," I greet them with a small wave. See? I'm trying to be nice.

Madison gives me an undoubtedly fake smile and continues to sip her bright blue drink while she takes her seat next to Zach. The princess cannot be bothered to verbally acknowledge the peasant.

"She just said hello to you," Ronnie informs Madison, staring her down.

Madison snaps her head up to meet Ronnie's glare. "I heard her."

"Hi, Samantha," Ashleigh interjects. "Congrats, by the way."

Almost everyone sitting at the table, including Miles, stares at her. Ashleigh is well aware I despise being called by my full name, yet she constantly still uses it. This bitch.

"Thanks, Ash," I reply with a smile so fake it could rival Madison's. I know damn well she hates any abbreviation of her name. Two can play that game.

Miles quickly interrupts Ashleigh's and my tense exchange by pulling her chair toward his own and lightly kissing her on the lips. Gross.

Ronnie turns and makes hushed gagging sounds at Brett. He instantly bursts into laughter. I can't help but chuckle too. Zach kicks my foot, signaling for me to behave myself. I give him my signature eye roll.

As Miles finishes locking lips with the Devil, he slides another vodka cranberry across the table to me.

"I saw you were empty."

"You're the best." I give him two thumbs up.

"Dork."

Out of the corner of my eye, I notice Ashleigh looks extremely perturbed. She abruptly stops drinking her own vodka cranberry, setting it down on the table a little too hard. I watch as liquid spills over the top of her glass. She dramatically flips her hair, turning to glare at her boyfriend. What is this chick's problem?

"Baby, I thought you ordered that second drink for me. I'm almost done with mine," she whines.

"Well, you are now that you spilled half of it on the table," Brett chides. Miles immediately glares at him, warning him to stop talking.

"No one was talking to you," Madison sneers as she locks eyes with Brett.

Before Brett can reply, Jill jumps out of her chair and runs over to him. "Let's go do a shot!" Jill tugs his arm and starts pulling him toward the bar.

"You wanna do a shot?" Brett is clearly surprised. Honestly, all of us appear a bit surprised. Jill never does shots.

"Heck yes!" I know Jill is only trying to distract Brett to prevent him from getting into an altercation with Madison. She hates taking shots.

Well, it works. At this moment, Brett only has eyes for Jill.

"Hell yes!" he responds with a laugh. He suddenly sweeps Jill off her feet, throws her over his shoulder, and starts carrying her to the bar. She shrieks with surprise before breaking into uncontrollable giggles. She waves back to us from Brett's arms as they walk away. Jealousy is emanating from Madison where she's sitting beside Zach.

My best friend Jillian Moore is what I consider to be drop-dead gorgeous. Not only is she physically attractive, but she's one of the best people I've ever known. There isn't a more beautiful combination.

Zach looks at me with wide eyes, obviously trying not to laugh. I take a huge gulp from my vodka cranberry to prevent myself from laughing as well. As I set my glass back on the table, I notice Ashleigh is staring daggers at me.

"Aren't they cute together?" Ronnie asks Madison, feigning sweetness. She's definitely trying to get under Madison's skin right now.

Madison glares at Ronnie as she finishes her last sip of Smurf blood. What the hell is she even drinking?

"I'll go get you another drink, babe. It's no problem," Miles softly reassures Ashleigh.

"You know what? I think we all need another round," Zach decides. I can tell he feels bad for Miles who is about to get his ass reamed by his lovely girlfriend. "Craig, wanna help me grab some drinks?"

"Sure thing, buddy." Craig happily jumps up out of his chair. "Madison, what is it you're drinking?"

She bats her long, fake eyelashes at him as she purrs, "It's called a Blue Bayou. Could you make sure they put sugar on the rim? Pretty please, Craigy?"

*Craigy? I cannot stand this woman.*

Craig is visibly flustered by Madison's over-the-top flirting. "You got it, Maddie. I, uh, didn't know Van made drinks like that."

"He does it special for me," Madison boasts. Like we actually give a shit.

Ronnie looks incredibly pissed off. Personally, I think she even looks a tiny bit jealous, but I'd never dare utter that aloud. She stands from her chair and steps toward where Craig is still standing. She lightly places her hand on his shoulder.

He turns to look at her and an effortless grin takes over his face as their eyes meet.

Brett once told me that I have a special smile I give him. Now I'm concluding, however, that if anyone has a special smile they give to a particular person, it's Craig to Ronnie.

"I'll just take a Jack and Coke, Craigy," Ronnie purrs, mimicking Madison.

What she does next shocks us all—but especially Craig. She gently grabs Craig's face between her petite hands, leans in, and softly kisses him on the lips. An audible gasp makes its way around the table. Craig's mouth falls open as Ronnie pulls away from their kiss. He stares at Ronnie, stunned.

"Thanks, Craigy-Boo." Ronnie's sultry tone has Craig at a complete and utter loss for words.

Oh, Madison. I hope you've learned your lesson. Never try to one-up Ronnie. She will always win.

"Maybe this 'major crush' isn't as one sided as I thought," Zach whispers to me before he walks over to Craig. Zach then grabs Craig by the arm, pulling him away from the table and towards the bar.

"You have officially ruined that man," Miles chuckles as he tosses a balled-up napkin at Ronnie.

"Maybe we'll ruin each other," Ronnie ponders, shrugging her shoulders and discreetly biting her lower lip as she stares after Craig.

# CHAPTER EIGHTEEN:

"So, Samantha, when are you going back to school?" Ashleigh questions.

"What?" I ask, completely baffled. Doesn't she know I just graduated?

"Well, Miles said you only completed your associate's degree. I was just wondering when you were going back for a *real* degree."

I stare at Ashleigh, my mouth agape. I cannot believe she just said that to me. She is unbelievable. "I'm sorry, remind me of what *you* have a degree in, Ash?" I snap.

I notice Miles growing increasingly uncomfortable. He nervously runs his fingers through his trademark mess of curls. My glare moves from the She-Devil to settle upon his face.

"I'm sorry," he mouths at me.

"Oh, Sam. You didn't hear?" Ronnie cuts in. I turn to look at my best friend. "Ashleigh just graduated with a bachelor's in not knowing when to shut her big fat mouth."

Miles gasps. Ashleigh whips her body around in her chair to face him.

"Are you going to let this bitch talk to me like that?" she screams at him.

"Oh, I forgot to mention. Ash is going back for her master's in being a stupid whore!" Ronnie yells, slamming both of her hands onto the table.

Tony spits the water he was drinking across the table. He starts uncontrollably laughing, which only serves to piss off Ashleigh even more.

There's no going back now—no more playing nice.

Suddenly, Ashleigh stands to face me, thrusting her hands onto her hips. "Stay the hell away from my boyfriend, Sam!" she screeches.

Where is this even coming from? Ronnie was the one who called her a stupid whore. Why is she screaming at me?

"What are you talking about?" I ask, dumbfounded.

"I know it's hard for you, but don't play dumb," she hisses at me.

Miles stands from his chair to place his hand on Ashleigh's shoulder. "That's enough, Ashleigh."

"Miles tells me everything. I know you're in love with him," she spits.

What is she talking about?

"What are you telling her, Miles?" I demand. Is he seriously feeding her these bullshit lies?

"Nothing!" Miles yells. "What are you even talking about, Ashleigh?"

I guess Miles and I have the same question.

I look over to Ronnie who's still standing at the other side of the table. She's glaring at Ashleigh, looking like she may pounce at any moment. I can hear the faint sound of Ronnie's tongue clicking against the roof of her mouth. When she turns to look at me, I try giving her a look to convey that she isn't worth it. I'm not going to let her get under my skin. I know that's what she's trying to do.

"Miles and I laugh at how pathetic you are, Samantha. He'll never want someone like you," Ashleigh snorts, motioning to me with her well-manicured claws.

By this point, I'm physically shaking from the words she's hurled at me. I always knew Ashleigh wasn't a very nice person, but damn. She's vicious.

"That's ENOUGH!" Miles bellows, attempting to intervene before this gets out of hand.

Although I'm aware Miles is yelling (something I've rarely heard him do), I can barely hear him over the pounding of my heart. I can feel my anger start to consume me as I clench my fists at my sides.

"Okay, now I'm gonna kick your ass!" Ronnie shouts before she suddenly throws herself at Ashleigh. Before she can reach her, however, Tony quickly stands, catching Ronnie in a bear hug and trying his best to prevent her from tackling Ashleigh to the hardwood floor.

"How cute. Pathetic little Sam needs her friends to fight all her battles," Ashleigh snarls. As a finishing touch, she lifts her glass from the table and hurls the remainder of her vodka cranberry all over my brand-new white dress.

After this, everything happens rather quickly. It's almost as if I've left my body, watching my actions as I hover over myself, no longer in control of my movements. I've gone into some kind of animalistic auto-pilot mode. All I see is red. The voices around me are distant and muffled;

the only coherent thought I can make is "*attack*."

I dive across the wooden table, hurling myself at Ashleigh. Miles and Ashleigh both stand wide-eyed and frozen as I lunge towards them like a lioness about to rip apart her prey. The impact of my flailing body promptly throws Ashleigh to the floor of the bar. Before I know it, I'm sitting on top of her, releasing a series of punches and slaps. She attempts to block her face with her hands, crying and screaming for help.

I can't stop myself; there's no going back. I want to hurt her like she's hurt me. In the distance, I can hear a roar of screams and shouts. I feel hands around me, attempting to pull me away, but I fight them off.

I've never hit another person before—at least not seriously. It's a feeling I can't describe. A mix of revenge and guilt, relief, and remorse. I know physical violence is wrong, but all I can think is that she pushed me to this point. She deserves this.

"The way you spell your name is stupid!" I scream at Ashleigh as I rear my arm back to throw another punch. Not my best of insults, but something I've always wanted to say to her.

Before my fist can reconnect, I've been pulled off of her. Large arms wrap around my waist as I'm hoisted away. The arms continue to hold me tightly, afraid to release me, I'm sure. I wouldn't trust me either right now.

"Stop, Sam. An assault charge would end your career before it even starts." I hear the person holding me mutter into my ear, out of breath.

I can see clearly again, the red tinge to my vision having dissipated. I notice Ashleigh sitting on the floor, crying hysterically, with her nose bleeding and her lip split open. Tony and Miles are both kneeling before her, examining her injuries.

Madison appears to be crying, too. She's also bleeding. I have a sneaking suspicion that Ronnie busted Madison's lip open. In my opinion, she also deserved it. Craig hovers over Madison in what looks like an attempt to console her.

A few feet away I spot Jill attempting to calm a seething Ronnie. If anyone can talk some sense into Ronnie, it's Jill. Beside them stands Zach, who appears to be pleading with Van about something. I'm sure he's begging him not to call the police about our not-so-little dispute.

If Zach's over there, then whose arms are around me?

I turn my body around and look up to see Brett, his arms still wrapped around my shaking body. He tilts his head down to meet my gaze, icy blue eyes boring into mine.

To my surprise, I feel warm tears stream down my cheeks. I bury my head into my friend's chest and bawl.

"She ruined my dress. Jill spent an hour ironing it for me tonight. It was brand new," I cry. I know my tears are about more than just a dress, but it's all I can manage to communicate right now.

He pulls me away from his body, meeting my gaze once more. He gently wipes a tear from my cheek with the pad of his thumb. "You still look beautiful," he whispers. My breath catches.

"Am I interrupting something?"

I abruptly turn to see Miles standing behind me. His eyes slowly take in my tear-stained cheeks and my even-more-stained dress.

"You ruined everything," I whisper to him.

He snaps his head up, his hazel eyes meeting mine. He runs his fingers through his thick hair as his mouth opens, but no words are spoken.

"If you think I'm so pathetic, why do you pretend to be my friend? Just so you can have something to laugh at?" I ask through tears. My anger has morphed into a sinking feeling of betrayal.

Miles steps towards me, attempting to place his arms around me. I instinctively step back and collide with Brett's tall form. The last thing I want is for Miles to touch me.

"You can't really believe I would say all that shit," Miles says.

"I don't know what to believe."

"Ashleigh made all of that stuff up."

"If that's the type of person you choose to date, then I don't think you're the type of person I'll choose to be friends with anymore."

"Don't do this, Sam," Miles pleads. I can hear Brett's harsh intake of breath behind me. I know he wants to tell me that I'm over-reacting, but for the second time this evening, Brett remains uncharacteristically silent.

Just last night, I made a vow to remain friends with all of these people for as long as I live. Now, only twenty-four hours later, I'm saying goodbye to one of them.

"You did this. Not me. I think you should go, Miles. And please don't contact me anymore." I wipe one last tear from my cheek.

Miles's eyes appear to glisten under the bar's fluorescent lighting. I watch as he silently nods his head, then turns and walks away.

His long legs stride toward Ashleigh and Madison, who now stand at the opposite side of the bar. When Ashleigh sees Miles walk her way, she quickly turns and stomps out of the bar, Madison hot on her heels.

To my surprise, Miles doesn't say goodbye to any of our other friends. Instead, with his head hung low, he quietly follows Madison and Ashleigh out of the bar.

And just like that, he was gone, without even a simple farewell.

*Goodbye, Miles.*

# CHAPTER NINETEEN:

Luckily Van agrees not to call the police. He also knows how important tonight is for me, so he even allows our group to stay and drink at the bar. Since Ashleigh and Madison left, he figured there won't be any further altercations this evening. We assured him there wouldn't be.

I've told Van I would pay for all the damage caused by the fight, which fortunately was only a few broken glasses. Van declined my money for the broken glasses. I apologized to him repeatedly. I hate that I caused a scene in his bar. I'm usually not that kind of person.

When Zach didn't think I was looking, I noticed him slip Van a hundred-dollar bill for the broken glassware, to which Van silently nodded his thanks and walked back to the bar.

In the hour it's been since the incident, I've already downed four more vodka cranberries. I finally feel like I've calmed down.

I look over to Zach who's sitting beside me with his hand resting atop my thigh, chatting with Tony and Craig. He throws his head back and laughs loudly at something Tony said.

"So, what happened to 'she isn't worth it,' Sammie Bear?" Ronnie asks with a laugh. I'm not the least bit surprised she was able to pick up on the look I gave her before all the chaos ensued. I grin at how well she knows me and at our innate ability to communicate without words.

"Nobody fucks with Jill's ironing," I snicker. Jill and Ronnie both burst into laughter. My favorite sound.

"Come on, Jilly Bean. You're doing a shot with me," Ronnie states matter-of-factly.

"But who's gonna drive us home?" Jill squeaks. Jill is already buzzed. There's no way any of us are letting her drive.

"Tony said we're all piling into the back of his truck. He'll get us home," I reassure her.

"Plus, you took a shot with Brett. You've never even taken a shot with me!" Ronnie whines.

Jill glances at Tony who's slowly sipping on his glass of tap water as he chats with Craig and Zach. She nods her head, then gracefully lifts her lean body out of her chair. "I'm buying you a shot, Veronica Mae," she announces.

Ronnie stands, preparing to follow Jill to the bar. "Oh, yeah? What's the special occasion?"

"You punching that horrid Madison in her big ol' mouth," Jill snickers. Ronnie and I both laugh. It's quite out of character for Jill to celebrate anyone getting hit in the mouth.

"Sam and I should've fought those bitches a year ago, outside of theatre three," Ronnie chuckles.

"What?" Jill questions.

"Oh nothing," I giggle. Jill shrugs her shoulders and turns to head towards the bar, Ronnie following close behind.

"Bring me back another drink, please," I call after them. Ronnie throws a thumbs-up into the air to indicate she got the message.

"You know this is going to get really awkward, right?"

I turn to look at Brett, confused at what he means. Does he think it will be awkward between us because he called me beautiful? I won't make it awkward if he doesn't.

"What do you mean?"

"With Miles," he sighs. "He's Tony's partner. And, you know...my roommate. Not to mention my best friend."

"I thought *I* was your best friend?" I dramatically grab my chest, then give him my cheesiest grin.

"You're definitely up there," he chuckles. He slowly exhales before continuing, "Miles is to me what Jill is to you. I've known him longer than I haven't known him. He's always been there. And he always will be."

"That's fine, Brett. I'm not asking you to stop being friends with him. I just don't want to be." I take another sip of my drink.

"How is that supposed to work? Two of my best friends hating each other?"

"I don't hate him."

"You have to know he'd never purposefully hurt you, Sam. He's not that kind of person. Plus, he really cares about you."

"And how exactly would you know that?"

"Because he and I feel the same way about you." He gives me a playful nudge.

I shrug him off and move to stand. I don't feel like talking about this anymore, just when I'm finally starting to enjoy myself. I decide to go take a shot with Jill and Ronnie when I feel Brett grab my hand. I turn to look at him.

"Yes?" I ask impatiently.

"Will you do something for me, Sam?"

"Of course."

"Forgive him."

"No."

"Forgive him. For me. Please."

I give a dramatic sigh as I collapse back into my chair. I pull my phone out of my small, cross-body purse draped over the back of my chair.

"If you buy me a shot, I'll text him," I propose.

"One vodka shot coming right up," he laughs, right away jogging toward the bar.

"Make it top shelf!" I yell to him. He pulls a Ronnie and throws a thumbs-up into the air, and I can't help but giggle.

I open my phone's lock screen and search for Miles's name in my text messages. I open our last chat and am stuck staring down at my phone. I have no idea what to say to him.

Brett, Ronnie, and Jill return to the table with their hands full of shot glasses. Brett sets a vodka shot on the table in front of me. I immediately bring the shot to my lips, throwing it back. The old, familiar burn engulfs me.

I guess it's time to text Miles. A deal is a deal. Besides, Secret Santa would be pretty strange if I didn't resolve this. Kind of hard to buy a gift for someone when you aren't on speaking terms.

I drunkenly compose my text.

**Miles, I'm sorry for what I said. It wasn't your fault. Come back to the bar.**

I press send. Hopefully, he knows when I say come back to the bar, I mean without Ashleigh. Before I can stop myself, my intoxicated fingers take it upon themselves to type out another message.

**I love you.**

My finger hits the send button before I realize what I've just done. I'm mortified. I can't believe I just wrote that. Especially after Ashleigh just accused me of being in love with him. I mean, I love him as a friend. ...Maybe I should send another text and add that?

Before I can overthink it any further, I hear the text alert on my phone ding.

*Oh, God.*

My trembling fingers open my home screen to see a text from Miles. I'm terrified to open it. He probably thinks I'm, well...pathetic. I open his text, quickly shutting my eyes before I read it. I take a deep breath. Here goes nothing. I slowly open my eyes and focus on Miles's text.

**I love you, too.**

When I read his message, I can't help but smile. Maybe he doesn't think I'm pathetic? Suddenly, another message comes through.

**I'll be there in 30.**

Just about thirty minutes later, I see the heavy, wooden door of the bar open. I watch as Miles walks into the bar holding a grocery bag in his hand. My friends grow oddly silent as I slowly stand and head towards Miles.

Once he notices me approaching, he stops walking. When I reach him, I gaze down to the Walmart bag clasped in his hand. He notices me staring at the bag before slowly handing it to me. Giving him a confused look, I timidly take the bag from him.

"I bought you a new dress. I spent like ten minutes trying to pick one out. I was totally out of my element and—"

Before he can finish his sentence, I throw myself into his arms, hugging him. He wraps his arms around me and briefly lifts me off of the ground.

We both have huge smiles plastered on our faces as we hear all of our friends cheering. My pack is whole again.

I beam up at him. "Will you be my friend again?" I ask softly.

Oh, geez. I sound like a kindergartner.

He stares down at me and breathes, "Sam. No matter how mad you are at me, no matter what happens, I'll never stop being your friend."

# CHAPTER TWENTY

## (August 2013):

All I can say is, a lot has happened in the last eight months.

Zach and I are still going strong, and I couldn't be happier. Let me clarify that—most of the time, I couldn't be happier. That's when I'm not overthinking everything and driving myself crazy over the fact that he hasn't said "I love you" yet. We're quickly approaching a year together and according to every romantic comedy I've ever watched, we are well within "I love you" territory. Ronnie keeps telling me I'm overthinking it, that I can't base my life off a "stupid rom-com." Her words, not mine.

A few nights before Ronnie left for Nashville, she and I were snuggled up on our old, hand-me-down sofa, snacking on a garbage bag filled with pilfered Cinedome popcorn while we watched a movie. Ronnie had just worked her final shift at The Cinedome, and, thankfully, we had plenty of leftover snacks from our private viewing in her honor the night before. But now, it was my turn to choose the movie and Ronnie couldn't have been more annoyed. She was mildly relieved that I at least wasn't forcing her to watch the *Twilight* Saga again.

In the middle of our movie, Ronnie suddenly suggested I tell Zach that I love him first. Shocked, I immediately pulled my vision away from Harry meeting Sally to stare at her, completely dumbstruck. I promptly informed her there was no way I'd be doing that. Absolutely not. Ronnie rolled her eyes at me before turning her vision back to the television.

I wish I was brave enough to tell Zach that I love him. I've always envied Ronnie's confidence and down-right courage. She is who she is, and she makes no apologies for it. Sometimes I have no idea who I am at all. I could never say those three little words first in any relationship.

Now, when it comes to Jill, she has a completely different outlook on the situation. She thinks I might be trying to force feelings I may not even have. She also thinks I'm obsessed over the progression of my relationship solely because I have this imaginary timeline in my head of how a relationship should be. Damn you, again, romantic comedies. I just need to stick to superhero movies from now on.

Jill asked me if I thought I was truly in love with Zach or if I just wanted to be. What happened to Jillian Moore, the hopeless romantic? And why does she always have to sound so annoyingly intelligent?

While we're on the topic of Jillian, I must say that I couldn't be prouder of my best friend. This summer, Jill graduated at the top of her class as a full-fledged respiratory therapist. Without missing a beat, she landed her dream job, working as an RT in the Summit Valley neonatal intensive care unit, or NICU. They would've been stupid not to hire her.

Soon after Jill started her new position, she traded in her Toyota Corolla for a brand-new, black Audi A5. She looked like a local celebrity driving away from the dealership in her sleek new convertible with her oversized black sunglasses on, her blonde hair whipping in the wind. Jillian Moore was simply not meant to drive a Corolla.

As for our beloved Veronica, like I previously mentioned, she finally made the big move to Music City, USA. Ronnie was supposed to transfer to Belview University in the spring, but her plans were derailed by one minor slip-up.

A few months ago, she stayed out drinking a bit too late the night before her Sociology class final. She ended up sleeping through her alarm, completely missing the exam. Due to a history of poor attendance, her professor refused to allow her to make up the exam, and Ronnie inevitably failed the class. Before she could transfer to Belview as she'd planned, she had to retake her Sociology course which, unfortunately, postponed her plans an entire semester. But, in true Veronica Sanders fashion, she prevailed. At the end of July, she made her big move to Nashville. She was finally able to enroll in Belview's social work program for the fall semester.

Before she left, Brett would tease Ronnie about Belview being a well-known Christian university. He'd say they must've been crazy to accept her. Ronnie didn't find this funny at all. She informed him she was, in fact, a devoted Christian, and that she prayed every night.

I knew this to be true. I'd seen my best friend drop to her knees in front of our hideous, hand-me-down sofa and pray every night before she fell asleep. She never forgot to say her prayers, even if it was in the wee hours of the morning when she finally came home.

When he learned how religious Ronnie actually was, Brett looked thoroughly stunned and was at a loss for words. I love seeing him speechless. It doesn't happen often enough.

As for Brett, he's been excelling in his position with the Bristol County Fire Department. Just like we all knew he would. One night at The Barn Door, Tony revealed to our pack that he aspired to make a similar career move.

Tony became Miles's new partner right after graduating from paramedic school. Tony had been an EMT, or emergency medical technician, prior to becoming a paramedic. Paramedics can administer drugs, insert intravenous lines, and perform various other procedures that aren't within the scope of an EMT's practice. If I'm being honest, until Miles informed me, I hadn't known there was a difference between the two.

Tony said he'd decided to go back to school to become a paramedic all in the hopes of increasing his chances of getting accepted into the fire academy. His dream is to one day become a firefighter, just like his dad.

Brett was ecstatic with Tony's news and instantly began talking his ear off about the academy. He's stoked about the prospect of having a real friend at the firehouse. Of course, he's friendly with all his fellow firefighters, but he often complains that they're just not on the same wavelength as him. To put it simply, they weren't his pack. They weren't us.

I've been keeping my fingers crossed that Tony will be accepted into the academy sometime soon. I know how much this means to him. And if something means a lot to my friend, it means a lot to me.

Miles and I have kept up our weekly coffee get-togethers. We still don't speak about what happened on the night of my pinning ceremony last year. All that's important is that we've made amends. No use in digging up old wounds.

What may be even more important, though, is that Miles broke up with Ashleigh. There was a unanimous sigh of relief from our entire pack upon hearing the news that the lovebirds were no more. Well, at least Miles was a lovebird. I'd describe Ashleigh as more of a rude and vengeful pigeon.

Unbeknownst to me, Miles had actually broken up with Ashleigh when they left the bar the night she and I got into our brawl. I told Miles I didn't want him to break up with his girlfriend just because of the things I'd said to him. As much as it pained me, I finally admitted I may have overreacted a tad bit that night. But just a tad!

Miles had reassured me, however, that he broke up with Ashleigh because he was no longer happy dating her. He didn't want to be with someone who treated his friends like she did.

If you ask me, I think it might've had something to do with how stupidly she spells her name—Ashleigh. I know that's technically her parent's fault, but still. That girl was as extra as the unnecessary letters comprising her name.

I'm thankful Miles and I were able to put the Ashleigh debacle behind us because it would've made for an awkward Secret Santa exchange over Christmas. Instead, everything turned out great. As she always does, Jill came through and helped me find the perfect gift for Miles. Per her suggestion, I ended up gifting him a fancy bag of hazelnut coffee (his favorite) along with a fancy French press. It was my own idea, however, to finish off the gift with a framed picture of Miles and me at our favorite coffee house.

Needless to say, he absolutely loved it. He even declared the coffee I bought him to be "the best coffee he's ever had," and he still uses his French press religiously. Sometimes he even asks to skip our coffee house meet-ups so he and I can enjoy a cup of coffee from his French press instead. He even recently bought himself a milk frother. That boy is becoming quite the barista, and I get to reap all the benefits.

In a strange turn of events, Miles pulled my name out of Craig's cowboy hat for Secret Santa, too. What are the odds? I thought my gift to him was pretty clever. That is until I opened his gift to me.

Miles bought me the Littmann stethoscope. The one I wanted more than anything. I was finally able to retire the garbage stethoscope I was still carrying around from nursing school.

I knew instantly that he'd spent well over the fifty-dollar gift limit. In my eagerness to buy myself one, I had been thoroughly researching these stethoscopes for months. The one he bought me was close to two hundred dollars. He repeatedly informed me this was both a graduation gift and a Christmas gift, that I should stop questioning him.

To make it even better, not only did he buy me the exact stethoscope I wanted, he had it personalized, too.

It was Superman colors!

The tubing of the stethoscope is bright red, while the headset and bell of it are a sheen of deep blue. The best part, though, is the fact that he had the diaphragm of the stethoscope engraved with my name. I felt tears well in my eyes as I lightly traced my finger across "Samantha Carter, RN" engraved into the cool metal.

He confessed that he went back and forth between engraving "Sam" or "Samantha" onto the gift. He hoped I wasn't upset that he chose to go with my full name. I assured him it was perfect exactly how it was.

Finally, there was our Captain Cowboy, Craig. He'd worn his personalized t-shirt so often that he'd started wearing holes into it. Jill insisted upon making him a new shirt on her Cricut as soon as she found out. Craig sat nervously on our sofa as he waited for Jill to finish making his new shirt. You could've sworn he was waiting for a loved one to come out of a life-threatening operation. He'd been so upset when Ronnie made him throw his first t-shirt away, but he appeared completely blissful when Jill presented him with his freshly made shirt.

When Ronnie first moved to Nashville, she tried to convince Craig to make the move with her. She argued this was the best move for him to make to pursue his dreams of becoming a country singer. She gushed about the adorable apartment she'd found for them and how close it was to Lower Broadway. But sadly, against what Craig truly wanted, he had to decline Ronnie's offer. His mom's condition had progressed immensely over the last eight months. He said he just couldn't leave her. He didn't know how much time he had left with her.

One may wonder why Veronica would ask Craig to move with her to a different city and share an apartment in the first place. Well, the answer was quite simple. Who wouldn't want their boyfriend to make that big move with them?

I must say, the vote on this coupling was a unanimous "yes" from our pack. Three weeks after the night of my pinning, Craig confessed to Ronnie that he was in love with her. Craig revealed to me that he'd never fully realized the magnitude of his feelings for her until the night she kissed him. His feelings were far more than just a "major crush."

I had my suspicions for some time that Ronnie had feelings for Craig, too. She always tried to hide it, but I know her better than that. Initially, she declined Craig's declaration of love. Ronnie recited the same, worn-out excuse. A two-year age difference was just too big for her. He was just too young.

That night, after Craig declared his love, Jill, Ronnie, and I sat in silence together on our sofa. Jill and I patiently waited for Ronnie to speak. Only hours earlier, Craig mustered up every ounce of courage he had and confessed his feelings to Ronnie at The Barn Door in front of us all.

Back at the apartment, Jill and I sat uncomfortably on either side of Ronnie. The silence was deafening. When I finally reached for the television remote hoping to ease the tension, I felt Ronnie smack my hand away from it. I hesitated before glancing up at her.

Ronnie finally spoke. "Do you think he meant all those things he said?"

"I don't think Craig ever says things he doesn't mean," I replied. It was the truth; Craig is an open book.

"Aw! That was so cute, Sam," Jill squealed as she clasped her hands together. "I'm totally shipping you two!" I smirked at Jill for using one of Ronnie's favorite phrases on her.

Ronnie stayed silent, her vision traveling between Jill and me. She stared at me expectantly, waiting for me to weigh in on the situation.

I turned to face her, sitting cross-legged on the sofa. I placed my hands on both of her shoulders, then playfully shook her. She looked back at me wide-eyed.

"Um, Sam? Why are you shaking me?"

"Just trying to knock some sense into you."

She gave me an exaggerated sigh. "Well, I guess I'm about to be Craig Corey's girlfriend." She stood from the sofa and reached for her purse.

"Where are you going?" Jill exclaimed.

"To go get my man," Ronnie declared, swinging open the front door to our apartment.

At this, Jill and I both stood, then wildly jumped up and down on our sofa cushions like Tom Cruise proclaiming his love to Katie Holmes on *Oprah*. Ronnie giggled at our spectacle before rushing out the door. Jill and I fell into each other's arms before plopping back onto the sofa as the door shut.

"They grow up so fast," Jill sighed, wiping an imaginary tear from her cheek.

I slowly turn my Blazer onto Main Street as I try focusing my eyes on the road. Driving at night has always been a challenge for me with my astigmatism. The fact that I was too cheap to upgrade my glasses to anti-glare lenses isn't helping.

Seeing Summit Valley Hospital in the distance, I realize it isn't that my job doesn't bring me happiness. I smile to myself as my thoughts suddenly drift to my friends and my boyfriend. To be honest, they're *truly* what make me the happiest. But I do love being a nurse. I'm no longer an "almost-nurse;" I'm now legitimately a registered nurse!

To my relief, I passed my boards exam on my first attempt. That doesn't mean I still didn't cry like a baby when I left the testing center. I had to be consoled by the worried parking attendant before I was composed enough to drive home. I felt like I utterly bombed it. I had to wait a full, tortuous week to find out I didn't. Then I cried again, but this time it was joy-filled tears.

I felt like since starting the nursing program, I'd been holding my breath. After seeing the notification on my laptop screen that I passed, that I was a registered nurse, I finally allowed myself to exhale.

As I was saying, it's not like being a nurse doesn't make me happy. It does. It's just that somedays, I feel like the pressure of it is all too much. Sometimes I wonder, what did I get myself into? Am I really cut out for this? These are thoughts I feel guilty for. Thoughts that I feel I could never truly voice to anyone without total embarrassment.

It's my duty as a nurse to serve others, to care for the ill, to aid the dying. I signed up for this, so I have no right to complain.

As I turn into the hospital parking lot, I force myself to take a deep breath. I'm working my third consecutive twelve-hour graveyard shift tonight, and I'm emotionally, mentally, and physically exhausted. This week has just been tough.

To make matters worse, I'm convinced that my charge nurse, Marilyn, has a personal vendetta against me. She always seems to give me the impossibly difficult patient assignments, while other nurses are given substantially lighter workloads. In all of our interactions, she's incredibly short and noticeably unpleasant towards me. I have no idea what I did to piss her off so badly. My guess is my existence is enough.

Tanya has assured me on multiple occasions this is just the way Marilyn is towards new nurses; it's not me specifically that she despises. I just can't fathom why this type of behavior is so widely accepted in the field of nursing. If you ask any human resources department, they'd tell you it's not acceptable. But the fact is, they're often not around to witness what happens on the floor.

It's the whole "nurses eat their young" ideal. Of course, this doesn't hold true for all seasoned nurses, but it sure does for my charge nurse.

I just don't understand why someone would wish for one of their co-workers to fail at their job. In turn, by not giving your fellow nurses the tools to succeed, you're ultimately failing your patients. Why does it have to be "sink or swim?" Why can't it be "let me help you to float until I can teach you how to swim?"

I've also been having an increasingly hard time with sleep. I know working graveyard has been taking a toll on my body, but that's the life of a new grad nurse. It's extremely rare for a new nurse to be offered a day-shift position.

Most nights, I'm chugging coffee to keep myself awake during my shift. Then, when I arrive home in the morning, sleep is simply unobtainable, without a few glasses of pinot noir, or whatever else happens to be in our pantry. I prefer to drink wine on work nights (or should I say mornings) so I'm not battling a potential hangover on my next shift.

I often feel Jill's judgmental eyes on me in the mornings when I pop the cork on a bottle of red wine after one of my night shifts. But Jill is one of the lucky ones. Even though she works a lot of weekends, she was lucky enough to be offered a day-shift position in the NICU. So, she isn't allowed to judge me. She doesn't understand how hard my shifts are.

I park my forest green Blazer in a spot toward the back of the parking lot. I prefer to park in the back. Not only does it free up the closer spots for patients' family members, but the long walk to the hospital doors gives me an opportunity to suppress my pre-shift anxiety before I step through them.

I sling my Superman backpack over my shoulder, shutting my car door. Once I enter those double-doors I know the next twelve hours of my life are not my own. For the next twelve hours, my patients' problems are my problems. Their family's despair is my despair. Their pain...is my pain.

I allow myself to take a deep breath, then slowly exhale to rein in my anxiety. With each passing year of my adult life, I feel my anxiety worsening. Why can't I just be normal?

"Hey, Sam!"

My hand still clutching the strap of my backpack, I swiftly turn around to see Miles jogging through the parking lot in my direction. A few yards behind him, I spot Tony leaning leisurely on the hood of their ambulance. He waves at me, and I happily wave back.

"Tony and I bought you dinner." Miles holds out his hand, offering me a bag with a Subway sandwich inside of it. "It's the pizza sub. I know it's your favorite."

I beam up at him, greedily snatching the bag from his hand. I haven't eaten anything today. The only thing in my stomach is a glass of red wine from this morning. I felt too nauseous to eat when I woke up for my shift this evening. Now, I'm starving.

"You guys didn't have to do that, but thank you," I say, cradling my sub like a newborn baby.

"I know the cafeteria's night-shift cook isn't the best," Miles chuckles. "Plus, I know you've had a really hard week. Hang in there. It'll get better."

I drop my backpack off my shoulder to the asphalt—I wouldn't dare drop my sandwich—and hurl myself into Miles's arms. He drives me insane sometimes, but he's always there for me. Even when I don't ask. He wraps his arms around me and momentarily lifts me off of the ground.

"I'll see you tomorrow night, right?" Miles asks. He picks up my Superman backpack from the parking lot ground and hands it to me.

Tomorrow is Sunday, which is my first of four days off, so that means we're having dinner at Margo's. It is going to be one of those rare Sundays where we're all off work. I can't wait!

"You know it," I respond with a smile.

Miles gives me his trademark sideways smirk, a smile I've grown to adore.

"Have a good shift," he says before jogging back to where Tony's been standing. He turns back mid-jog to give me a wave.

I look down at my nursing clogs and chuckle. If I ever tried something like that, I'd sprain my ankle.

"Bye, Sam. Love your face!" Tony shouts from his spot across the lot.

"Bye, Tony Cakes. I love you more!"

I turn to continue my trek to the entrance of the hospital, suddenly feeling lighter. The weight of my anxiety has lifted, and I know I can handle anything that happens after I enter those automatic doors.

My friends are my therapy. With them in my corner, I can overcome any obstacle. And as long as I have them, I have everything I need.

# CHAPTER
# TWENTY-ONE:

I place my backpack into my locker after stocking the pockets of my scrubs with pens, Sharpies, scissors, and my handy-dandy hemostat. I drape my stethoscope around my neck and leave the break room.

As I approach the nurses' station, I see Tanya leaning leisurely against the counter, awaiting her patient assignment. Tanya is one of the lucky ones who normally works the day-shift, but she picked up an overtime shift tonight. I often tease her that she only picks up these extra shifts because she loves working with me. My companionship is so much more valuable than the overtime pay. She always laughs, puts her arm around my shoulder, and tells me I may be delusional, but I'm indeed her favorite deluded person.

Tanya has been working as much as humanly possible these last few months. In my time working with her, I've learned she's a single mother to two fairly young children. Her sorry excuse of a husband left her about two years ago for a younger woman who he met at work. His name is James. *We don't like James.*

Thankfully, Tanya knows she's better off without him. She'd rather be alone than with a man who doesn't respect her. She recently decided she wanted to buy a home of her own, for her and her children. She said she's tired of apartment living and wants her kids to have a yard to play in. That means she has worked many night-shifts beside me these last few months.

Over these past few months, I've come to realize that Tanya is one of the strongest women I've ever met. She's become an amazing mentor to me at work, as well as a great friend.

"Hey, Sam! Happy Friday!" Tanya exclaims. It's actually Saturday night, but I'm off tomorrow. So, it's *my* Friday.

"T-G-I-F!" I thrust my hands into the air in a "raise the roof" motion.

"Girl, no one does that anymore," she laughs.

"Okay, ladies. Time to get to work," Marilyn announces as she exits the nutrition room, sipping on a pilfered carton of juice. She hands each of us an assignment. "Sam, you'll be getting the first admission. It's for very extensive wound care, so I recommend you properly prepare your supplies."

I stare down at my assignment and sigh. Of course, I'm getting the first admission. I'll probably get the second one, too. This is just how it is with Marilyn as my charge nurse.

"I'll take the first admission," Tanya graciously offers. "My patient assignment has been pretty light. Sam has had a rough week."

"Sam can handle it," Marilyn asserts before she turns and walks away.

I'm not surprised one bit by her reaction. This is always how it is. I try to tell myself that, when all is said and done, it will make me a better nurse.

"Bitch," Tanya mutters under her breath. "Don't worry, Sam. I'll help you."

"Thanks." I give her a small smile. I don't know what I'd do without Tanya. Marilyn would probably eat me alive.

As I begin making my initial rounds, I feel my cell phone vibrate in the pocket of my scrubs. I quickly pull it out of my pocket and unlock the home screen. I smile when I see a text from Zach.

**Would you be up for breakfast after your shift?**

I lean against the wall in the middle of the hallway, my fingers rapidly composing a response.

**Will there be mimosas? And can I take a nap at your place after?**

Zach's reply is immediate.

**Yes and yes. I'll go to the store tonight. See you in the morning babe.**

I can't help but blush whenever he calls me babe, be it over text or in-person.

**I can't wait to see you.**

I hit send and slip my phone back into my pocket.

After taking a few steps forward, I realize I'm now standing outside my patient's room, 542. Okay, Sam. Back to reality. I need to mentally prepare myself before entering this room.

The patient lying in the hospital bed behind this door is forty-four-year-old Collette Simmons. I admitted Mrs. Simmons to the hospice floor on Thursday night, which was essentially my Monday morning. Now it's Saturday night, which is again, *my* Friday morning. I know. Confusing, right?

Collette was in excruciating pain when she was initially transferred to our floor. I couldn't stand seeing her in such distress. It was awful. She had tears streaming down both of her cheeks; she screamed in agony when the two men transferring her moved her from the gurney to the hospital bed. The men were as gentle as possible, but it was no use. The slightest movement caused Collette immense pain.

Mrs. Simmons has a hospice diagnosis of end-stage metastatic breast cancer. This means her cancer, which originated in her breast, has spread to her lymph nodes. Despite chemotherapy and radiation treatments, her cancer continued spreading to her bones before finally spreading (or metastasizing) to her brain. This is when Summit Valley's lead hospital oncologist regretfully informed Collette and her husband, Roger, that her situation was terminal.

Collette and Roger have two school-aged children, Liam and Macie. On the night she was first transferred to our floor, Roger disclosed to me that he didn't know how he'd raise his children without his wife. He said Collette was the backbone of their family, the glue that held them all together. He feared that if he lost his wife, everything he had and everything he was, would shatter into a million pieces.

I held this man in my arms as he cried. He cried for the years he spent working too late and the countless home-cooked meals he'd missed. The anniversaries he'd forgotten and the phone calls he'd sent to voicemail because he'd just been too busy to talk. He mourned the years that were being stolen from them. He begged for more time.

That night, after Roger released me from his embrace, I left room 542 and walked straight to the supply room. Once inside, I leaned my back against the supply room door, unable to keep my body from sliding to the unforgiving hospital floor. There, alone on the cold, sterile tiles, I cried.

I cried for the man who had been uncontrollably sobbing in the arms of a stranger, only moments before. For the two children who would be forced to face life without a mother. For the woman currently lying in the hospital bed of room 542, who wouldn't live to see her forty-fifth birthday.

After giving myself a minute, I picked myself up from the hospital floor and forcibly wiped away one final tear from my cheek. I smoothed out the few wrinkles in my scrub top, adjusted the stethoscope hanging around my neck, and walked out of the supply room. I returned to work, acting as if my heart hadn't been ripped from my chest just fifteen minutes prior.

**Because that's what nurses do.**

Before I left work Friday morning, Roger told me that if he'd only known how short his time would be with Collette, he would've done it all differently. He would've worked less and taken his family on more vacations. He told me Collette had always wanted to go to Hawaii, he'd just never gotten around to taking her there.

Becoming a hospice nurse has forced me to come to terms with how fragile life really is.

One day, you feel as if you have your entire life planned out to perfection. It seems like everything is going according to plan. You're on top of the world. You're invincible. You have it all.

Then, with one sentence, your entire world comes crashing down around you.

"There's nothing more that can be done."

Suddenly, everything you've worked so hard for, everything you've obtained, seems worthless. Nothing in life has meaning without her. If you lose her, then you've lost it all.

And, unfortunately, Roger said he realized this truth too late.

Dr. Lee, our hospice and palliative care medical director, suspected Collette's uncontrolled pain was primarily due to the cancer spreading to her bones. Collette was begging for some relief from the pain; she was no longer able to endure it. But Roger was skeptical of her receiving pain medication. He didn't want her to be sedated. He wanted her to be alert enough to speak with him and their children.

The issue was oral pain medications were no longer managing Collette's pain. She was already taking high doses of long-acting and short-acting oral painkillers. Despite this medication regimen, her pain level never dropped below a nine out of ten.

That Friday morning, as I was finishing the final rounds of my Thursday graveyard shift, I was performing a final assessment on Mrs. Simmons. As I was examining her, she grabbed my hand, holding me in a firm grip. This startled me because I could've sworn she had been sleeping. I was intentionally being as quiet as possible to keep from waking her. I didn't even turn on a light. Fortunately, graveyard nurses are accustomed to functioning in the dark.

With her hand clasping mine, Collette started to whisper. "I don't want to do this anymore. I'm so exhausted, but I just can't sleep. I'm tired of being in pain." She started to cry. "I don't want Roger to hate me. Please convince him that I need the Morphine drip."

Dr. Lee had previously suggested starting Collette on a continuous Morphine drip to better control her pain. Roger had vehemently refused.

"I know I can make these decisions alone, but I don't want to do anything without Roger's consent," Collette explained. "We've always operated as a team; I don't want that to change now. I don't want him to think I'm giving up." She briefly removed her hand from mine to wipe a tear from her cheek.

"The three of us will talk to Roger together. You, me, and Dr. Lee," I assured her. Collette managed to smile at me through her pain and tears as she clutched my hand once more.

This wasn't the first time I'd dealt with this type of situation. Hospice and palliative care wasn't black and white. Everything was gray matter. Having extremely tough conversations with people was informally part of my job description. It's true, it never gets easier. But every day, I become better at handling these difficult situations.

When I came back to work Friday evening (after only getting a few restless hours of sleep from my previous graveyard shift) the three of us did indeed have a conversation with Roger. A conversation that nearly lasted an hour. Roger finally agreed it was time for Collette to begin a Morphine drip to help manage her excruciating pain. When Dr. Lee left the room to write the order for the drip, Roger's cellphone rang. He stepped into the hallway to take the call.

Suddenly, as I lifted my body from where I'd been sitting at her bedside, I felt Collette grab my hand, her grip more gentle than before. On instinct, I sat back down when I felt her touch. I gazed at her, waiting for her to speak.

"I'm scared," she croaked, holding back tears.

I delicately placed my free hand over her trembling one. You never know the right thing to say in a moment like this. I'm not going to tell her not to be scared. She is allowed to feel afraid—this is all pretty damn scary.

"I will do everything in my power to make this less scary for you," I softly replied.

"Thank you," she mouthed, before laying back down onto the pillow beneath her.

I gently pulled the pale, pink, hospital blanket over her frail body as her eyelids began to close. Collette deserved to finally be able to rest.

Collette finally looked free from the pain she had been battling when I left work Saturday morning, or should I say this morning. Working three consecutive twelve-hour graveyard shifts will really destroy your concept of time. Who even knows what day it is anymore? They all seem to meld together anyway.

Collette had been on the Morphine drip for almost twenty-four hours when I left work this morning, and the medication appeared to finally be managing her pain.

A common misconception about treating chronic, severe pain is that you can take a single dose of pain medication, and your symptoms will automatically be under control. The truth is, the drug actually needs time to take effect within your body. It needs to be administered continually, in measured increments of time, to prevent any breakthrough pain.

In Collette's case, she was on a drip, which meant she had a continuous infusion of Morphine. So, the likelihood of her suffering breakthrough pain was minor, as long as the infusion was maintained. Sometimes the rate of the infusion would need to be increased if the patient grew tolerant to the dosage they were receiving, but I hoped that wouldn't be the case for Collette.

This morning, Dr. Lee had also ordered Collette to remain on a small dose of intravenous Lorazepam to keep her from feeling anxiety or agitation during the dying process. The dosing regimen wasn't meant for sedation but simply for symptom management. Another common misconception.

Although Collette's symptoms may be managed now, as a consequence, she's much drowsier than she was before the Morphine drip. This was a side effect of changing her medication regimen, which was something she and her husband had been thoroughly educated on by Dr. Lee and myself prior to the change.

The unfortunate truth of Collette Simmons's circumstance was, regardless of whether or not the drip was started, she would pass away. The difference now was she could die on her own terms—free from pain, no longer afraid.

I hope she's not afraid. She's no longer able to tell me, no longer able to grasp my hand with her own. At least, she wasn't able to when I left work this morning. But I try to find comfort in knowing that I helped her advocate for herself. I sadly couldn't change when Collette's story would end, but I did help her decide *how* it would.

Peacefully. She would leave this world peacefully. Just how she wanted.

Please let my last shift of the week be better than the previous two, I silently pray. I take a deep breath and allow myself to fully exhale before I turn the door handle to room 542.

# CHAPTER
# TWENTY-TWO:

As I enter room 542, I'm relieved to see Mrs. Simmons resting peacefully in her hospital bed. I hear the faint, familiar whirring sound of the Morphine drip. I remove my stethoscope from around my neck, carefully moving towards Collette to perform my initial assessment.

Before my shift tonight, I barely slept. I couldn't stop thinking about Collette. I couldn't shake the feeling of her slender hand grasping mine, begging me to help her. I tossed and turned as the image of her tear-stained face appeared ingrained in my mind. I couldn't rest until I knew she'd found comfort.

Finishing my assessment, I sigh with relief. She appears peaceful, free from pain.

Suddenly, I hear a whoosh of air as the door to her hospital room swings open. I turn, seeing her husband rush into the room, frantic.

Before I greet Roger, I take in his overly-tense posture, his shaking hands.

*Oh no, this is going to be bad.*

"The Morphine is killing her! You're killing her!" Roger screams at me.

His shouting leaves me stunned speechless. This isn't the first time a patient or their family member has yelled at me, but something about this feels more upsetting. I'm usually able to take these situations with a proverbial grain of salt. Everyone grieves differently. Sometimes, grief can bring out the worst in people. As a nurse, you quickly learn there will be times when you're essentially a human punching bag.

I take a harsh swallow, trying to compose myself before I respond. No nursing textbook can prepare you for the verbal assault of a grief-stricken husband who's about to lose his wife.

"Mr. Simmons, it's true the Morphine drip is making Collette more drowsy. But it's her disease—her cancer—that's taking her life," I say softly, stepping towards Roger in an attempt to calm him.

But there is no calming this man down.

"You're killing her!" He points his index finger at me. "Turn that drip off. NOW!"

"I completely understand your concern, but I fear if we suddenly stop the drip, Collette will be in excruciating pain and may go into terminal agitation."

In a slightly calmer tone, he replies, "I just need her to wake up. I need you to turn it off."

I'm relieved to see he's become less aggressive. I don't think this man would try to hurt me physically, but as I said, grief can bring out the worst in people. It wouldn't be the first time my life has been threatened for simply trying to do my job.

"Okay. I understand, Mr. Simmons," I say, nodding my head. "Let me see if Dr. Lee is still here finishing his rounds."

I quickly turn and jog out of room 542, into the hall. Hopefully, Dr. Lee is still here to be able to speak with Roger. Maybe he'll be able to convince Roger that Collette should remain on the Morphine drip.

The truth is, even though Dr. Lee may tell him the same information I already have, Roger might actually listen to Dr. Lee. Sometimes, people listen more intently when a man in a white coat is speaking, even if he says the same exact thing a girl in wrinkled blue scrubs just said.

As I jog down the hallway, I notice Dr. Lee leaning against the counter of the nurses' station, writing in a patient's chart. Hearing the galloping sound of my nursing clogs as I run down the hall, Dr. Lee turns to look in my direction.

"Moving awfully fast this evening, Sam," he comments with a laugh.

I glance down at my watch, recognizing that I only have fifteen minutes until my new admission arrives. The extensive wound care patient that Marilyn so graciously assigned to me.

Not fast enough, Dr. Lee. *Not fast enough.*

"If you can spare a moment, I need a huge favor," I say breathlessly, most likely a combination of my growing anxiety and my quick jog. Like I've said, cardio just isn't for me.

"I think I can spare a moment for one of my favorite nurses."

He is such a nice man. I knew from the second I met him that I wanted to work alongside him. That I wanted to learn everything he was willing to teach me.

"Hey! You said *I* was your favorite nurse Doc," Tanya jokes, giving Dr. Lee a huge smile.

"All the nurses I work with are my favorite," Dr. Lee professes. Like I said, so darn nice.

"Mr. Simmons, in room 542, is requesting his wife's Morphine pump be discontinued. He fears the Morphine is what's killing her. I tried to explain to him that wouldn't be a good idea, but to no avail," I pause briefly before continuing. "I was wondering if you could speak with him?" I give Dr. Lee a pleading look, silently begging him to have a conversation with Roger.

"The patient would be in severe pain if we abruptly stopped the Morphine drip at this stage. I'll speak with him." Dr. Lee closes the chart he was writing in.

"Thank you," I say on an exhale. I didn't realize I was holding my breath.

I watch as Dr. Lee takes long strides towards room 542, adorned in his white coat.

"Looks like your week isn't getting any better," Tanya chuckles, lightly smacking her hand on my back. "I'll handle your admission. You go get this situation sorted out."

"But there's extensive wound care..."

"Girl, I've never met a pressure ulcer I couldn't cleanse, measure, and dress."

I throw my arms around Tanya, pulling her in for a hug. "Thank you," I sigh.

"You don't need to thank me. This is how it's supposed to be. If I was a charge nurse, I'd never let my nurses drown the way Marilyn does."

"You would be a great charge nurse."

"You're just saying that because I'm doing your wound care. Now, get out of here," She laughs, playfully bumping me with her hip and pointing down the hall.

"Wish me luck." I turn and walk back down the hallway, back toward room 542.

Just as I reach the entrance to Mrs. Simmons's hospital room, I nearly collide with Dr. Lee as he exits the room. I look up at him in surprise. I recognize the exhaustion on his face, even though he tries masking it with a smile.

"I tried my best, Sam. But Mr. Simmons is insistent on discontinuing the Morphine pump and holding all pain and anti-anxiety medications," Dr. Lee confirms.

My stomach drops. I suddenly feel lightheaded. My breath quickens and my hands tremble as I struggle to formulate a coherent response. This was exactly what I'd been fearful of. Collette dying in pain, dying afraid.

"I'm writing the order to discontinue all scheduled medications per her husband's request, but I'll leave the order in place for 'as-needed' doses."

"But...she's gonna suffer," I mutter, barely able to find the words to summarize the dread I'm feeling.

"Sam, sometimes people need to see things for themselves. This is, unfortunately, the case for Mr. Simmons. He wants to speak to his wife one final time."

"But she most likely won't be coherent when the meds leave her body. She'll probably just be writhing in pain. Or worse, screaming for help."

"Yes, Sam. You and I both know that, but this isn't something that's apparent when you're losing someone you love." He sighs before placing a hand on my shoulder. "This is one of those instances where our hands are tied, but we've done everything we can. You did your best, Sam."

But what if my best just isn't *good enough*?

Despite starting off extremely hectic, tonight's shift has surprisingly calmed down. Tanya, amazing as she is, completely admitted my new patient. She dressed the woman's wounds to perfection and ensured she was resting comfortably by the time I was able to check in on her. Tanya even went so far as to call the patient's family, letting them know she had arrived to our unit safely and was now resting peacefully.

Of course, charge nurse Marilyn was nowhere to be found. If I tried to hold my breath until Marilyn came to help her floor nurses, I'd end up dying from lack of oxygen.

It's been almost six hours since Mrs. Simmons has been given any medication for her symptoms. Since I'm unable to stay at her bedside and she can no longer use the call light, I insisted her husband remain at her bedside to alert me immediately if she becomes distressful. Thankfully, he agreed.

Between my nursing aide and myself, we've been rounding on Collette every thirty minutes. My CNA, or certified nursing assistant, Lucie has been excellent tonight. Lucie just graduated from her CNA program and has been working on our floor for about a month now. If you think I'm young, Lucie is *really* young. Last night, she informed me she only just turned nineteen. I instantly felt geriatric.

Though Lucie's experience was minimal, her caring nature and hard-working mentality made her a perfect fit for our unit. She's fairly quiet and reserved but working with us will pull her out of her shell soon enough. Tanya and I have also made it our personal mission to protect her from the wrath of Marilyn.

"I'm sorry to bother you, Sam," I look up from my computer to see Lucie standing timidly on the other side of the nurses' station.

"You're never bothering me," I assure with a smile. "What's going on?"

"It looks like Mrs. Simmons is starting to get pretty restless. Her husband is really upset."

"Shit," I mutter under my breath. "I'll be right there. Thanks for alerting me, Lucie. And please, don't ever be afraid to come to me."

She gives me a shy smile and nods.

A smart nurse knows that their CNA is invaluable. In my opinion, CNAs are the backbone of the nursing field. Without them, we nurses would undeniably be lost. A nurse that treats their nursing aide like a personal assistant rather than a valuable member of the healthcare team is the kind of nurse I never want to be.

"What can I do to help?" she asks me.

"Maybe we can reposition her together? Hopefully, that will make her more comfortable." Since Mr. Simmons won't allow me to medicate Collette, repositioning her is now one of my only options to improve her comfort.

As Lucie and I walk into room 542, I'm momentarily taken aback. I see Collette's rigid body thrashing in the hospital bed where she once rested so peacefully. She moans loudly and unintelligibly, her face contorted in pure agony.

My fears have come to fruition. It appears Mrs. Simmons has entered full-blown terminal agitation. Terminal agitation can sometimes occur at the end of life when a person's symptoms aren't properly managed. It often presents as severe restlessness, uncontrolled pain, shortness of breath, and sometimes even hallucinations.

One of our hospital chaplains once told me he believed terminal agitation was a person's soul fighting with their failing body. I honestly don't think I could describe it any better.

At Collette's bedside, I see her kneeling husband. His body is hunched over hers as he sobs. Upon hearing us enter the room, his head shoots up. His vision meets mine.

"Help her. Please, help her," he begs.

I rush to Roger's side, placing my hand on his shoulder in an attempt to console him. Lucie instinctively moves to the other side of Collette's bed to ensure she doesn't fall. I nod towards her to reassure her that she made the correct move. Lucie is a natural at this.

"Your wife needs medication," I reply gently. "Is it okay if I give her something for comfort?"

"Whatever you need to do. I can't stand to see her like this," he cries.

My heart hurts so deeply for this man. I don't blame him for his wife's current distress. This isn't his fault. It's exactly as Dr. Lee said—sometimes, people have to see it for themselves. To finally understand, Roger had to see that his wife wouldn't be coming back to him. At least not in the way he wanted.

I'm thankful Roger decided not to let his children stay tonight; they were sent back to their grandparents' house. This shouldn't be a child's last memory of their mother.

As soon as Roger gives his consent, I lift myself from where I was kneeling beside him and dart through the door, towards the pharmacy. I've almost reached the pharmacy on our unit when I lose my footing, and I trip. Damn nursing clogs.

"Hey, Sam—everything okay?"

I turn to see Tanya standing behind me, wide-eyed.

"I need a narcotic waste," I respond breathlessly.

I know Tanya can see how frantic I am. She quickly punches in the code on the pharmacy door's keypad. She swings open the door for me, and I dash to our electronic medication dispenser. I quickly pull up Collette Simmons's orders in the machine, silently thanking Dr. Lee for leaving her "as-needed" medication orders in place. It saves me from having to make a phone call to our on-call provider in the middle of the night, but more importantly, it saves me time. Right now, time is something we have very little of.

I pull a vial of Morphine and a vial of Ativan out of the machine, the former for her pain, the latter for her agitation. I verify Collette's medication orders with Tanya, then pierce the top of the Morphine vial with a needle.

I watch as the syringe fills with medication. I draw five milligrams of Morphine out of the vial, then with a separate syringe, I draw one milligram of Ativan from the other vial. Her "as-needed" medications, or PRN as we call them, are to be administered by intravenous push. Fortunately, this is one of the fastest ways for a drug to enter a person's bloodstream.

*Please, don't let me be too late.*

The instant the syringes are ready, I race out of the pharmacy, cradling Collette's medications in my hand. Hopefully, this will grant her some relief. Sprinting towards room 542, I notice Tanya is following closely behind. I'm so thankful she picked up an extra shift tonight. God knows my charge nurse is useless to me.

As I reach the entrance to Collette's hospital room, I hear a scream.

It's a man's voice. Roger's voice.

*Please, don't let me be too late.*

Tanya and I barrel through the door. Once inside the room, I'm engulfed by the sound of Roger's sobs. He is splayed out, crying uncontrollably on the hospital floor. Lucie kneels beside him in her best attempt to console him, but how do you console someone who has just lost everything?

My eyes dart from Roger's heaving form to the middle of the room, where Collette's lifeless body rests within the confines of the small hospital bed.

I walk to Collette's bedside while Tanya joins Lucie and Roger on the floor. She kneels to the left of Roger, with Lucie remaining on his right, and lightly places her hand on his shoulder. He looks at Tanya with tears streaming down his face and falls into her arms.

Sometimes, compassion is a wordless act. Sometimes, we need to be reminded that we're not alone, even when we're in a world that can feel so lonely.

Remembering the medication in my hand, I set the syringes on the bedside table before slowly removing my stethoscope from around my neck. I look into Collette's eyes. Her soft brown eyes now appear empty, her pupils completely dilated.

I place the earpieces of my stethoscope into each of my ears, then lightly place my stethoscope diaphragm over Collette's chest. I listen for over a minute to her lack of lung sounds and the silence of her heart, no longer beating.

*This is one of the longest sixty seconds of my life. I knew you were gone from the moment I set foot into your hospital room. You don't always need a stethoscope to tell you these things. Yet I continue to listen to your silence, nonetheless.*

I hear Roger say he can't stay in this room any longer, that it's too difficult. Tanya and Lucie help him up off the floor and into the hallway.

A lone tear falls to my cheek as I imagine the conversation he will soon have with his children, telling them their mother is gone.

Then I think of Collette Simmons—the woman who never got to see her forty-fifth birthday.

Collette, I'm sorry.

I'm sorry that your last breath on this earth was labored. That you left this world in pain. That I allowed you to die afraid.

Once again, my best just wasn't good enough.

*I've failed you.*

As I finish straightening Collette's body, my vision catches on a sound machine on the bedside table. I slowly walk to her bedside table and press the "on" button. I shuffle through the sound options until I find the one labeled "ocean waves."

With a push of a button, Collette and I are surrounded by the sound of waves crashing to the shore. I reclaim my place at her bedside and place my gloved hand inside Collette's, a hand that now lies limp, no longer able to grasp my own.

With one final tear streaming down my cheek, I whisper to Collette's lifeless form, "It may not be Hawaii, but I think you found paradise."

# CHAPTER TWENTY-THREE:

# COLLETTE SIMMONS

**August 11, 2013, 02:42**

The pain has finally subsided. It feels like years since I've known an existence free from pain.

I can hear his voice now. Roger. I hope he can forgive me for giving up. I just couldn't endure the pain any longer.

Some time ago—I'm not sure how long—I heard the voices of my babies. Liam and Macie.

Take care of our babies, Roger.

When the years have passed and my memory fades, remind them of how fiercely their mother loved them. How they'd been my world. How I wished, more than anything, that I could've stayed.

But I cannot stay. It's my time to go, and I'm no longer afraid.

I hear the voice of my husband once more. But now there is another voice, one not so familiar. A woman's voice—the nurse. I can't remember her name, but I remember the feel of her hand in mine.

*Suddenly, I hear Roger yell. But why? And at who?*

*When the yelling ceases, I feel a pair of gloved hands on my forearm. They're unscrewing the tube connected to my vein.*

*Please... No...*

*Time has passed. Has it been a minute? An hour? An eternity?*

*I have no way of knowing. Just please, don't let it return.*

*But then it comes. Just as I feared it would. The pain has returned, and now it consumes me.*

*Fire...I am on fire.*

*I try screaming for help, but I can't form the words. Instead, my mouth releases a guttural moan.*

*I hear Roger yell once again.*

*Fire. I'm on fire.*

*How does Roger not know? How can he not see that my body is engulfed in flames?*

*I dig, desperately grasping for any remaining strength that lies dormant within me. I move my finger, then my hand. I'm clutching, reaching, ripping, pulling... Somebody, help me.*

*I hear footsteps. They become louder and louder. And now a voice. It's the nurse, again.*

*She and Roger speak. They speak of me as if I'm no longer present. But I'm present. I'm here, and I'm burning alive from the inside out. How can nobody see it? Why can't they see me?*

*Help me.*

*I hear Roger cry. Until this past year, I'd never seen my husband cry. Now, it's like I can't remember a time when his eyes weren't brimming with tears. Tears for me.*

*The pain radiates to every square inch of my body. I'm burning. It's as if my soul is on fire. The numbness has long dissipated. In this moment, I can feel it all.*

*They said I wouldn't hurt anymore.*

*If that was true, then why is pain all that I can feel?*

*I hear the nurse's voice. She tells Roger I need medication. Roger agrees.*

*Please my love, let me go.*

*Please Nurse... Help me.*

*The nurse—she understands. She's heard my pleas and held my hand. She sees my fire, knows my pain. She said she would help me.*

*Fire. I'm on fire.*

*My strength is drifting. The fire is winning. I can't go on any longer. I'm ready now. I can't bear this pain another minute; my body has been ravaged by it. My breath is ragged. I am too weak.*

*But then, the fire does what it does best. It destroys everything.*

*It's time for my fire to be extinguished.*

# CHAPTER
# TWENTY-FOUR:

When I exit the automatic doors of Summit Valley Hospital, the sun's bright rays momentarily blind me. I'm a night shift vampire; I've become allergic to sunshine.

I snicker to myself, thinking of Jill's and my impromptu reenactments of *Twilight* scenes and how embarrassing Ronnie finds it.

I miss Ronnie. Our sofa seems so empty without her.

As I reach my Blazer, I unlock the driver's side door and throw my worn-out self into the vehicle, tossing my Superman backpack onto the passenger seat in the process. Before putting my key in the ignition, I rest my forehead against the steering wheel.

I'm so incredibly exhausted. And that exhaustion isn't just from lack of sleep.

For the first time in over twelve hours, I allow my body to truly relax as I take a deep breath. As I exhale, I feel a wave of emotion crash over me. Warm, unwanted tears are now streaming down my face.

All I can see is her face, contorted in agony. I feel as though I failed her.

Sometimes I wonder if I'm cut out to be a nurse. Although I'm almost twenty-three years old, more often than not, I still feel like that scared, seven-year-old little girl with the far-off notion that one day she'd be a real-life superhero.

Well, superheroes don't let the people they protect die in pain. They don't let them die afraid.

I'm too tired to think straight. That must be why I'm so emotional right now. I find an old stack of fast-food napkins in my glove compartment and wipe the streaks of bleeding mascara from my cheeks.

Remembering that soon I'll be at Zach's side, I can't help but allow myself to smile. Everything will be okay once I'm in his arms. He's become my safety net.

By the sound of it, Zach has something special planned for me. Last night, he sounded uncharacteristically excited while he planned this morning's brunch date. I can't help but wonder if he's finally going to tell me he loves me. Merely the idea of it leaves me with butterflies fluttering in my stomach.

I finally place my key into Old Faithful's ignition and start the engine. It's time to pull myself together and enjoy my morning with my amazing boyfriend.

I won't allow myself to think of last night's shift again.

Pulling up to the front of Zach's apartment, I park my Blazer into an empty space. I can't help but feel nervous; this feels like it might finally be the day we're going to take our relationship to the next level.

Putting aside my nerves, I hop out of Old Faithful and trudge up the steps to Zach's apartment where I'm greeted by my boyfriend standing on his porch, holding out a mimosa for me. Well, more like a glass of champagne with a splash of orange juice, just how I like it. I knew Zach and I were meant to be.

"Good morning, beautiful," he says with a faint smile.

"My Prince Charming."

"But instead of a white horse, I have white wine."

"This better be champagne, not wine."

"It's champagne," Zach chuckles. "Just trying to be clever."

"Stick to bartending," I tease.

He takes my hand and leads me through the entryway. Zach lives alone in a studio apartment. It's small, but it's private. Considering I've always had roommates, it's nice to have a place where he and I can be alone together.

My eyes grow wide as I take in the glorious spread across his kitchen counter. I'm ecstatic to see that he bought *two* bottles of champagne. After this week, one just won't do.

"You made cinnamon buns?" I squeal.

"With the orange cream frosting. Your favorite." He leans over, giving me a soft kiss.

Holy crap, he's totally about to say, "I love you."

"How did I get so lucky?" I whisper as our lips part.

"I often ask myself the same question." His fingers slowly tuck a loose tendril of hair behind my ear.

By this point, the butterflies in my stomach are no longer fluttering; they're slamming into each other in a full-blown mosh pit.

"All right, let's dig in." Zach pulls out a barstool, indicating for me to sit.

I slide onto the barstool, kick off my nursing clogs, and waste no time in grabbing a cinnamon bun. I gaze down lovingly at the pastry in my hand before taking my first bite. This man sure does know the way to my heart—mimosas and carbohydrates.

"Sam," Zach starts. "There's something I wanted to tell you."

I look up from my cinnamon bun and stare at him expectantly. This is it. He's about to say those three little words I've been longing to hear these last few months...

"I got accepted into law school," he announces.

...Okay, maybe not what I had expected him to say, but amazing news, nonetheless.

"That's incredible, babe!" I throw myself into his arms, cinnamon bun still tightly in my grasp.

I knew Zach had applied to a few different law schools in Virginia and Tennessee, but I wonder which one he was accepted into. Hopefully, it's not too far of a drive. We've already decided we'll alternate driving out to visit one another each week, no matter where he has to move.

"The school I was accepted into... well, it's..." he hesitates.

"It's what?"

"...It's in San Diego."

"As in California? *That* San Diego?"

Well, that is definitely not a drive to be made weekly.

"Yes," he whispers.

Although still stunned, I instinctively take another large bite of the cinnamon bun I'm holding. Why is it that every time Zach tells me something that will completely alter my world, I'm holding food in my hand?

"Wait...I'm confused. How did you get accepted into a law school in San Diego when you didn't apply to any law schools in San Diego?" I ask, my mouth still full of cinnamon bun.

"I *did* apply to one." He looks down abashedly at his feet.

I instantly feel betrayed. Why wouldn't he tell me he applied to a school across the country? My emotional shift last night may be partly to blame, but I'm suddenly extremely angry.

"Why the hell didn't you tell me this, Zachary?"

"Sam, please," he begs. "It was a complete shot in the dark. I never thought I'd actually get accepted. I didn't think it was even worth mentioning."

"Seems pretty mention-worthy now."

"Come with me." His statement sounds more like a command than an offer.

This can't be happening right now. I haven't slept in what feels like days. I'm in no state to be making major life decisions right now. I blame my sleep-deprived mind for the next words that come tumbling out of my mouth.

"Are you in love with me?"

If this man expects me to move with him across the country, he damn well better be in love with me.

"Um, what?" Now, Zach looks like the dumbfounded one.

"I believe my question was pretty clear. Are you in love with me, Zach?"

"I think one day that I could be," he reveals, beautiful brown eyes meeting mine.

Oh Zach, I truly wish that answer was enough for me.

For the second time this morning, I feel warm, unwanted tears impeding my vision. I suspected our morning brunch would change Zach's and my relationship, just not quite like this.

"A possibility isn't enough for me, Zach. It's not enough for me to up and leave my entire life here in Bristol. I can't risk everything for a maybe," I cry.

What was the use in even wearing mascara to work last night? People should be given some type of warning before they have their hearts broken. That way they don't waste their time applying makeup just for it to be smeared all over their face.

Suddenly, Zach's arms are around me. He runs his fingers through my hair, gently pulling my head into his chest. I can't help but cry harder when I come to the harsh realization that I'm losing my safety net.

"We'll just do the long-distance thing, okay? It's only three years." Zach seems to choke on his words, as he tries to keep from joining in my tears.

Pulling myself out of his arms, I grab both his hands with my own. Looking into his gaze, I see his beautiful brown eyes now brimming with tears.

"Zach, I think we both know a long-distance relationship isn't in the cards for either of us."

He pulls one of his hands out of mine to quickly wipe away one of his tears before it falls from his cheek.

"Then it's settled," he announces. "I'm not going to San Diego."

"No!" I yell, shocking us both. "You're going to San Diego. You worked your ass off for this! I'd be a shitty person if I let you turn down this opportunity."

Wow, I actually just sounded like a mature adult. How out of character for me.

"So, then I guess that means we're done..." Zach whispers, bowing his head.

I lift my hand to tenderly stroke his cheek. He lifts his head, studying my face.

"We'll never be done, Zach. I'll always be rooting for you. And you'll always be one of my best friends."

He smiles down at me, then places a light kiss on my forehead.

"You'll always be one of my best friends, too, Samantha Carter." He grins when I make exaggerated gagging noises at his use of my full name. "But can I ask a favor?"

"Of course."

"Can you wait 'til tomorrow to be my best friend? Can you still be my girlfriend for the rest of the day?"

"Only if I'm still allowed to take a nap in your extremely comfy bed," I chuckle.

His laughter melds with mine as he quite literally sweeps me off my feet and into his arms. He carries me to his bed, lightly laying me down onto the mattress before turning to walk back towards the kitchen.

"Wait," I grab his hand, stopping him. "Lay with me? One last time."

He smiles down at me. "Well, duh," he laughs. "I was just going to get the champagne first."

"I'm sure going to miss you," I whisper.

"Wait to miss me until tomorrow, Sam. Today is still ours. Now, take those off," he commands, pointing to my scrub top.

"How forward of you, Zachary Ryan," I laugh.

"Strictly a sanitation thing," he says with a smirk.

My eyes follow him as he saunters back to the kitchen. He leisurely pulls off his t-shirt, throwing it onto the back of his futon. As I take in the toned muscles of his back, I can feel the heat rise to my cheeks.

Grabbing the hem of my top, I begin to remove my scrubs— strictly for sanitation purposes, of course. As I lay in bed, I reach down to the floor and pull my cell phone out of the pocket of my scrub top, deciding to send a quick group text to Ronnie and Jill.

**Zach and I broke up. I'm okay. We're still friends.**

I hit send, then immediately press the power button on my phone, shutting it off. I really don't feel like being bombarded with questions right now. I just need a few uninterrupted hours of sleep.

Even though I know everyone will find out the news at Margo's for dinner tonight, I feel a sense of loyalty to ensure that Jill and Ronnie know first. Ronnie's still in Nashville, meaning she won't be able to come to dinner tonight. I'll have to call her after my nap so she doesn't have a conniption fit.

As I watch a shirtless Zach stride back towards me with a bottle of champagne in his hand, I can't help but feel a pang of sadness. I know Zachary Ryan will always be in my life, but unfortunately, not in the way I'd hoped. But as Zach said, today is still ours.

My heart will just have to wait until tomorrow to break.

# CHAPTER TWENTY-FIVE:

A loud banging jolts me awake. I'm not sure how long I've been napping, but apparently, Zach decided to do the same. I turn my body to face him. Looking at his sleeping form, I can't help but admire how handsome he is, even when fast asleep.

The banging sound grows louder. Zach begins to stir, while I sit upright in bed. What is that noise?

"Coming!" Zach yells at the front door, still in bed half-asleep.

Oh, someone's at the door... Duh.

"Open the door, asshole!" a voice growls from behind the front door. A woman's voice.

What the hell? Is Zach cheating on me? Or *was* he cheating on me? Since we're not exactly dating anymore.

"What the hell?" he mutters, confused.

"Who is that?"

"Your guess is as good as mine," he responds with a shrug.

The banging continues as I scurry to find the scrub-pants I haphazardly threw on the floor this morning. Currently, I'm only wearing my underwear and one of Zach's t-shirts. I look to the alarm clock on his dresser—it's nearly 4:00 PM. Geez, we've been asleep a full six hours.

I watch as Zach rushes to his dresser, pulling on a pair of sweat-pants as he heads towards the door.

"You can't hide from us!" the voice screams out, once again.

Us?

Zach pauses briefly, looking back at me with apparent confusion. I decide to follow close behind, just in case he's about to get attacked by an angry mob of women he's somehow wronged.

"Maybe they have the wrong apartment," I whisper.

"Open this door, gosh darn it!" a gentler—yet somehow equally as angry—voice shouts.

Zach and I both turn to each other, simultaneously asking the same question: "Jill?"

Zach swings open the front door. He's immediately confronted by my two furious best friends. I don't have time to comprehend what's happening before Jill swings her giant tote bag with all her might, pelting Zach in the arm. "How dare you break Sam's heart!"

Zach instinctively lurches back, trying his best to avoid Jill's oncoming assault. Before I can stop him, he slams into me. My sock-covered feet slip across the surface of his tiled entryway, bringing Zach and me crashing to the ground.

"Shit! Sam are you okay?" he worriedly asks from where he's sprawled out next to me on the ground.

"Ugh, I think I broke my butt," I whine, grabbing my backside which managed to break both Zach's and my fall. I seriously think I just fractured my sacrum—the medical term for "I think I broke my butt."

"Sam? What are you doing here?" Ronnie asks. Both she and Jill appear surprised to see me.

"I should be asking you two the same question," I grunt as I attempt to lift my beaten body off the tile floor. Seeing my obvious struggle, Zach helps gently lift me off the floor and onto my feet.

"We were coming to kick Zach's ass for breaking your heart," Ronnie speaks matter-of-factly, as if their reason for being here should be glaringly apparent.

"I expected more from you, Zachary!" Jill scolds, angrily pointing her finger at him.

"Why am I automatically the bad guy here?" he questions, throwing his hands up in the air in exasperation.

"Wait! How are you even here right now, Ronnie? You were in Nashville this morning," I exclaim, suddenly even more confused.

"Sam! You send Jill and me a cryptic text saying you two broke up, then you turn your damn phone off! Of course, I'm jumping in my car and hauling ass back to Bristol!"

Okay, so maybe sending my two best friends a text, then turning off my phone wasn't the most considerate thing to do. I was just so exhausted, both physically and emotionally. I couldn't handle having this conversation with them before I gave my body the sleep it so desperately needed.

"I'm sorry. To both of you. I just didn't want Jill to find out at dinner tonight. Or for you to find out through Craig or someone else." My gaze alternates between Ronnie's glaring emerald green eyes and Jill's soft blue ones, trying to convey my apology to them both.

Just then Zach cuts into the conversation, probably in an attempt to break the awkward tension between Ronnie and me.

"I was accepted into a law school in San Diego, which means I'm moving to California in a couple weeks," Zach informs Ronnie and Jill.

Jill audibly gasps before flinging herself at Zach, giving him a giant hug. "Oh my gosh, Zach! That's great news!"

Before Zach has a chance to thank her, Ronnie turns her anger at Jill. "Seriously, Jill? He's dumping Sam for San Diego, and you're congratulating him?"

Jill suddenly looks as if she's about to cry, her soft blue eyes appearing tearful. I understand that Ronnie's upset and is only trying to defend me, but she's crossing the line—Jill doesn't deserve to be yelled at.

I turn to Jill, placing my hand on her shoulder. "Jill, it's fine. Zach deserves to be congratulated. He worked his ass off to get into that school," I assure her. She gives me a slight smile, quickly wiping away a tear before it falls from her cheek.

When I look at Zach, he's beaming at me. He mouths the words "thank you." I nod at him in return. I'm so glad he and I will be able to stay friends after all of this. See? Margo was worried for nothing.

I finally tear my vision away from Zach and begrudgingly face Ronnie. The woman is visibly seething. Well, I guess it's time to do some damage control.

"To be clear, I actually think I'm the one who ended things," I tell her.

"I'd much rather be moving to California with Sam," Zach professes. "But I respect her decision to stay in Bristol."

This time, both Jill and Ronnie gasp.

"You were going to try to take Sam away from us?" Ronnie shrieks at Zach.

Zach sighs, saying as he walks off, "I seriously can't win with her, Sam. I'm gonna go take a shower. Good luck."

I shake my head in exhaustion before focusing on my two best friends once more. I can't fault Ronnie for the way she's acting. Her passionate nature is one of the reasons I love her so much. She's an extremely loyal and protective friend. No matter how old we are, that will never change.

"I'm staying in Bristol," I promise them. "I'm happy for Zach, and I want him to go. Even if, selfishly, it hurts my heart. Zach and I will always be friends. Look, at the end of the day, I'm going to be fine. Mainly because I have two crazy-ass best friends to make sure that I am."

"Who is this reasonable and mature adult, and what have you done with my Sammie Bear?" Ronnie breaks into a laugh, as Jill and I join her, all of us collapsing into a group hug. Their laughter will always be one of my favorite sounds; being in their arms, one of my favorite places.

Before we break apart, Ronnie whispers something in my ear that only I can hear: "I'm proud of you."

# CHAPTER TWENTY-SIX:

As we gather around Margo's massive dining table, I suddenly become nervous. I hate that Zach and I have to announce our break-up like this, but I guess there's no easy way to do it.

I take my self-assigned seat between Zach and Jill, which also situates me directly across from Miles. On our first Sunday night dinner almost a year ago, when we first chose our place at the table, little did we know these would become our permanent seats for many meals to come. Even when a member of our pack isn't able to attend a Sunday night dinner, no one dares sit in that person's spot. We all look at it as a sign of respect.

Many years ago, Margo had this dining room table custom made, leaf extension and all, in the hopes that one day she and her then-husband Peter would have a family big enough to fill every seat. She told us once that after her fifth miscarriage, she realized fate had other plans.

I watch as Margo and Tony walk into the dining room holding two large dishes full of food. I can't help but notice that Margo is glowing with happiness as she looks at her crowded table. Sometimes family isn't defined by blood but by love, and we all love Margo like she was our own mother. We're Margo's family, and we'll always crowd this giant dining room table of hers.

"Dinner is served!" Tony hollers above the chatter as he and Margo place the casserole dishes in the center of the table.

"About time. I'm starving," Brett mutters. Margo lightly smacks him on the back of the head as she walks past him to take her seat at the head of the table.

"That's what you get for being impolite," Jill scolds him. Brett gives Jill his devilishly handsome grin, and just like that, she's putty in his hands. I wish she would just admit she has a crush on him already.

As we all pass around dishes and shovel food onto our plates, I see Craig stand from his chair.

My stomach instantly drops. Please just be stretching your legs, Craig.

"Alright y'all, I just want to say that tonight sure is a great night!"

Okay, maybe that's all he wanted to say. Seems harmless enough.

"My lady surprised me and drove into town today," he continues, grinning down at Ronnie. "And my best buddy just got accepted into one of the best law schools San Diego has to offer!"

Damn it, Craig.

Everyone immediately turns to Zach—everyone but Miles. When I look up from my trembling hands, I see Miles's hazel eyes boring into me. There's an enormous pit in my stomach, and I can taste the bile rising in my throat.

I feel like I can't breathe. The walls of Margo's dining room are closing in on me. I have to get out of here or I'm sure I'll spontaneously combust.

Launching myself out of my chair, I hear a muffled sound as it crashes to the floor. My thoughts are so loud, the other noises surrounding me seem faint and distant. I race out of Margo's dining room and through her back door, where the warm summer air invades my lungs as I gasp for breath. I feel like I'm going to cry and scream at the same time. All my strength, maturity, and newfound sense of reason from earlier today is now crashing down around me.

What is happening to me?

"Sam."

I quickly whip my body around, expecting Zach to have followed me out to the backyard. I'm momentarily taken aback when I find Miles standing before me.

"Miles." I try to regain my composure, but as I speak his name, my voice falters. I know I can't hide my distress from him. At this point in our friendship, he knows me too well.

He shouldn't be out here. There's nothing he can say that will make this feeling go away. There isn't anything he can tell me that will make this hurt less.

As if reading my thoughts, Miles doesn't speak at all. Instead, he simply wraps his arms around me. In this moment, his embrace speaks louder than his words ever could have.

To my surprise, I suddenly feel calmer. My panic starts to fade, and I no longer feel as if I'm breathing through a straw. After each inhale of Miles's cologne, I slowly exhale my dread.

"Is anyone going to tell us what the hell is going on?" Brett's voice echoes through the trees that surround Miles and me.

I lift my head from Miles's chest and realize our entire dinner party has joined us in the backyard. I step out of his embrace to face my friends—my family.

Zach walks toward me, and I stare at him as he stands beside me. He gently interlaces his fingers with mine. I'm granted a small reminder that today is, in fact, still ours.

I finally break the silence. "I think I was having an anxiety attack."

"Anxiety attacks are trash," Tony blurts out. We all laugh, and the awkward silence is officially no more.

"But in all seriousness, Sam. I get them too," he confesses.

I look at him stunned. I had no idea Tony dealt with anxiety too. He always seems so carefree. I guess you never truly know what internal battles people are fighting, even when those people are your friends.

"Are you moving to San Diego?" Miles asks, his eyes locked with mine.

"Of course he is! He isn't going to commute to class from across the darn country," Craig chuckles.

"Baby, I think he was asking Sam," Ronnie points out as she lovingly pats him on the head.

"Oh. Yeah, that makes more sense."

"Well, are you?" Brett demands.

All eyes are on me, and I suddenly start feeling anxious again. I try moving my mouth, but no words emerge. I really need to start getting more sleep. Or switch to day-shift. Maybe then my brain will start functioning properly.

"I asked Sam to move with me," Zach says. "But she declined, and I completely understand. We've decided to end our relationship and remain friends."

Internally, I thank him for saying the words I couldn't.

"Then why are you holding her hand?" Brett asks, his tone rather abrasive.

"We aren't breaking up until tomorrow," I explain.

Oh, so now my mouth wants to start functioning.

"Are we voting on whether people in our pack should break up too? Because I vote no," Craig says, as serious as can be.

Zach smiles at his best friend. This morning, he asked me if he could tell Craig about his acceptance into law school. How could I tell him no? This was exciting news, and Craig is his closest friend. Best friends have an absolute right to share this type of news with one another. It wasn't Zach's fault that one of the best days of his life happened to be one of the saddest of mine.

"It's okay, Craig," I reassure him. "This is what's best for both of us. Zach and I are good."

Well, eventually I'll be good, and this won't be a lie. But tomorrow, I'm absolutely planning on being extremely not good.

# CHAPTER
# TWENTY-SEVEN:

To my dismay, tomorrow has come, and I'm officially single once again. I'm so happy I'm off work today because I don't think I'd be able to make it through a shift in my current state.

I thought Zach would be able to help ease the stress that work has been causing me. I never thought he'd inadvertently add to my dismal state of mind. I miss him already. Even though I know he's still my friend and I can call him anytime, it's just not the same.

For what feels like the hundredth time today, I cry. I roll over in bed and stare at my alarm clock. It's almost 2:00 PM, and I've made zero effort to drag myself out of bed.

Hearing a light tap at my bedroom door, I instinctively throw my comforter over my head. I'm never getting out of this bed—never. "I'm asleep. Go away!"

I hear my bedroom door open slowly. Tightening my grip on my comforter, I burrow deeper into my cavern of blankets.

"People don't talk in their sleep," Jill says gently.

I rip off the comforter and sit up straight in bed.

"Yes, they do, Jill. It's, like, a common thing," I sneer.

"Yeah, Jill. I've heard you say some pretty crazy shit in your sleep after watching all those ghost shows," Ronnie laughs, peeking out from behind my bedroom door.

"I do not talk in my sleep." Jill's hands fly defensively to her hips. She breaks into a visible pout, and I can't help but laugh.

Jill turns back to me and smiles. "It's good to hear you laugh, Sam."

"We were getting really tired of hearing your blubbering," Ronnie jokes.

"Aren't you going back to Nashville yet?" I snap.

"I'm only joking, Sammie Bear." Ronnie throws herself onto my bed, while Jill politely takes a seat on the other side.

"We brought you food," Jill informs me, handing me a plate with a tuna fish sandwich on it.

"We also wanted to make sure you weren't dead," Ronnie adds.

"You couldn't tell I was alive by my blubbering?" I chuckle, giving Ronnie a light shove.

She dramatically flings her body off my bed and onto the floor, at which point we all burst into laughter.

"I guess I'm gonna make a pretty crappy social worker then, huh?" Ronnie quips.

"Shush, you'll be amazing," Jill exclaims.

"Alright, alright. Enough about me," Ronnie says. She's never been good at receiving compliments. "Sam, eat your sandwich. Then, we're officially cheering you the fuck up!"

"I don't want to be cheered up," I sulk. "I want to cry and feel sorry for myself, damn it!"

"Eat your sandwich!" Ronnie demands before strutting out of my bedroom.

"You really should eat something," Jill insists. To appease her, I begrudgingly take a bite of my tuna fish sandwich.

It took almost an hour, but Ronnie and Jill were finally able to coax me out of my bed with the promise of a full glass of red wine.

Now, I'm currently wearing an adult onesie, snuggled up on our sofa watching *Sleepless in Seattle*. I sniffle as I watch Tom Hanks take Meg Ryan's hand in the final scene. Such a beautiful ending. Why can't real life be like the movies? Where's my happy ending?

I wipe my nose on my onesie sleeve before taking another gulp of Pinot noir.

"You poor thing," Jill murmurs, softly shaking her head.

I know, Jill. I'm a complete train-wreck.

A loud knock at the door pulls me from my rom-com stupor.

"Eww, don't answer it," I moan, to no one in particular.

"I'm not going to answer it, you are," Ronnie asserts.

"The hell I am," I hiss back before trying to burrow under the blanket on my lap.

"Give me that!" Ronnie takes hold of the blanket and rips it away from me.

"You're mean," I pout, crossing my arms in front of my chest like a petulant child.

"And *you're* answering that damn door."

"Fine!"

I reluctantly pull my body from the sofa and sulk towards the front door in my Superman onesie, the glass of wine in my clutches.

"Should we brush her hair?" I hear Jill whisper to Ronnie.

Another loud knock rings out just as I reach the entryway to our apartment. Unwillingly, I turn the knob and open the door. My vision slowly adjusts to the sunlight as I take in the presence of four men standing on my patio.

"I brought three different flavors of ice cream and lots of toppings because I wasn't sure which was your favorite," Tony announces.

I chuckle seeing Tony, Brett, Craig, and Miles standing awkwardly on our patio, all of them with their arms full of goodies.

"I bought wine and champagne. I'm pretty sure y'all ladies drink both, right?" Craig asks.

"We sure do, honey!" Ronnie shouts from where she currently sits on the sofa.

"Well, I was instructed to bring romantic comedies, but I don't own any of that shit. So, I brought *The Shining* and *Die Hard*. Sorry," Brett apologizes as he offers up the movies he's holding.

I laugh, taking them from him. I actually really love *The Shining*, so I'm not the least bit disappointed by his selections. I should probably take a break from my rom-com binge anyway.

"You had one job, Brett," Ronnie gripes.

"Ronnie, I already told you I don't watch that shit!" Brett shouts above me. "Why didn't you ask Tony to bring the movies?"

"Hey! Just because I'm gay doesn't mean I watch romantic movies," Tony says in his defense.

"Sorry, dude," Brett replies, putting his arm around Tony.

"Except for *The Notebook*, of course." Tony gives me a wink then proceeds to quote Nicholas Sparks word for word.

Jill, Ronnie, and I burst into hysterics while the other three men look extremely confused.

"The book was better." I smile at Tony.

"Isn't it always?" he laughs.

Tony, Brett, and Craig eventually squeeze past me, joining Jill and Ronnie in the apartment. However, Miles remains on the patio, watching as I chug the remnants of my wine glass.

"You look good," he remarks sarcastically.

"Shut the hell up," I snarl.

"And as sweet as ever, I see. Singleness really becomes you."

"Are you done mocking my heartache?" Why is he being such an asshole?

He silently runs his fingers through his thick curls. Figuring our conversation over, I move to head back inside the apartment, but before I can take a step, I feel his hand lightly touch my forearm. I turn back to face him.

"Hey, I'm sorry," he starts. "I was just joking with you. We always give each other crap, Sam. It's kind of our thing."

"I'm just really sensitive right now. And sad... I'm really sad, Miles."

"Well, I have something for you that will hopefully make you less sad." He thrusts a dingy teddy bear towards me. "You're always kind of sensitive though, so I don't think it'll fix that," he chuckles.

I glower at him before reluctantly taking the tattered stuffed animal from him. I look back up at him with what I can only assume is a very confused look, because he proceeds to explain. "My mom gave me this bear when I was a kid. Somehow, he always made me feel better when I was sad. I thought you might need to borrow him for a bit."

"That's pretty adorable," I profess, changing my glower to a giant grin. I know this bear must mean a lot to him, especially after losing his mom.

"Shut the hell up," he laughs.

"Does he have a name?"

"Of course he does. It's Teddy."

"Real original," I chuckle.

"Give me a break, I was four." He gives me his signature sideways smirk.

"Thank you," I reply, gazing down at the worn teddy bear in my hands. "I'll be sure to return him in one piece."

"Good. I'll need him for my next heartbreak."

"Hey, now! Maybe the next girl you date will be the one," I propose, giving him a reassuring smile.

God knows he can't do any worse than Ashleigh.

"Maybe she will be," he murmurs under his breath.

# CHAPTER
# TWENTY-EIGHT:

Miles and I enter the apartment together, but as Miles gently shuts the front door behind him, I slip into my bedroom undetected. Once inside my room, I carefully prop Teddy up against the pillows at the head of my bed. A worn stuffed bear seems like a strange gift to give someone going through a break-up, but it's the thought that counts. Well, I guess Teddy isn't technically a gift; he's more of a loan.

As I leave my room, I find all my friends huddled around our sofa, watching Brett place a disc into the DVD player. I really hope he chose *The Shining*. In my opinion, *Die Hard* is a Christmas movie, and it's only August.

"We were worried you had crawled back into your dungeon of despair," Ronnie jokes.

"Wow, you're so hilarious, Veronica," I mock, sticking my tongue out at her. "So, what movie has the pack chosen?"

"*The Shining*," Brett says. "Miles seems to think *Die Hard* is a Christmas movie." He rolls his eyes.

I smile at Miles, but he doesn't notice as he's too busy arguing with Brett. This is one of the many reasons he and I are such great friends—he just gets it.

We all settle in as the movie begins. Before the opening credits roll, I scurry to the kitchen to refill my wine glass, still decked out in my Superman onesie. Happiness is, indeed, a full glass of wine.

When I return from the kitchen, I wedge myself between Miles and Jill on the sofa. On the other end of our infamous hand-me-down floral couch, Ronnie and Craig are snuggled up.

I'm truly elated that they're so happy together, but at the moment, their adorableness makes my stomach churn.

I can't believe I'm single again. It all happened so fast. On the plus side, I guess now I have more time and energy to devote to not being a terrible nurse.

But today, I'm allowing myself to remain in a state of full-blown self-pity. Tomorrow, I'll try to become a respectable human being again.

Jill leans over to me and offers in a hushed voice, "Do you want me to brush out the tangles in your hair for you?"

"It's okay. I'm embracing the bedhead today," I respond, taking another gulp of wine.

Unfortunately, our couch isn't big enough for us all, so Brett and Tony are currently splayed out on the fuzzy rug in front of the sofa. When Jill and I finally pull the trigger on new furniture, we're definitely splurging on a sectional.

Before I can stop myself, I think aloud, "This just feels weird without Zach here. Should we invite him?"

"We can't have a breakup party and invite the person you just broke up with," Ronnie moans.

"Is that what this is? A breakup party?" I ask, feeling rather annoyed. Am I that pathetic that my friends think they need to throw me a "party" all because I went through a completely normal breakup?

I subconsciously try running my fingers through my hair as I ponder this idea, but to my horror, one of my fingers gets caught in a huge knot of my tangled hair.

*Yeah, I guess I'm, in fact, that pathetic.*

"Sam, this isn't just for you," Craig informs me. "We all got dumped for San Diego. We're all losing Zach." A small frown comes over his face.

As I look at Craig, I realize he's right. I may be losing Zach as a significant other, but in a way, we're all still losing him. Even though I know he's only moving, it's a far move. It's not like Nashville. Zach can't just jump in his car and drive back to Bristol whenever Craig sends him an upsetting text.

In one way or another, we're all losing Zach. We're all losing a member of our pack.

"We actually were at Zach's before we came here," Tony admits to me.

"You were?"

"He's sad too, Sam."

Tony's words resonate with me slowly, and I decide to pull my cell phone out of my onesie pocket. Side note, I really need to start wearing onesies more often. They're comfortable and convenient.

I unlock my phone, find his name, and press the call button before I can overthink it.

"What are you doing?" Jill asks.

I smile at her. "The right thing, Jill."

I'm doing the right thing.

"Hello?" Zach answers, sounding somewhat confused.

"Hi. It's Sam." Now, all my friends are staring at me as I initiate an awkward telephone conversation with my ex-boyfriend.

"I know," Zach chuckles.

"We're all watching *The Shining* at Jill's and my place. Do you want to come over?"

"Are you sure? It won't be weird for you?"

"Honestly, it's weird not to have you here," I confess.

Out of my peripheral vision, I see Craig pump his fist into the air in triumph.

Don't celebrate yet, Craig. Zach hasn't quite accepted my invitation.

After what feels like an eternity of silence, Zach finally responds. "Can I bring anything over?"

"Zach wants to know if we need him to bring anything," I announce to the crowd in my living room.

"We're completely out of dish soap," Jill answers.

"I think he meant snacks, not dish soap," I giggle.

Jill immediately blushes. "You said anything. You didn't specify snacks!"

"It's okay," Zach says through the phone. "I have an extra bottle. I'll bring it."

I give Jill a thumbs-up. "You're in luck, Jillian."

"Hopefully it's Seventh Generation. Their bottles are made of one-hundred percent recycled plastic," she informs me, even though I already know this.

Only Jillian Moore has a favorite dish soap brand.

Zach arrives about twenty minutes later, dish soap in hand. The dreary mood I'd been feeling today immediately lifts when he walks through the door. This is how it should be. No uncomfortable awkwardness. My friends shouldn't have to split their time between Zach and me. We should all be together—always.

"Thank you for bringing the soap, Zach," Jill graciously greets him. He gives her a big hug, then proceeds to work his way around our small living room delivering hugs and handshakes to the rest of our friends.

"It's not Seventh Generation," Jill whispers to me.

"It'll be okay just this once," I whisper back, trying not to giggle.

I know how serious Jill is about using recycled products, and I don't want to upset her by laughing. Before living with her I never recycled anything. Now, I consider myself a fairly decent recycler, all thanks to Jill. So, I commend her for her environmentally-friendly ways.

After we finish the movie, I wander over to my Victrola record player and try deciding on which album we should listen to. I would love to say I own an old Victrola, but it's actually fairly new. It even has Bluetooth. My dad bought it for me for my birthday two years ago.

The coolest part of my birthday gift that year, however, wasn't actually the player itself. Along with the record player, my dad also gifted me all of his vintage vinyl records. I inherited my taste in music from my father, so getting all his old vinyl albums was an absolute dream.

"What do you guys want to listen to?" I call out through the chatter.

"Your choice!" Brett shouts back before chugging the rest of his beer.

Miles walks towards me; I watch as he takes in my huge collection of vinyl albums.

"This is awesome," he murmurs.

"I know, right? You want to choose an album?"

"Hell yeah, I do."

I smile as I watch him excitedly shuffle through my albums. After a minute, he thrusts his choice into my hand.

I gaze down at the album he handed me. "Solid choice."

"What can I say? I have superb taste," he boasts. I dramatically roll my eyes at him, then carefully slip the vinyl from its sleeve.

As I drop the needle of the tonearm onto the outer groove of the record, I see Tony and Ronnie prancing around our kitchen peninsula together.

Tony is holding the two bottles of chocolate syrup he brought over for our ice cream. Why he thought we'd need two bottles, I have no idea. Meanwhile, Ronnie is holding the bottle of dish soap. I stare at my friends in complete and utter confusion.

The sound of white noise invades my ears before the music begins playing. Call me a hipster, but that noise is probably my favorite thing about listening to vinyl.

"We're going skating!" Ronnie shouts.

"You mean, syrup-soap skating," Tony laughs.

"...What?" Miles and I ask in unison as the opening guitar solo of AC/DC's "Highway to Hell" starts blaring through the speakers of my Victrola.

Tony and Ronnie nod at one another. Then, out of nowhere, they start squirting dish soap and chocolate syrup all over our linoleum kitchen floor.

"What are you doing?" Jill gasps. She has turned ghostly white, as if she may faint at any moment.

"Just go with it, Jill," Brett urges. "It's about time you lived a little!"

Jill nods at him, then slowly exhales. She walks over to where Ronnie and Tony are currently destroying our kitchen floor and shocks us all by throwing the full glass of water she's holding into the soap-syrup mixture.

"Everyone knows water makes soap more slippery," Jill giggles, shaking her head in disbelief. "I can't believe I'm allowing this to happen."

"Don't worry, Jilly Bean. We'll clean it all up later," Ronnie assures her.

"Well, here goes nothin'!" Craig shouts, barreling through our tiny living room and into our even tinier kitchen.

As soon as his sock-covered feet hit the wet linoleum, he goes flying. His feet slip out from under him, and he comes crashing to the disgusting-looking floor, cowboy hat and all.

Our entire pack bursts into laughter as we all go running towards Craig. My onesie-clad feet hit the soap-syrup floor, and I immediately do a *Risky Business* slide through the kitchen. If only I was wearing sunglasses and Bob Seger was blaring through my speakers, it would have been perfect.

In mid-slide, I start to lose my footing. Instinctively, I grab onto Miles's shirt to brace myself but end up taking him down to the floor with me. For a moment, I'm fearful for my life as I watch his tall frame nearly topple onto me. Luckily, he's able to somewhat catch himself. We end up landing with me flat on my back in a pond of muck and Miles in a kneeling position, straddling me.

I silently thank him for not crushing me to death. I'm still sore from my fall with Zach yesterday. It seems as if falling on my ass has become a very undesirable hobby of mine.

Looking up, I notice Zach slip through the kitchen in an attempt to help Craig to his feet. Instead, they both end up joining Miles and me on the floor.

Brett and Ronnie drag Jill into the kitchen, and I watch as the three of them go sliding in different directions. Jill grasps the kitchen countertop trying to keep herself from falling but still ends up kneeling into a puddle of chocolate syrup.

Finally, Tony and Miles are able to help pull me off of the soiled floor. Once I'm standing, I stupidly decide this is the perfect moment for me to attempt one of my signature pirouettes. I twirl my body, end up spinning out of control, and smack directly into Brett's back. The force of my body crashing into his takes both of us tumbling back to the ground.

In the process, Brett inadvertently sweeps Ronnie's feet out from under her as he falls. She flops onto her stomach and goes sliding towards the refrigerator like a penguin down an icy slope.

I think our combined laughter is louder than "Highway to Hell" blasting in the other room. The eight of us continue slipping, sliding, badly singing along, and crashing into each other in our tiny kitchen as AC/DC proudly serenades our shenanigans.

I have no idea what highway we're actually on. All that matters is that we're on it together.

While the final seconds of my AC/DC record play, I hear a forceful knock at the front door. That's the one downside of listening to music on vinyl; eventually, the record needs to be flipped.

Another forceful knock, this time sounding louder and angrier than before, shakes our front door.

"Who's answering that?" I ask, pushing a strand of my syrup and soap-covered hair out of my face.

"I've got it," Jill answers cheerily as she attempts to wipe a smudge of chocolate syrup from her cheek to no avail.

Now, the knocking has turned to pounding.

"I bet it's the cops," Brett groans.

"It's not the cops," I snap.

As if on cue, a voice screams from the other side of our door, "IT'S THE POLICE!"

Shit! It really *is* the cops.

Jill looks back at me with wide, stunned eyes before slowly cracking open the door.

"I'm sorry, were we being noisy?" she asks sweetly, opening the door a bit wider.

By this time, the rest of us have managed to pull ourselves off the kitchen floor and are now standing a few feet behind Jill.

Two male police officers are standing on our front patio. One looks to be in his mid-forties, the other appearing to be around our age. Both officers look extremely confused as they take in our dirty, disheveled appearances. We must be quite the sight.

"So, are y'all cooking drugs, or is this like...a cult situation?" the young officer asks with a laugh.

We all snicker as we struggle to refrain from laughing. I don't think it's technically illegal to laugh at a police officer, but I also don't want to risk it.

Jill can't help it though, and she starts giggling uncontrollably.

Jill, NO! You'll never survive prison.

But, as I often forget, Jill looks like a supermodel. The younger officer is completely enchanted by the sweet sound of her laughter. He grins at her, unabashedly before the older officer speaks up. "You got a noise complaint from one of your neighbors."

"Bastards," I whisper. Standing on either side of me, Miles and Brett both chuckle at my outburst.

"Keep it down, okay? We don't want to come back here," the older officer says, mildly annoyed.

"We understand. Thank you, officers," I reply.

The older officer nods to me, before turning and walking down the steps to our apartment. Before following, the younger officer slightly hesitates. He waits just long enough to take one final look at Jill as she leans her slender body gracefully against the door frame.

"Yeah. I'd hate to have to come back," the young officer jokes as he grins at Jill once again. And just like that, he turns on his heels and jogs down the cement steps.

Jill stands frozen in our open doorway, staring after the young (and did I mention extremely handsome) officer.

"You can close the door now," Brett calls to her.

This instantly snaps Jill out of her trance, and she slams the front door just a bit too hard.

"Now, *he* was cute," I blurt out.

"No girl, he was *fine*," Tony corrects me.

"You move on pretty fast, don't ya?" Zach laughs.

"Not for me—for Jill," I clarify.

"What? Why for me? Why would you say that?" Jill stammers, clearly embarrassed.

"Because he couldn't stop staring at you. Duh!" Ronnie rolls her eyes exaggeratedly.

"He wasn't staring at me," Jill maintains, her cheeks now turning bright red. She instantly goes to change the subject. "Alright, everyone! Let's clean up this disaster."

We all groan when we look at the gross film of soap and syrup covering our once-sparkling kitchen floor.

"You promised," she whines at our reluctance.

"She's right, we did," Ronnie admits.

"Welp, let's get 'er done!" Craig hollers.

Jill looks around our apartment, then her eyes meet mine. "Well, we're out of dish soap again," she giggles, giving me a shrug. I join in with her laughter, even though her statement is not necessarily true— there's plenty of dish soap spread across our kitchen floor.

"We're gonna need more music for this," Miles insists.

"I'm on it!" I tiptoe across the living room trying my best to avoid dirtying our apartment any further.

Picking up the record, I gently turn it over and am once again engulfed by the sound of AC/DC flowing through the speakers. I join the cleaning crew in the kitchen as we proceed to dance, sing, and, of course, painstakingly clean.

But, with this group of individuals, I must admit, even cleaning is pretty damn enjoyable.

# CHAPTER
# TWENTY-NINE

## (February 2014):

Over the last few months, work has gotten a lot easier. Primarily because my charge nurse Marilyn has retired. I'm not saying she wasn't a good nurse. All I'm saying is, she was extremely burnt out. And unfortunately, her floor nurses suffered for it.

I'm also not saying that I blame her. An entire career in nursing can do that to a person. Not to sound wildly dramatic, but it can break a person's soul. I just never want to get to the point where I think it's acceptable to treat others poorly in the workplace simply because I'm no longer happy.

*Please, never let me get that way.*

Another reason things have also gotten so much better for me at work is that Tanya accepted Marilyn's old position as the night-shift charge nurse on weekends. Although Tanya wasn't thrilled about leaving her coveted day-shift position, the promotion made the move worth it for her. Not to mention she's getting shift differential now too. Which means our hospital pays us an extra two dollars an hour to work night-shift and another dollar on top of that to work weekends. With the extra bump in pay, she's able to save money for a down payment on her first home without having to work crazy amounts of overtime the way she did before.

Tanya told me I should try switching to her old day-shift schedule. She knows how difficult it is for me to sleep when I'm working graveyard. But I can't leave my schedule now that one of my best work friends just became my charge nurse. And I just couldn't stomach losing the extra three dollars an hour. There's no way I'm switching schedules.

Plus, Lucie and I have become extremely close over the last six months. I don't want to stop working with my favorite CNA either. She and I make an excellent team, and I truly enjoy working with her.

She's also become my post night-shift breakfast buddy—mainly because she's not yet old enough to drink with me at The Barn Door. Lucie and I (and sometimes Tanya, too) love going to breakfast at the restaurant across the street from the hospital after we get off of work. Personally, I'm a huge fan of their Bloody Marys. They're the perfect way to wind down from an excruciatingly long twelve-hour shift.

The idea of working a somewhat-normal schedule is appealing, but now that I've found my "work pack," I can never leave them.

As for my actual pack, everyone seems to be doing really well.

Zach is excelling in law school and is absolutely loving life in San Diego. We text and talk on the phone frequently. Sometimes, we even FaceTime even though I hate it. But for him, I do it.

He often tells me how much he thinks I would have loved living in California. I always laugh it off and tell him I'm not California material. But I would certainly love to visit someday.

Brett and Miles are also both doing well. Miles decided to adopt a one-year-old black lab from the local shelter last November. He named him Scout. That dog has completely stolen my heart. I wish I could spend every minute petting and cuddling him. He's big, goofy, and undeniably lovable—just like his owner.

Recently, Miles and I have been meeting for our coffee "get-togethers" exclusively at his and Brett's place because Miles doesn't like to leave Scout alone in the apartment if he doesn't have to. He already spends enough time alone while Miles and Brett are working.

It'd be perfect if we could find a dog-friendly coffeehouse, but apparently, they don't exist in Bristol. Trust me, I've looked.

All in all, Tony's doing well too, but he's had a bit of a tough time lately. Although he's tried multiple times, he still hasn't been accepted into the Bristol County Fire Academy. He's even contemplated moving, in the hopes that maybe another county's fire department would give him a shot. I understand his thought process, but I'd be devastated if he moved away.

It's well-known in the medical community that becoming a firefighter is an extremely competitive process. Some people just happen to have better luck than others.

Take Brett, for example. He made the entire process look so easy. He was accepted into the fire academy after his first application and subsequently passed with ease.

Tony in no way resents Brett. He whole-heartedly loves his friends and wants nothing but the best for them. But he's still human, and sometimes he gets frustrated at the whole process.

But where there is a will, there's a way. Tony has so much will, there's no doubt in my mind he'll find a way.

Jill and I are still happily living in roommate bliss. At this point, I can't remember what my life was like before I lived with Jillian Moore.

She and I still can't go into our tiny kitchen without thinking of that one night last August where things took a super weird turn. Three weeks after the syrup-soap skating incident, we discovered an overlooked puddle of chocolate syrup and dish soap concealed under our trash can. Upon discovering the hidden trash lake, which at that point closely resembled raw sewage, we laughed so hard tears streamed down our faces.

Ronnie is still living in Nashville and doing well in her social work program. I can't believe Veronica Sanders is going to have a master's degree. She and Craig are still going strong, making long-distance relationships look like a cakewalk. Ronnie keeps begging Craig to move to Nashville with her. It's not only because she misses him, but because she's urging him to pursue a career as a country musician.

We've all had the pleasure of witnessing how talented Craig is. Recently, he performed at open mic night at The Barn Door which blew us all away.

It's no wonder Ronnie's pushing him to chase his dreams; however, Craig says he doesn't have the luxury to think about himself right now.

Sadly, he has a point. His mother's multiple sclerosis has progressed quite rapidly, and Craig and his father were told by her physician that she doesn't have much longer.

I splash cold water from the bathroom sink onto my face, bracing myself for another long night-shift. After giving myself a moment, I rush out of the staff bathroom to grab an assignment sheet from Tanya before settling in behind my computer. Looking over the sheet, I quickly open the charts of the patients I'll be caring for tonight.

I'm relieved it's my Friday and that I'll be off for four days after tonight.

Most of the patients I'm assigned I'm already familiar with and have cared for all week. All except for one. She was a new admission during today's day-shift. Tanya didn't want to overwhelm me. She offered to be the nurse for the new patient in room 542 tonight, but I insisted on doing it myself.

*I have to be her nurse. I have to do it for him.*

With my pockets full of supplies and stethoscope around my neck, I walk down the hallway towards room 542. Before entering the room, I glimpse at the patient's name on the report sheet in my hands.

*Susan Corey.*

But I know her better as Craig's mom.

# CHAPTER THIRTY:

Although the door to Mrs. Corey's room is ajar, I still lightly knock before entering.

"Come on in," I hear Craig holler from inside the room. I recognize my friend's distinct southern twang.

As I make my way into the room, my heart slowly breaks when I see Craig and his father, John, sitting on either side of Susan's bed.

Susan Corey lies motionless in her hospital bed. Her complexion is pale and waxy. I immediately notice her breathing is agonal with approximately twenty-second periods of apnea. In laymen's terms, one moment she is taking short, shallow breaths and the next it appears like she's holding her breath entirely. This is what we refer to as end-of-life breathing.

The first time I saw anyone breathe this way, I was seven years old.

I know Susan is unresponsive now; she has been for the last four days. In her current state, John didn't want to transfer Susan from home hospice to Summit Valley for inpatient hospice, but that was Susan's wish.

Susan made it clear to her husband and son that when she was close to passing away, she wanted to be transferred to Summit Valley. She didn't want to die in the home the three of them shared for twenty years. She didn't want their last memory of her to be of her dying in their family home.

She would rather they remember all the cookies she baked for them in their kitchen, their Monopoly game nights in their den that she always won, and the many Christmas trees she decorated in their living room. After she was gone, she didn't want them to think of her final breaths anytime they sat on their sofa.

Not everyone's wishes are the same. Many people with terminal illnesses would rather pass away in the comfort of their own homes; however, for some people, that's the last thing they want.

At my last visit to the Corey home, about a week ago, Susan was still alert and able to communicate. She had been resting peacefully in a hospital bed they had set up in the middle of their living room. The home hospice company delivered the hospital bed and various other medical supplies when Susan first signed onto hospice four months prior.

When Craig briefly left the living room to grab a glass of water, Susan confided in me. She motioned for me to place my hand in hers. I obliged, and our eyes met, her eyes looking so weary, yet still so beautiful.

"I'm not afraid to die. I'm ready," she said.

In response, I simply nodded, not knowing what else to say.

"What I'm afraid of is, if I die in our home, my death will taint all the wonderful memories we've had here." She spoke the last word just as Craig turned the corner into the living room.

Once again, I didn't know how to respond. All I could do was nod my head, attempting to portray my understanding. Even though I have plenty of these tough conversations with patients and their family members when I'm at work, this felt so much different.

Susan wasn't one of my patients—she was Craig's mom.

But now, she really is one of my patients.

"Ronnie's driving up as we speak," Craig tells me, pulling me away from my thoughts about Susan's and my last solemn conversation.

"I'm so glad she's making the trip up here," I reply. Ronnie has a remarkable way of making tough situations a bit more bearable.

"Zach's flying out tomorrow morning," he adds.

I grin at discovering this news. Sometimes, all it takes is an upsetting text from your best friend, and you're on the next flight to them. Even when you live all the way across the country.

All of us deserve a friendship like that, but especially Craig. He's one of the most selfless and kind people I know. I'm sure he gets that from his mom.

"We're so thankful you're her nurse tonight, Samantha," Mr. Corey addresses me, a sad smile on his face.

"Pops, I told you a zillion times she likes to be called Sam," Craig reminds his father.

"I apologize, Sam."

"Craig, it's fine." Then, I turn to John, giving him a smile, "It's fine, Mr. Corey. Really."

"Well, if we're getting technical about names, it's John," he chuckles.

This family is so damn nice. I hate that they're going through this. They don't deserve this. Susan doesn't deserve this.

I gently assess Mrs. Corey. I'm thankful she appears comfortable. Although her breathing is irregular, it's not abnormal for this stage of the dying process, and I don't believe she's short of breath.

Craig and John did an excellent job of caring for Susan at home. Her skin is perfectly intact. They managed to prevent her from acquiring any pressure wounds or becoming contracted while she was bedbound. Contractures are fairly common in patients with these types of diagnoses. Since they don't have a lot of mobility, their muscles can easily contract, becoming deformed or rigid. Thankfully, Mrs. Corey had none of that.

After completing my assessment, I spend a bit of time talking with Craig and John and attempting to answer any questions they may have about this process. Susan has been battling an aggressive form of MS for years. As such, John and Craig have had plenty of time to prepare themselves for this day.

Yet it still doesn't make this any easier.

Surprisingly, tonight's shift has been pretty quiet. The word "quiet" is taboo in the medical field. Every time you utter the "q-word," shit inevitably hits the fan. Frankly, that's why I'd never say it aloud. Hopefully thinking it won't do any harm.

Ronnie got to the hospital around 10:30 PM. She decided to stay the night in Susan's room with Craig and John. Susan absolutely adored Ronnie, so it only felt right for her to stick around.

With Craig's permission, Margo also briefly dropped by, following the end of her shift in the ICU. She only stayed for about fifteen minutes, but I think the fact that she came meant the world to Craig.

Margo has truly become a shoulder for Craig to lean on during his mom's illness. Before Margo left Susan's room, Craig told her she'd never know how much he appreciated her being there for him. When he spoke those words, I swear I saw a tear in Margo Hatcher's eye.

The rest of our pack reached out to Craig via text, phone calls, and even FaceTime. But, overall, they've respected the need for him to be alone with his family right now.

Lucie and I have continued to make constant rounds to ensure all of our patients are safe and comfortable. We both only just caught up with our charting a few minutes ago. Now, we're passing the time chatting at the nurses' station until our next rounds.

Like I said, tonight has totally been the "q-word."

"Any plans on your days off?" I ask before taking a huge sip of my steaming hot cup of coffee. Fortunately, Lucie and I have the same schedule, so it's her Friday too.

"No, not really. Maybe hang out with some friends."

"Any of those friends a boyfriend?" I joke.

"I've never had a boyfriend," she murmurs.

"What? How? You're so beautiful!"

"I was just...um...never really into that." I can tell she's starting to feel uncomfortable, so I decide to quit my line of questioning.

"Well, you're young. You have plenty of time," I assure her. "You want some coffee? I just made a pot."

"You always make the coffee really strong," she snickers.

Just as I'm about to defend my coffee-making skills, I see Craig step out of room 542. He softly closes the hospital room door behind him and slowly walks towards the nurses' station.

Quickly, I rise from my seat, draping my stethoscope around my neck out of habit. I start walking towards Craig. Lucie stands as well, then follows close behind.

Lucie and I don't need to speak—we just know.

Meeting my friend in the center of the hallway, I wait for him to speak first. I can tell his eyes appear redder than normal; however, he isn't crying. I've never seen Craig cry. Not once. Even despite everything he's endured.

"She's gone, Sam," he whispers.

Without a moment's hesitation, I wrap my arms around my friend.

Susan didn't deserve this.

Craig doesn't deserve this.

But sometimes life doesn't consider what you do or don't deserve.

# CHAPTER THIRTY-ONE:

# SUSAN COREY

**February 9, 2014, 05:57**

'm not afraid to die. I'm ready.

But are they ready? Will they be okay?

John, the only man I've ever loved. Thank you.

Thank you for all those amazing years, for showing me what it means to be loved unconditionally. You're such a wonderful man. You deserve to love again, one day.

Promise me you'll allow yourself to love again. And to be loved. Though I doubt anyone can ever love you as much as I did—as much as I do. But I hope they come close.

Craig, my sweet boy. My sweet boy who's no longer a boy. You've become such a wonderful man, just like your father. I'm so proud of you.

The moment you were born, you became your father's and my entire world. My favorite part of this life has been watching you grow. Watching you learn, laugh. Watching you fall in love.

*Promise me you'll always follow your heart and chase your dreams.*

*Now that I'm leaving, it's your time.*

*Promise me you'll stay true to yourself and continue to be the goofy, fun-loving person we all adore. I know now, it's not only* **my** *heart you've stolen.*

*Promise me you'll continue to dance like no one is watching. Promise me you will sing. If not for you, then for me. More importantly, promise me you'll sing like everyone is listening.*

*These are the words I wish I could have told them before I could no longer speak. I pray they know how much I love them.*

*Though it's my time to leave this world, my love for them will remain. As the years pass, and they forget the sound of my voice or the feel of my touch, my love will still surround them.*

*My love for them is eternal. Even though, sadly, I am not.*

*As the voices surrounding me fade, my consciousness drifting further away, I know I'm finally ready. I'm not afraid to die. I will leave this world at peace with my life, knowing I truly had it all.*

*I had both of you—***I had everything***.*

# CHAPTER
# THIRTY-TWO:

I hang up the phone at the nurses' station after speaking to the mortuary Susan Corey made prior arrangements with. Honestly, it's such a relief for families when a patient already has funeral arrangements in place prior to their death. Choosing a funeral home, whether to have your loved one buried or cremated—it's an impossibly huge decision to make on the spot. Especially, when you're wracked with grief, having just lost someone you love.

Summit Valley Hospital doesn't have a morgue. This means we don't have any way to store a patient's body after they pass. To put it bluntly, we have about a four-hour timeframe to work with before the process of rigor mortis sets in. It's our goal to transfer the patients' remains to the mortuary or funeral home before it hits that point.

Rigor mortis occurs naturally after a person has passed away. Their limbs stiffen, which is caused by chemical changes in their muscles that occur after death.

This information isn't always widely known, making it extremely hard to discuss with patients' family members after they've lost their loved ones. I've had families tell me they feel as though we're rushing their grieving process by asking them to choose a mortuary so soon after death. As a hospice nurse, I can assure you that's never our intention. Rather, the rush is solely to preserve their loved one's remains.

As I said, this is a very uncomfortable conversation to have.

I'm relieved this isn't the conversation I need to have with Craig and his dad. About four months ago, as soon as Susan signed on for home hospice, she took it upon herself to get her arrangements in order.

She even left John a notebook in which she had handwritten all of their account passwords.

These are types of things people don't often think of before it's too late. But not Susan—she thought of everything.

She was such an amazing woman.

"You almost ready?" Lucie asks.

I pull myself away from my computer, watching as she seats herself next to me behind the nurses' station. Lucie and I are both still at work, even though it's an hour past the end of our scheduled shift. Neither of us could stomach leaving Craig and John so soon after Susan's passing.

Besides, with every death comes charting and death notifications. I didn't want to dump all that extra work onto the day-shift nurse.

As a nurse, you basically spend half of your career charting. They always say, "If you didn't chart it, you didn't do it."

I'm not sure who actually started that; odds are it was someone being sued.

"I'm just finishing up charting. You don't have to wait," I tell Lucie.

"It's okay. It's Friday!" She gives me a quick smile.

Just then, we see the call light flashing outside of room 540. On cue, Lucie immediately gets up to assist the patient, Mr. Mitchell, even though the day-shift is already here in full force doing their morning rounds. Many nurses and nursing aides would never answer a call light after shift change, but not Lucie.

Maybe I'll buy her breakfast this morning to thank her for all her help tonight. When Susan passed, she was amazing with Craig and his father. I could tell her presence was of great comfort to them.

This was the first time any of my friends outside of work had met Lucie. I think even Ronnie is a fan of her, which is saying a lot because Ronnie doesn't always take kindly to new people.

Finally, I finish my charting and log off my computer. I start gathering my things, which I've managed to inadvertently spread about the nurses' station throughout the night when I notice Lucie speed-walking back in my direction.

Well, *someone's* excited to get off work.

"What's up, Luce?" I ask.

"We have a problem." Lucie now stands frozen before me. Her eyes wide, an undeniable look of horror on her face.

I set my water bottle back down on the countertop, mentally preparing myself for whatever she's about to say.

"Is Mr. Mitchell okay?" I didn't think he was close to passing away, but sometimes, you never actually know.

"He's fine. But...I think he has bed bugs," she blurts out.

Ok, I was in no way prepared to hear that.

"Excuse me? He has what?" Now it's my horror that's glaringly apparent.

"The day-shift CNA was giving him a bath. She pressed the call light because she found some bugs in his bed," Lucie details. "We Googled them. I think they're bed bugs."

"Shit."

Lucie and I have cared for Mr. Mitchell all week. We've bathed him together and helped reposition him in bed countless times.

"How did we not see any bugs?"

"They're tiny. I don't even know how she found them this morning," Lucie explains.

"Bad news ladies," Tanya announces as she approaches us.

"Why are you still here?" I ask. Tanya never stays at work this late.

"Because we, unfortunately, have a situation. The patient in room 540 has bed bugs."

"Shit," I groan once more.

This *cannot* be happening. It's the prime example of why you never utter the "q-word" when you work in the medical field.

Trust me. Don't even think it.

# CHAPTER
# THIRTY-THREE:

With shaking hands, I unlock my phone and dial Jill's number. I suddenly have the urge to vomit as I wait for her to answer.

"Hello," Jill's sweet voice trills through the phone.

"Jill, where are you?!" I demand.

"I'm at home, just drinking a cup of coffee," she responds, sounding somewhat confused. "I already heard the news. I'm so devastated about Craig's mom."

"I know. Me, too." For a split second, I forget why I called her before I remember. "But I'm actually calling because we have a problem."

"Oh, no! What's happening?"

"One of my patients has bed bugs," I groan. This isn't how I hoped to start my weekend.

"That's awful. I'm sure you wore the proper PPE, though, right?"

Needless to say, I surely would have worn personal protective equipment if I knew I needed it.

"So, here's the thing..." I pause, hating the news I have to break. "We only just discovered he has bed bugs this morning. I've been his nurse for the past three nights."

"Oh my gosh!" Her shriek causes me to instinctively pull the phone from my ear.

I would argue this news called for the use of a curse word, but that's just not Jillian's way.

"I need you to check our mattresses. Check around the seam at the foot of the bed," I instruct her.

"Oh my gosh! What am I looking for?"

"A lot of black spots. That's their feces."

"They *poop*?! On our *beds*?!" Somehow, her shrieking gets even higher.

Jill is the epitome of a neat freak. I knew she wasn't going to handle this well. There's silence coming from the other end of the phone which lasts about a minute. I can only assume this means Jill is still examining her bed.

When she breaks the silence, my stomach drops. "Oh no, Sam!"

My worst fears have become a reality. I know that if they're on Jill's mattress, they're most definitely on mine.

*We have bed bugs.*

"What do we do?" Jill asks.

"Tanya said we should call the office of our apartment complex. Maybe they can help us. She also said we have to throw away our mattresses. And probably our sofa, too."

"Our sofa? But we love that old sofa!"

"I guess we're finally getting that sectional," I joke.

"This isn't a joke, Sam," Jill chastises me.

"I'm sorry. I'm on my way now. I'll be home soon."

"Okay. I'll call the office. Or should I walk over there?" Her voice cracks as she speaks, and I can tell by the tone of her voice that she's panicking. In her emotional state, she shouldn't be walking anywhere. As someone who deals with anxiety on a daily basis, I know how panic feels. I don't want to cause her any further distress.

"I think calling is fine."

"I'm hanging up on you so I can call them right now."

"I don't think you're technically hanging up on someone if you warn them first," I laugh.

At that, she hangs up on me. Apparently, she didn't think my joke was very funny.

Luckily, our property manager informed us the first bed bug extermination is covered under our lease. If it happens again, though, we'll be responsible for the cost. Jill politely informed them that we don't plan on having bed bugs again anytime soon.

The property manager told us to immediately put all our clothing into garbage bags, then wash and dry each piece on high heat.

Consequently, Jill's and my Sunday morning has been filled with load upon load of laundry. For once, Ronnie wasn't staying at our apartment while she was in town. She decided to, understandably, stay at Craig's house this visit. Personally, I'm just glad she doesn't have to witness her favorite sofa being tossed in the dumpster.

The exterminator should be arriving in two hours to bomb our apartment—or at least that's what it sounded like he'd be doing. Apparently, the chemicals they use to exterminate bed bugs are so strong that Jill and I can't come back into our apartment for almost three days.

It looks like we will need to get a hotel room for the next three nights. I told Jill to look at it as an impromptu staycation; instead, she burst into tears.

We need to dispose of our mattresses and our old floral sofa before the exterminator gets here. Thankfully, there's a giant dumpster at our apartment complex that we can throw them into.

I'm certain Jill and I could get our mattresses down the stairs and into the dumpster no problem, but the sofa is a different ball game.

"We need to call in reinforcements," I decide, as Jill actively throws more clothes into a garbage bag.

"No, Sam. It's too embarrassing," she pleads.

"It's not our fault. Everyone knows how tidy you are, Jill."

"Who would you call?"

"Definitely not Craig or Ronnie."

"Of course not," she agrees. We both know that they would drop everything to come help us, but with Susan passing away this morning, we would never ask that of them.

"Tony's working overtime today, and I don't think Zach's landed yet," I say.

"We can just slide it down the stairs ourselves. It'll be fine," Jill tries reassuring me.

"I think Miles and Brett are both off today," I ponder aloud.

"No!" she shrieks.

"Why?" I snap, my impatience growing. I assume this has something to do with the crush she has on Brett which she still won't admit.

"I just don't want to bother them."

"They're our friends. We reserve the right to bother them," I tell her.

Jill covers her face with her hands, shaking her head as she sighs, "Fine."

I immediately grab my phone and call Miles. After I quickly update him on our disastrous morning, I plead for his and Brett's help. Without a moment's hesitation, Miles agrees to come over.

And although I didn't hear a verbal confirmation from Brett through the phone, I know he'll be here, too.

About twenty minutes later, Jill and I hear a knock at our front door. Miles and Brett slowly tiptoe into our apartment, their hesitation glaringly apparent. I can't say that I blame them.

If you've ever worked in the medical field, you know bed bugs are one of our deepest, darkest fears.

"I didn't know you guys were getting a pet. Or should I say pets?" Brett laughs.

"Shut up, Brett!" I hiss.

I snap my head toward Jill; now, she officially looks horrified. Sometimes Brett can be such an asshole.

"Alright, let's do this," Miles announces, rolling up his sleeves.

"Hold on," Jill cuts in. "I need to call the Marriott first and see if I can book our reservation."

"Why are you staying in a hotel?" Miles asks.

"We can't come back to the apartment for three days after they bomb it," I groan.

Brett surprises me by saying something very non-assholey. "You're not staying in a hotel. You guys can stay with us."

"We couldn't put you out like that," Jill insists.

"Really, it's no problem," Miles adds.

"Y'all aren't wearing any of those contaminated clothes into our place though," Brett chuckles.

"We can go to Walmart and buy a few new things," I offer.

"I hear they have super cute dresses there," Brett jokes, giving Miles a light elbow.

I think back to the night of my pinning and the dress Miles bought me after his atrocious ex-girlfriend threw her cranberry vodka all over me. I actually love that dress.

"There is one thing I *need* to bring," I stress. "Don't worry. Jill and I have washed and dried him on high heat, and he's now safely sealed in his own clean bag."

"He?" Miles and Brett ask in unison.

I scurry into our laundry closet and run back out, holding a plastic bag tied closed at the top. Inside the plastic bag is Teddy, Miles's stuffed bear that he loaned me after my breakup with Zach. I admit, at first, I thought it was a super strange gift; now, I find myself cuddling him almost every night. I couldn't leave him behind.

Brett looks utterly confused, staring at the worn stuffed animal in the plastic bag before him.

Miles softly chuckles. "Yeah, you can bring him."

# CHAPTER
# THIRTY-FOUR:

The four of us had just finished lugging the mattresses and sofa to the dumpster when the exterminator arrived.

As a paramedic and a firefighter, this wasn't Miles's and Brett's first rodeo with unwanted house guests. Brett even had a recent run-in with scabies. Honestly, if I was forced to make the awful decision, I think I'd choose bed bugs over scabies or lice.

The boys came prepared with a change of clothes and garbage bags to throw their possibly contaminated clothing into. See, Jill? They were definitely the right people to call.

As Miles and Brett changed clothes, Jill and I packed up our cars with the list of items we were allowed to bring with us. We awkwardly tried not to watch as the boys stripped down to their boxers in front of our apartment building. I practically had to lift Jill's jaw off the asphalt.

Now, Jill and I are in Walmart purchasing our wardrobes for the next three days. Since today is Sunday, luckily both Jill and I don't work again until Thursday. That's what happens when you're still new in your profession. You almost always get stuck working weekends.

Since I didn't have to work and had no plans for the next few days, I'd only be buying comfortable clothing. Craig's mom, Susan, didn't want to have a funeral which meant Jill and I didn't have to buy any formal clothing for our three-day staycation.

"Jill, why are you buying a bunch of fancy shit?" I ask.

"A dress and a pair of slacks is not fancy."

I look down at the two pairs of sweatpants, three t-shirts, one oversized sweater, and the pair of matching Superman pajamas currently cradled in my arms. I was so excited to find this pajama set in my size. One of the perks of being short, I can still fit into clothes from the children's section. I'm putting these pajamas on as soon as we get back to the guys' apartment. I haven't slept in nearly twenty-four hours. I'm allowed to put on my pajamas at 2:00 PM.

"Whatever you say," I laugh.

"Fine," she sighs. "I'll go find a sweatsuit, too."

"I'll find some mattress protectors, and I'll meet you at the register."

Jill nods at me in agreement then trudges off towards the junior's department. Sadly, unlike myself, Jill is just too tall to shop in the boy's department.

After some online research, I decided the courteous thing to do was to purchase mattress protectors for both Miles and Brett. Despite all of our precautions, we couldn't guarantee a little demon bug didn't hitch a ride with us to their apartment. This would ensure their mattresses were protected.

After all is said and done, Jill and I will also be purchasing mattress protectors for the new mattresses we have yet to buy. It's starting to make sense to me why hotels always have them on their beds.

You live and you learn, I guess.

When I reach the registers, Jill has already made her purchases, but she waits with me until I've checked out.

"I guess we'll just change in the bathroom?" I ask.

"Ew!" Jill suddenly looks as if she's smelled something rancid. I can't lie, I find it mildly amusing that she thinks changing in a Walmart bathroom is the most disgusting part of this whole ordeal.

"Unless you want to change in the parking lot?"

"Fine, we can use the bathroom," she begrudgingly agrees.

Once I'm finished checking out, Jill and I head to the bathroom. We enter parallel stalls and change into the clothes we just purchased. The bathroom is indeed disgusting—I don't think I've ever seen a big-box store bathroom that wasn't. Thankfully, we both wore clothing here that we didn't mind tossing after we changed. We technically could have bagged up the clothes we changed out of to wash later, but quite frankly we're both fed up with laundry.

"I never thought I'd be buck naked in a Walmart bathroom," I chuckle.

"My life is spiraling out of control," Jill moans. I can't help but laugh harder. I may be delirious from lack of sleep.

"Are you ready?" she asks.

I turn the lock on the stall door and exit my makeshift dressing room. Taking one look at each other, we both burst into laughter. Somehow, Jill and I chose—and are now wearing—the same exact oversized sweater and sweatpants.

You can't make this shit up.

The only difference? Jill is built like a supermodel. She looks much better in the ensemble; she can make anything look good. Looking in the mirror, I realize in comparison, I more closely resemble a troll in our matching outfits.

In my defense, I'm a very comfortable-looking troll.

"I'll change," Jill giggles.

"Absolutely not!" I nudge the bathroom door with my shoulder, then prop it open with my foot as I usher for her to exit. "We're rocking it."

Even though Jill and I drove our own cars, Miles and Brett insisted on waiting for us in the Walmart parking lot. As Jill and I exit the Walmart, we head towards where our three vehicles are parked side-by-side. When we approach, we find Miles and Brett sitting in the bed of Miles's pickup truck sharing a twenty-piece order of chicken nuggets. Suddenly, I'm aware of how hungry I am.

"We bought you and Jill some food." Miles tosses a McDonald's bag to me.

Immediately, I dive into the bag. "Thanks. I'm starving."

"I figured as much."

He's such a great friend.

Actually, he and Brett both are.

"Wait. Are you nerds actually matching?" Brett chuckles.

Jill instantly blushes at Brett's remark.

"Shut up, Brett!" I hiss, shoving a chicken nugget in my mouth. I turn to Jill, "Ignore him."

"He's just jealous—he could never pull off that sweater," Miles adds. "Gray totally washes him out."

The four of us break out in laughter.

Even on days that seem pretty crappy, you can always find something to laugh about. Having great friends helps, too.

Once we get back to Miles and Brett's apartment, I waste no time changing into my new Superman pajamas.

Scout, Miles's black lab, is almost as excited to see me as I am to see him. I love that dog. Being around him so much lately has convinced me I want to adopt a dog of my own. I'm still trying to convince Jill of this plan, but I think three days around Scout will definitely win her over.

After changing into my pajamas, I step out of the bathroom and join Jill, Miles, and Brett on the couch.

"Do y'all want to watch a movie?" Brett asks.

What I really want is to take a nap. By this time, it has officially been over twenty-four hours since my head has touched a pillow. The problem is, I'm not sure where Jill and I will be sleeping. If it's on the couch, I currently have three people sitting on my bed.

"Um...I would actually love to take a nap," I say.

"Oh shit!" Miles blurts out, startling me. "You haven't slept yet, have you?"

"No. Not since my shift ended."

"Miles, you wanna sleep in my room? Give the girls your bed for the next few days?" Brett proposes. He points his thumb at Miles. "His room's cleaner."

"Yeah, of course," Miles agrees. "Let me just put some clean sheets on the bed."

Jill chimes in, "You guys don't have to do all this!"

"Yeah. I'm fine with a blanket on the floor," I add.

"No," Brett says definitively. "Our moms raised us right. You're not sleeping on the floor."

I try to imagine Brett and Miles as children. I know they grew up together and have been friends since they were in grade school, but it's hard to picture them as kids. I wonder if their mothers were friends, too. This thought makes me suddenly realize Brett has never talked about his family. I wonder if he has any siblings, where his parents are.

"Thank you, both," I respond.

I don't know if they'll ever truly know how much today meant to Jill and me.

Miles finishes prepping his bedroom for our stay rather quickly. I don't know many single men who have a spare set of sheets, let alone a *clean* spare set of sheets. I'm officially impressed.

"Alright, the room's all yours," Miles announces. "I already put yours and Jill's bags in my room. Hope that's okay."

"You're a sweetheart," Jill beams. Miles immediately turns beet red from Jill's compliment.

"Ass-kisser!" Brett shouts, hurling a couch pillow at Miles.

"Sam, is it okay if I nap with you?" Jill asks. "This day has worn me out."

Jillian Moore? *Napping*? Jill never naps. This day really must've kicked her ass. "Of course!"

Jill and I shuffle into Miles's room, both of us overcome by exhaustion. Glancing around Miles's room, I realize I've never actually been inside his bedroom before. I've been in this apartment plenty of times but never really had a reason to go into his or Brett's bedroom.

I take note of the neatly made bed in the center of the room. Teddy is thoughtfully sitting propped up at the head of the bed. Miles obviously must've freed him from his plastic bag prison.

"Aw, he even made the bed!" Jill gushes.

Snatching Teddy off the bed, I give him a brief squeeze. I've grown to love this tattered little bear. I hope Miles doesn't want him back just yet.

The familiar ring of my cellphone catches my attention, and I quickly rifle through my purse to answer it. On the screen, I see Zach's name along with a picture of the two of us from when we were dating. I haven't had the heart to change his caller ID photo yet.

"Hello," I answer.

"Who is it?" Jill mouths at me.

"Zach," I mouth back.

"Hey, Sam," Zach's voice chimes through the speaker.

Jill climbs into bed. "Tell Zach I said hello."

"Jill says hi," I pass on. "How was your flight?"

I'm sure by now he's heard that Craig's mom passed away this morning; if not, I don't think I should be the one to tell him.

"Tell Jill I said hello. And our flight was pretty smooth," he replies.

One word catches my attention, so I decide to put Zach on speakerphone. Jill looks at me confused as I burrow into bed next to her. I gently prop Teddy up against the pillow between us. I have a sinking feeling this is a conversation we're *all* going to need to hear.

"Our?" I ask.

"That's why I'm calling. I know I should have said something to you before, but everything happened so fast..."

I'm silent. Jill is silent. Teddy is *extremely* silent.

Zach continues, "I knew you were working last night and didn't want to call you while you were sleeping today..."

Little does he know; I haven't slept at all today.

Just spit it out, Zach.

"...I've kind of been dating someone. Only for about a month or so," he says. "She asked if she could fly back to Bristol with me. I was really upset about everything happening with Susan and she didn't want me to have to travel alone."

Great. So, I'm about to meet my ex-boyfriend's new girlfriend.

*Today sucks.*

"I'm sorry, Sam. I didn't want you to find out like this."

"Jerk," Jill whispers. Or was it Teddy? I'm not sure—they both look pretty upset.

Well, I'm definitely changing his caller ID picture now.

"It's okay," I mouth to my best friend. She scoots closer to me, lovingly wrapping her arms around me.

"It's okay," I repeat, this time to Zach. I sigh to myself before continuing, "I'm excited to meet her. If she makes you happy, then I'm happy."

As I speak these words, I'm acutely aware I've heard them before. Miles may not have said the exact same thing to me that I just uttered to Zach, but it was pretty damn close.

"Thank you." He lets out an audible breath, and I can tell he's relieved I didn't rip his head off.

I won't lie and say it doesn't hurt that Zach has already moved on—it does. But I also didn't lie when I said I was happy for him. I would be an awful friend if I wasn't.

Besides, I think deep down I've always known Zach wasn't my person, even though at times it sure did feel like it. Maybe now Zach actually has found his person.

*One day, I hope I find mine.*

After Zach's revelation, the remainder of our conversation is pretty brief. Once we say our goodbyes, I hang up the phone.

"Are you sure you're okay?" Jill asks.

"I'm okay this time. I promise," I assure her.

"In other news," she says, completely changing the subject, "Miles has a framed picture of the two of you on his nightstand." She holds up a photograph in a wooden frame.

It's the picture I gave Miles the Christmas before last, along with the French press and bag of hazelnut coffee. The photo of the two of us at our favorite coffee shop.

I take the picture from Jill's hands, examining it. It's been months since we've been to this coffee shop. Now that Scout's in the picture, we'd rather have coffee here at the apartment.

Speaking of Scout, I think I could use some Labrador cuddles right about now.

"It's just the picture I gave him for Christmas," I tell her. "I wonder if Miles will let me steal Scout for a bit."

"It's interesting that he decided to put it by his bed."

"What do you mean?" I ask.

"You can't tell me you don't see it, Sam."

What is she talking about?

"See what?" I look at her, my confusion apparent.

"Miles totally has feelings for you! I mean he tells you he loves you for goodness sake!"

My mouth falls to the floor in utter disbelief. Has Jill lost her mind?

"All of our friends tell one another they love them," I explain.

"Not in the way Miles says it to you," she retorts. "Honestly, Sam? I think he's in love with you."

"I think the bed bugs have invaded your brain, Jill," I joke, giving her a nervous laugh. "He is one hundred percent not in love with me."

Worried I may have missed the signs, I think back to when Miles and I first met and how he fervently insisted he wasn't asking me out on a date.

No. Point blank, Miles thought of me as nothing more than a friend.

Jill rolls her eyes at me then proceeds to toss Teddy at my head.

"Hey! Don't throw him," I scold.

"I apologize. I will never throw your future husband's teddy bear ever again," she snickers.

"Well then, Brett's *your* future husband," I mock her, sticking my tongue out at her. Two can play this game.

"You, shush!" she snaps.

I start singing loudly, "Jill and Brett, sitting in a tree..."

In an attempt to shut me up, Jill tackles me, and we both start giggling like we're thirteen-year-old girls. It takes me back to Jill's and my preteen years when we had countless sleepovers at one another's houses.

Now, here we are at twenty-three years old, cuddled in bed together, gossiping about boys. The only difference being that now, we know what responsibility is. We both have professions where people's lives are in our hands.

Our laughter is silenced by a light tapping at the bedroom door. Hopefully, Miles and Brett haven't been listening in on our conversation. That would make the next three days extremely awkward.

"Come in," Jill squeaks. I can tell she's thinking the same thing I am.

The bedroom door opens, and a blur of black fur comes barreling into the room. Scout hurls his big body onto the bed where he promptly lays on my lap. My heart swells as I wrap him in my arms.

"Hi, Scout," I say.

Miles peeks his head around the corner. "He was whining to come in."

"He can stay," Jill insists. Scout's winning her over already, I see. "But you have to go," she giggles, pointing at Miles.

"I don't think I'd fit anyway," Miles chuckles, watching as Scout's large body lays curled up on my lap. "Let us know if you need anything."

After Miles softly shuts the bedroom door, Jill, Scout, and I maneuver ourselves in bed until we're all comfortable. I grab the television remote, click the "on" button and randomly choose a channel for background noise. Although I prefer to sleep in silence, I know Jill finds the silence unnerving.

"Sam?" Jill whispers.

"Yes?"

"Can we watch *Ghost Adventures*?"

"Jill, you always have nightmares when you watch that stuff," I remind her.

"I have you and Scout to protect me. I won't be afraid this time," she claims.

I smile at her, then surrender the remote. She greedily grabs it from my hand and begins flipping through the channels. Jill is probably the only person I know who loves scary things just as much as she's terrified of them.

"I'll always protect you, Jill," I respond, putting my arm around my friend.

I'll protect her from ghosts. I'll protect her from bed bugs. I'll protect her always.

# CHAPTER

# THIRTY-FIVE

## (October 2014):

W ork has been oddly slow tonight—I don't dare allow myself to think the "q-word."

After tonight's shift, I'll be off for four full days. Having three consecutive twelve-hour shifts is beyond brutal but having four days off every week is hard to give up. I guess everything comes with a cost.

Tomorrow morning, Miles and I are having coffee together at our favorite coffee shop once I get off of work. We decided to treat ourselves and go out for coffee in honor of his birthday this week.

I won't lie. Miles has gotten pretty skilled with his French press and milk frother, but nothing compares to drinking a fresh cup of steaming hot coffee in the middle of a bustling coffee house. Plus, Brett's off work tomorrow, so Scout will have company.

My phone begins vibrating in my scrubs pocket. I pull out my phone and glance down at the screen.

A text from Ronnie.

***Are we out of milk?***

I quickly send her a response.

**We have almond milk.**

She instantly texts back.

***Gross!***

I can't help but chuckle. Personally, I think almond milk is pretty delicious.

As for why Ronnie's texting me about our groceries? She's currently living with Jill and me once again. Don't get me wrong, Jill and I are happy she's back in Bristol, but we wish it was under better circumstances.

Apparently, Veronica had been stretching the truth a tad when she would repeatedly tell us she was doing well in her social work program. It turns out in reality she had been failing multiple classes.

After what happened the semester before she moved to Nashville, when she failed her Sociology course because she slept through her final exam, she had been too embarrassed to tell us the truth. With her love of partying, Nashville's Lower Broadway had been too much of a temptation. She spent the majority of her nights barhopping when she should have been studying.

Subsequently, she was kicked out of her social work program last semester for her poor grades.

When Ronnie moved back to Bristol, Craig convinced her to reapply to work at The Cinedome. Craig took on Zach's old position when he moved to San Diego, so he was now the swing shift supervisor. Ronnie begrudgingly agreed and was immediately hired back as a snack bar attendant. On multiple occasions, she's divulged that she's ashamed to be working back at The Cinedome. I know she feels like a failure, but she's not. I'm constantly reassuring her this is just a speed bump on her road to success. If anyone can pick themselves up and start over again, it's Veronica Mae Sanders.

Although Ronnie may be having a rough time right now, things are finally starting to look up for Tony.

Earlier today, I found out Tony was finally accepted into the Bristol County Fire Academy. I couldn't be any prouder of my friend. According to him, the fire academy takes place Mondays through Thursdays and is four months long. He'll have to switch around his work schedule so he can continue as a paramedic on his days off from the academy. Sadly, though, this means he'll no longer be Miles's partner at work. We also won't see very much of him over the next four months. But you have to make sacrifices to make your dreams come true, and Tony is so close to finally living his dream. I can just feel it.

Pouring myself my third cup of coffee of the night, I hear a patient's call light ring. Earlier, I had told Lucie to call for me if she needed help with the bed bath she was administering. The patient in room 541 is probably triple Lucie's weight and I don't want her injuring herself by trying to reposition him on her own. I made that mistake a few months ago and have been seeing a chiropractor regularly ever since.

For the sake of my back, I've learned to ask for help at work when I need it. Tanya constantly reminds me I only get one back, so I better take care of it.

Before heading off to help Lucie, I quickly send a response to Ronnie.

**Beggars can't be choosers.**

If she wants regular milk, she can buy groceries for once.

After I hit send, I slip my cellphone back into my scrubs pocket. Then, setting my cup of coffee down in the break room, I start towards room 541 to assist Lucie.

Tanya, Lucie, and I sit together behind the nurses' station as we wait for the day-shift to arrive. We only have twenty minutes left until shift change, but time feels like it's dragging. This night has gone by so slowly. Tanya helps time pass a bit quicker by showing us pictures of the house she recently put an offer on. I'm crossing my fingers for her that it gets accepted. This house would be perfect for her and her kids.

"I think I want to go to nursing school," Lucie suddenly blurts out. Tanya and I both pull our vision away from the computer screen to gaze back at her.

"You should do it," Tanya encourages as she swivels her chair around to completely face Lucie, a huge grin spreading across her face.

"You'd be a great nurse, Luce." I give her an effortless smile as I follow Tanya's lead and turn my chair around. Lucie now has our undivided attention.

"Do you really think so?" she asks. Lucie's gaze momentarily drifts down to her hands resting in her lap.

"I most definitely think so." She slowly looks up. Her eyes find mine as she shyly starts to smile.

"My mom was a hospice nurse for like ten years before she started working in oncology," Lucie informs us.

"No way!" Tanya exclaims. "It's in your blood, girl!"

Lucie's smile grows wider as she looks toward Tanya. "I just finished all my pre-requisite courses," she discloses. "I think I'm going to start my application for the nursing program tomorrow."

"That's amazing, Lucie!" I lovingly throw my arm over her shoulder.

"Now, you definitely don't have time for any silly boyfriends," Tanya laughs as she gives her a playful nudge.

Lucie has made it clear to us that she has no interest in dating right now. I can't say that I blame her. I haven't been on a single date since I ended my relationship with Zach. Nor do I care to go on one. Not like anyone is asking me out anyways. Meanwhile, Zach has been dating his girlfriend Sarah for nearly eight months now.

"There's something else I wanted to talk to you both about." As she speaks, for some reason, Lucie appears extremely nervous. The silence grows as she tries mustering up the courage to go on, growing increasingly uncomfortable. She starts awkwardly shifting positions in her seat, and I notice her hands slightly shaking in her lap now.

I try reassuring her. "It's just us, Luce." I place my arm back around her and give her shoulder a light squeeze.

"You can tell us anything," Tanya adds.

"I don't want you guys to think I'm weird," she whispers, refusing to look up at us.

"Lucie, I work with Sam. No one comes close to her level of weird," Tanya chuckles, pointing at me. Lucie looks up from her trembling hands and gives Tanya a timid smile.

"Hey!" I feign offense before immediately joining Tanya in laughter. Before long, Lucie is softly chuckling as well.

When our giggles fade, Lucie continues. "Since I was about eleven years old, I knew there was just something...different about me. I never felt the same way about boys as all my friends did. I never had crushes."

At these words, Tanya and I both can tell Lucie's about to open up about something serious.

She goes on, "I always felt kind of broken." She once again looks down to her hands.

"You're not broken!" I chime in, feeling the need to defend her.

"I'm not done yet," she replies softly, a small smile spreading across her face. "I used to think I was broken—but not anymore."

A single tear falls down her cheek which she quickly wipes away with the back of her hand. "I recently came across something online that made a lot of sense to me. I discovered there's a name for the way I've always felt. That I'm not the only one who thinks this way. Who *feels* this way." She hesitates momentarily, then announces, "I'm asexual."

Tanya briefly glances over to me, giving me a look of confusion, before directing her gaze back to Lucie. "What's asexual?" she asks genuinely.

If I'm being honest, I'm not quite sure what it means to be asexual either. If that means Lucie's gay, then she should've known she had no reason to be nervous to tell me. One of my best friends is gay. I would never judge her or treat her differently; I love her unconditionally.

"Asexual people don't experience sexual attraction. I've never felt any form of sexual attraction to someone," Lucie explains. "One day, I'd like to have a romantic relationship. I'm just not interested in a sexual relationship with anyone."

I decide not to beat around the bush. I'll just ask Lucie the question that keeps bouncing around in my head.

"Does being asexual also mean you're gay?" I hope that question didn't somehow offend her.

"No, not necessarily," she responds sweetly. "You can be both asexual and gay, but I'm not gay."

I'm relieved she doesn't seem even remotely taken aback by my question.

"I'm proud of you," Tanya tells her. "It takes a lot of courage to be true to yourself. Promise me you'll continue being unapologetically you, Lucie."

Tanya always knows the right thing to say.

"I promise," Lucie gulps, tears welling in her eyes.

I stand and instinctively take a few steps, stopping in front of Lucie. "I'm proud of you, too."

Lucie stands with me and, suddenly, we're wrapped in each other's arms. Tanya walks over and joins our hug, wrapping her arms around the both of us.

Lucie might be a couple of years younger than me, but I truly look up to her.

I didn't think it was possible to love Lucie, my newest friend, any more than I already do. Until today, that is.

# CHAPTER THIRTY-SIX:

I arrive at the coffee shop before Miles. Since I know what he likes, I order for both of us. While our coffees are being made, I find us a table in the middle of the cafe.

I forgot how much I love being in an actual coffee shop. This would be perfect, if only we could bring our big, goofy black lab.

I mean, Miles's big, goofy black lab.

"Sam, right?"

Quickly looking up from my cellphone, I see Dr. Connors (a.k.a. Dr. Jackass) standing before me, holding a large cup of coffee. It takes me a second to recognize him in street clothes, as opposed to his normal white coat.

Meanwhile, I'm still wearing my scrubs from my shift last night. It makes sense why he recognized me. "Good morning, Dr. Connors."

"Call me Richard," he requests.

"Hmm...Dr. Richard," I ponder aloud.

He chuckles before taking a seat at my table, in the chair across from me. "Just Richard is fine."

He does not look like a Richard. Whatsoever.

"How are you?" he politely asks me.

It feels awkward making small talk with Dr. Jackass at my favorite coffee shop, but I'll go with it. "I'm doing quite well. How are you?"

*Doing quite well?* What kind of a response was that?

"I can't complain. I'm currently drinking a great cup of coffee and I have a beautiful view," he says.

Holy shit! Is Dr. Jackass flirting with me?

"Yeah, the coffee's really good here." I can feel the heat of embarrassment overtaking my cheeks

"Are you waiting for your boyfriend?" Dr. Connors asks as the barista places two cups of coffee on the table before us.

"Just my friend. I don't have a boyfriend."

He smiles and nods his understanding. He does have a really nice smile, and eyes—beautiful green eyes. I still think hazel eyes are my favorite, but his are a close second.

I hear the chime of the bell above the coffee shop door, then I notice Dr. Connors's vision briefly focus on something behind me.

His eyes once again meet mine. "Have dinner with me tomorrow night." It comes across as more of a command than an offer.

My mouth falls open as I stare at Dr. Connors. I am completely taken aback by his proposition.

Do I really want to go to dinner with Dr. Jackass? Oh, Hell. Why not?

I manage to squeak out a simple "okay," not knowing what else to say. I wonder if he notices my sudden nervousness.

Dr. Connors then hands me his cellphone. Looking at him in utter confusion, I timidly take the phone from his hand.

"Put your number in my contacts," he instructs, giving me another handsome smile.

My nervous fingers begin to fumble as I type my number into his contacts. Why am I so nervous?

Oh, yeah. Maybe because I haven't been on a date in over a year.

"Am I interrupting something?"

I look up from the phone still in my hand. Miles is hovering over where Dr. Connors currently sits.

After years of friendship, I know Miles. And right now? I know he's pissed off.

"You must be the *friend*," Dr. Connors says with a smirk. It's not lost on me how he emphasizes the word "friend."

He stands from the chair he was in, then ushers for Miles to sit. Miles doesn't obey, continuing to stand, towering over Dr. Connors.

If I had to guess, I'd say Dr. Connors is probably about 5'10" which is by no means short but standing next to Miles can make anyone look short.

"I believe we've met," he observes, staring back at Miles.

"We have," Miles scowls.

I know Dr. Connors was sitting in Miles's seat, but I don't think that necessitates his current behavior. In short: Miles is being a total asshole.

"I'll call you later about our plans for tomorrow night, Sam," Dr. Connors announces. He gives Miles another smirk, before turning to give me one more handsome smile.

I awkwardly wave goodbye to him, then watch as he exits the coffee shop.

"Do you just want me to leave?" Miles sneers.

Is he being serious?

I sigh—I'm too tired to deal with a grown man throwing a temper tantrum. "Miles, what are you talking about?"

Still standing, he crosses his arms in front of his chest and pouts. "Just seems like I'm not wanted here."

"Sit your ass down. Your coffee's getting cold."

Miles shrugs, continuing to sulk, but he heeds my request and sits. I can't help but think how adorable he is when he's pouting like a giant child.

"Miles, you know I love you."

"I love you, too," he mumbles, still grumpy.

"And—I have a birthday present for you!" I cheer, throwing my arms into the air.

He can't help but chuckle, finally giving me one of his infamous sideways smirks. The small scar above his upper lip is barely notice-able to me now. It's just part of what makes him who he is.

But I'll always be blown away by the color of his eyes. The truest hazel eyes I've ever seen.

Miles holds his arms out like an excited kid, waiting to receive his gift.

"I love presents," he grins.

"I know you do."

"So, are you still mad at me?" I hold his gift hostage in my arms until he gives me the answer I'm looking for. He doesn't get his present until he stops acting like a brat.

"I just don't like that guy," he reveals. "He seems like a dick."

I can't help but laugh. Miles looks at me confused, waiting for me to explain my sudden outburst.

"I just found out his first name is Richard!"

"I call 'em like I see 'em," Miles chuckles.

"Okay, you can open your present now." I hand the small gift bag to him, and I can see the excitement in his eyes as he slowly removes the tissue paper from the bag, piece by piece. He pulls out his gift from inside the bag and closely examines it.

"I love it," he announces with a big grin. "You always give the best gifts."

He proudly holds up the custom coffee mug with a silhouette of a Labrador on it and the words "Dog Dad." Jill helped me make it with her Cricut.

Somehow, all the gifts I give Miles end up being coffee-themed. I guess it's kind of our thing.

"Are you really going out with him?" Miles asks suddenly.

"I think I am."

Honestly, what do I have to lose?

"If he hurts you, I'll kick his ass."

I can't help but chuckle at Miles's comment. "Since when are you the violent type?"

The only time I've ever seen Miles engaged in violence was when Craig pummeled him that night at The Cinedome, which some could argue was strictly in self-defense.

"I'll be whatever type of person you need, Sam," Miles answers.

His words catch me off-guard, and I look up from my cup of coffee to meet his hazel eyes.

I don't need Miles to be anything besides himself.

Exactly who he is—that's the person I'll always need.

# CHAPTER
# THIRTY-SEVEN:

I've been feeling anxious about my upcoming date with Dr. Connors—I mean Richard—all day. I hate every article of clothing I own, and my hair is refusing to do anything except look extremely frizzy. Lucky for me, I live with two of my best friends.

Ronnie forced me to borrow her favorite little black dress. I think it's a bit snug on me, but she insisted I look stunning in it. She and I also happen to be the same shoe size, so she convinced me to wear her sparkly, silver stilettos along with it. Since tonight felt like a special occasion, I ditched my signature black cat-eye glasses for the night and popped in my contacts. I miss my glasses already.

I tried curling my hair earlier, but Jill had to redo it for me. I guess I did a piss poor job at styling it myself. Meanwhile, Ronnie applied my makeup. I asked her to go light on the makeup since I rarely ever wear it. But alas, you don't tell Ronnie what to do; she does what she thinks is best. So, I ended up with a dark smokey-eye, fake eyelashes, and deep red lipstick.

Now, I'm sitting in my Blazer outside of the Italian restaurant Dr. Con—uh, Richard—chose. I pull down my visor to examine myself in the small mirror. I don't even recognize the girl staring back at me.

Although I'm a bit uncomfortable with how heavy my makeup is, I must admit, Ronnie did an excellent job. She could do this professionally.

*Alright, Sam. Stop stalling. Just go inside the restaurant already.*

I turn the key, removing it from the ignition. After one last look in the visor mirror, I open my door and step out of the car. Please, don't let me fall in these shoes. If I'm constantly falling in nursing clogs, in these, I'm bound to end up on the floor tonight.

Entering the restaurant, I'm taken aback by how busy it is for a Monday night. I nervously glance around the restaurant looking for Richard, but I don't see him anywhere.

What if he stood me up? How embarrassing would that be?

"May I help you, ma'am?"

Carefully, I turn around so as not to fall, and I see the hostess staring at me from behind her podium.

"I'm meeting someone, but I'm...uh...not sure if he's here."

"What's his name?" she asks politely.

"Doctor...uh...I mean, Richard Connors." I sound like a damn fool. Suddenly, I'm feeling quite anxious; I have the urge to dart out of this restaurant and never look back.

What if he's not here?

"Oh, yes. Please follow me." The hostess turns from her station and starts toward the dining area.

I breathe a sigh of relief. At least he didn't stand me up.

As we're walking, the hostess points to my feet. "I love your shoes."

"Thanks, they're my roommates." They're also probably going to cause me to fracture my ankle tonight.

I follow the hostess towards the back of the restaurant. We turn a corner, and I instantly spot Richard sitting at a table, his back facing me. I tell the hostess, "I see him. Thank you." She nods at me, before turning back towards the front door.

After taking a deep breath, I approach the table where Richard sits. "Sorry I'm late." Only by five minutes, but late is late.

Richard quickly looks up from his cellphone. I can feel his eyes travel over me, and I notice them widen as he takes in my tight dress and six-inch heels. "You look stunning."

He stands to greet me, then gives me a quick kiss on the cheek, lightly placing both his hands on my shoulders. My stomach does cartwheels at his touch.

He pulls my chair out for me, motioning for me to sit. Maybe he's not such a jackass after all.

I timidly take a seat, trying to prevent my dress from riding up my thighs. I'm not accustomed to wearing something this short—or this tight.

"You have really beautiful eyes," he says as he takes his seat once more.

"Thank you." I know I'm blushing, but I can't help it. I'm terrible at receiving compliments.

"Have you been here before, Sam?"

"No." I briefly look around the restaurant, taking in my surroundings. "This place seems pretty fancy."

He smiles at me. "How about I order for both of us since I'm familiar with the menu?"

"But you don't know what I like." How would he order for me if he doesn't know me?

"How about I order a few different things, and we can find out what's your favorite?" he smirks. "Are you allergic to anything?"

Leave it to a doctor to ask about my allergies.

"Just Augmentin," I grin.

"Okay," he chuckles. "I'll try not to order you any antibiotics."

To my surprise, I'm actually really enjoying myself. We're about an hour into our date, and my anxiety has passed. It feels pretty comfortable carrying on a conversation with Richard. On a first date, you always fear there will be an excess number of awkward silences, but so far that hasn't been an issue. The conversation between Richard and me has flowed easily and continuously thus far.

I wanted to be a brat and tell him I didn't like any of the food he insisted on ordering for me, but I truly loved it all. If I had to choose a favorite though, it would hands-down be the eggplant parmesan.

Not only did Richard insist on choosing what I ate tonight, but he also chose what I had to drink. His pick was a bottle of red wine that I'm pretty sure costs more than what Jill and I spend on groceries in a month. I consider myself a lover of red wine, but if I'm being honest, I have no clue what type of wine I'm currently drinking. Not wanting him to think I'm some sort of uncultured swine, I didn't ask. All I do know? This shit's delicious.

Taking a long sip of the delicious shit in my glass, I listen to Richard tell a story from his med school days. From only one date, it's already apparent he and I had drastically different upbringings.

The man told me he got a brand-new Mercedes Benz for his sixteenth birthday. That was six cars ago. Now, he drives a Tesla.

Meanwhile, I'm still driving my first car, and I assure you it was nowhere near brand new when I purchased it. It also isn't a Mercedes.

"I almost forgot...the ICU has a current opening for an RN," he says, randomly changing the topic after he finishes telling me about his father who is, of course, a doctor as well.

"Oh, did they find anyone for the position?" I'm not exactly sure why he's telling me this. Maybe he's wondering if I know any nurses who would be interested.

"Not yet," he replies. "You should apply. I'm sure Margo would give you a good recommendation. She seems fond of you."

"But—I already have a job."

Richard takes a long sip of his wine before setting his glass back on the table. "Aren't you ready to be a real nurse?" he questions, studying me.

My jaw hits the floor, as I stare at him dumbfounded. A real nurse? What the hell is that supposed to mean?

"Last time I checked, I *was* a real nurse," I say sarcastically, showing my irritation. I exaggeratedly pinch my own arm. "Yup, still real!"

"Don't get offended, Sam. You know what I mean." He reaches across the table in an attempt to hold my hand.

"Actually, I *don't* know what you mean, Richard!" I put my glass of wine down, looking him square in the face. "Please, elaborate."

He slowly retracts his arm as he becomes aware that there's no way in hell I'm going to let him touch me now. "You're a smart girl, Sam. I just think you should work in a department where your skills are more utilized," he discloses. "Don't you want to save people? Isn't that why you went to nursing school?"

By this point, I'm fuming. I can feel my hands shaking. Reaching for my wine glass, I quickly chug the remainder in an attempt to calm my nerves. Then, I reach across the table, grab Richard's glass out of his hand, and chug the rest of his wine, too. Fuck him.

He looks at me stunned.

"For your information, Dr. Jackass, I *am* a real nurse. I care for *real* people and use my *real* nursing skills every day I step through those hospital doors." He has pushed me past the point of caring. It's about time I gave this man a piece of my mind. I take a deep breath before continuing my rant. "I may not be saving people, but I'm sure as hell helping them. Not like it's any of your business, but that's why I went to nursing school—because I wanted to help people. To help the people *you* couldn't save."

Richard stares at me in silence, very apparently at a loss for words.

Shuffling through my purse, I search for my wallet. Once I pull it out, I throw three twenty-dollar bills onto the table as I stand from my seat. I'm sure my meal and wine cost more than this, but it's all the cash I have on me.

"I'm not going to let you pay, Sam," Richard says as he stands, attempting to keep me from bolting out of the restaurant.

"Here's the thing, Richard," I snap. "You don't get to 'not let me' do anything. You don't get to just order my food for me, and you sure as hell don't get to tell me what kind of wine I want to drink."

"I'm sorry," he mutters. "I didn't realize my ordering for you would make you so upset. A lot of girls like that."

"I'm not a lot of girls." Technically, I'm not upset he ordered for me. It was annoying, yeah, but it wasn't what sparked my rage. What I'm actually upset about is the fact that he just belittled my entire nursing career on our first—and final—date. But I'm not going to waste my breath trying to explain that to him.

I look down at our table noticing the half-full bottle of wine. I'd be lying if I said that this wine wasn't downright delicious. I swipe the bottle of ridiculously expensive wine from the table, then stare into Richard's shocked green eyes.

"This is for my pain and suffering," I claim, before stomping off towards the exit. I don't even bother looking back at Richard.

I just pray I never have to work with that man again.

Now, *that* would be awkward.

Once I climb into my car (that isn't a Tesla), I take a long sip from my pilfered bottle of wine. The liquid warmth rolls down my throat, feeling like a familiar friend. Pulling my cellphone from my purse, I scroll through my contacts until I find her name. She answers on the second ring.

"Hey, honey." Margo's motherly voice sounds from the other end of the line.

"I did a bad thing," I whisper.

"What did you do, Sam?"

"I went on a date with Dr. Connors."

She immediately interrogates me: "Why is that bad? Did you two sleep together? Did you use protection?"

"I didn't sleep with him," I tell her. "But I definitely called him Dr. Jackass, ripped him a new one, stole the bottle of wine off our table which he bought, and ran away."

Margo's laughter comes booming through the other end of the phone. "Now why on earth would you do all of that?"

"He told me I wasn't a real nurse because I work on the hospice floor."

"Fuck him!" Margo exclaims. "I'll have a word with him tomorrow morning."

I laugh. "That's not necessary. I think I handled it, Mama Margo." If Margo heard me chew out Richard, I think she would've been proud.

"The work you do makes a difference, Sam. Don't let anyone make you think otherwise."

"Thank you," I reply softly. "I needed that."

"You shouldn't be drinking and driving though, Samantha," she scolds.

"I'm just drinking *inside* of my car. I'm not currently driving it."

"That isn't funny. Where are you?"

"I won't drive. I'm going to call Miles to pick me up."

"Promise me, Samantha." I hate how she always uses my full name when she's irritated with me.

"I promise, Margo."

After we hang up, I call Miles. He told me he didn't have any plans tonight, so I could call him if I needed him. Hopefully, he meant that.

He answers on the first ring. "Are you okay?"

"Well, hello to you, too," I giggle.

"What happened?"

"I'm fine. I think I'm too tipsy to drive, though."

"Are you at his house?"

"Ew, no!" I shriek. I would never go home with that asshole. "I'm outside the restaurant."

"That asshole just LEFT you there? Drunk?!" Miles booms.

"I walked out on our dinner. He pissed me off. I'll tell you more when I see you." I shouldn't assume he'll just drop whatever it is he's doing to come and pick me up...but I know he will.

"I'll be there soon. Stay in your car. And lock the doors," he instructs before hanging up.

That's fine by me. I'll happily stay in my car, finishing off this expensive bottle of wine.

I don't need to tell Miles where I'm at; he insisted on knowing what restaurant we were going to tonight. He said it was for my safety. So did Jill and Ronnie.

I can't wait to tell the girls about my catastrophic date. Then we can all talk shit about Dr. Connors together.

*In other news, I'm officially going to be single forever.*

# CHAPTER
# THIRTY-EIGHT:

see Miles's pickup truck pull into the restaurant parking lot as I finish my last sip of wine.

About ten minutes ago, I watched as Richard finally exited the restaurant, got into his Tesla, and drove away. Thankfully, he has no idea what car I drive, so I was able to snoop undetected. I'm just glad he left the general vicinity before Miles pulled up. I had no desire to see if Miles was serious about kicking his ass.

Tossing the empty bottle of wine into the back seat of my car, I reach over and grab my purse. I guess I'll just have Jill or Ronnie bring me to pick up my car in the morning. I carefully step out of my car, wiggle my dress back down my thighs where it has risen up, and begin stumbling towards Miles's parked car.

When he steps out of his truck, I notice he scans the parking lot in search of me. He's wearing a t-shirt, basketball shorts and...boots. At the sight of him, I can't help but laugh out loud. He must've just thrown on his boots and left his apartment. Luckily, it's an abnormally warm evening for October in Bristol. I'd been excited the weather was warm enough for me not to need a sweater. Ronnie said covering up this dress would be a travesty. Little did I know that this date would be the real travesty; a sweater would've been the least of my worries.

"Hey, butthead," I call out to him.

Miles quickly spins his body around to face me as I approach him. His mouth falls open, staring at me. I come to a standstill before him.

I watch as his eyes slowly travel down the length of my body. He's stunned silent for an uncomfortable amount of time.

Suddenly, I wish I had a sweater.

"You look so different," he finally gets out.

I give Miles an effortless smile. I love how awkward he can be at times. I find it endearing. I would choose Miles's awkwardness over Richard's arrogance any day.

"I don't want to go home yet!" I whine, changing the subject. I've decided I'm not letting this makeup and dress go to waste.

"Um..." Miles looks down at his basketball shorts and cowboy boots, then back to me. "Where do you want to go?"

"I was going to say The Barn Door. But you're dressed a lil' too fancy." Looking at his outfit, I can't help but laugh. His ensemble reminds me of when my dad and stepmom, Amanda, allowed my half-sister, Taylor, to start picking out her own outfits.

He smirks at me, running his fingers through the thick mess of curls on his head.

"You need a haircut," I point out.

Laughing, he replies, "You want to take me to get my hair cut at 9:00 PM on a Monday? Not exactly my idea of fun."

"Let's go back to your place. We can play Trivial Pursuit and drink some more," I propose.

Miles bought me Disney Trivial Pursuit for my birthday last year. I decided to leave it at his place, so we can play it together on Sundays during our "coffee get-togethers." He knows a shocking amount of Disney trivia which, again, he claims is only because he grew up with a sister. Deep down, though, I think he's just as big a Disney fan as I am.

"Brett has a girl over."

"When *doesn't* Brett have a girl over?" He's literally dating a new girl every month. "We can just play in your room."

Miles slowly looks me up and down once more, continuing to run his fingers through his hair. I know this is a nervous habit of his.

Why is he acting so weird? It's just me. Unless...

"Wait, do you *both* have girls over?"

"The girl Brett's been seeing—Emily—she brought a friend with her tonight. But...I'm...uh, not interested in her or anything," he stammers.

It all makes sense now.

I feel terrible about pulling him away from his plans to come and pick my drunk ass up. I should have called Jill or Ronnie.

"Shit, I'm sorry for assuming you weren't already doing something tonight." Something...or some*body*. But that truly isn't my business. I smile sweetly at him. "You can just take me home."

"I want to be with you, though—I mean—I want to spend time with you," he stutters.

"Wouldn't it be weird if I crashed your guys' party though?"

"You're one of our best friends, Sam. It won't be weird," he reassures me.

"Good, because I want to see Scout!" I giggle.

Walking around Miles's truck, I go to open the passenger door, but Miles beats me to it. This is nothing new; Miles always opens doors for me. He says it's just how he was raised.

I'm only 5'3", so to get into his truck, I usually have to jump up for the grab handle, then pull myself up the remainder of the way. After almost an entire bottle of wine and in six-inch heels, this is going to be interesting. Here goes nothing.

Leaping towards the grab handle, I miss it by a mile. There's absolutely no way I'll be able to regain my footing in these heels once I hit the asphalt.

Just when I think it's over for me, Miles catches me around the waist, pulling my body into his before I can fall. My back rests against him as he slowly removes his hands from where they were grasping my hips.

I look down, and, to my horror, I realize my dress has bunched up around the top of my hips. Which, of course, means my underwear is completely visible.

Miles politely looks away as I yank my dress back down my thighs. Actually, not my dress—Ronnie's dress. It's glaringly obvious I'm not cut out to wear a dress like this.

At least I know Miles won't care much about accidentally seeing me in my underwear. Over the years, he has made it obvious he's not attracted to me in that way. So, I'm trying not to feel too embarrassed right now.

"I'm going to pick you up and put you in the truck."

"You don't have to do that. I'll just take off these stupid shoes."

"Technically, I think I do," he laughs.

Before I can object further, he sweeps me into his arms, then gently places me into the passenger seat of his truck before walking back around to the driver's side. I'm impressed how easily he just picked me up.

"Since I'm never getting married, I guess that's as close as I'm going to get to being carried over the threshold," I joke.

Miles slides into the driver's seat. "Why do you think you won't get married?"

Sighing, I explain, "I think someone has to actually want to date you before you can get married."

As he reverses out of his parking spot, Miles shoots me a brief glance. "You're crazy, Sam."

"That's probably part of the problem," I groan.

"Tell me what happened tonight."

"I don't want to bore you."

"In all the years I've known you, you've never bored me."

Before I explain my horrendous date, I let out a long sigh. "He asked me if I was ready to become 'a real nurse.' Then he said I wasn't utilizing my skills by working in hospice."

We're currently stopped at a red light. Miles shifts his body to partially face me. "He actually said that?"

"More or less, yes."

"Unbelievable," he mutters. The light turns green, and he accelerates.

"He just made me feel so...insignificant." My voice involuntarily cracks.

Oh no, please don't get emotional. I don't want to cry in front of Miles.

Taking me by surprise, he grasps my hand in his. He interlaces his fingers with mine, then places our intertwined hands onto his lap while he drives. I've never held Miles's hand before. We've hugged one another hundreds of times, but somehow this feels more intimate. This feels different. His hand is nearly double the size of mine, yet, somehow, with my hand woven in his, it feels like the perfect fit.

"You're so many things, Sam, but insignificant isn't one of them."

I look up from our interlocked hands to rest my gaze on his face. His eyes remain focused on the road as we drive down Main Street. The pad of his thumb lightly brushes, back and forth, across the top of my hand.

My stomach does Olympic worthy acrobatics at his touch as, hand-in-hand, we settle into a comfortable silence the rest of the drive.

# CHAPTER

# THIRTY-NINE:

Miles doesn't release my hand until after he's parked in front of his apartment building. I'm trying not to overthink what's happening between us right now; he was probably just trying to console me. If so, it worked. I've completely forgotten about Richard.

"I'll help you out," Miles says, opening his door.

"I'll be okay," I protest.

He stares at me momentarily. "I'll help you out," he repeats as he climbs out of his truck.

I concede, patiently waiting for Miles to walk around and assist me. He's probably right—I'm sure I would end up tumbling out of the truck if I tried to get out alone in these shoes. He's probably trying to spare himself from me flashing him again.

When Miles opens the truck door, I grab my purse. He gently slips his arm beneath my knees, scooting my body towards his until I'm flush against him. I wrap my arms around his neck as he lifts me out of the passenger seat. He continues holding me as he bumps the truck door closed with his hip. I expect Miles to set me on the ground—because I can in fact walk—but he continues carrying me to his apartment.

"You know I can walk, right?"

He grins down at me in his arms. "I'm not in the mood to risk it." He effortlessly climbs the stairs up to his apartment, all while continuing to cradle me in his arms.

"Are you going to carry me over the threshold now?" I ask with a laugh.

"Not until you're my wife," he says, giving me his sideways smirk.

My breath catches as I glance up at him. That was a joke, right?

Once we reach the top of the stairs, he gently sets me on my feet.

"Do you think they'll want to play Trivial Pursuit?" I ask.

"Probably not," he chuckles, as he unlocks the door to his apartment. As he opens the door, I hear a woman's playful shriek, followed by a chorus of giggles.

"So, are you ladies up for strip poker or what?" I hear Brett ask. Yup, they probably don't want to play Disney Trivial Pursuit.

Following Miles into the kitchen, I see Brett and two women, about my age, seated around the small dining table.

"What do you want to drink?" Miles asks me. The group must have overheard us because the three of them turn around in unison to look at us. The apartment has suddenly gone silent.

"Holy shit," Brett mutters.

"So, that's where you went," the woman (who I assume is not Emily) says, shifting her glare between Miles and me.

*Maybe this was a bad idea.*

I decide to awkwardly introduce myself. "Hi, I'm Sam."

"You look super hot, Sam!" Brett blurts. The heat rises to both of my cheeks. Suddenly, I'm feeling extremely self-conscious. I wonder if Miles will let me borrow a t-shirt and a pair of his shorts.

"Isn't that kind of inappropriate to say to your best friend's girl-friend?" Emily asks Brett. At least I'm assuming she's Emily because she's currently sitting on Brett's lap. She also appears to be incredibly annoyed.

"Sam's not Miles's girlfriend. She's one of our best friends," he corrects her.

The girl on Brett's lap then turns back to face me. "I'm Emily, Brett's girlfriend," she says, obviously staking her claim.

You're his girlfriend for the *month*, I want to correct her. Instead, I reply with a pleasant smile. "It's nice to meet you."

"I'm Alyssa," the other girl chimes in. "So, Miles, are you playing strip poker with us?"

Looks like Alyssa is attempting to stake her claim, now.

"I'd say you should play, Sam, but I'm afraid if you lost a single hand, you'd be naked," Emily laughs.

"She's barely wearing anything to begin with," Alyssa remarks snidely.

Despite having only heard it once, their combined laughter has already become one of my least favorite sounds. I figure they're laugh-ing at me, but I honestly couldn't care less. This isn't my first rodeo with the mean girls that Brett and Miles date.

I'll never understand why women think they need to be so nasty to one another. If we think it's appropriate to "slut-shame" each other, can we really be upset when men treat us the same way?

"Nobody wants to see that." I join in on their joke, refusing to let them get under my skin. Emily and Alyssa look at each other, obvi-ously confused as to why I'm now laughing with them—technically laughing at myself.

Brett unexpectedly stands from his seat, knocking Emily off his lap, and slams his hands onto the table. All of us, including Miles, jump at his sudden outburst. "I guess you didn't hear me!" Brett bellows.

"Sam's one of our best friends. If either of you feels the need to disrespect her again, you can fucking leave!" He then grabs a half-empty bottle of beer from the table and hurls it against the kitchen wall. The sound of shattering glass immediately engulfs the small space.

I experience a sudden flashback to the last time I saw Brett lose his composure like this—when he hurled an entire tub of popcorn at me. This side of Brett undeniably scares me. Miles and I both rush to his side in an attempt to calm our friend.

"Hey, look at me," I whisper to him. Brett's icy blue eyes lock with mine. I place both of my hands on his shoulders, giving him a reassuring smile. "We were just joking around. I don't feel disrespected—everything's okay."

He takes a deep breath and slowly exhales. It's as if I can feel the tension leaving his body. "You do look really beautiful tonight," he quietly murmurs as his eyes lose their icy edge.

Miles takes in a sharp breath behind me.

"Thanks, bro." I playfully punch Brett's arm. I told you I was terrible at receiving compliments.

"Remind me to never compliment you again," he laughs, exaggeratedly cradling his punched arm. I love the sound of Brett's laughter.

"I'm sorry, Sam," a woman's voice squeaks. Turning away from Brett, I'm face-to-face with Emily. She's nervously chewing at one of her fingernails as she looks at me, her eyes filled with tears.

I don't think Brett realizes how scary his outbursts can be. According to Miles, they've thankfully been few and far between over the last few years. This is only the second one I've witnessed.

"It's okay." I smile at her, and she smiles timidly back at me.

Alyssa meanwhile doesn't apologize. She remains silent, and I couldn't care less.

On the other hand, I do feel like Emily and I could actually become friends if I had the opportunity to get to know her better. I think we just got off on the wrong foot.

Alyssa? Not so much.

Regardless, I'll be kind to both of them.

"Let's go to the bar," Brett suggests, already in a better mood. "Van just texted me. He said there's a band playing tonight."

"Who's Van?" Alyssa asks.

"He owns The Barn Door," I reply, which she doesn't acknowledge.

"It's pretty rare for a band to be playing on a weeknight," Miles says.

"All the more reason we should go," Brett replies.

The majority of our pack—Brett, Miles, and I included— are usually stuck working on the weekends which means, we rarely get to see any of the local bands perform at The Barn Door. The last performer I saw there was actually Craig.

I don't know if Craig will ever truly know how talented he really is, even though our pack tells him quite often. I hope one day he'll decide to share his talent with the rest of the world. He's currently writing a secret song for Ronnie. I have a sneaking suspicion that once he sings it for her, a proposal may follow. Nothing would bring me more joy than for the two of them getting their happily ever after.

"Let's go!" Emily agrees. She looks towards Miles and me. "You guys should totally come."

"Of course they're gonna come," Brett responds for us.

My feet are already killing me in these shoes, but I did say I didn't want this dress and makeup to go to waste. Hopefully, one of the girls happens to drive a small sedan and offers to drive. I don't really feel like being carried in and out of a truck again tonight. And Brett's truck is even bigger than Miles's, so if either of them drives, I'm doomed.

"Sam and I were actually planning on playing some Disney Trivial Pursuit," Miles speaks up. I turn and look at Miles, giving him a huge grin, which he returns with one of his infamous sideways smirks. Staying in and playing trivia with him sounds so much better than a night out at the bar.

"You two and that game—I'll never understand it," Brett moans. "Trivia is so lame."

"Just because you're stupid doesn't mean trivia's lame," Miles jokes, giving him a lighthearted shove.

"I'm sorry I don't lock myself in my room, watch Disney movies all day, and cry," Brett mocks, shoving Miles back.

Miles pulls out his usual defense: "For the last time, I grew up with a sister!"

Brett and I bust out laughing. Miles can't help but join in, while Emily and Alyssa once again look completely confused.

"Well, if you nerds get tired of arguing about when *The Little Mermaid* was released, you know where to find us," Brett announces.

At the same time, Miles and I shout: "1989!" We both turn to look at each other and smile, as Brett shakes his head in disgust.

As the trio walks out of the kitchen together, I hear Alyssa whisper to Emily, "It totally seems like they're dating."

It leaves me thinking of how Miles's hand felt in mine. How he lightly stroked my hand with the pad of his thumb. How even though his hands felt rough, his touch felt so gentle. I can't help but allow myself to wonder what it'd be like if Miles and I were dating.

"Sam, you want to help me set up the game?" Miles calls from the living room.

I force myself to abandon my current train of thought. Miles is one of my best friends—I could never risk ruining that.

# CHAPTER FORTY:

"I have an idea!" I squeal.

Miles pauses from setting up the game board to stare at me, waiting for me to share my newest idea.

"Every time you get a wedge, the other person has to take a shot," I propose.

If you've ever played Trivial Pursuit, you know your game piece looks like a round, empty pizza. Every time you answer a question correctly on a category, you place a wedge into your empty game piece. Each category has a different color wedge, and there are six different categories. So, altogether, Miles and I really only have the potential to take six shots each in a single game. I doubt that would lead to either of us getting plastered.

"Did you forget my birthday party is tomorrow? I don't want to be hungover all day," Miles whines.

Although he and I already celebrated at the coffee shop, his actual birthday is tomorrow. Our pack has decided to celebrate together at The Barn Door. Even Zach and his girlfriend, Sarah, are flying in for the party. Miles is turning a quarter of a century old. That's a big deal.

"You're like 6'4"—you can handle a few shots," I laugh.

"Why do I get the feeling it'll end up being more than a few shots?"

"Well, I guess you better be on top of your trivia game tonight." I give him a huge smirk.

His hazel eyes bore into mine. "You're going down!"

"Bring it!" I shout, meeting his glare with my own.

Did I forget to mention Miles and I are both extremely competitive?

We're now in the middle of our third game, and I've officially lost count of how many shots of vodka I've taken. Meanwhile, Miles has been shooting whiskey, so I believe he's now equally as drunk as I am.

I won the first game, so, of course, Miles demanded a rematch. After he won the second game, I knew a third was in our immediate future. We couldn't settle for a tie. Now, Miles and I are both sitting cross-legged on the floor, side-by-side, hunched over the coffee table where the Trivial Pursuit board is splayed out. Since the two of us ended up taking a lot more shots than initially anticipated, we decided it'd be best to keep ourselves close to the ground. With how drunk I am, I know there's a high probability I would take a tumble off the couch simply attempting to move my game piece across the board. Miles isn't as clumsy as I am, but he chose to join me on the floor anyways.

"It's your turn." With all the alcohol Miles has consumed, his speech is now slurred.

I look over at him, noting his usually bright, hazel eyes appearing glazed and slightly red. Yet, they're still so lovely to look at.

Before my drunken mind can stop my stupid mouth, I blurt out one of the most embarrassing things I could possibly say to him: "Your eyes are my favorite color."

Instantly, I slap my palm over my mouth. Did I really just say that? And I thought Miles could be awkward. Turns out *I'm* the most awkward person on earth. His eyes go wide at the sheer randomness of my compliment. I can tell he's at a loss for how to respond to me. Looking down at my lap in embarrassment, I can feel the heat rising to my cheeks and immediately know I'm blushing.

Maybe he's drunk enough that he won't remember this.

His hand gently grazes my cheek, and I jump at the sudden feeling. My eyes dart up to meet his, and he gently tucks a tendril of my hair behind my ear. My heart starts racing as he stares at me.

"Everything about you is my favorite," he whispers.

It's as if my breath was just stolen from me. I gasp at his words, losing every ounce of cognitive thinking I once possessed. His large palm momentarily lingers on my cheek before falling away. I know sober me will regret this, but I need to feel his touch again. I slowly lean my face towards his, closing my eyes.

I know that if I kiss him right now, it will change everything. Not just for us—for all of our friends, as well.

My face is mere inches away from his now, the warmth of his breath brushing against my lips. Tilting my face upwards to kiss him, I hear him whisper my name. "Sam...you're drunk."

I immediately jerk my body away from his, feeling humiliated. What was I thinking?

Watching as he runs his fingers through his thick mess of curls, lightly shaking his head, I can't help but wonder what it would feel like to run my own fingers through his hair. As quickly as the thought came to me, I banish it from my head. Miles isn't attracted to me. That much is obvious.

"I think I should go home," I whisper.

He studies me for a moment before responding. "Neither of us can drive, Sam."

He's right, we're both undeniably drunk.

"I'll call Jill. Or Ronnie," I mutter, looking down at my fidgeting hands. I can't help but feel embarrassed by his rejection.

"But...it's like one in the morning."

Why do things suddenly feel so uncomfortable between Miles and me?

I turn to grab my purse from where I left it on the couch behind us. Yanking my phone out of my bag, I open the screen, shocked to see that Miles is correct—it's 1:37 AM. I guess I don't have much of a choice.

"You can sleep in my bed," he says. I can only stare at him wide-eyed. "I'll sleep on the couch, of course," he adds quickly.

"No, I can sleep on the couch."

"Don't be ridiculous." It may be all in my head, but I have a strange feeling that Miles is upset with me. Did I just ruin our friendship by trying to kiss him?

"Can I borrow something to sleep in?" I ask timidly, as I slowly stand from my seat on the floor.

I hate that he's upset with me. I'm not sure why, but I feel as if I'm going to cry. Oh, yeah—maybe it's because I'm mortified and embarrassed.

Miles can sense my sudden shift in mood. He grants me one of his sideways smirks as he lifts himself off the ground. When he smiles at me, the tears once threatening to release instantly vanish.

"You didn't pack your Superman PJs in that bag of yours?" Miles laughs, pointing to my extremely small purse.

"You're just jealous," I giggle. "You only *wish* they made those bad boys in your size."

"I wouldn't want to outshine you like that," he chuckles, motioning for me to follow him to his room. Scout immediately leaps up from his spot on the couch to follow us.

I'm relieved things between Miles and me feel normal again.

Once we're in his room, I watch as he rifles through one of his dresser drawers. After about a minute, he tosses me a Chicago Cubs t-shirt and a pair of boxer shorts. I stare down at the pair of boxers in my hands.

Possibly noticing my confused look, he says, "My basketball shorts would drown you." I nod my understanding, before secretly smelling the shirt in my hands. It smells like him.

"Did you just smell my shirt?"

Ok, maybe I was not-so-secretly smelling it.

"I was making sure it was clean," I lie, giving him a joking glare. He laughs, smirking back at me. Why does he always have to be so observant?

"Well...goodnight," he murmurs, as he walks towards the bedroom door, Scout at his heels.

"Hey, Miles?"

He stops just before getting to the door, then turns to gaze at me, waiting for me to continue.

"We're okay, right?" I ask quietly.

"We're okay." He nods his head, giving me a small smile. "Even though you've gifted me an inevitable hangover for my birthday."

"Oh! Happy birthday!" I squeal, running over to give him a hug. "I love you!"

He pauses for a split second before he returns my hug. When we part, he awkwardly runs his fingers through his curls.

"Thanks, Sam," he replies faintly, before turning and walking out of the bedroom, softly shutting the door behind him and Scout.

I'm not oblivious to the fact that—for the first time—he didn't say "I love you" back.

*Maybe we aren't okay?*

# CHAPTER FORTY-ONE:

If this was one of your run-of-the-mill rom-coms, I'd ask Miles to help me unzip my dress so I can change into the t-shirt and boxers he gave me to sleep in. We'd have a passionate encounter, start a loving relationship, and subsequently live happily ever after.

But this isn't a rom-com and I'm no Meg Ryan. This is the real world. And in the real world, Miles has brutally rejected me. So, instead, I painfully bend my arm behind my own back, struggling with the zipper of this extremely snug-fitting dress. After uttering approximately six curse words, taking three breaks, and contemplating ripping the dress in half and just buying Ronnie a new one, I finally manage to free myself from its confines.

There was—without a doubt—nothing sexy about that.

After throwing on Miles's t-shirt and boxers, I crawl under the comforter. I've decided, screw it I'm leaving my contacts in and my makeup on. I'm honestly too drunk to care right now. I'll deal with the repercussions tomorrow.

As I reach over to turn off the lamp on Miles's nightstand, I notice the framed photograph of the two of us, still sitting in its same spot. I think about what Jill said when she and I stayed in this room during our bed bug fiasco. Is it really *that* strange to have a framed picture of you and one of your best friends on your nightstand? Well, after what happened tonight, now I'm positive Miles isn't in love with me like Jill once thought.

I wonder if the girls he brings home think it's weird our picture is there? Would Alyssa have been upset by it? If I hadn't come over tonight, would he have slept with Alyssa? He probably would have. But why does the thought of them together make my stomach churn?

Maybe because now, I know he doesn't want me.

*Okay, Sam. Time to turn off your brain and force your drunk ass to go to sleep.*

Just as I switch off the small, bedside light and lay my head on the pillow, I hear a soft knock at the bedroom door. Immediately, I jerk upright in bed. After I flick the light back on, I hear another soft knock, followed by the whines of an adorable black lab. I knew Scout would want to sleep with me, but if Miles wasn't offering, I didn't want to ask.

Jumping out of bed, I scurry towards the door. When I swing it open, I watch as a black, furry blur comes barreling into the room, leaping onto the bed. Scout then paces in precisely three tight circles before finally plopping his large body at the foot of the bed.

As always, seeing him really makes me want a dog of my own. I know I can pretty much visit Scout anytime I want, but at the end of the day, he's still Miles's dog. I turn away from Scout to see Miles standing awkwardly before me in the bedroom doorway.

His demanding voice cuts through the uneasy silence. "Promise me something."

I'm a little taken off-guard by the seriousness in his tone, but I'll go with it.

"Okay...?" I respond, unable to completely disguise my confusion.

"Promise me—no matter what happens, you'll never stop being my friend."

How strange? This doesn't seem like something a drunk Miles would say to me as much as it's something a drunk Jill would say. Then, she and I would vow to be best friends forever. We'd plan to buy houses next door to each other one day. We'd even make sure to have children around the same age, so they could grow up to be best friends, too.

Just hypothetically speaking, of course. It's not like Jill and I have ever drunkenly planned out our future as besties...just kidding, we totally have. On numerous occasions.

"I'll never stop being your friend, Miles," I assure him. "Why would you—"

Before I can finish my sentence, his mouth is on mine. I gasp against his lips, but he continues kissing me. He gently leads my body further into the bedroom, shutting the door behind us with his foot. He slowly maneuvers me so my back rests against the wall. Before I can comprehend what's happening, he leans down, grasps both of my thighs, and lifts me up, his lips never leaving mine. Instinctively, I wrap my legs around his waist.

Meanwhile, my hand wanders into his curls, where I desperately grasp a handful of his hair—just as I'd imagined doing. He softly moans into my mouth, and it's as if my body's been electrified. His tongue tastes like whiskey and spearmint—the combination is absolutely intoxicating. His mouth finally leaves mine, only to slowly travel down my neck, as he pulls down the t-shirt I'm wearing, baring one of my shoulders. I shudder as his lips lightly trace the outline of my collar bone. I'm about to lose all common sense and allow myself to fall under his spell. But, before I do, I can't help asking him what's on my mind.

His lips momentarily leave my body when he grabs at the hem of my t-shirt. Before he can go any further, I place my hand on his. "Wait, I'm confused," I gasp. They're the only words my brain is able to formulate at the moment.

He begrudgingly stops removing my shirt to stare down at me. He's still holding me up, pinned against his bedroom wall. My legs are firmly wrapped around his waist.

When I look up to meet his gaze, he smiles down at me. "What part are you confused about?"

"I—I thought you weren't attracted to me?" I stutter, my eyes falling.

He tenderly lifts my chin, so I meet his gaze once more. "Why would you think that?"

"When you asked me to coffee, and I asked you if it was a date, you seemed disgusted. And not to mention, just earlier, you rejected me when I tried to kiss you." I'm rambling, but I can't stop myself.

Miles sighs then, with me still in his arms, he walks towards his bed. He sets me onto the bed, next to where Scout is curled up, then sits beside me.

"Have you really held on to that for all these years?" Miles asks.

"Of course, I did. You made me feel ugly and unwanted." The words spill out of me. I guess we are laying it all out on the table now.

He gasps, taken aback. "I made you feel ugly?"

"And unwanted," I correct him.

Suddenly, he moves from where he was seated to kneel before me. Why is he on the floor? He then takes both my hands in his own. I look down at him in shock.

"Don't worry, I'm not asking you to marry me," he chuckles.

"I didn't think you were."

"Don't get mad at me, Sam," he pleads. "I think you're the most beautiful person I've ever known, and I've wanted you since the moment I first saw you."

"But why didn't you kiss me in the living room? I don't understa—"

"Please, let me finish," he gently interrupts me. I nod at him in understanding, and he continues. "I was nervous. I didn't want to risk losing you. You have a bad habit of always trying to say goodbye to me," he says, running his fingers through his hair, as is his nervous habit. "That first day we met, when you asked me if going to coffee was a date, I panicked. I didn't want you to say no. I had to see you again."

I move my hand up to cup his cheek. "I wouldn't have said no."

He stares up at me, stunned. "Really? You would've gone on a date with me?"

"In a heartbeat," I say, lightly tracing his bottom lip with the pad of my thumb.

He softly kisses my thumb as it moves across his lip. "Sam, will you get coffee with me in the morning?"

I'm officially putty in his hands.

I smile at him. "Are you asking me on a date Mr. Streelman?"

"Absolutely. Better late than never," he grins, pulling me down onto his lap.

His lips find mine once more, and I know it's over for me. I've allowed myself to fall—for him. Or maybe I've just finally allowed myself to realize that I've been falling for this man since the day I met him.

**All I know for certain—there's no going back.**

# CHAPTER

# FORTY-TWO:

I wake up with a pounding headache. My mouth is miserably dry, my eyes are ridiculously blurry. All in all, I feel like shit. Rolling over in search of a water bottle, I smack into another person's body. I frantically rub my eyes until I can see somewhat clearly. I've never slept in my contacts before—now I know why. Once I'm able to see again, I realize it's Miles lying beside me. He's fast asleep, snoring softly.

Timidly, I lift the comforter and glance under the covers. Yup, he's completely naked. Then I look down and realize I, too, am completely naked. The events of last night come flooding back to me. The things he said. The way he touched me. The way he tasted.

I hope he remembers. I hope he meant everything he said last night.

Moving towards Miles, I lie my head against his chest, letting the sound of his soft snoring ease my anxiousness. For some reason, being hungover always causes me anxiety. He had to have meant what he said last night. There's no way he'd risk our friendship, all for a one-night stand.

In that case, we'll probably have a *real* coffee date this morning. I can't help but feel butterflies when I think of Miles and me on a legitimate date.

I think I'll let him sleep in, though—it's his birthday, after all.

Closing my eyes, I try to will myself to go back to sleep, but almost instantly, I hear Miles's bedroom door open.

"Happy birthday, bro! Wanna hit the gym with me before—" At the sound of Brett's voice, I instinctively pop up from Miles's chest. For just a moment, Brett and I stare at one another, before I burrow my head under the comforter to hide from my embarrassment.

This isn't how I wanted our friends to find out about us dating.

"What the fuck?" At the sound of Brett's raised voice, Miles immediately sits up in bed. Peeking my head out from under the comforter, I sneak a look at Brett whose icy glare is currently shooting daggers at Miles. Brett remains frozen in the doorway, dressed in gym attire, his hands balled into tight fists.

Where the hell are my clothes? And why is he so pissed off? Is it because we didn't vote on this? Honestly, the whole voting thing is so ridiculous.

"Get out of here, Brett," Miles groans, motioning for Brett to leave. By the cracking of his voice, I can tell that Miles also feels like shit this morning. He tiredly rubs at both of his eyes before letting his head fall into his hands.

"Not until you tell me what the hell is going on here," Brett demands. "I already saw you, Samantha. You can stop hiding!"

Miles's head snaps up as he glares at Brett. I finally jerk my head completely out from underneath the covers. Wrapping the comforter around my bare chest, I sit and watch as Brett and Miles start yelling at each other.

"Get the hell out of my room!" Miles shouts.

"How long have you been screwing her?"

Miles ignores Brett and, instead, reaches down, grabbing off the ground the Chicago Cubs shirt and boxers I was borrowing last night. He tosses them to me. "Put these on."

"Yeah, Sam. You should probably put your clothes on," Brett sneers.

"Shut the hell up, Brett!" Miles shouts. I then watch as he stands from his bed, still completely naked, and walks to his dresser. He pulls out a pair of sweatpants from one of the drawers and slips them on.

Meanwhile, I sneak beneath the comforter once again to slide on the boxers and throw the shirt on over my head.

I can't believe this is happening right now.

When I come out from under the comforter, I can hear Brett's voice echoing off of the walls, he's so pissed off. "Answer my question, asshole! How long have you been fucking her?"

Suddenly, Brett is in Miles's face. Knowing Brett's anger issues, I'm instantly worried he's going to completely lose it and hit Miles. Miles does not back down though—he squares off his shoulders and glares right back.

Sliding out of bed, I move towards the two men. Although I know I won't be able to physically pull them apart if an altercation breaks out, maybe if I stand between them, they won't start fighting to begin with.

"It was only last night," Miles reveals, maintaining his staring contest with Brett. "Sam and I got way too drunk and hooked up. It's not a big deal—it doesn't mean anything."

Once again, I feel as if my breath has been stolen from me. Only this time, Miles hasn't just stolen my breath—he's ripped my heart out. I can feel hot tears streaming down my face. I'm distantly aware Brett and Miles are still speaking, but all I can hear is the pounding of my own heart.

Looking around, I start searching the floor for my dress and purse. I find them splayed out on the floor nearby. My hands are shaking so badly, I have difficulty grasping them.

I'm about to have a panic attack—I can already feel it happening. I have to get out of here.

How could I have been stupid enough to think Miles had real feelings for me?

Through tear-filled eyes, I see that Brett and Miles are still deep in conversation. This is my moment to escape and never look back. Before I dash out of Miles's bedroom, I kneel beside where Scout lays on the floor. I wrap my arms around the dog I've grown to love, one last time.

"You're the best boy, Scout," I whisper into his fur.

I can no longer be friends with Miles—not after this. Not after his betrayal. I'm well aware this will probably be the last time I get to see this big, goofy black lab. Another reason I want my own dog. If Scout was mine—I wouldn't have to say goodbye.

Finally, I stand and make a mad dash out of the bedroom. Seeing the sparkly six-inch heels I wore last night on the floor in the living room, I scoop them up as I run towards the front door. It's only at this moment that I recall I didn't drive myself here.

This is literally about to be a walk of shame.

When I reach the front door, I hear both Miles and Brett yelling my name. But I refuse to turn around. I have to leave. I have to get out of here before my anxiety consumes me.

Grasping the door handle, I start pulling the front door open, but before I can, I sense someone standing directly behind me. Suddenly, an arm reaches above my head and the door is slammed closed.

"Sam, where are you going?" It's Miles standing behind me.

I don't want to speak. I don't want to turn around. If I do, then he'll know I'm crying.

I'm mortified and embarrassed, but, most of all, I'm heartbroken. I just want to leave.

"Sam, answer me!" His tone is frantic. He pauses for a moment, collecting himself. Then he whispers, "Why are you leaving me?"

I'm leaving him? What a joke! Abruptly, I spin around to face him, the tears still streaming down my face. He looks down at me, wide-eyed, while Brett stands just a few feet behind us.

"Hey, why are you crying?" He tries consoling me, lightly rubbing both of my arms.

Last night his touch made me feel electrified, but now, all I feel is disgust. His hands feel like lies, just like his words. "Don't fucking touch me!"

Miles looks shocked, as he drops both of his arms to his sides. "I don't understand," he whispers.

"I don't mean anything to you? It was nothing?"

"That's not what I said."

"I heard you!"

"That's not what I meant," he corrects himself. "Just let me explain—I'm begging you."

"How could you do this to me? Was getting laid really worth ruining years of friendship? You couldn't find anyone else to have sex with?"

"What are you talking about?" Miles is yelling now. He's only yelled at me once before, years ago. "Why do you always have to do this shit?" At his words, I start to cry harder.

Off to the side, Brett remains silent, watching me sob. He looks extremely uncomfortable, but, for the moment, he stays out of our dispute. He realizes this really has nothing to do with him.

"What 'shit' is it that I do, exactly?" I wipe the stream of tears from my face with the dress in my hands as I try to compose myself.

"Make a huge deal out of nothing, then act fucking crazy! Do you really think if I was looking for a one-night stand, I'd choose *you* to sleep with?"

As someone who deals with chronic anxiety, one of the most hurtful things someone can do is call you crazy. Hearing those words come from someone I thought was one of my best friends makes this even more hurtful.

If I could change my anxiousness, my overthinking, doesn't he think I would? If I could choose to live without a constant pit in my stomach, wouldn't I? If I didn't have to constantly worry about what people thought of me—whether I said the wrong thing or not, whether I'm making the right decision—doesn't he think I would choose to live in peace rather than with constant dread?

But it's not that easy. And if I wasn't in the midst of a panic attack, I would try explaining all of that to him.

Instead, I decide to slap him in the face—*hard*.

As my hand falls back to my side, Miles stares at me, stunned. His mouth has dropped open, and his hand moves to touch his cheek. Immediately, Brett sprints over to where the two of us are standing and tries to pull Miles away from me.

I can't believe I just hit him. Maybe he's right; maybe I *am* crazy.

Brett finally succeeds at pulling Miles away from me. When he does, I can hear Miles mutter, "I would never hit her."

"I know you wouldn't. I've just seen that shit too many times to chance it." Brett whispers.

What has Brett seen too many times? Suddenly, I'm thinking of his family—the family he never talks about. What else is there that he refuses to talk about? But then I think about my brother—the brother *I* refuse to talk about. Matty wouldn't be proud of me, of the way I just acted. I know he wouldn't be proud of me because I'm not proud of myself.

"I'm sorry, Miles," I manage to choke out.

Brett and Miles both stop whispering to each other and turn to stare at me.

"I'm sorry I hit you," I snivel. "And I'm sorry, but I lied to you last night—I can't be your friend anymore."

"Please, Sam. Don't do this," Miles begs, taking a step back towards where I'm standing.

How can this man beg me to remain his friend after I just smacked him across the face?

"Happy birthday," I whimper before wrenching the door back open and darting outside. As I wobble down the cement stairs leading to their apartment, my cries turn to sobs once more. I thought last night was only the beginning for Miles and me. At the time, I had no clue that it would actually be the end of our story.

I'm walking barefoot on the sidewalk alongside their apartment complex, contemplating whether or not to put on my heels. It's about a three-mile walk to my apartment. I'm too embarrassed to call either Jill or Ronnie to come and pick me up.

How am I going to explain this to them?

I decide to slip on Ronnie's sparkly stilettos. I must be quite the sight, walking down the street at 7:00 AM in six-inch heels, an oversized shirt, and men's boxer shorts.

"Hold on, Sam!" When I turn around, I see Brett running towards me. I stop, waiting for him to approach. Only moments later, he's standing before me.

"Miles said you don't have your car. Let me give you a ride home," he offers.

I pause to think about it. "...Okay," I mutter. This is no time to be stubborn. I probably wouldn't have made it a mile in these shoes.

"Were you really going to walk five miles in glittery high heels?" Brett laughs.

I quickly correct him. "It's only about three miles."

I remove Ronnie's heels, deciding to walk to his truck barefoot. I know I wouldn't be able to climb into the front seat with them on anyway. He and I walk the rest of the way to his truck in silence.

Once we're both inside, Brett turns to look at me before starting the engine. "Be honest with me."

"I don't want to talk about this."

"How do you know what I'm going to ask you?"

I move to face him. He gives me a devilish grin, as he grabs his aviators from the center console and puts them on.

He was at The Barn Door ridiculously late last night—I'm sure of it— yet he looks perfectly groomed and well-rested. How is he not hungover at all?

"Fine, I'll be honest. What is it?"

Brett starts pulling his truck out of the parking spot. "Do you have feelings for him?"

"Who?" I obviously know who he's talking about.

"Don't play dumb, Sammie," he says, keeping his eyes on the road.

"Don't call me that!"

He briefly glances at me. Lowering his sunglasses, he gives me an exaggerated wink. "Then don't avoid answering my questions."

"I do," I whisper. "That's why I can't be his friend anymore."

"He hasn't admitted it to me yet, but I know he's crazy about you, too," Brett says.

At his words, I abruptly turn my entire body to face him. The seatbelt semi-chokes me, but I don't care. I can't help but stare at him.

Is he being serious?

"Why would you say that?"

"Because it's the truth," he maintains.

"You couldn't be more wrong." I spin back around to stare out the passenger-side window.

We are silent for the remainder of the ride. A few minutes later, Brett parks his truck in front of my apartment building. He turns off his truck engine and opens his driver-side door.

"You don't have to walk me up," I tell him. "I'll be okay."

He grins at me. "I was raised better than that." Then he slams his truck door shut. He saunters around the truck, casually opening the passenger-side door for me when he reaches it.

I hop out of the truck with my dress, shoes, and purse tucked under my arm. I'm crossing my fingers Ronnie is still passed out on our sectional. She usually isn't awake this early unless she has to be.

Jill, on the other hand, is always up early, whether she has something to do or not. This morning, though, she's having breakfast with her mom, so I know she won't be home.

I've always been secretly jealous of her relationship with her mom. I haven't spoken to my own mother in years—since the night of my pinning ceremony, actually.

Brett watches me struggle to hold last night's outfit under my arm. "Can I carry anything for you?"

"I'm okay, thank you."

We walk together up the cold cement stairs to my apartment. I've never walked them barefoot before, so I never realized how cold they are.

When we reach the front door, he asks, "Do you have your keys?"

I quickly rifle through my purse, pulling out my keys by the Superman keychain. I hold them up for Brett to see. "They're right here."

He smiles, then takes a step closer to me. I'm not sure how I'm going to hug him with all this shit in my hands.

Suddenly, he's stopped smiling and is now staring at me, his light blue eyes boring into mine.

"Forgive me," he murmurs. "I just know this is my last chance to do this. 'Cause tomorrow, you'll be my best friend's girl."

"What does that—" But before I can finish my question, his mouth is on mine. He wraps both his arms around me, pulling me deeper into his kiss. I end up dropping everything I was holding onto the ground, sparkly stilettos, and all.

Finally, he pulls away from me, studying me momentarily before, without warning, he rushes down the stairs. Without turning back around, he yells up to me, "I'll see you tonight!"

My mouth falls open in shock. What the hell just happened?

I know Brett only kissed me for a few seconds, but, somehow, time felt as if it stood still. I'm left standing on my front porch, staring after Brett as he jumps into his truck and peels out of my apartment complex.

I'm still so confused—why would he do that?

My life is officially a mess, and it's all my fault. I should never have tried to kiss Miles last night. I certainly should never have slept with him.

I don't know how I'm supposed to feel right now, but I do know that I feel confused, hurt, and ashamed all at the same time. But the only thing I *want* to feel is numb.

Walking through my front door, I head straight into my kitchen and open the pantry. My hand grips the clear bottle sitting on the top shelf. I'm as quiet as possible, in the hope I don't wake Ronnie. I don't want her to see me like this. I unscrew the cap, place the bottle to my lips, close my eyes, and chug. The familiar burn of vodka brings me some comfort. I shuffle into my bedroom with the bottle in my hand. Once it no longer brings me comfort, it'll grant me sleep. If I could, I'd sleep for the next two days, until I have to go back to work on Thursday. Until I'm forced to face the world again.

But right now, *I just want to forget it all.*

# CHAPTER FORTY-THREE:

'm awoken by the vibration of my cellphone on the nightstand. Grabbing my phone to silence it, I see Zach is calling. I've finally removed the picture of him and me from his contact. As for why he's calling, if he's looking for someone to pick him and Sarah up from the airport, I'm not the one. So, I ignore his call—I don't feel like talking to anyone, right now.

I stare at the time. My phone reads 5:47 PM. I've successfully slept the day away. Miles's birthday party starts at 7:00 PM tonight. There is absolutely no way I'm going. I sit up in bed and lazily rub the sleep from my eyes. I feel better than I deserve, but I might actually still be drunk. It's too soon to tell if I'll have a raging hangover.

I hear a forceful knock at the door, followed by Ronnie shouting, "Wake your ass up, Sleeping Beauty!"

"Go away!"

Then Jill softly chimes in, "Are you okay, Sam?"

I groan, forcing myself out of bed. I unwillingly drag my feet to my bedroom door, swing it open, and find Ronnie and Jill standing side-by-side, completely ready for the night.

"Wow, you look terrible," Ronnie says.

"Thanks." Taking a couple of steps, I collapse back onto my bed.

"Are you going to start getting ready soon?" Jill asks politely. "We really should leave for the bar within the next hour."

"I'm not going."

"What the hell do you mean you're 'not going'?" Ronnie demands.

Jill takes on a more curious tone. "Did you pick up an extra shift?"

"No, I'm off tonight. I just don't feel like going." Eventually, I'll have to tell them what happened between Miles and me, but I don't have the energy for it right now.

"How was your date last night? Did y'all get down 'n dirty?" Ronnie asks with a smirk.

"Veronica Mae! That's none of your business!" Jill scolds, giving her a disapproving look.

"Oh, cut the crap, Jilly Bean," she groans in response. "You know you're just as curious as I am." Then, she and Jill turn to stare at me, awaiting my response.

I'm quick to dash their hopes. "Dr. Jackass lived up to his nickname. There will be no second date."

Jill's mouth falls open in surprise, while Ronnie's hands fly to her hips as she clicks her tongue against the roof of her mouth. Tony once compared her clicking to the sound of a snake's rattle. If you heard it—you knew shit was about to go down.

When Jill breaks the silence, I can hear the concern in her voice. "Did he cross the line, Sam?"

I close my eyes and purse my lips together. Clawing its way through the vodka induced haze, the events of last night and this morning come flooding back to me.

"Did that asshole try to take advantage of you?" Ronnie orders, obviously taking a different tactic than Jill. "Where does he live? What floor does he work on?"

I jerk my body into a sitting position, my eyes now wide-open and meet their concerned stares. "What? No! Nothing like that," I assure them. "He was just rude—he implied working in hospice wasn't 'real' nursing. It pissed me off."

"Well, screw that jerk-head!" Jill cries out. At her reaction, Ronnie and I both turn to her, trying to stifle our laughter. Only Jill can sound absolutely furious without uttering a single curse word.

"Yeah, what Jill said," Ronnie chuckles. "Fuck him!"

"I did *not* say that!" Jill gives Ronnie an exaggerated glare, which makes us laugh openly. Jill can't help but join in.

Being around the two of them makes me feel instantly better. No matter what the chaos is, wreaking havoc on my life, I know I'll always have my two best friends.

Jill and Ronnie finally convinced me to go tonight. Even though I wanted to tell them everything about last night and this morning, I just couldn't bring myself to reveal what I'd done.

I'm completely embarrassed at how I acted this morning—I still can't believe I slapped Miles in the face. At the same time, I'm heart-broken by Miles's rejection. And, to make matters worse, I'm utterly confused by Brett's kiss.

Tonight, pretending as if none of this happened, is going to be complete hell for me. That is if Miles doesn't immediately kick me out of his party when I walk through the doors.

Ronnie suggested I wear another one of her outfits this evening, and Jill repeatedly offered to do my hair again. I politely declined both of their offers, letting them know I didn't have the energy to get all dolled up. Tonight, I just want to feel like me.

So, I ditched the contacts—donning my glasses once more, opted out of applying any makeup—except for a little mascara, and pulled my freshly-washed hair into a messy bun. For the rest of my ensemble, I've decided to keep it simple this evening, choosing to wear my favorite pair of light-washed jeans, and a black V-neck t-shirt with a red and black flannel tied around my waist.

After experiencing this morning's horror of almost having to walk three miles home in six-inch heels, I decided to play it safe for tonight, finishing off my look with a pair of black, high-top Converse. With this choice of footwear, I'd be able to make it home by foot tonight if need be.

Jill is our self-appointed designated driver, per usual. She traded shifts with a co-worker and has to work tomorrow morning, so she won't be drinking tonight. She hardly drinks anyways, though. I can't say the same for Ronnie and me. While I was getting ready, I decided to have a couple drinks to ease my increasing anxiety. And Ronnie is always willing to drink with me. She never turns down the opportunity to "pre-game," as she puts it.

I wish I could explain to my friends the dread I feel knowing I have to see Miles again, so soon after he ripped my heart out. I'm just too embarrassed to tell them. Instead, I attempt to return to my haze with the aid of more vodka. I'm trying to ignore the fact that I barely ever drink wine anymore (except for pilfered wine from a fancy Italian restaurant, of course). Vodka has become my drink of choice these days, even after my graveyard shifts. Somehow, it always makes the unbearable things in life a little more manageable.

Now, as I'm sitting in the back of Jill's car, I realize I'm already pretty buzzed. But I'm not drunk. I'll fix that soon enough.

"We're late," Jill notes, glancing at the time as she pulls her Audi into the parking lot at The Barn Door.

"It's a party, Jill," Ronnie tells her. "Only nerds are on time to parties."

"Miles is one of our best friends," she replies. "We should've been on time."

Ronnie groans in response. "We're only fifteen minutes late!"

While they go back and forth, I remain silent in the back seat. I can feel my anxiety, fighting its way through the haze of vodka. I shouldn't have come here. I should've just stayed home.

I try calming myself—inhaling then slowly exhaling. Once we're stopped, I climb out of the backseat and silently follow behind Ronnie and Jill, as we make our way through the parking lot.

"You're quiet tonight," Ronnie observes.

"I'm just tired," I lie.

"How're you tired? Your ass slept all day," she laughs.

"Do you think you're coming down with something?" Jill adds.

"I'll be fine." My response is clipped as we walk into The Barn Door.

As soon as he sees the three of us enter, I hear Tony yell, "It's about time!"

Immediately, the rest of the party turns to watch as we approach—or the majority of the party does. I notice Brett doesn't turn around to look our way. He appears unfazed at our arrival, engaged in a conversation with Emily and Alyssa. I have to admit, I'm actually kind of relieved to see Emily and Alyssa here tonight. Maybe Miles and Brett will just hang out with them. Then I can safely hide in the corner all night, unnoticed.

Miles is currently talking with one of Brett's co-workers, a fellow firefighter named Nathan. From the few conversations I've been forced to endure with Nathan, I've come to the conclusion that he's completely full of himself, and a total asshole.

But I guess I thought that of Brett, too, when I first met him. Maybe I should give Nathan another chance.

My plans of going unnoticed tonight are quickly foiled, when Miles abruptly stops his conversation, then turns to stare at Ronnie, Jill, and me. As his eyes pass over the three of us, his gaze locks on mine, and I instantly feel like I'm going to vomit. All I want to do is turn around and run out of here.

I rapidly avert my eyes, looking at the ground as we join our group at the back of the bar.

"Hey, baby," Craig drawls, scooping Ronnie into his arms and giving her a kiss.

I smile as I watch them—Ronnie deserves this happiness.

"Howdy, gals!" Craig calls to Jill and me.

I imitate Craig's drawl and give him my best finger guns. "Howdy, cowboy."

Craig roars with contagious laughter, but all I can focus on is how Ronnie smiles at him.

"Sam, right?"

At the sound of my name, I whip around, almost crashing into Emily. "Sorry," I mumble. "And yes—Emily, right?"

"It's good to see you, again," she smiles sweetly. I watch as she glances curiously at Jill, who is now standing beside me.

I introduce them. "This is my roommate, Jill."

Emily holds out her hand in greeting. "Nice to meet you."

"It's nice to meet you, too." Jill takes Emily's hand in return. "I'm also Sam's best friend," she adds.

Turning to look at Jill, I smirk. Is Jillian Moore jealous?

"It's, uh, again, nice to meet you. See you around, Sam," Emily says nervously before walking back to join Brett and Alyssa.

"I didn't know you had a new friend," Jill says.

"She's Brett's newest girlfriend," I explain. "I must admit, she's much nicer than the last one."

"Oh."

"Don't worry, Jill...there's no replacing you." I wrap my arms around her, giggling as I try lifting her off the ground. She squeals with laughter until I set her safely back onto the wood floor.

"I see nothing's changed here." The sound of Zach's chuckling voice grabs our attention. Jill and I watch as Zach and his girlfriend, Sarah, approach us. Sarah must've decided Zach is moving too slow because she abruptly runs past him to pull Jill and me into a giant group hug.

I can't lie. I absolutely adore Sarah.

Understandably, I was nervous, at first, to meet my ex-boyfriend's new girlfriend, but after spending only an hour with Sarah, all my worries dissipated. She's truly wonderful, and I know how happy she makes Zach.

Out of the corner of my eye, I notice the way Zach smiles lovingly at his girlfriend when she hugs us. Zach deserves this happiness, too.

"Sam, I've been trying to call you all day," he claims when he reaches us. "I kind of wanted to talk to you before the party."

"*We* wanted to talk to you," Sarah corrects him.

"Okay..." I'm a bit confused. Did I do something to upset them?

Jill covers for me. "Sam has been sleeping all day. That's probably why she didn't answer."

"Oh, I thought you were off last night," Zach voices.

"She was. She went on a horrible date last night." Jill makes a cringing face, and I glare at her, trying to signal her to stop talking. Totally oblivious to my message, she proceeds to compliment Sarah on her outfit. I abandon my attempts at giving Jill non-verbal cues, then turn back to face Zach.

I'm mortified to find that Miles has now joined us, staring at me as he stands beside Zach. "Sam, we need to talk," he says.

"Wow—*everyone* wants to talk to you," Jill giggles.

Before I'm forced to respond to Miles, I'm saved by the sound of Craig, banging his pocket-knife against a beer bottle. He's currently standing on top of a chair at our favorite table. "I want to make a toast," he announces.

From behind the bar, I hear Van shouting, "Get off the chair, Craig!"

"Sorry, brother!" Craig calls back, hopping down from his impromptu stage.

It wouldn't be one of our pack get-togethers without an infamous Craig Corey speech.

"I want to start off by wishing a happy birthday to one of the best guys I know. The first time I met Miles—I kicked his ass." Craig laughs, and the rest of the party joins him.

"Hey, now! I think I held my own against Captain Cowboy," Miles chuckles. I steal a glance at him as he speaks, wishing more than anything that I could just have my friend back. How is it that I miss him already and we're standing just two feet apart?

"Yeah, Captain Cowboy versus the Jolly Green Giant," Brett howls.

"Alright, alright," Craig shouts, calming down the group so he can finish his toast. "I just want to say thank you for always being there for me. This year has been a tough one for me but being your friend has made it less tough. I love you, man."

"I love you, too, brother," Miles replies.

Craig raises his beer. "Happy birthday, Miles! Cheers to you!"

A chorus of "cheers" and "happy birthdays" surrounds me before everyone takes a sip of their drinks. I wish I had a drink, right about now. Why didn't we stop at the bar before walking over here?

"Happy birthday, Miles," I whisper, looking down at my Chucks.

At the familiar sound of Craig, once again, tapping his beer bottle with his pocketknife, I look back up. My breath catches when I see that Miles has turned around and is now staring, his hazel eyes boring into me. He takes a few steps in my direction until he's standing directly in front of me.

I'm distantly aware that Craig is still speaking, but I can barely hear anything he's saying over the pounding of my own heart.

"Sam," Miles whispers. He lifts his hand as if he's about to touch me but lets it drop back to his side.

My voice is hushed in reply, trying to remain unheard by those around us. "We can't do this." I'm not even sure what it is I mean by "this"—I just know I don't want to fight with him here and ruin his birthday party.

"All I want is *this*," he tells me softly.

"No more lies."

"I never lied to you," he says, his voice rising slightly. "I was just trying to calm Brett down until I could talk to him one-on-one. I wanted to tell him about us myself—not for him to find out like he did."

"Why would it even matter how Brett feels about us?"

"It matters more than you know. He's my best friend—" he pauses. "—Brett said that this morning when he drove you home, he told you he used to have feelings for you."

Suddenly, my mind drifts back to Brett kissing me on my patio this morning. Does Miles know he kissed me? Does Brett actually think a kiss equates to disclosing that he used to have feelings for me?

...Wait? Brett had feelings for me? What the hell?

I can't process any of this right now. "None of this even matters. There will never be an 'us' anyways—not now."

Just then, Craig's loud cheer interrupts our conversation: "Congrats to my best friend, Zach—he's getting MARRIED!"

My jaw hits the floor in disbelief as I stare towards where Zach and Sarah are standing. This must be what they wanted to talk to me about before the party.

The bar erupts in a chorus of cheers, as everyone moves to crowd around them. Everyone but Miles and me.

Miles stares down at me, lightly placing his large hands on my shoulders. He whispers to me, "Are you okay?"

I am actually extremely happy for Zach and Sarah. Maybe there's a small part of me that's jealous I'm not the one with the engagement ring on my finger, but I know Zach is marrying the person he's supposed to.

Zach isn't the one for me. Miles isn't either, for that matter.

"Don't touch me!" I snap, wrenching myself away from him.

I realize Jill and Ronnie must've heard me since they're now staring at Miles and me. I lower my voice before confronting him again. "Why don't you go make out with Alyssa? I bet you wouldn't be embarrassed to be seen with her."

I know I'm acting childish, but I can't help it—he hurt my feelings. The wound is still so fresh. Which is exactly why I didn't want to do this tonight.

"You think I'm embarrassed to be with you?" Miles asks (very loudly, I might add). Everyone must be staring at us now. How could they not be?

"You seemed pretty ashamed this morning. You know, when you were claiming how I meant nothing to you," I hiss under my breath. Terrified to confirm my suspicion that everyone is, indeed, staring at us, I refuse to take my eyes off Miles.

"You mean everything to me!" Miles shouts.

I hear someone gasp—I'm not sure who.

He takes another step towards me, our bodies almost touching. Before I can formulate a response, he leans down and kisses me. With one hand, he runs his fingers through my hair; with the other, he finds the small of my back, gently pulling me in closer to him.

I can hear Jill squeal, "Oh my gosh." Ronnie shout, "What the hell?" And a voice that sounds like Tony's yells, "Hot damn!"

I allow myself to kiss him for a few seconds more before coming to my senses. He tastes like an intoxicating combination of whiskey and spearmint. Then, abruptly, I jerk my body away from him. I take a few steps backward, then stare up at him in shock. Before I can stop myself, I'm yelling at him. "You don't get to do this! I'm not going to let you screw with my emotions anymore!"

Ronnie and Jill have started approaching me now. They know me well; they're aware I'm on the verge of losing my shit. Craig, Brett, and Tony are drawing near, as well.

It appears all of my friends are in some kind of unspoken agreement that I look unstable and may end up needing to be restrained. I should leave before I say or do something I regret—again.

"I'm going home," I say as I turn to leave, suddenly thankful I wore my Chucks. I had a sinking suspicion I'd be hoofing it home tonight. I knew I shouldn't have come.

The sound of Miles's shouting voice stops me in my tracks: "No!"

Hesitantly, I turn back around, meeting his eyes. "*You* don't get to do *this*," he asserts, pointing at me. "You don't get to keep leaving me like this."

"What do you want from me, Miles?" I throw my hands into the air, exasperated.

We're really becoming quite the spectacle, him and I.

His next words catch me off guard. "I didn't use to like coffee," he blurts out.

I stare at him in utter confusion. Then, I look over to where my friends are standing—they all look equally as confused.

He continues, "When I met you, I didn't like coffee. I used to drink an energy drink every morning. You can ask Brett."

"Oh yeah! You used to drink a shit ton of Red Bull," Brett chimes in.

"I'm confused," I mumble.

Jill raises her hand adding, "I'm also confused."

"Let the man finish his speech," Craig insists.

"It's not a speech," Miles explains.

Tony chuckles, "It totally sounds like the makings of a speech."

"Just get on with it already," Ronnie groans. "I need to know why you two were just swapping spit in the middle of The Barn Door."

Miles puts his focus back on me. "I never used to like coffee," he repeats. "But the first day I met you, I asked you to go get coffee with me. I needed an excuse to be able to see you again."

He takes a deep breath before continuing, as he takes a step closer to me. "As the years passed, I grew to like coffee more and more. Coffee just kind of became our thing, Sam." He pauses briefly. "...And now—no matter where I'm at or who I'm with—I can't drink a cup of coffee without thinking of you."

I stare into his hazel eyes, the truest hazel I've ever seen. I watch him nervously run his fingers through his hair, noticing his curls are slightly less wild than they were last night. Taking a small step towards him, I examine him closer. "You got a haircut."

He smirks. "You told me to."

"...You really never used to like coffee?"

"Not at all. But look at me now. I'm a man that owns a French press. And a damn milk frother," he chuckles softly. He reaches out, clasping both of my hands in his own. This time, I don't pull away from him. I allow my hands to fit perfectly into his. "Now, I can say, without a doubt, I'm in love with coffee," he starts. "...But not nearly as much as I'm in love with you, Sam Carter."

I can't help but smile up at him as he gazes down at me. That was officially the best "non-speech" I've ever heard.

"OH MY GOSH!" Jill shrieks.

I briefly turn away from Miles to grin at Jill. I knew she'd be just as impressed as me. His declaration of love—for coffee and myself—was definitely cinema-worthy. Actually, it was even better than the movies.

"I vote yes!" Craig exclaims, pumping his fist into the air.

"Babe, we're twenty-five now. Please tell me we aren't still doing this ridiculous voting thing," Ronnie sighs.

"*You're* twenty-five, darlin'. I'm still a spring chicken," he jokes back.

"I always forget you're a cougar, Veronica," Tony teases, while Ronnie dramatically rolls her eyes at him.

"Well, if we are voting," Brett starts. "It's a yes for me."

At this, Miles turns from me to lock eyes with Brett. I watch as he mouths "thank you" to his best friend, and as Brett subtly nods back in response.

Miles's eyes then return to mine. His hand gently tucks a loose tendril of hair behind my ear, before softly grazing my cheek with his thumb, as he gazes down at me.

"So, what's your vote, butthead?" His trademark sideways smirk forms across his face.

I'm fully aware at this moment that my cheeks are fire engine red from blushing. No one has ever looked at me the way he's looking at me right now.

"YES!" I exclaim, throwing myself into his arms. "A million times, yes."

He effortlessly lifts me into the air as he hugs me. The bar breaks into a chorus of cheers for the second time tonight. I guess love is in the air at The Barn Door this evening. Well, love and the familiar smell of spilled Budweiser.

As Miles sets me back onto the ground, he tenderly kisses me. "I love you, Sam," he murmurs softly as our lips part.

Maybe—just maybe—*I deserve this happiness, too.*

# CHAPTER FORTY-FOUR

## (September 2015):

Today is my twenty-fifth birthday, and I'm stuck working a graveyard shift.

Although it's a Wednesday night, and, technically, I should be off. I switched shifts with a co-worker this week so I could take a long weekend instead.

One might ask why I would need this weekend off. Well, the answer is, in fact, pretty self-explanatory: Zach is getting married on Saturday!

So, working on your twenty-fifth birthday seems like a fair trade to be able to travel to San Diego for your friend's wedding. It'll also be my first-time visiting California, so I couldn't be more excited.

Our entire pack—including Mama Margo—is flying to San Diego for Zach and Sarah's wedding.

While most of us—Jill, Ronnie, Craig, my boyfriend, and me—are flying out tomorrow afternoon, unfortunately, Margo and Brett had to book a later flight due to their work schedules. They won't be leaving Bristol until Friday.

There isn't actually an airport in Bristol, Virginia. The closest one is Tri-Cities Airport, located in Blountville, Tennessee. Thankfully, even though we have to drive to a different state, it's a little more than a twenty-minute drive if traffic is light.

And, if you're wondering who my boyfriend is...it's Miles, of course. He and I have been officially dating since his birthday last October, meaning we've been together for almost a year now.

I've been trying not to drive myself insane worrying about relationship timelines the way I have in the past. I've simply allowed myself to enjoy being in love with my best friend.

Being with Miles feels so natural to me now. Don't get me wrong—we'll still have our arguments and disagreements—but we always work it out in the end.

He's always urging me to communicate my feelings rather than constantly internalize them and push him away. My lack of communication is the root of most of our disputes, I know. But I'm steadily working on being more open with him.

Luckily, he's an extremely patient man.

Recently, Miles decided to go back to school to finish his bachelor's degree in biology. After he graduates, he hopes to get accepted into a physician assistant program at a nearby university. His dream job is to be a physician assistant working in an emergency department.

I'm so proud of him for making the decision to go back to school. I know he'll make a great PA one day. I'm also thankful he hasn't put any pressure on me to go back to school, too. For now, I'm content with my associate's degree.

Unfortunately, Tony wasn't able to complete the fire academy last year. He said he hadn't been accustomed to working under that level of stress. By the time he finally started to adjust after a few weeks in, he'd already accumulated enough points against him to be released from the academy. Tony beat himself up pretty badly about it all. The day he was released, he got drunk for the first time in almost four years.

In all my years of knowing him, I had never seen Anthony Hernandez drunk. When he entered our pack about three years ago, he had already decided to live a sober lifestyle. I never understood why, at just twenty-four years old, Tony had decided he never wanted to drink alcohol again. But after seeing him that night? I finally understood.

After Tony received the news that he was being let go from the academy, he went straight to The Barn Door, then proceeded to get dangerously intoxicated, alone, on a Tuesday afternoon. Miles, Jill, Brett, and I had been watching a movie together at Jill's and my apartment when Brett received a call from Van—the owner of The Barn Door.

Van had to cut Tony off because of how drunk he was. This caused Tony to become angry and overly aggressive. Van told Brett if he didn't come down to the bar to pick Tony up, he'd be forced to call the police because he was starting to cause a scene.

This wasn't the Tony we knew. Tony was never angry or aggressive; he was only ever lovable and kind.

So, the four of us drove down to The Barn Door that Tuesday afternoon to help our friend. I'll never forget how we found him. He was barely recognizable. Thankfully, his anger simmered at the sight of the four of us. It was a bit of a struggle, but Brett and Miles were finally able to drag Tony into the back seat of my Altima.

Yes, it's true. I was finally forced to purchase a new car. After many years of faithful service, my 2001 Chevy Blazer died on me; smack dab in the middle of the intersection at Main and Spruce. They informed me the repairs would cost me more than the car was worth, so I made the difficult decision to trade it in for a brand-new Nissan Altima.

As I drove the five of us back to our apartment, I glanced in my rearview mirror, watching as Tony began sobbing in my backseat. He sat in the middle, between Jill and Brett, both of them wrapping their arms around him without hesitation as he cried. Tony repeatedly uttered the word "failure" until his sobs became so heavy, he could no longer speak. I felt my own warm tears streaming down my cheeks, my heart breaking for one of my best friends.

Miles must've noticed my silent tears because he gently placed his large palm on my thigh as I continued driving. Then he leaned in and whispered, "He has us. He's going to be okay."

I nodded my head in agreement, pulling into the apartment complex.

Thankfully, Miles was right; somehow, he always is. The following morning, Tony once again made the decision to part ways with alcohol, saying, "It's never too late to start over."

I'm happy to report that he hasn't had a drink of alcohol since that emotional night last November. He's even been volunteering at a firehouse in a nearby county for the last few months. He hopes his volunteer firefighting will outweigh the blemish on his record of failing out of his first academy, as well as help prove his skills and competency. Where there's a will, there's a way. Anthony Hernandez has so much will, I'm positive that, one day, he'll find a way.

Another huge development from the past year? Ronnie has, once again, moved off Jill's and my couch. This summer, Ronnie and Craig made the giant step of moving in together. Craig was promoted to assistant manager of The Cinedome, and, with his pay increase, he and Ronnie were able to snag a lease on a beautiful condo. I have a sneaking suspicion he'll be proposing to my gorgeous friend any day now. He keeps saying he just needs to finish writing her song—when Veronica's song is finished, he'll be dropping on one knee.

An arguably even bigger development? Jill and Brett recently started "dating"—I use the term loosely. They both keep reassuring us they aren't labeling whatever it is that they're doing. They're just having fun. Honestly, I think Jill is trying to convince herself of that, too. I know she's had feelings for Brett, pretty much since the day she met him, and would prefer if the two of them were in a committed relationship. But as we all know, Brett doesn't really date and if he does, it usually doesn't last longer than a month.

I'm hoping that's not the case this time. Because I'll kick his ass if he breaks my best friend's heart.

At this point, we're no longer doing that ridiculous voting thing since all of us are pretty much coupled up. But rest assured, if we were, I would've voted "no" on this pairing.

It's not that I don't love Brett, because I do—I just know him too well.

Finally, the absolute biggest development over the past year in my own life—at long last, I adopted a dog of my own. I am officially a dog owner!

Initially, I was hell-bent on adopting a Labrador like Scout. I'd fallen so madly in love with that dog, I was convinced I had to have one of my own. Miles encouraged me to keep an open mind when we went to the local animal shelter, but I knew what I wanted. Sometimes, though, what we want isn't always what we need.

That morning, I ended up leaving the animal shelter with a one-year-old black pug cradled in my arms. As soon as I saw his large, sad eyes staring at me through the kennel bars, I knew we were meant to be. I named him Archie, and I can't explain how much joy he has brought to, not just me, but our entire pack. That dog has such a huge personality, and he's so incredibly loving.

It was also a pleasant surprise to both Miles and me to see how quickly Scout and Archie bonded. Sometimes Miles and I joke that we should just hurry up and move in together, so we don't have to keep separating them. If I'm being honest, though, I don't know if I'm ready for that yet.

While we're out of town for the wedding, Scout and Archie will be spending the weekend at my dad's house. My half-sister Taylor couldn't be more excited. She's been begging our dad to let her adopt a dog since she could speak. Maybe after this weekend, he'll finally cave.

Now, sitting behind my computer at the nurses' station, I can't help but stare at the clock on the screen, willing the time to move faster as I think of this weekend. Only twelve more hours until I'm off work and able to rapidly finish packing for my trip. I really shouldn't have put that off until the last minute.

Seeing the call light illuminate above room 542, I force my exhausted body out of the uncomfortable rolling chair I've been sitting in. I guess it's time to get to work.

Since Wednesday nights aren't my normal shift, I'm not working with Lucie and Tanya tonight. The three of us work so well together at this point, it feels odd to be working with anyone else.

As for Lucie, though, she was just accepted into the community college's nursing program for the fall semester. So, I'm sure she'll have to alter her schedule depending on her clinical rotations. I'm so incredibly proud of her. She has really come into her own over the last year. Although I once thought that Tanya and I would be the ones to pull Lucie out of her shell, I was wrong. Lucie has come out of her shell all on her own, and on her own terms.

Walking towards room 542, I finally realize how tired I am. I think the night shift is really starting to wear on me. But as I said before, there's no way I can abandon my work pack.

Coffee will fix my exhaustion.

Coffee fixes everything.

# CHAPTER

# FORTY-FIVE:

Before walking into room 542, I quickly glance down at my report sheet. The patient currently in this room is Mr. Henry Thomas, a ninety-eight-year-old man with end-stage cardiac disease. I was able to skim through his chart after receiving the report from the day-shift. According to his chart, Mr. Thomas is "alert and oriented times four," which is medical lingo to explain that he's fully awake and knows who he is, where he is, and the date and time.

As a nurse on the hospice floor, I find a good majority of patients, by the time they're admitted to our unit, are somewhere between deeply lethargic to unresponsive. So, it's refreshing to have patients that I'm able to hold a conversation with once in a while.

Mr. Thomas is in heart failure. To measure how well your heart is pumping blood, we use something called an ejection fraction. A normal ejection fraction is anywhere between fifty to seventy percent; Henry's ejection fraction is only fifteen percent. In layman's terms, his heart was no longer functioning properly. When someone is in heart failure, they can experience a lot of unpleasant symptoms.

Oftentimes, people exhibit shortness of breath and extreme fatigue. It's not uncommon for people with end-stage cardiac disease to even develop massive amounts of fluid retention—or edema.

Fortunately, the report from the day-shift nurse shows Mr. Thomas has been very comfortable, remaining symptom-free throughout the day. I was told his condition had stabilized over the last week, so his family made the decision to have him transferred to a group home tomorrow morning.

A common misconception is that when someone signs onto hospice care, they die immediately. In reality, it's possible for hospice and palliative care patients to live months—sometimes even years. When you're given a terminal diagnosis, choosing hospice care isn't a death sentence. Rather, it's an opportunity to live out the remainder of your days on your own terms, however many days that may be.

Our unit inside Summit Valley isn't a long-term care unit— another common misconception among some of our patients' family members. Although we do often care for patients actively dying on our floor, we also help manage hospice and palliative care patients' symptoms, even when they aren't yet near the end of life. If the patient's symptoms are managed properly, and they remain stable, they're transferred back home, to a group home, or some other type of care facility.

Deciding on the right group home, assisted living, or long-term care facility for yourself or a loved one is extremely stressful. It's a huge decision that most people aren't ready to make when the time arises. Luckily, we have amazing social workers to help patients and their families make these hard decisions.

After one final look over my report sheet, I fold it, shoving it into my scrub top pocket. Since this is my first time as Mr. Thomas's nurse, I wanted to familiarize myself with his story before meeting him. In my opinion, every patient has a story that goes beyond their diagnosis.

Mr. Thomas is a veteran, having fought in two wars. After his time in the military, he was able to return to college and finish his master's degree. He then had nearly a thirty-year career as a high school history teacher and football coach. He was married for almost seventy years until his wife passed away about two years ago from emphysema. They had three children together, two of which are still living; one of his sons passed away in a motor vehicle accident in 1982.

Sadly, I don't always have the time to dive this deeply into a patient's "story,"—it would be ideal if I did. It can make such a huge difference in how we provide care to our patients.

As healthcare professionals, sometimes we forget we aren't just treating an illness or a disease—we're treating people. Real people who have loved and lost, many of which have lived amazing lives we rarely get to know anything about.

I'm a nurse that cares for patients at the end of their stories. If I get the opportunity to hear a patient's story in their final chapter, before their book is closed, I take advantage of it.

Before I enter, I lightly knock on the door of room 542.

"Come in," a voice calls.

As I enter the hospital room, I find Mr. Thomas propped up in bed, watching The History Channel. Knowing Henry's background as a veteran and history teacher, this makes perfect sense.

"Good evening, Mr. Thomas. My name is Sam. I'll be your nurse tonight."

"Please, dear. Call me Henry," he corrects me, then adds, "You look awful young to be a registered nurse."

I grin back at him. "Thanks." I get this comment a lot. I've learned to take it as a compliment rather than an insult.

Henry gives me a smile in return. "What can I do for you, Sam?" I'm assuming he must have turned his call light on by mistake.

"May I do a quick assessment?"

"Of course," he replies, pulling the blanket from his legs. I can already tell he knows the drill; this definitely isn't the first time he's been assessed.

Making small talk with Henry while I perform my initial assessment, I ask him if he's a football fan. I assume so, considering he was a high school football coach for almost thirty years.

It turns out, Henry is a fan of all types of sports. He even played football, baseball, and basketball in his youth. When he discloses to me that he's a diehard fan of The Chicago Cubs, I instantly think of Miles—the other diehard Cubs fan I know.

From my assessment, I deduce that he appears comfortable. His respirations appear even and non-labored on two liters of oxygen via a nasal cannula, and his lung sounds are clear. However, I did note that he had two-plus pitting edema—or swelling—to both of his feet. The two-plus refers to the severity of the edema. The way we measure it is by lightly pressing your finger into the area that's swollen, then counting the seconds it takes for the finger indentation to return to normal. The scale is from one to four, so two-plus means it took less than fifteen seconds for the slight indentation from my finger to rebound. All and all, not terrible for someone suffering from end-stage cardiac disease.

Once I'm done, I decide to take a few minutes to chat with Henry. It is a rarity for me to have spare time, so I thought I'd take advantage of it by having a conversation with my only alert patient of the night. "Are you excited to transfer to the group home in the morning? I hear it's one of the best in town."

"Can I be honest with you, Sam?" Henry's question catches me slightly off-guard.

"Of course you can."

"I don't know if this ninety-eight-year-old heart has another move left in it," he sighs. "Unless it's a move upstairs to see my Gertrude."

"I read in your chart that your wife passed away about two years ago. I'm very sorry for your loss."

"My heart breaks a little more each day I've had to live without her. I've tried to stay strong for my son and daughter, but this life has been so lonely without my wife." Henry hesitates before proceeding, "I know Gerdy is with our son Jimmy. He's been gone for many years now...I know they're waiting for me."

This is one of the many instances in my career where I have no idea what to say. So, instead of struggling to find the right words, I simply place my hand in his. He meets my gaze, tears brimming his eyes, then grants me a soft smile as he lightly squeezes my hand. I notice a lone tear roll down his cheek.

"I know I'll be reunited with them soon," he murmurs.

I gently nod my head, reassuring him as I continue holding his hand.

"Tell me, Sam. Have you ever lost anyone you love?" My eyes widen in surprise at Henry's sudden question. I don't think I've ever been asked this before. I hesitate briefly, trying to decide how to answer.

Finally, I resolve to tell this man the truth. I'm going to tell him something I never speak of—something I haven't even told my own boyfriend.

"My brother died when I was seven. He was only nine years old. He had a brain tumor." These words sound foreign leaving my mouth.

"What was his name?" Henry asks.

"Matty," I say as I hang my head and shrug. "Well, Matthew. But I called him Matty."

"Since it will be a long, long time until you're able to..." Henry pauses, gently squeezing my hand. "I'll be sure to tell your Matty hello for you, Nurse Sam."

I quickly wipe a tear from my eye before it has the chance to fall. "Thank you." It's all I can manage to say.

I'm an hour and a half into my shift, and I've finally finished my first rounds of the night. Usually, it only takes me about thirty minutes to do my initial rounds, but the patient in room 545 required impromptu extensive wound care. So, that set me back about forty-five minutes.

After leaving my last patient's room, I rush into the break room to make myself a fresh cup of coffee before beginning my first medication pass. When my coffee is finished brewing, I take a long gulp, then reach into my pocket to retrieve my favorite pen so I can inscribe my name on the side of the Styrofoam cup.

To my horror, I realize my favorite pen is no longer in my pocket. I start to panic—if nurses are absurdly particular over anything, it's our pens.

I can't believe I lost my favorite pen. This shift is beginning to go downhill fast. Thinking back, I realize it must've fallen out of my pocket when I sat at Henry's bedside. It's imperative for me to find my pen before I begin my med-pass. It just writes so well. I can't stomach having to try and find a new favorite.

Setting my cup onto the break room table, I then speed-walk down the hallway. I'm going to perform a quick sweep of room 542 before I start the other thousand and one tasks I need to complete.

It has to be in there.

Assuming Henry is still awake—it's only been a little over an hour since I chatted with him last—I lightly knock before entering.

This time, he doesn't answer. I guess he must've fallen asleep.

Upon entering the room, I notice The History Channel and the overhead light above the bed are both still on.

"I'm sorry to disturb you, Mr. Thomas," I begin, taking a step toward his bed. As my vision focuses on Henry, I stop in my tracks.

Henry is still sitting up in bed, propped up by multiple pillows, only now, his body is motionless. His complexion has taken on an alarming pallor that wasn't present an hour ago.

Immediately, I can tell he's gone. Sometimes you don't need a stethoscope to tell you these things.

Nonetheless, I approach Henry's bedside, checking for a pulse—I feel nothing. Removing my stethoscope from around my neck, I move to listen to his lung and heart sounds. Finally, I examine both of his pupils with my pen light.

Nothing.

*I can't believe he's gone.*

Slowly, I flatten the hospital bed. I need to straighten Henry's body before calling his children to inform them of his passing. It can be extremely difficult for people to view their family member's body after death. We try not to make it more traumatizing by leaving patients' bodies in an unpleasant-looking position.

As I glance down at the bed controls, I spot my favorite pen lying on the floor at my feet. Instinctively, I lean down to retrieve it. As I begin to stand, I hesitate when something catches my eye. I see the corner of what looks like a piece of paper poking out from beneath the bed. Henry must have dropped whatever it is after I left his room earlier. I bend back down and carefully grasp the piece of paper. I quickly realize it's not paper, but rather a black-and-white photograph that was lying underneath Henry's hospital bed.

Hesitantly, I examine it. It's an old photo of a beautiful young woman. In her arms is a tightly swaddled newborn baby. Slowly, I turn the photograph over to see "Gerdy and Jimmy" scrawled in faded black script.

This photograph doesn't belong on the floor. Before leaving room 542, I gently place the picture on Henry's chest, directly over his heart.

No longer would his ninety-eight-year-old heart have to break. No longer would it have to go through another move.

Henry's heart was finally home.

## CHAPTER FORTY-SIX:

# HENRY THOMAS

### September 2, 2015, 20:42

don't want to disappoint my children—Martha and Daniel. They've done so much for me over these last two years. I know they want me to move in the morning.

They tell me I'll be happier in the group home—that there'll be more for me to do.

But, I'm tired. I'm tired of living without her.

I saw her tonight—Gertrude. She was here. As soon as the nurse left me. Gertrude stood before me, in the corner of this very room. I saw her, clear as day.

She had finally come to take me home. Because the only home I've ever truly known was with her.

The house she and I shared for all those years was our home. But after she died—after she left me—it was only a house. A very empty house. She had taken my home with her.

*The doctors tell me my heart is failing. Any day could be my last. But I could have told you that without all those fancy tests they ran on me.*

*My heart was doomed the day my Gertrude died. Every day without her, my heart has failed me a little more.*

*But, tonight, I saw her. I saw my Gerdy.*

*It ruined me to tell her goodbye. But, now, I'm ready to say hello again. I'm ready to be home once more.*

*Then, there'll be no more goodbyes for her and me. Never again will I have to say goodbye to my Gerdy.*

*I'm also ready to tell my Jimmy hello once again. Oh, how I have missed my son. I know I'll find him with his mother.*

*And a promise is a promise. I mustn't forget to say hello to Matty for a kind, young nurse.*

*After ninety-eight beautiful years, leaving this world doesn't feel like goodbye.*

***This is hello.***

# CHAPTER
# FORTY-SEVEN:

As I swipe my badge to clock out, I can't help but think of Henry. His son, Daniel, had been shocked when I told him of his father's passing. Daniel argued that he'd just spoken with his father on the phone that afternoon, and he'd sounded fine. How could he have died only hours later?

Unfortunately, when it comes to matters of the heart, people can pass away quite suddenly. At least that's what I had tried explaining to a devastated Daniel.

I hate when I have to inform a patient's family member of difficult news like this over the phone, but sometimes we have no other choice. Still, I'm always left with a pit in my stomach, even after years of hospice nursing under my belt.

Imagine being the person who calls to tell someone, arguably, the worst news they will receive in their existence. Hearing the screams, cries, and howls from the other end of the receiver. Knowing you're the one who just delivered the news that shattered their whole world. It sucks being that person. Occasionally, I wonder if my anxiety would be less severe if I'd chosen a different career. A career that wasn't entirely about life and death—where people's lives weren't constantly in my hands. A career where I wasn't surrounded by continuous despair and devastation.

Honestly, I'm embarrassed to even think these thoughts, let alone verbalize them to anyone. I chose to become a nurse to help people, no matter how hard that may be at times. I know I need to remain strong for my patients and their families. Sometimes, though, it sucks being strong.

As I stand at the hospital elevator, impatiently waiting for the doors to open, I try forcing myself to stop thinking about how weak I feel. I audibly groan, remembering I still have to finish packing for San Diego when I get home. I think I definitely deserve a Bloody Mary to take my mind off last night's shift. On second thought, maybe I should have a vodka Red Bull instead. I won't be able to get any sleep until we're on the plane this afternoon. I don't even have time for a power nap. Even though I love the night-shift—I make an extra two dollars an hour and get to work with some of my favorite people—I think it's slowly killing me.

Hearing the ping of the elevator as it reaches my floor, I quickly squeeze through the doors as they open, jabbing the button for the hospital lobby. The sooner I get home, the sooner my vacation can start.

"I would ask if you've been avoiding me, but the answer is fairly obvious."

Immediately, I recognize the voice, my eyes darting up from my clogs, to find Dr. Connors standing next to me in the elevator. I'd been in such a rush; I didn't even notice him standing there when I hurried inside. I haven't seen Richard since our awful first-and-only date almost a year ago. Working night-shift and weekends has helped me avoid running into him in the hospital. Only now do I realize that switching shifts wasn't conducive to my attempts at avoiding Dr. Jackass.

"Oh, I didn't even notice it was you," I mumble in response.

"Ouch," he laughs uncomfortably.

"I didn't mean it like that."

"Can we talk?"

At his request, I randomly blurt, "I have a boyfriend now."

"...And I have a fiancé," he chuckles.

I stare at him wide-eyed, my mouth falling open. I was *not* expecting that. "Um—congrats," I finally manage to respond.

"Thanks." Richard grins as we both step out of the elevator, into the hospital lobby. "What I wanted to tell you, though, was...I'm sorry, Sam."

And I *definitely* wasn't expecting that.

I put my hand up, signaling for Richard to stop talking, in an attempt to hurry along with the conversation. "Really, it's fine."

Miles switched shifts to have this weekend off, so he also worked a graveyard shift last night. He's supposed to be meeting me in this very lobby, any moment now. I don't think Miles was serious when he threatened to kick Richard's ass last year but still. I don't want to chance it.

"No, please let me finish," he pleads. When I nod at him to continue, he reveals, "I lost my grandmother to end-stage colon cancer in January."

Instinctively, I try consoling him. "Oh, I'm so sorry."

"Thank you. She went into an inpatient hospice facility back in Arkansas. That's where she spent the final three days of her life." He sighs, pausing momentarily to compose himself. "The hospice nurses and nursing aides were amazing. I never truly understood what it is you do until then. Just because it isn't life-saving work doesn't mean it's not life-changing work. The world needs nurses like you, Sam. I'm sorry for trying to convince you otherwise."

"Thank you," I whisper. Never in a million years did I imagine I'd receive this type of an apology from Richard. "...I'm sorry I called you Dr. Jackass." He softly chortles. I can't help but giggle as I think about our disastrous first date.

He grins at me. "No hard feelings. I can kind of be a jackass sometimes."

Just then, a familiar voice breaks up our conversation. "Am I interrupting something?"

I quickly whirl around to face Miles, still dressed in his paramedic uniform. His mouth is drawn into a distinct frown, as he visibly straightens his shoulders, flaunting his full height.

"This must be the boyfriend," Richard comments, offering his hand for Miles to shake. "I was just apologizing to Sam for how rudely I behaved last year."

For a moment, Miles looks confused, obviously thinking this encounter was going in an entirely different direction. He hesitates for a few seconds but finally accepts Richard's handshake.

I smile up at Miles—my patient, kind-hearted, forgiving boyfriend.

"I was worried she was about to beat the shit out of you," he jokes, releasing Richard's hand.

The sound of Richard's laughter echoes through the bustling hospital lobby. He turns to me then, giving me his handsome, million-dollar smile. Now, he offers his hand to me. "Friends?"

"Friends," I confirm, shaking his hand.

"Well, I better hurry. I promised Margo I'd get her a coffee—Lord knows I don't want to be on that woman's bad side," he chuckles softly.

Well, we're minutes from boarding our flight, and I can confidently say that I'm drunk. When I finally got home after my shift to finish packing, I proceeded to take three shots of vodka on top of downing a vodka Red Bull. Then, at the bar inside the airport terminal, I drank at least four beers with Ronnie and Craig as we were waiting to board.

Jill forced us to arrive at the airport almost three hours before our flight was scheduled, so we had plenty of time to kill. For some reason, Miles didn't want to drink. So, while the rest of us got properly plastered, he, Jill, and Tony decided to hang out at the gate. Jill just so happened to have UNO and Skip-Bo in her Mary Poppins-sized carry-on, so they passed the time playing cards.

Thankfully, it's finally time for us to board our flight. As we walk through the jet bridge to board the plane, I try my best not to stumble. Moments ago, I was forced to chug my last beer because they called our boarding group. I feel Miles's arm around my waist as he guides me to walk in front of him. He grabs my tote bag off of my shoulder, slinging it over his own. Then, he rests both of his hands on my hips in an attempt to steady me as we board.

He leans down to whisper in my ear, "You need to keep it together, Sam. If you seem too drunk, they'll kick us off the flight." I can tell he's annoyed with me.

"Why would they kick you off?" The question didn't seem stupid in my head, but by his reaction, I realize it must be.

He stares back at me blankly. "Well, I'm not going to leave my girlfriend behind—especially not alone and intoxicated."

"I'm sorry," I whisper to him, as I clumsily scoot down the center aisle to our row. "I have to pee." By this point, all of my words are coming out slurred.

"Hold it," he snaps. Yup, he's definitely annoyed with me.

As we reach our row, I turn to face Miles. "Can I have the window seat?" Glancing behind him, I see Ronnie, Craig, and Tony sliding into the row in front of ours.

"What if Jill wants it?" Miles is no longer hiding his irritation.

Jill is standing directly behind Miles, with her huge tote bag slung over her shoulder, patiently waiting for us to sit our asses down.

"I don't mind the aisle," Jill chimes in sweetly.

"So, you want my 6'4" self to squeeze into the middle seat?" Miles gripes at me.

"Pleaseee," I whine, purposefully pouting my lips and batting my eyes as I look up at him. I know I'm being wildly selfish. Miles also worked graveyard last night, so he hasn't slept either. But I also know he can't say no to me. I shouldn't take advantage of this, but I'm drunk, and I want to sleep. Everyone knows the window seat is the best seat for sleeping.

"Fine," he grumbles, ushering me to sit down.

"I love you." Then I slide into our row, seating myself beside the window.

"I love you, too," he mutters, trying to load our carry-ons as quickly as possible into the overhead compartment. Then he turns to Jill and offers to load her giant tote into the overhead compartment, as well. "Sorry, she's pretty drunk," he says to her as she hands him her bag.

Jill smiles at him in return. "It's no problem."

Do they think I can't hear them? I'm drunk—not deaf. Why the hell is Miles apologizing to my best friend for me being drunk?

"Ignore those party poopers," Ronnie whispers to me from the seat in front of mine. She's turned around to peek at me through the space between the seats, and she gives me a smug smile. "We're not drunk—we're fun."

I can't help but grin back at her. Ronnie's right. Jill and Miles are just being party poopers. I'm not going to let them ruin my buzz. I'm allowed to be drunk. I'm on vacation.

Miles awkwardly situates his tall form into the narrow seat beside mine. He mumbles under his breath, "I should've upgraded to extra legroom." Then at me, "Put your seatbelt on."

"Don't tell me what to do," I hiss back at him.

"Jesus, Sam. Stop acting like a brat."

I whip around to glare at him, while Jill hesitantly seats herself in the aisle seat beside Miles, staring at me with weary eyes. I can tell she's internally begging me not to lose my shit right now.

After over a decade of friendship, she knows me well. And, for Jill, I try to remain calm.

Instead, I whine. "Stop being mean to me." I know Miles hates it when I whine, so I purposely do it to piss him off.

"I'm not being mean to you. Try to get some sleep." He hands me his neck pillow.

I stubbornly refuse to take the pillow from his hands. "What will *you* use for a pillow?"

In response, he places his pillow gently around my neck. Before I can argue further, he kisses me softly, the pad of his thumb grazing my cheek. "I'll use my stubborn, bratty, beautiful girlfriend," he murmurs, wrapping his arm around me.

"Get a room!" Tony hollers from in front of us, at which Miles and I both start to laugh.

"I'm sorry I was a brat. Thank you for letting me have the window seat." I know he's just as exhausted as I am.

"You know I'd do anything for you, Sam," he whispers, reaching over and buckling my seatbelt for me.

He's right. I do know he'd do anything for me. But I also know it's wrong of me to keep taking advantage of that fact.

# CHAPTER FORTY-EIGHT:

The wedding ceremony was breathtaking. Zach and Sarah recited their vows on a private section of the beach, just as the sun was setting. The ocean waves crashed to the shore as Zach kissed his stunning bride. It truly could've been a scene from a Disney movie—a happily ever after of cinematic proportions.

Now, I'm waiting impatiently to enter the hotel where the reception is being held. I won't lie, I'm thankful Jill convinced me to bring a sweater. I was convinced people didn't wear sweaters in California, but it's surprisingly chilly on the beach after nightfall in September.

I'm relieved to see a hotel staff member start ushering wedding guests inside. I'm in desperate need of a cocktail. Although Ronnie and I pre-gamed back at our hotel before the ceremony, that was hours ago. My buzz is almost completely gone now.

Jill, Ronnie, Margo, and I excitedly enter the hotel lobby. By this point, we're all just happy to be inside. The boys are all Zach's groomsmen, so they're currently busy taking pictures with the rest of the bridal party.

As the four of us enter the banquet hall, I'm disappointed to find out the bridal party will all be sitting together at a long table in the front of the room. Which means I'll be separated from my boyfriend for pretty much the entire night.

Great.

"Well, I guess we're not sitting with our men," Ronnie states the obvious, as she examines the seating chart prominently displayed at the entrance of the banquet hall.

"It's quite common for the bridal party to sit together during the reception," Jill informs us.

I let out an audible groan. "It's stupid." I resist the urge to kick over the stand displaying the stupid seating chart.

Suddenly, Margo starts power-walking ahead of us when she spots a smorgasbord of appetizers beautifully arranged on a banquet table across the room.

"I'd want my whole bridal party to sit together," Jill points out, pulling Ronnie's and my gaze away from Margo's mad dash to the food.

Ronnie turns to Jill, giving her a teasing smirk. "Already planning your wedding to Brett, Jilly Bean?"

Jill doesn't seem to find Ronnie's joke all that funny. "That's not what I said, Veronica." She thrusts both of her hands onto her hips. "Plus, we've only been dating a month."

"It's already been a month?" I blurt, a sudden pit forming in my stomach. Considering Brett's dating history, the one-month mark usually isn't a good thing. But there's just no way he'd do that to Jill...I mean, it's Jill. Who could hurt her? She's literally the sweetest person alive.

"A month to the day," she announces with a giggle, a visible blush forming on her cheeks. "I guess that makes this our one-month anniversary."

"Ew—gag." Ronnie starts making exaggerated gagging noises as the three of us join Margo at the appetizer table.

"Ronnie!" I scold, giving her a disapproving look.

Margo turns around with a full plate of food in her hand and immediately notices how upset Jill looks. "What's going on?"

"Oh, just Jill going on and on about Brett," Ronnie groans as she dramatically rolls her eyes. Jill has grown extremely silent and looks like she might cry. I know neither of us approve of Brett and Jill dating, but now Ronnie is just being mean.

Margo glares daggers at Ronnie. "Behave yourself, Veronica Mae." She then turns to Jill and smiles at her sweetly before taking a huge bite of a cucumber sandwich. "I'm happy for you and Brett," she says with her mouth full. Margo must be ravenous, it's unlike her to talk with food in her mouth.

"Thank you, Margo," Jill replies, before turning back to glower at Ronnie.

As we move to fill our plates with appetizers, I mutter under my breath, thinking nobody can hear me, "I'll kick his ass if he hurts you."

Ronnie leans over to whisper in my ear. "*We'll* kick his ass."

About an hour later, I'm excited to hear the DJ finally start playing music we can dance to. I'm currently five vodka cranberries in, and I'm just drunk enough to bust a move on the dance floor with my girls.

We were briefly able to chat with Miles, Brett, Craig, and Tony before they were ushered off to their assigned seats at the head table. I loathe seating charts. I have to admit, though, the boys all look extremely handsome. They all clean up well.

In more shocking news, Zach finally cut his hair. The man bun is officially no more.

For some reason, it almost seems like a different lifetime when Zach and I dated. I wonder if this is always how it feels to attend your ex-boyfriend's wedding.

Zach has found his person, and I couldn't be happier for him.

As I watch guests start to shuffle onto the dance floor, I decide to drag Jill and Ronnie out there with me. Margo vehemently refuses, and I don't push the matter because she still scares the shit out of me. I strongly agree with Dr. Connors—she isn't someone whose bad side I want to be on.

The three of us start jumping around like fools when the song "Down" by Jay Sean comes on. Jill is oddly obsessed with this song. She, Ronnie, and I have danced together around our apartment to it many times.

I spot Miles striding onto the dance floor. All of our friends look handsome tonight, but Miles takes the cake. Granted, I'm a little biased.

Miles approaches the corner of the dance floor where my two best friends and I are flailing around more than dancing. He's wearing a sharp, navy-blue suit. His usually wild curls are tamed and styled tonight. This past year, he decided he wanted to grow a mustache. I don't dislike his mustache, but I miss seeing the small scar above his upper lip. It's one of the million things I love about this man.

He grants me one of his infamous sideways smirks, sweeping me into his arms. My breath catches as I stare up into his beautiful hazel eyes.

"Hey, you," he murmurs into my hair.

Zach may have found his person, but I'm pretty sure I've found my person, too.

"Somehow, you're my real-life Prince Charming, my Superman and my best friend all rolled into one."

"I'll be whoever you want me to be," he whispers. I'm suddenly reminded of that day at the coffee shop, before my date with Richard, when Miles vowed something similar.

"You're already exactly who I want you to be," I tell him. He leans down to me, and I close my eyes as his lips meet mine. He tastes like whiskey and spearmint.

When our lips part, I find myself wishing the reception was already over. Being able to be alone with Miles in our hotel room these past two nights has been pure bliss. Maybe the two of us moving in together isn't such a bad idea.

"I'm sorry to interrupt," Jill squeaks. Miles and I look over to see Jill awkwardly standing beside us.

"No need to be so formal, Jill. It's just us," Miles chuckles.

"I know. It just looked like you two were having a moment."

"It's not like Miles was asking me to marry him or anything," I remark sarcastically, smirking at Miles.

Miles softly kisses me on the cheek. "...Yet," he faintly whispers, his lips grazing my earlobe.

Alright, we're going back to our hotel room right this instant.

"I think this kind of stuff is what Jill meant by 'having a moment,' y'all," Craig cuts in. I turn away from Miles to smile at him. He's looking extremely dapper this evening—especially with a drop-dead gorgeous red-head on his arm.

Ronnie comes running up behind Craig, wrapping her arms around him. "Found my man!"

"Oh, trust me, darlin', I'd never hide from you," he drawls, turning to tip his cowboy hat at Ronnie.

Sarah requested that Craig not wear his cowboy hat for the ceremony and pictures, but she gave him the okay to don it for the reception. Zach tried to convince Sarah of how cold and lonely Craig's head gets without his hat, but she wasn't budging on the matter.

"Have any of you seen Brett?" Jill asks. "I've been looking for him everywhere."

"He and I were smoking cigars out on the patio not too long ago," Tony tells her.

Jill seems appalled. "Ew! Cigars? Brett's not a smoker!" Jill, a respiratory therapist, would never date a smoker.

"It's a special occasion. People smoke cigars on special occasions, Jilly Bean," Ronnie says. "It's just as normal as the bridal party all sitting together."

"If you say so," Jill replies. "I'll look for him out on the patio."

Tony offers to go with her in search of Brett.

"Aw! You're so sweet, Tony Cakes," Ronnie coos.

"Sweet as candy," Tony purrs, winking at Ronnie.

Miles pouts, "Am I ever gonna get a nickname?" The five of us laugh as he continues to sulk. I guess he was serious.

"It just has to come organically. It's nothing against you personally," Ronnie explains. "You know I love you, Miles. You put up with all of my Sammie Bear's bullshit."

"Hey!" I shout trying to sound angry, but my laughter betrays me. Ronnie is one hundred percent correct. Miles does, indeed, put up with all my bullshit.

Jill tries to stifle her giggles before turning to address Tony. "It's okay. Thank you for offering, though, Tony. I'll be back in a couple minutes." As she walks away from us, we hear her ponder aloud, "I wonder if the DJ will play "Down" again."

It's been almost forty minutes since Jill went to find Brett, and now I'm starting to worry.

"Do you think Jill's okay?" I whisper to Ronnie as she, Miles, Craig, and I stand at the bar, waiting to order our drinks. Tony is sitting at our table chatting with Margo.

We all offered not to drink tonight if Tony thought it would be a trigger for him. After that terrible night last November, our pack became much more careful about drinking in front of Tony. But he has sworn up and down that our drinking around him isn't a trigger. He revealed the only thing that's ever triggered him to drink were his own self-deprecating thoughts.

Recently, Tony joined a small CrossFit gym in Bristol where he's made a few new friends who are also sober. He told me that he and three other members created a small group outside of the gym which seems to have become their own form of Alcoholics Anonymous. He refers to his new friends as his "Sober Squad" and meets them religiously for coffee, once a week.

It comforts me knowing Tony has found the type of support we simply can't give him. He's found people who understand—it's an understanding one can only possess when they've fought the same battle as you.

"Maybe she and Brett are doing it on the patio," Ronnie replies, waggling her brows, seemingly unconcerned.

I laugh. "Jill would never."

"Hey, weddings make people do crazy things," she shrugs, as she hands me a vodka cranberry.

I turn to Miles and tell him, "I'm going to go find Jill."

"Ok, we'll be over with Margo and Tony. Hurry back," he grins at me, lightly smacking my ass.

I glance at his empty hands, realizing he didn't order a drink from the bar. Actually, I haven't seen him drink all night. But he had to have drunk whiskey at some point in the evening—I distinctly tasted it when he kissed me. "Why didn't you get a drink?"

"I don't really feel like drinking tonight," he tells me. "I just had a glass of whiskey to toast Zach."

Come to think of it, Miles has barely drunk this entire trip. Maybe he's just trying to be respectful of Tony.

I gently pull Miles down towards me by his tie, kissing him before I run off in search of Jill. "I'll be back in a couple minutes."

As I head out, I decide to search the patio first. Hopefully, I don't find her and Brett doing it out there as Ronnie had suggested. When I step out onto the patio, I see a group of mostly unfamiliar-looking men smoking cigars. The only familiar face I see is the groom himself.

"Sam!" Zach calls, raising his hand, motioning for me to walk over to him.

"Congrats, Zach!" I exclaim, moving in for a hug. The smell of his cigar is awful, and I immediately start coughing.

"Sorry," Zach laughs, now holding his cigar away from me. "Special occasion, ya know."

"Of course."

"Sam, these are some of my law school buddies." He motions to the other men standing around the patio. Then, he puts his arm around my shoulder. "Guys, this is my friend, Sam."

"Hi, guys," I greet them with a small wave. The group welcomes me, and a man—about my height—offers me a cigar which I politely decline.

One of the men drunkenly yells, "Hook it up!" at Zach, throwing me an exaggerated wink.

Zach lets them down with a chuckle, "Sorry, boys. She has a boyfriend." A chorus of loud boos follows, and I can't help but laugh. It's definitely a different vibe out here on the patio.

"You look happy, Sam," Zach says to me before taking a long drag from his gross-smelling cigar.

I grin back at him. "So do you."

"I never knew I could be this happy," he divulges. Then, he unexpectedly blurts out, "Ya know, I always kind of thought you'd end up dating Brett. But I'm glad it's Miles. Nothing against my boy Brett, though."

"*Brett* and me? Oh, hell no!" His comment caught me off guard, but now I'm cackling. "I think that cigar smoke is altering your brain function!"

"I just always thought he had a thing for you. Even when we were together."

Okay, it's officially time to change the subject. "Have you seen Jill?" I ask him.

"Last time I saw her, she was going into the bathroom," Zach informs me. "That was about thirty minutes ago, though."

"Ok, I'll look for her there. Congrats again, Zachary," I say, purposely articulating his full name.

"Thanks for actually being on time for something today, Samantha," he teases.

In response, I simply shoot him some of Craig's signature finger-guns, before heading back into the banquet room. I hear Zach break out in laughter behind me as I walk away.

"Hey, Sam?" he then calls.

I stop walking and spin around to look back at him. "Yes?"

"I know I'm three days late but...happy birthday."

I stare back at him in surprise. With everything he's had going on, I can't believe he remembered. I grant him a small smile before mouthing "thank you." As I notice some of the other men turning to glance at me, I quickly turn on my heels and scurry back inside.

It seems like only yesterday that Zach, Craig, Ronnie, and I all worked at The Cinedome together. I won't lie, sometimes I do miss those days. Everything just felt less complicated then. We were merely a group of best friends who got paid to work together. Who wouldn't miss having regular private movie viewings while you got to drown yourself in free popcorn?

After a few minutes of searching, I finally locate the women's bathroom in the back of the large, open reception hall. As I enter the bathroom, I immediately notice two older women standing by the sink, talking to one another. I assume they're family members of Sarah due to their undeniable resemblance.

Then I hear the faint sound of a woman crying. The noise is coming from one of the bathroom stalls.

One of the women motions to me, saying, "Go ahead, honey. We aren't waiting."

The other woman then chimes in. "We're just worried about that poor girl in the stall. She's been sobbing for at least thirty minutes." She shakes her head. "She won't come out of there for anything."

The pit in my stomach has grown even heavier.

Placing my vodka cranberry on the bathroom counter, I walk over to the occupied stall. I lightly tap on the door with one of my knuckles, aware that both women standing at the sink are now staring at me.

"Jill?" I whisper.

The crying immediately ceases. "Sam?" Jill sniffles.

Both women nod to me, signaling their understanding, before exiting the bathroom. I'm glad they realize this needs to be a private conversation between friends—the conversation I've dreaded since the day Jill told me Brett kissed her. Jill slowly opens the stall door, allowing me to squeeze into the tiny space with her. My heart breaks for my best friend as I take in her appearance. The whites of her eyes are rimmed with red, and black mascara is smeared down both her cheeks.

She daintily blows her nose into the wad of tissues she's clutching. "I went looking for Brett," Jill begins. "Oh, did I find him—making out with one of Sarah's bridesmaids by the emergency exit." She starts sobbing. "How could he do this to me?"

"That asshole!" I hiss. "He's not going to get away with this!" Abruptly, I barrel out of the tiny bathroom stall, heading for the exit.

"Sam, no! WAIT!" Jill shrieks after me, as I snatch my vodka cranberry from the counter and storm out of the bathroom.

*Where the fuck is he?*

My eyes furiously scan the room until my vision locks on my target. Brett stands at our table beside where Miles is sitting. They appear to be deep in conversation. I'm sure he's trying to defend his inexcusable actions. I stomp angrily towards our table, my cocktail still clutched in my hand. Margo and Tony are chatting, so they don't notice my approach—but Craig and Ronnie do.

When I reach the table, my body language must say it all. Craig's eyes grow wide, while Ronnie instantly stands from her chair. I don't have to say a word to her. Ronnie just knows—it's about to go down.

"Sam!" I hear Jill yell from a few feet behind me. At the sound of her voice, our entire table turns. Straight away, Brett and I lock eyes. I notice his stance subtly widen, attempting to brace himself for my arrival. He knows I'm coming for him.

I come to a stand, directly in front of Brett. I continue to glare at him while he stands motionless, staring back at me. Miles tries to stand quickly from his chair, but he isn't fast enough.

"YOU ASSHOLE!" I scream, hurling the contents of my drink into Brett's face.

"What the hell did he do?" Ronnie screeches.

Turning to look at her briefly, I watch as she tries lifting a chair off the ground. Craig is successfully able to remove the chair from Ronnie's grasp and pull her away from the table.

Times have changed, Brett! Ronnie has upgraded her weapon of choice from soft pretzels to chairs.

Brett continues standing motionless in front of me, my drink still dripping down his face. He knows he deserves this.

I feel Miles wrap his arms around my waist and begin pulling me towards the exit.

"Your girlfriend's a fucking lunatic, Miles," Brett sneers, as Miles leads me away.

*Oh, I'll show you a fucking lunatic!*

I rapidly spin my body around, somehow managing to escape Miles's embrace. I don't think—I just move. Kicking off my high heels, I charge towards where Brett is standing. He isn't paying any attention to me; instead, he's arguing with Margo about something. The impact from my thrashing body catches him completely off guard.

I ram my shoulder into his abdomen with the full force of my 5'3" body, able to momentarily knock the wind out of him. The two of us go crashing down to the banquet hall floor. Luckily for Brett, the floor is carpeted. He falls to his ass but is able to brace his fall, landing with both of his hands behind him. Since I'm drunk and uncoordinated, I'm completely unable to catch myself, eventually landing directly on top of Brett.

The only game plan I had was to pummel my body into his as hard as physically possible. Now, he has the upper hand. He wraps both arms around me, managing to flip me onto my back. Thankfully, at least, he doesn't allow my head to slam onto the floor.

He's left straddling my body with his own, kneeling above me. I reach up in an attempt to smack him, but he's too fast for me. He wraps his hands around my wrists, successfully pinning my arms to the floor on either side of my head. I try bucking my body beneath him, but it's no use. He's substantially stronger than me.

I'm really wishing I had a Plan B right about now. Maybe Plan A shouldn't have been to physically attack this man in the first place. It's then that I hear the distinct pounding of my own heart. The harsh intake of Brett's breath. The roar of Miles's voice. Ronnie's frantic screams. Jill's hysterical sobs. But—above all else—I hear Margo shriek Brett's name.

At the sound of her voice, Brett visibly flinches. At first, it seems as if he's about to remove his body from where it's perched atop my own; instead, he shouts in my face. "WHY DO YOU KEEP FUCKING WITH ME, SAM?"

*Me*? Fucking with *him*?

He's the one who completely shattered Jill's heart over a girl he just met today. Not to mention, this is the same man who randomly decided to kiss me on my patio last year, then never say another word about it. How dare he accuse me of fucking with *him*!

"You're a piece of shit!" I hiss.

He snarls back, "And you're a selfish little bitch!" Someone—I can't tell who—audibly gasps at his words.

I refuse to let him think I'm scared of him. I'm not afraid of him. Not anymore. His icy blue glare bores into me, but I hold my own, glaring right back at him. We're in a stand-off now. Neither of us is backing down.

"Get the fuck off of her!" Miles bellows, pulling Brett back by the collar of his suit jacket. Tony and Zach proceed to help pull Brett off of me. When I sit up, I notice Zach is now standing next to us. I stare at him, suddenly feeling ashamed. I've just single-handedly ruined the best day of Zach's life.

Brett's right. I am selfish. I'm an awful friend.

Miles now stomps over to me with my heels in his hand. He lifts me from the floor and throws me over his shoulder like a rag doll. I don't fight him as he marches towards the exit, my body slung over his shoulder. This time, he's not taking any chances when it comes to my escape.

"Keep her away from me. I mean it, Miles!" Brett yells after us.

Miles doesn't respond. I make the smartest decision I've made all night—I keep my mouth shut.

When we're halfway to our hotel, Miles finally sets me back onto my feet. After setting me down, he drops my shoes on the ground before me, then continues walking without uttering a word. I slip my heels back on before I start to follow him.

I know he's angry with me. I shouldn't have caused a scene. I acted without thinking.

*I blame the vodka.*

"Miles." It's all I can think to say.

He stops walking, turning to stare at me in silence.

"Say something," I whisper.

"What the hell were you thinking?"

"I wasn't," I admit. "I was just so pissed at Brett for cheating on Jill."

"He *didn't* cheat on Jill. He was honest with her from the beginning about not wanting a committed relationship. She agreed to that!

He's been seeing other women the entire time they've been fooling around!"

My jaw hits the floor. "Are you defending him?"

"No! I'm not defending him. The way he acted tonight was wrong. He shouldn't have done that with Jill there." Miles inhales, then slowly exhales before continuing. "But I'm not defending you either. How you acted tonight was way out of line!"

I cross my arms in front of my chest. "He deserved it."

"No one deserves to be physically attacked, Sam! Period!"

"He called me a selfish bitch," I pout.

He groans, "I'm pissed about that, too."

"I need a drink." Maybe the bar in the hotel lobby is still open.

"No, you don't," Miles tells me.

"Excuse me?"

"You heard me. You don't need a drink," he maintains. "Honestly, that's part of the problem." He runs his fingers through his unusually tame curls.

"What is 'the problem' supposed to mean?" I ask, making air quotes with my fingers.

He lets out a sigh. "Your drinking. It's a problem."

I stare up at him, dumbfounded. "Are you serious right now?"

"Do you want to know why I barely drank on this trip?" Miles asks. I simply stare at him until he resumes speaking. "I knew you'd get wasted all weekend—like you always do—and I'd have to babysit you."

I'm now standing before him speechless. I feel both as though I'm going to burst into tears and vomit, all at the same time. Does he really think I have a problem with alcohol? What the hell does he mean by "babysit" me?

I point my shaking finger in his face and shriek, "You're an asshole!"

"I'm an asshole because I care about you enough to tell you the truth?"

"You don't care about me!"

"How can you say I don't care about you? I fucking love you, Sam!" By this point, he is shouting—we both are.

"You don't love me!" If he loved me, he'd never say those things to me.

"Why would I put up with all of this shit—," he motions to me with his hand. "—if I wasn't in love with you?"

"Well, don't worry, Miles. You won't have to put up with my shit anymore," I inform him. "IT'S OVER!"

"NO!" Miles bellows. "Breaking up with me won't fix this. You can't run away forever!"

"And what is it exactly that I'm running away from?" I snort, before turning to walk back towards our hotel.

His voice comes out in a little more than a whisper: "Yourself."

For some reason, his last word strikes a nerve with me. My entire body shakes, as I angrily ball both my hands into fists at my sides. Feeling warm tears begin to stream down my cheeks, I choke out, "It's inevitable. I'm going to be just like her."

"Like who?"

"Like my mother," I sob, turning back to face him. "My alcoholic mother, who destroyed my family and ruined my entire childhood. The woman who constantly made me feel as if she wished *I* had been the one to die that day. Instead of her son. Instead of my brother."

*There it is. My deepest, darkest fear, forced to the surface.*

Now, it's Miles's turn to look dumbfounded. His mouth falls open as he stares at me. He appears speechless. Finally, I tear my vision away from him. When I do, I'm shocked to discover Brett, standing about ten feet behind Miles. He must've decided to walk back to the hotel, as well. Now he's come across Miles and me fighting. I wonder how much of it he actually heard.

Miles finally speaks up. "I thought you only had a half-sister?"

"I had an older brother. He died of a brain tumor." At this point, I'm weeping. I didn't want to talk about this, let alone cry about it. Especially not in front of Brett.

"Sam," Miles whispers, taking a step towards me. He tries wrapping his arms around me, but I jerk my body backward before he can touch me.

"I don't need your sympathy," I snap. "And I meant what I said. It's over between us. Trust me, Miles—you're better off without me."

"Don't do this, Sam," he pleads, trying to approach me once more. I take a full three steps back to avoid his embrace. I think I've always known I'd have to tell Miles goodbye—it's the only chance he has at happiness. And if I feel his touch, I know I'll be too weak to walk away from him.

"I'll destroy you, eventually," I whisper, looking up at Miles, tears streaming down my face. His hazel eyes, normally warm and bright, are now bloodshot. I watch the tears fall from his beautiful eyes—tears I caused him to shed.

Brett stands, still as a statue, behind Miles. He doesn't move, doesn't speak.

See, Brett? Once in a while, I'm not a selfish bitch.

I kick off my heels again, then reach down and grasp them with my shaking hand.

"Goodbye, Miles," I whisper before turning and running back to the hotel.

# CHAPTER
# FORTY-NINE:

When I enter the hotel lobby, my high heels still in hand, I notice the bar is still open. We've all booked rooms in a hotel that's walking distance from where Zach and Sarah's wedding reception was held. Since the reception was at a hotel directly on the beach, it would've broken the bank for all of us to stay there for three nights.

Now, I stand frozen at the entrance to the bar. I want a cocktail more than anything. It's the only thing that'll make me feel better—the only thing to numb my hurt and anger, taking the edge off. But more than I want a drink, I want to prove Miles wrong: I am *not* an alcoholic.

Instead of entering the bar, I trudge over to the vending machine next to the elevators. Pulling my incredibly small wallet out of the pocket of my dress (yes, my dress is awesome and has pockets—which wasn't by chance, but rather a highly calculated purchase), I shove a dollar bill into the vending machine. I jab the button on the machine, selecting a cold bottle of Arrowhead water. Arrowhead isn't my preferred brand of water. If you're an avid water drinker, like me, you know not all water tastes the same. I'm in no condition to be picky, though.

Twisting the top off my bottle of water, I move back toward the elevators. Noticing an elevator about to go up, I slip through the open doors just before they close. Inside are a few men in suits, who stare at me as I barge in. I really hope they weren't guests at Zach's wedding—the one I just single-handedly destroyed.

One of the men slurs, "What floor, sweetheart?"

"Six, please." I can feel their roaming eyes on me, wishing they would stop staring. Can't a girl just ride an elevator in peace?

"Calling it a night this early? Seems like a waste of a pretty dress," another man remarks, grinning at me. "We're going for drinks at a bar down the street in a bit. You should join us."

I take a long sip of my water as I eyeball the three men, weighing my response. This seems like the makings of a horrible decision. I know Miles would be royally pissed if I went out for drinks with three total strangers. I'm being presented with the opportunity to hurt him—just like he hurt me, tonight.

The thing is, though, I've already hurt Miles. Again, and again.

"This pretty dress is just a disguise," I blurt, exaggeratedly crushing the empty plastic bottle between my hands like a psychopath. "A disguise to help distract you from the fact that I'm actually bat-shit crazy and will ruin your entire life."

The three men stand gaping at me, wide-eyed, as the elevator dings, alerting our arrival to the sixth floor. My little outburst was probably a bit dramatic...but it wasn't a lie.

"Have a great evening, gentlemen," I add in a sing-song voice, prancing out of the elevator onto my floor.

When I reach Miles's and my hotel room, I unlock the door with the hotel key in my pocket. Again—dresses with pockets are awesome.

Once inside the room, I collapse onto the king-sized bed, then crawl under the fluffy, white comforter. Eventually, I know Miles will have to come back to this room. His suitcase and all of his things are here. I also know that when he gets here, he and I will probably continue fighting, right where we left off.

It's like a cycle: he'll tell me I'm childish for running away from him, literally and figuratively; I'll tell him he's a complete asshole for insinuating I'm an alcoholic.

I'm *not* an alcoholic! ...At least I don't think I am.

Just thinking about having another conversation about this with my boyfriend makes me exhausted. Or ex-boyfriend—I guess I technically broke up with him.

Maybe I overreacted.

Pulling the comforter over my head, I shut my eyes, wishing I could just hide under here for the rest of my life.

A knock at my hotel room door wakes me. I flip the comforter off of my head, sitting straight-up in bed.

How long was I asleep for?

The knocking continues. Why wouldn't Miles just use his key? Maybe he lost it.

I roll out of bed and scurry to the door. Apparently, I was asleep long enough not to feel drunk anymore. Now, I only have a pounding headache. Before I yank open the door, I brace myself, taking a deep breath. To my surprise, it isn't Miles standing before me—it's Jill and Tony. Jill has brought her suitcase and tote bag along.

"I know you said you danced ballet when you were young, but I really think you should've played tackle football," Tony laughs.

I groan, rolling my eyes at him. "Not funny."

"Honestly, I'm impressed," he responds, patting me on the back as he squeezes past me into the room.

"Come on in, I guess," I remark sarcastically.

I turn back to Jill, instinctively leaning in to hug her. She drops her tote bag to the ground and wraps her arms around me. Holding her shaking body, I can feel her crying before I hear her.

"I'm so sorry, Jill," I murmur.

She finally pulls away from me. "I should've known better. It's my own fault," she sniffles.

"This isn't your fault," I assure her. I pick her tote bag off the ground, then motion for her to come in.

Jill rolls her large suitcase into the room. "Would you mind if I stay with you tonight? I can't fathom staying the night with Brett after everything that's happened."

I shut the door behind her. I completely forgot she and Brett had been sharing a room.

"I'd offer—" Tony cuts in. "—but Miles is staying with me tonight. I'm just here to pack up his stuff for him."

I whip my head around to stare at him. "What do you mean?"

"Uh..." He hesitates momentarily. "He said you two broke up."

Jill's eyes go wide as she gasps. "Wait! What? When? How?"

"We got into a huge fight. I overreacted and broke up with him," I sigh.

Tony gives me a knowing look. "It seems as though you did a lot of overreacting tonight, Sam."

Turning to look at Tony once more, I start feeling sick to my stomach. Tony's words feel harsh, but I know they're true. Your friends wouldn't be your friends if they didn't call you out on your bullshit.

My stubborn self-righteousness from the vodka has finally faded. I know I screwed up. "I messed up," I whisper, looking at the floor. Without a moment's hesitation, Tony and Jill pull me into a group hug.

"You're human, Sam. We all mess up. Remember last November?" Tony asks, gently lifting my chin to meet his gaze. I nod.

"It happens to the best of us," he grins. Jill smiles at Tony, lovingly placing her hand on his shoulder.

"How do I fix this?" I ask him.

"I think you need to start with Brett," he says.

Jill looks between us, confused at Tony's suggestion. "Brett? Not Miles?"

"No, Tony's right," I admit. "I physically attacked him in front of a hundred people. I was way out of line."

"I agree that violence is wrong, and you shouldn't have tackled Brett to the ground," she expresses, kicking off her flip-flops. "But still—thank you for always trying to protect me, Sam." She smiles at me as she crawls under the comforter, grabbing the television remote. She turns the tv on, beginning to leisurely flip through the channels as Tony packs Miles's suitcase. "Oh! *Ghost Adventures* is on!"

"Jill," I sigh. "You've already had an upsetting night. Do you really want to have nightmares, too?"

She gives me a sweet smirk, telling me, "I never have nightmares when we bunk together."

About twenty minutes later, I stand outside of Brett's room, second-guessing my plan to talk to him. I'm not afraid of him after tonight's events. I know he would never physically hurt me. I simply have no idea what I'm going to say to him.

The door to his room is slightly propped ajar by the door's dead-bolt. He must be expecting someone—someone that isn't me. One of Sarah's bridesmaids, maybe?

I knock lightly on the door with my knuckle, letting out a slow exhale. Why am I so nervous?

"Come in," Brett calls from inside.

Cautiously, I push open the door and slip into the room. Brett stands with his back to me, pulling clothes out of his suitcase. His hair appears wet, and he has a towel loosely wrapped around his waist.

Great. He only has a towel on. "Uh, I'll come back later. Or not come back at all. Or...uh...I'm just gonna go," I stutter nervously.

Suddenly, he drops the shirt he was holding back into his suit-case, then rapidly spins around to face me for the first time. He looks as surprised to see me standing in his hotel room as I do to see him wearing only a towel. I definitely wasn't the person he was expecting.

"I should go," I mutter.

"Why are you here?"

"Are you naked?" I blurt, feeling the heat invade my cheeks. There's no doubt I'm blushing like a tween girl.

"Well, I usually shower naked," Brett remarks with a smirk. It's obvious he's enjoying my embarrassment. "Why are you here, Sam?"

I take a deep breath, then walk over to where he's standing, his icy blue gaze never leaving me. I come to a stand directly in front of him. Staring up at him, I meet his gaze with my own. I'm not sure why, but I decide at this moment to wrap my arms around his waist and hug him.

I hear his sharp intake of breath as my skin touches his. He gently wraps one of his arms around my back, while his other hand, thankfully, secures his towel. "I'm sorry," I whisper. Pulling myself away from him, I look up into his eyes once more. "I was a shitty friend to you. It doesn't matter how upset I was. I never should have treated you the way I did."

Brett doesn't speak. He just continues staring at me.

"Can you forgive me?" I ask.

After a moment's hesitation, he finally replies. "You're not scared of me, now?"

"I'm not scared of you," I assure him.

"I lost my cool tonight. For some reason, you always seem to bring out the worst in me."

I laugh, "That's the meanest thing anyone's ever said to me." I don't know why, but I find this funny.

He gives me a devilish grin before joining in my laughter. "I didn't mean it to be hurtful."

"Why—Why do I bring out the worst in you?"

"You push my buttons like no one else, Sammie."

"Stop calling me that," I say jokingly, pushing my finger into his chest. As soon as my finger touches his skin, I'm instantly reminded that he's not wearing a shirt. I immediately jerk my hand back and shove them both into my dress pockets.

He grins as he playfully pushes his index finger into my forehead. "Then, stop pushing my buttons."

We're then met with a painfully awkward silence as we continue looking into one another's eyes. I'm not sure what else to say to him. Thankfully, though, he breaks the silence first.

"I hate that I've done this to you twice, now," he divulges.

"You're not the only guilty party here." I slowly exhale before continuing. "Besides, I barely ever think of the whole 'Cinedome brawl' thing."

"I think about it every day," he murmurs. "I don't want to be that person, Sam."

"I don't want to be that person either—the person who keeps drinking too much and hurting the people she loves."

"We have a lot in common."

"Yeah, we both have some gnarly tempers," I laugh. "Well...I have a long list of people to apologize to tonight. I better get going."

Before I move to leave, Brett asks, "How pissed is Miles at me?"

I sigh. "Probably not nearly as pissed as he is at *me*."

"You haven't talked to him yet?" He looks surprised.

"Not since our fight walking back to the hotel. He never came back to our room. Not that I blame him. I was a total bitch."

"Will you do me a favor at least?"

"Stop tackling you in public places?" I giggle.

"Well, you can still tackle me in private," he smirks.

Instantly, I turn beet red. Once again, I'm overly aware he's only wearing a towel. "That's not what I meant," I squeak, purposefully averting my eyes from his bare chest.

He quickly turns serious. "Go talk to Miles," he says. "Even though he's not talking to me right now, I know he's a wreck. That kid loves you."

"He's my next stop," I say, smiling up at him. "But first, I need you to do me a favor, too."

"No, Samantha. I will *not* remove my towel!" Brett says, letting out an exaggerated gasp as he thrusts one arm across his bare chest, feigning modesty.

"Oh, shut the hell up," I groan, giving him a light smack on his arm as he laughs. Now, it's my turn to be serious. "Patch things up with Jill," I say.

Immediately, Brett stops laughing. "Jill and I will never be a couple. Everyone—including myself—knows she's way too good for me. She deserves everything I can't give her. I should never have allowed anything to happen between the two of us in the first place. But hell... she's so beautiful."

"Trust me, Brett. We're on the same page about all of this," I explain. "I meant, patch up your friendship. Tell her everything you just told me."

He nods in understanding. "I'll call her. I highly doubt she wants to see me."

I give him another quick hug to convey my thanks. I would hate for this whole debacle to destroy their friendship. Sometimes, people are just better off as friends. Unfortunately, though, you usually don't figure that out until you've already tried being more than friends. As they say, hindsight is twenty-twenty.

As I turn to leave, I tell him, "I'll see you tomorrow." Walking towards the door, I pull my cell phone out of my pocket to check the time—10:23 PM.

Just as I reach the door, I hear Brett's voice once more. "I have a brother," he says. I stop walking, and when I turn around to face him, he goes on. "I have a little brother. I couldn't imagine how it would feel to lose him."

"What's your brother's name?"

"Aaron."

"I bet he's way nicer than you," I joke.

"Oh, he definitely is," Brett chuckles. He subtly adds, "...I'm here if you ever need to talk."

"Thank you," I reply before walking out of his room.

I'm standing frozen outside of Tony's hotel room, the next stop on my apology tour. So far, on top of meeting with Brett, I apologized to Zach and Sarah. As I trudged down the hallway to Tony's room, I successfully sent off texts to the newlyweds, apologizing for my outburst at their reception. Neither of them has replied yet, but I didn't expect them to. It is their wedding night after all.

Just as I move to knock on the door, I stop. I didn't think it was possible, but I'm actually feeling more nervous to talk to Miles than I did Brett. Hopefully, he and Tony aren't already asleep.

Mustering every ounce of courage inside me, I manage to lightly tap on the hotel room door. After a few seconds, Tony opens the door. He immediately smiles when he sees me.

Turning to look over his shoulder, he hollers, "Miles, did you order room service?" I roll my eyes at him.

There's no response from Miles. Tony ushers me into the room anyways. "I was just about to swing by Ronnie and Craig's room for a nightcap," Tony tells me.

"Wait—you're not drinking again, are you?" I question, suddenly worried.

"By nightcap, I mean they ordered every dessert off the room service menu, and I'm going to join them," he says with a wink. He then guides my body around his, gently pushing me further into the room. Instantly, I spot Miles sitting on one of the two queen beds, staring at his cell phone. By this point, he knows I'm here, but he refuses to look at me.

"I'll be back, Miles," Tony announces.

"See you in a bit, bud," Miles responds, still not looking up from his phone.

Before leaving, Tony whispers into my ear, "You got this."

As the door slams shut, Miles's eyes dart up, locking with mine. My stomach drops, and I suddenly have the urge to vomit.

"What do you want from me, Sam?"

"I would love for you to forgive me," I say, giving him a sheepish grin and clapping my hands together in a praying motion.

His face remains emotionless. "Was that supposed to be an apology?"

"No, this is my apology," I claim. "I'm sorry I caused a scene tonight. I'm sorry I always try to run away when things get hard. I'm sorry that sometimes I drink too much and make poor decisions." I pause, taking a deep breath. "That's something I'm going to try to work on."

I walk over to where he sits on the bed, hesitantly seating myself beside him. He looks down at his feet instead of at me. My heart sinks. I continue on, "Most of all, I'm sorry for the way I treated you tonight. You didn't deserve that—any of that. I don't want to break up. I love you, Miles." My voice cracks when I say his name, and I begin to cry, hot tears start streaming down my face.

"Why didn't you tell me about your brother?" He still hasn't looked at me, but at least he's speaking.

"I never talk about Matty. With anyone. It hurts too much." I slowly exhale, trying to rein in my emotions, before continuing. "... Well, I never used to talk about Matty. Until my shift on Wednesday. My patient asked me if I'd ever lost anyone I loved. For some reason, I decided I wanted to tell him about Matty."

Finally, Miles turns to look at me, his hazel eyes glistening. He reaches over, placing his large hand on top of mine, which makes me cry harder. There goes reining in my emotions. "I've thought about him all weekend," I sob. "The only people in my life who know about Matty, aside from my family, are Jill and Ronnie."

"I wish you would've told me sooner," Miles whispers, softly squeezing my hand. "I want you to tell me everything."

"I almost did once. When you told me about your mom."

"Sam, I want to spend my life with you. I want us to have a future together. But in order for that to happen, you and I have to be honest with each other. Relationships are work. And we have a lot of work to do."

I scoot my body closer to his. "I'm willing to put in the work if you are."

"I will always fight for us," Miles says, gently pulling me onto his lap.

I lean into him, whispering, "I'm going to try to be better for you." Then, my lips find his, and I greedily run my fingers through his unusually tame curls.

Suddenly, Miles pulls his mouth away from mine and scoots me off his lap. He stands, walking briskly towards the door.

Wait, is he leaving? I stare after him, confused. What did I do wrong? What did I say?

Timidly, I ask, "Did I do something wrong?"

Instead of leaving the room, I watch as he bolts the door's deadlock before turning around and giving me a mischievous look. Miles grants me one of his infamous sideways smirks as he pulls his shirt over his head, tossing it to the ground. He points at my dress. "Your turn."

"You might have to help me." I stand, turning my back to Miles so he can unzip my dress.

He walks back to me and starts slowly taking off my dress. When the zipper reaches my hips, he calls out with a surprised laugh, "Whoa! This thing has pockets!"

I turn to face him. "I know!" My dress falls to my feet. For a moment, he looks my body up and down before pulling me into his arms. "Will you be mad if I stay with Jill tonight?" I ask. "She needs me."

"Not at all. I understand," he murmurs into my ear, as he leads me over to the bed. Just before he tosses me on the bed, he adds, "But only if I get you for however long it takes to eat everything off the dessert menu."

# CHAPTER FIFTY

## (December 2015):

've tried really hard to cut back on my alcohol consumption over these last three months. Of course, I still drink, just not as often. And not as much, when I do. I'll never stop drinking completely, though. I can't imagine my life without getting to have a glass of wine with dinner or a Clamato and vodka—my new favorite, less-filling way to drink a Bloody Mary— after a hard shift at work.

Life would be so boring if I completely stopped drinking—*I* would be boring.

Regardless, Miles says he's proud of me. I've been extremely cognizant, lately, of how I treat him when I'm drinking. To put it bluntly, I try not to be a raging bitch.

I haven't gotten downright drunk since Zach's wedding at the beginning of September. These days, when I start feeling buzzed, I cut myself off. Some days are harder than others, I won't lie. It's impossible for me to have just one drink. I usually end up consuming three or four in the course of a night. But at least now I'm keeping count.

*Really, who can just have one drink?*

I've also made a new rule for myself: absolutely no shots. It never ends up being a good night for me—or anyone I'm with—when I start downing shots.

Currently, I'm sipping on sparkling water as I lounge on our sectional, aimlessly flipping through television channels in search of something to watch. A few months ago, it'd most definitely be a cocktail in my hand. See? I've made progress.

Archie, my adorable black pug, is curled up on my lap. The sound of his soft snores soothes me. Pug snorts, grumbles, and snores have become the soundtrack to my life. Who needs a sound machine to help you sleep when you own a pug?

Jill, on the other hand, is not lounging. She's currently rushing around our apartment like a madwoman, trying to pack for her trip tomorrow to Virginia Beach with her boyfriend. That's right—Jillian Moore is officially off the market. And no, it's not Brett she's dating. Thank the Lord!

As for how Jill met her new boyfriend (or met him again, I guess), in October, Jill had decided she wanted to live a healthier lifestyle. She also decided that Ronnie and I needed to live a healthier lifestyle too; Ronnie and I were *not* consulted on the matter. Anyways, the three of us started running together a few evenings a week. There's a relatively large park near Jill's and my apartment. It seemed like the perfect spot to start running. Well, Jill ran; Ronnie and I alternated between walking and jogging, all the while complaining about how much we hate cardio.

A few weeks into our new running regimen, the unthinkable happened—one of those things you think will never actually happen to you...until it does. It was about 8:00 PM on a Wednesday, and the three of us were just finishing our second run of the week. Suddenly, two men, both wearing all black, quickly approached us. It wasn't until they were mere feet away from us that I realized they were both wearing ski masks. At that moment, I knew something very bad was about to happen. Before I could comprehend what was happening, one of the men wrapped his arms around me and pressed something into my temple. It took me only a few seconds to realize the "something" was, in fact, a gun. The other masked man grabbed ahold of Ronnie, forcefully thrusting his own gun to the side of her head. Jill stood motionless, her bright blue eyes taking in the scene that was unfolding before her. It was apparent she'd gone into complete shock.

I'm fairly certain I was also in shock. It felt as if, in that very moment, I watched my entire life flash before my eyes. I thought of my dad, my stepmom, Amanda, and my little sister, Taylor. I thought of my brother, Matty. I thought of Miles and the life we may never get to spend together. I even thought of my mother—the mother I haven't spoken to in years. When you think you're about to die, your thoughts do as they please.

Ronnie, on the other hand, was not in shock. She was pissed.

"We don't want to hurt you," the man holding me claimed. He stood behind me, so I couldn't see him, but I could feel his hand trembling, the hand holding a loaded gun to my head. He may not have wanted to hurt me, but I was terrified he might just shoot me on accident.

"Then why do you have guns to our heads?" Ronnie hissed.

The man restraining Ronnie shouted then, "Just give us your phones and wallets!" Then, in a lower voice, "No one needs to get hurt, tonight."

"Fuck you!" Ronnie screamed.

"Ronnie, please," Jill begged. "It isn't worth it. Just give them your stuff." She then began sobbing, removing her cell phone and wallet from the pocket of her leggings, setting them down on the ground.

"No, Jill! Don't give these assholes your shit!" Ronnie barked at her angrily.

Even though I'd never been as petrified as I was then, I couldn't just stand by and watch my best friend get herself killed.

"Veronica!" I shrieked. Ronnie turned her head towards me slightly. She and I then both slowly faced one another, trying to refrain from making any sudden, swift movements that could get us killed. No sudden movements—it's a good rule of thumb when you have a gun jammed against the side of your head. "It's just stuff, Ronnie."

I could see Jill had fallen to her knees in my peripheral vision. The sound of her wailing sent chills up my spine. Over the years, I'd seen my friend cry on numerous occasions but never like that. Her sobs were reminiscent of those I hear in my line of work—the sobs of someone in mourning, of someone who's lost everything.

If I'm being honest, I'd been just as terrified as Jill. Terrified that we were about to lose everything.

"It's just stuff," I reiterated, internally begging Ronnie to concede. For what felt like an eternity, Ronnie stared back at me.

All I could feel was the cool steel against my skin. All I could hear was my own blood whooshing through my ears. All I could see was Ronnie, her emerald green eyes unblinking and steadfast.

Ronnie finally broke the silence. "Fine. Take our shit and leave us the hell alone!" She then unbuckled her fanny pack, throwing it to the cement. (Well, Ronnie called it a belt bag. It was totally a fanny pack, though.)

Meanwhile, the man holding me began frisking me in search of my personal belongings. I stood as still as stone while this masked stranger ran his hands all over my body. Then, without warning, he shoved one of his hands down the front of my pants. I whimpered for help, standing there completely defenseless, tears streaming down my face.

Two months later, I still have nightmares about that night. I can still feel that asshole's hands roaming my body.

"GET YOUR HANDS OFF HER!" Ronnie shrieked, attempting to lunge towards the man as he groped me.

"RONNIE, NO!" I shouted. By this point, Jill had started screaming unintelligibly.

At her outburst, the man behind Ronnie forcibly grabbed hold of her arm, throwing her to her knees before me. He finished off his attack, violently striking Ronnie on the side of her head with the handle of his gun. I watched in horror as her body slumped unnaturally at my feet.

That's when I started screaming for help, while Jill continued her frantic shrieks. I knew I was screaming, but I didn't recognize my own voice as it echoed through the trees. Those screams weren't my own. They were the screams of someone who thought they'd just lost everything.

In the distance, I could see two figures running towards us.

The man who assaulted Ronnie shouted at the other man, still restraining me. "Grab the shit! LET'S GO!"

He fumbled to collect Jill's and Ronnie's belongings off the pavement before taking off at a full sprint. Finally, the man behind me released me from his nauseating embrace. I watched as he sprinted after his accomplice, my cell phone in his hand.

After all was said and done, the only thing they got from me was my piece of crap iPhone 4 with its cracked screen. When we went jogging, I never carried anything on me besides my phone—almost five years old and worth absolutely nothing.

As soon as the man let me go, I fell to my knees next to Ronnie's crumpled form. A streak of crimson stained the side of her beautiful face. Without thought, I wrapped my arms around my friend, whispering, "Please be okay."

"I'm okay." Her response completely startled me. "I've got a godawful headache, though," she laughed.

"You scared the shit out of me!" I snapped, gently assisting her to a sitting position. I brushed her blood-soaked hair away from her face. As I tried tending to Ronnie's wound, Jill continued screaming.

"I was just as scared, Sam," Ronnie whispered back to me.

The two figures running towards us ended up being an extremely kind older couple. The woman, whose name I believe was Sally, immediately ran to Jill's aid. Meanwhile, Sally's husband kneeled next to Ronnie and me, informing us he was on the phone with 911. The entire night felt pretty surreal. Sally and her husband—I feel awful for not being able to remember his name—stayed by our sides until the police and ambulance arrived.

Sally's husband also allowed me to borrow his phone after he'd gotten off the phone with the 911 dispatcher. I immediately called Miles, but he didn't answer. He hates answering calls from numbers he doesn't know. So, I called again, and he picked up on the third ring.

He answered the phone like he was at work. "This is Miles."

"Miles," I sobbed into the receiver.

"Sam?" The concern was apparent in his voice. "Are you okay?" He knew the three of us were jogging at the park; I was supposed to go over to his apartment afterward.

"We were robbed at gunpoint. Ronnie's been hurt."

Immediately, I could hear him yell Brett's name. Then, he turned back to me. "We're on our way." He abruptly hung up the phone.

Somehow, Miles and Brett arrived at the park ten minutes prior to the ambulance and fifteen minutes before the police, that night. Miles showed up barefoot; Brett showed up with a hatchet in his hand. When Ronnie asked Brett why he owns a hatchet, he simply responded that every man should own one.

Brett had demanded to know which way, and I quote, "those pieces of shit" had run off to. Then, even though the men were long gone, he ran off in the same direction, hatchet in hand. When the police did arrive, I quickly explained to them that the man running around with a hatchet was in fact our overprotective friend, not the perpetrator.

About five minutes after the police arrived, Tony and Craig got to the scene. Miles called Craig on the way over to the park, alerting him that Ronnie had been injured. Ronnie did allow the paramedics to examine her, as well as to cleanse and dress her head wound, however, she stubbornly refused to be transferred to the hospital. She pointed at Miles and Tony, then informed the paramedics treating her that she had her own paramedics at her beck and call. Why the hell would she need to go to a hospital?

Miles and I both tried convincing her she needed to have an MRI to ensure she didn't suffer a traumatic brain injury. Tony even offered to drive her to Summit Valley, so she didn't have to go in an ambulance. I'm sure Craig would've offered the same, but he'd been downright hysterical upon seeing Ronnie in that state and was in no shape to drive. Brett ended up having to calm him down when he eventually returned from his hatchet-wielding, wild goose chase.

In the end, no one made Veronica Sanders do anything she didn't want to do. She stood her ground, refusing to go to the emergency room. However, Brett and Craig did end up making her stay awake all night in case she had a concussion or, even worse, a subdural hematoma. That's just fancy medical jargon for a burst blood vessel which causes pooling of blood in the brain.

Thankfully, Ronnie ended up being fine. The seven of us spent the night together at Jill's and my apartment that night, just to be sure.

Finally, to get to the point of this whole story, as fate would have it, one of the responding officers happened to be the extremely handsome, young policeman who responded to the noise complaint at our apartment a couple of years ago. You know, the noise complaint involving a floor full of dish soap and chocolate syrup.

When he approached, I instantly noticed the recognition in his eyes as he saw Jill. He remained completely professional, though, never once mentioning the night he came to our apartment and found eight adults completely covered in chocolate syrup and dish soap.

Max, as we came to learn his name, and his partner had been the ones to take Jill's, Ronnie's, and my statement. The other two officers that were there ended up leaving to respond to another call. After completing our statements, Max's partner, not the same man from two years prior, immediately began walking back to the patrol car. Max hesitated, addressing us all before departing. He informed us they'd do everything in their power to find the men that robbed us and assaulted Ronnie. He turned to follow his partner. And that's when Jill did something totally out of character. Later, she told me the adrenaline from thinking we were about to die had given her the courage.

"Wait!" Jill called after him.

Max stopped in his tracks and turned to face her. The six of us stared after them as Jill approached him. Initially, I'd thought she wanted to add something to her statement. When she came to a stop before him, I realized this was something different.

"Do you remember me?" Jill asked.

"I do."

"Good...take me on a date," she proposed. Max stood before her, spellbound and speechless.

"That's off the record!" Tony hollered at them, cutting the tension. At Tony's comment, Max started to chuckle, and Jill smiled at him in such a way that I couldn't help but smile myself. At that moment, I knew something very good was about to happen.

Grinning back at Jill, Max finally responded, "I would love nothing more."

The two of them have been practically inseparable ever since that night. As I watch Jill flutter around the apartment, preparing for her romantic getaway, I'm fairly certain I've never seen her happier. Dare I say it, she looks even happier than the day she graduated as a respiratory therapist. Jill deserves this happiness.

"Hey, Jill," I call to her.

She briefly stops running around to glance at me. "Yes?"

"You're not leaving until tomorrow, right?" I ask, scratching Archie's belly. He grumbles his appreciation.

"That's correct," she says matter-of-factly as she smooths out a wrinkle in the silky blouse she's wearing. It's a soft teal color that beautifully complements her bright blue eyes.

"Come watch a movie with me and Archie."

"Sam, you know I have to pack!"

"You started packing three days ago," I remind her playfully. "You must be pretty close to done by now."

"What movie do you want to watch?"

"*Man of Steel*," I tell her. "I need some Henry Cavill in my life." The first time I watched this movie, I finally understood Margo's obsession with Christopher Reeve. Henry Cavill is my Christopher Reeve.

"He's so cute," Jill whispers as if her boyfriend could magically hear her from fifteen miles away.

"Are you in? Or are you IN?"

"Darn you," she sighs. "You know I'm in." She giggles as she takes a seat on the couch beside me.

"Hold this," I instruct, plopping Archie into her lap. "He needs continuous belly rubs."

"Oh, but of course," Jill snickers, dutifully scratching Archie's round belly. This pug is spoiled rotten.

I scurry over to our entertainment center in search of my *Man of Steel* DVD. Just as I find it, I hear a knock at our front door.

I lock eyes with Jill. "Are you expecting anyone?"

"No," she replies. "Are you?"

I shake my head "no." Walking over to our front door, DVD in hand, I hesitantly peer through the peephole. I see a mess of auburn hair, immediately recognizing our visitor.

"It's just Ronnie," I announce, yanking the door open.

"Hey, we were just about to watch—" I realize Ronnie is crying, and I immediately lose my train of thought. I've never seen Ronnie cry before, not even the night we were robbed at gunpoint.

Beside her, I notice a suitcase.

"I fucked up," she whispers.

I can feel Jill's presence behind me now. Archie has also come to join us, sitting at my feet. "Ronnie, what do you mean?"

She looks at us, heartbroken. "I cheated on Craig."

# CHAPTER FIFTY-ONE:

ehind me, I hear Jill gasp. My mouth falls open as I stare at Ronnie in shock. This can't be happening. Ronnie and Craig should be getting engaged, not breaking up.

"I don't understand." What I really want to say is I don't understand why you would cheat on someone you love, but I leave that last part out. She's already upset. No need to pour salt in the wound.

"I don't understand why I do the things I do, either," Ronnie sniffles.

I usher her into the apartment. "Come inside."

"I've got your suitcase," Jill announces, rolling Ronnie's bag into the living room.

"I know I've been a burden on both of you over the years," Ronnie sighs. "But I have nowhere else to go." Her emerald green eyes are bloodshot, her cheeks stained with tears.

Jill immediately reassures her, "You are *not* a burden, Veronica Mae! You know you're always welcome here."

"What Jill said," I confirm. "No matter what couch we own, you can always crash on it." Jill and I both simultaneously wrap our arms around her. It doesn't matter what she's done. Ronnie's our best friend—we love her unconditionally.

Jill softly smiles at Ronnie. "Everyone makes mistakes."

"But here's the thing," Ronnie breathes. "I *keep* making them. Over and over again." She slumps onto our sectional, and Archie immediately jumps into her lap. "Hi Archibald," she whispers, lovingly scratching him behind his ear.

We've nicknamed Archie the Medicine Pug. Whenever someone is sad or not feeling well, Archie is on the case. He'll immediately crawl on said person's lap, consoling them with his grumbles of love.

"What do you mean?" I ask.

"Come on, Sam. You know I'm a complete fuck-up."

"No, you're not!" Jill and I both react in unison.

"Ohhh, let me count the ways for you," she laughs sarcastically, removing her purse from her shoulder, setting it beside her on the couch. "First, I almost didn't even get accepted to Belview because I got wasted, missed my final exam at the community college, and failed my Sociology class."

All of a sudden, she reaches into her purse, pulling her nine-millimeter pistol out and placing it on our coffee table.

"You brought your gun," Jill gasps—she's sure doing a lot of gasping today.

"Of course, I did. I don't go anywhere without it."

About a week after we were robbed, Ronnie and Craig both enrolled in a course to get their concealed carry permits in Virginia. After Ronnie received her permit, she immediately purchased her own handgun. She vowed she'd never again allow herself to be in a situation like we were that night. Never again would she be completely defenseless. She frequently urged Jill and me to do the same.

"I don't know how I feel about a gun in the apartment," Jill mumbles.

"Y'all honestly should get a gun of your own. Two women living alone? You're practically sitting ducks," Ronnie says, before turning to face Jill. "Plus, you're dating a cop, Jill. I know for damn sure Max carries a gun on him at all times."

"I'm still adjusting to that," Jill whispers.

"Brett carries a hatchet. Maybe we should just get a hatchet instead," I joke. The three of us can't help but laugh, recalling Brett's wild antics the night of the robbery.

I try changing the subject. "It was one slip-up, Ronnie. That doesn't make you a fuck-up."

"Oh, I wasn't done, Sammie Bear," she interjects. "Let us not forget about when I completely failed out of Belview and never became a social worker."

"Maybe that just wasn't your true calling," Jill offers, lightly rubbing Ronnie's shoulder, trying to comfort her.

"Well, all I know is having to go back to working at The Cinedome definitely wasn't my calling," Ronnie replies, turning to face Jill once more.

I take a seat beside her on the couch. "It's only temporary," I try to assure her.

"You're right about one thing. It sure was temporary," she sneers.

"What do you mean?" Jill asks.

"I was fired yesterday...by my own boyfriend."

I gasp. "What?!" I guess Jill isn't the only one gasping today.

"Craig fired me, yesterday."

Jill is the first to ask, "Why on earth would he do such a thing?"

"I guess he didn't have a choice." Tears begin streaming down Ronnie's face once more. "That didn't make me any less angry, though."

I decide to stop beating around the bush and ask her directly. "Why did he fire you, Ronnie?"

She turns her body to face me, her tear-filled eyes locked with mine. "Remember when we used to make our fruit punch vodka cocktails for our private viewings after our shifts?"

"I remember."

She hesitates for a moment before responding. "...I may have started making those vodka fruit punch cocktails—minus the fruit punch—during my shifts once in a while."

Jill's eyes go wide. "You were drinking during your shifts?"

"I *knew* you would judge me!" Ronnie shrieks. "Not all of us can be as perfect as you, Jillian!"

Immediately, Jill looks as if she's about to cry.

"Ronnie!" I scold her.

"I wasn't judging you," Jill whimpers.

Ronnie sighs. "I'm sorry, Jill. That was uncalled for. I just don't feel like myself anymore."

"How often were you drinking at work?" I ask.

"Every day."

I put my arm around Ronnie and rest my forehead against hers. "It's going to be okay."

"Craig wants me to go to rehab."

"Maybe it isn't a bad idea."

Jill remains silent. I know she's afraid to speak for fear of Ronnie lashing out at her again.

"I'm not going to rehab," Ronnie asserts, pulling away from my embrace.

"What about AA?" I propose. "Or what about talking to Tony? He's found a great group of sober friends at his gym."

She looks at me, furious. "How about you go to AA, Sam?"

I'm taken aback by both her tone and her words.

Jill's screeching shouts ring out across the room, surprising us both. "THAT'S ENOUGH!" She looks directly at Ronnie. "You don't get to be a...a...a BITCH to us! We're just trying to help you!"

Both of our mouths fall open as we stare at Jill in complete shock. "Did you just swear?" Ronnie asks.

"I can't believe I just swore," Jill mutters, cradling her head in her hands.

I start chuckling. "It was kind of awesome."

Ronnie turns to smile at me, before scooting over to sit beside Jill. "It was totally awesome." Jill meets Ronnie's gaze. "I'm sorry, Jill." Ronnie then looks between the two of us. "I'm sorry to both of you. Neither of you deserves this."

"It's okay," Jill replies, smiling back at Ronnie. "We know you're going through a tough time."

"Don't feel sorry for me, Jilly Bean. I did all of this to myself." Ronnies sighs before continuing. "Yesterday, after Craig let me go from The Cinedome, I went straight to The Barn Door for a drink. One drink turned into multiple drinks. I got completely shit-faced and went home with a guy from the bar."

"Just a random guy?" Jill asks.

"Not exactly," Ronnie mutters under her breath, looking down at her feet. "It was Nathan, Brett's co-worker."

"I've never liked that guy!" I blurt out. "He's an asshole."

Jill adds, "Doesn't he have a girlfriend?"

"To be honest, I barely remember anything. I'm so ashamed of what I've done. I immediately went back home when I woke up this morning and confessed everything to Craig."

"He kicked you out of the apartment after you told him?" I ask.

"Not exactly. He just said he needed some space to think about everything."

"Everything will be okay," Jill reassures her, grabbing her hand. "Contrary to popular belief, everyone makes mistakes—even me."

Ronnie shakes her head but doesn't pull her hand away from Jill's. "I just keep making the same mistakes over and over again." The frustration is apparent in her voice. "Do you remember that guy Kevin I dated a few years back? The one I lived with for a few months?"

"Yeah, the asshole that kicked you out for no good reason? I never liked him either," I tell her.

"I admit, he was an asshole. But he had a good reason to kick me out. I cheated on him, too," she discloses.

"You were young, Ronnie," Jill comforts her. "Don't beat yourself up about the past."

She groans. "Yeah? And what's my excuse now?"

"You're only twenty-six," I point out. "I still consider that pretty young. Just give Craig a little time. Jill's right—everything will be okay."

"I'm canceling my trip tomorrow," Jill announces, before turning to address me directly, "Ronnie needs us."

"No, you are not!" Ronnie declares, standing from the couch. "You're going on that trip, and you're gonna have tons of crazy sex with your hot cop boyfriend."

Jill's cheeks turn bright red. She covers her face with her hands in embarrassment, and I can't help but laugh. "I'll be okay," Ronnie assures her. "Plus, Sam's here."

"No trips for me," I say with a grin.

Once she's recovered from her mortification, Jill asks, "Are you sure? I really don't mind canceling."

"I'm positive, Jill." Then, she collapses back onto the couch. "So, what movie are we watching?" Archie immediately scurries back into Ronnie's lap. "You know, Sam, I was never a fan of pugs, but this little gremlin has swayed me," she laughs, cuddling him.

"He's totally the best," I admit, smiling at my adorable black pug. "We were just about to put on *Man of Steel*."

"Can we watch something funny instead?"

"*Step Brothers*?"

"I was thinking more like *Twilight*," she admits. "Don't you dare repeat this, but I kind of miss watching you nerds reenact it."

"Somebody, pinch me!" I shout. "Veronica Sanders just requested we watch *Twilight*. I always knew you secretly loved those movies."

Ronnie grins. "Maybe I just secretly love how much you two love them."

"Say it!" Jill blurts, jumping onto the sectional.

"Out loud!" I bellow, hopping onto the couch with her.

The three of us scream in unison, "VAMPIRE!"

As we curl up onto our sectional for the impromptu movie marathon, I can't help but feel thankful. Thankful that no matter what obstacles we're faced with—we'll always have each other.

**Nothing can tear us apart.**

# CHAPTER FIFTY-TWO:

ast night felt just like old times. Jill, Ronnie, and I stayed awake 'til almost three in the morning, binge-watching the *Twilight* saga. I know the times when Ronnie has lived with us haven't always been under the best circumstances, but we do always enjoy having her here. Honestly, our couch feels so empty without her on it—last night was a reminder of that.

Jill left early this afternoon for her trip with Max to Virginia Beach. She asked Ronnie at least three more times if she wanted her to cancel her trip, to which Ronnie finally said that if Jill didn't go to Virginia Beach with Max, she'd go in her place. Finally, she conceded and left for her vacation, but not before giving Ronnie a huge hug goodbye.

Earlier, Miles asked if I wanted to go to The Barn Door with him tonight to see a local band perform. It's rare for a band to play on a weeknight. Usually, I would never miss an opportunity to see live music, but, currently, I have higher priorities. My friend needs me. I didn't go into great detail about what's going on with Ronnie, but Miles said he understood.

I have a feeling, though, that Craig probably reached out to him. Probably Brett and Tony, too. I wouldn't be surprised if Craig called

Zach, as well. Just like Ronnie immediately sought out Jill and me. Sometimes, you just need your friends.

Scurrying out of my bedroom, a blanket draped over my shoulders, and Archie on my heels, I snuggle up to Ronnie on the couch. "Hi, friend," I say, giving her my biggest cheesy grin.

"Hey, dork."

Archie crawls from my lap onto Ronnie's and plops down with a grunt. "Traitor," I mutter.

"He just knows I need extra Medicine Pug cuddles, right now," she states, wrapping her arms around Archie.

"Wanna play a board game?"

"Aren't you going to the bar tonight?" Ronnie asks. "There's a band playing."

"I'm not leaving you here alone."

"I'm not alone. I have Archie. Plus, Craig is coming over. We're gonna talk."

"Oh...do you not want me here?"

"I always want you where I'm at, Sammie Bear." She wraps her arms around me. "But I want you to go see that band play tonight. I want you to go hang out with your boyfriend—just like I told Jill." She turns to me, laughing. "Sorry, I just can't call Miles hot, though."

I feign offense. "Miles is *super* hot."

She grins back at me. "He's adorable. Now, go get ready. You look awful." She leans over, giving me a peck on the cheek.

"You look worse," I tease, sticking my tongue out at her.

"I know," she sighs. Then she smiles as she adds, "Oh, by the way...tell Miles his new nickname is 'Miley Moo.' I know he's always wanted one."

I clap my hands together in excitement. "He's going to love it! He's finally the proud owner of a certified Veronica Sanders nickname."

Ronnie beams at me.

I turn serious once more, asking her a final time, "Are you sure you want me to go, Ronnie?"

She nods at me reassuringly. "Yes."

As I pull myself off the couch and start heading toward my bedroom to change, I feel Ronnie grab my hand. I turn around to look at her.

"He's your person, Sam. Don't let him go. Don't make my mistakes."

I squeeze her hand, staring into her watery, emerald eyes. "Craig will forgive you, Ronnie. I know he will. Everything will be okay."

"I love you, Sam," she whispers.

"I love you, too." Then, returning her sentiment, I lean over and give her a peck on the cheek.

Even though the band is terrible, I'm still having a great time. I've decided to have only a few beers tonight. I don't want to get too buzzed, and beer doesn't get me nearly as drunk as liquor.

I plan on calling it an early night, tonight. I don't want to leave Ronnie alone for too long, but I also don't want to come home too early and interrupt an intimate conversation between her and Craig.

I pull my phone out of my purse to check the time—almost 9:00 PM. I decide to send Ronnie a text to check in on her.

**Did Craig come over yet?**

I hit send. Then, I decide to send her one more text before shoving my phone back into my purse.

**Hang in there. I'll be home soon. Love ya.**

I grab my bottle of Bud Light off the table, taking a long sip. I'm not a huge fan of beer, but on the other hand, vodka's not a huge fan of me. I've come to realize I have a tendency to be really mean when I drink hard liquor.

"How's that Bud Light treatin' ya?" Tony's new friend Calvin comes up behind me. Calvin goes to the same CrossFit gym as Tony and is also sober. I won't lie, I'm curious if Calvin is possibly more than just a friend...but I don't want to be nosy. Either way, I really like him.

I laugh, "It's not my favorite."

"Even when I used to drink, I always hated beer."

"Does it bother you to be inside a bar and not drink? I don't know how Tony does it."

"Not anymore," Calvin says. "Especially if there are other things going on." He motions to the stage in the corner of the room. "Like a dreadful band performing."

I can't help but burst into laughter. "I couldn't understand a single word they were saying," I tell him.

Brett and Miles approach our table, having just returned from the bar. "We got you another Bud Light," Brett tells me, placing a fresh drink on the table.

"Where's Tony?" Miles asks.

"He went to tinkle," Calvin responds. Both Miles and Brett laugh—I think they like Calvin too.

I thank Brett for the beer, then pull my phone from my purse again. Ronnie still hasn't responded to my texts yet. I decide to send her one more message.

**Everything okay?**

I hit send and set my phone on the table.

A couple minutes later, Tony returns to the table with two glasses of ice water in his hands. He grins at Calvin as he hands him one. "There's a food truck outside. Should we go check it out?"

"Sure," I reply, grabbing my phone off the table, sticking it into the back pocket of my jeans as I stand from my chair. "Let's go."

The band is about to start their second set inside the bar, so there isn't much of a line for the food truck. Calvin and I may not be crazy about them, but they do seem to have a lot of loyal fans here, tonight. To each their own, I guess.

"A band and a food truck on a weeknight? Van is really starting to spoil us shift workers," Brett chuckles.

The five of us stand in front of the truck, checking out the menu. Everything looks extremely unhealthy yet equally delicious. Suddenly, I feel my phone start vibrating in my back pocket and quickly grab it. It's Craig. I stare at my phone screen, and I can't help wondering why he's calling me. Did he and Ronnie get into a fight?

"Hey, Craig," I answer. Miles, Brett, and Tony turn to look at me.

Craig doesn't respond. Instead, my breath catches in my throat as I realize Craig is crying. I instantly feel sick to my stomach. He sobs something unintelligible through the phone.

"Craig! What's going on?"

Still no response; I hear only crying. My hands are shaking. Actually, I think my entire body is shaking. Instinctively, I start walking back to Tony's truck. I don't know why, but I need to go. I need to get home.

"Sam!" Miles shouts. "Where are you going?" I turn around, seeing Miles, Brett, Tony, and Calvin, all follow me.

I come to a stand in the middle of The Barn Door parking lot, yelling through the phone. "Craig! Answer me!"

"She's gone, Sam," Craig finally sobs. "She's gone."

"Who's gone? What the hell are you talking about?"

"Ronnie's gone," he wails. "She shot herself—inside your apartment—she's dead, Sam."

The world moves in slow motion. My phone drops out of my hand, hitting the asphalt. I can't breathe. My vision blurs: I can't see. My throat feels as if it's closing.

**I can't fucking breathe.**

I collapse to my knees. Everything sounds so far away. It's like I'm underwater. Miles, Brett, and Tony are all crouched down around me. They're trying to talk to me, but I can't hear them. All I hear is screaming. Screams that sound foreign to me, that aren't my own. Screams of someone who has just lost everything.

My hands hit the pavement, and I'm now in a cat-like position on my knees. In between my screams and sobs, I start vomiting.

Now, I can hear Miles screaming. He's screaming for help. Little does he know; I can't be helped. No one can help me.

When there is nothing left in my stomach, I finally stop vomiting. But now I'm left gasping for breath. I've never felt such visceral pain like this. This isn't just pain—this is agony.

*She can't be gone. He's wrong. He has to be wrong.*

"Sam! Sam! What's wrong," Brett is screaming to me. He's kneeling before me on the asphalt, both of his hands on my shoulders. I'm finally able to focus on him through my stream of tears. I'm only just realizing I've thrown up on him, which he doesn't seem fazed by.

Looking to my left, I see Miles and Van running back to me. Van has a first aid kit and a bottle of water in his hand. They reach us within seconds.

"She wouldn't stop throwing up," Brett tells Miles.

"Here, drink some water, baby." Miles kneels beside me, offering me a bottle of water which I refuse.

"She's gone," I croak—I've lost my voice from screaming.

"Who's gone?" Miles asks.

"She gave you a nickname," I cry. "Ronnie gave you a nickname."

"I know," he replies, confused. "You told me."

"She was saying goodbye. How did I not see she was saying goodbye?"

"Who was saying goodbye?" Tony asks.

"Craig called me." I look vacantly at Miles, Tony, and Brett, all kneeling before me. My friends. Ronnie's friends. Our pack.

*None of us will ever be the same.*

"What'd he say?" Brett asks, his voice hollow.

"Ronnie shot herself," I choke out. "He said she's dead."

At first, I'm met with silence. Then, Tony starts to cry. Calvin kneels down at his side, trying to hold his shaking body. Van drops the first aid kit he was holding, letting it tumble to the ground. His mouth falls open in shock. Brett stands silently, then storms off without a word. Then I hear the deafening sound of metal crunching—I know he's just punched something.

Finally, I lock eyes with Miles. I watch as his hazel eyes fill with tears. Wordlessly, he pulls me into his arms and our sobs meld into one. I let my head fall back, then stare up to the cold, December night sky, hot tears rolling down my face, and realize what today is.

It's December 9th...the day my brother, Matthew, died.

And now...the day my best friend took her own life.

# CHAPTER FIFTY-THREE:

# VERONICA MAE SANDERS

# "RONNIE"

**December 9, 2015, 20:57**

Archie is whining—I can hear him. I moved him and his kennel into the laundry room and shut the door. I know the noise will scare him.

I'm sorry, Archie.

I didn't want to do this here, but I had nowhere else to go. If I'm being honest—selfishly—I wanted one more night with them. My best friends. The friends I never deserved, but that God gave me anyway.

God, please forgive me. I'm sorry.

I send one final text, telling him the front door is open. Within seconds, he replies; he'll be over soon.

I'm sorry, Craig. I'm sorry to do this to you, but I couldn't let it be Sam or Jill.

*I've betrayed you, in more ways than one. Let this be my last betrayal. Let this be the last time I break your heart. You gave me everything, and I threw it all away. I've loved you the only way I know how, but I've finally accepted that isn't enough. You deserve so much more than I can give you. You deserve so much more than me.*

*After I'm gone, you can finally start to heal. One day, when you meet the beautiful, kind, loving woman to become your wife, the mother of your children, you'll thank me. You'll thank me for setting you free.*

*I'm sorry. I'm sorry. I'm sorry.*

*Finishing off the bottle of vodka in my hand, I set it into the empty sink. I brought this bottle with me, tucked deep inside my suitcase. Sam doesn't keep liquor in the house anymore—she's trying to be better.*

*Please be better, Sam. Please do what I couldn't. And I'm sorry. Please, don't make my mistakes.*

*Willing myself to move, I walk into Sam's bathroom. Just as I place my phone on the bathroom counter, it vibrates. It's Jill. Against my better judgment, I read her text. She's checking in on me, again. My eyes betray me, tears streaming down my face.*

*I'm sorry, Jill.*

*I lock my phone screen—I don't return her text. Placing my phone back onto the bathroom counter, I resolve not to look at it again.*

*I'm sorry. I'm sorry. I'm sorry.*

*I step into the bathtub, closing the shower curtain behind me. I hear my phone vibrate again; a few seconds later, it vibrates once more. Momentarily, I think about checking on who's texted me now. But it's best if I don't.*

*My body slumps into the empty tub. I can feel the guilt crashing down around me. The guilt of doing this here, of being a burden once more—one final time.*

*I'm sorry, Sammie Bear. I'm sorry, Jilly Bean. I'm sorry.*

*This apartment feels so cold. The tub beneath me, the steel clutched in my hand. It all feels so cold.*

*My phone vibrates one last time. I ignore it.*

*I'm sorry. I'm sorry. I'm sorry.*

*I squeeze my eyes shut, yet the tears still fall.*

*I'm sorry. I'm sorry. I'm sorry.*

*I force my shaking finger to move.*

*I'm sorry. I'm sorry. I'm sor—*

# CHAPTER FIFTY-FOUR

## (Four Days Later):

The past four days have been a blur. I don't feel as if I even exist anymore. It's like I'm merely floating along, watching the world pass me by.

I can barely remember the night of Ronnie's suicide. I wasn't drunk, so I'm not sure why my memory is so poor. I remember Craig calling me while I stood in The Barn Door parking lot, waiting to order from the food truck. Even though I can't remember the exact words he said, I'll never forget what he told me:

*She's gone. She shot herself inside your apartment. She's dead.*

Then, there's nothing. No recollection of what happened next. Not until we were all huddled around Margo's dining room table. I don't remember vomiting on Brett, or telling Miles, Brett, and Tony that Ronnie died. I don't remember calling Jill and my dad, hysterical. I have no memory of the drive to Margo's house after Miles finally managed to calm me down. The next thing I'm able to remember—after Craig's phone call—is being at Margo's house. The police officers who responded to Craig's 911 call took some time to question him at the scene; afterward, he and his dad joined us at Margo's.

Craig had been sobbing when he finally arrived, cradling Archie in his arms.

At first, I was pretty upset to learn the police had questioned Craig in that state, but Max had assured me it's standard protocol whenever someone finds a body.

It feels so wrong to refer to Ronnie as just a "body." Is that all she is now?

In the early morning following Ronnie's suicide, Jill and Max drove back to Bristol, cutting their Virginia Beach trip short. I still feel bad that I had to break the news to Jill over the phone, ruining her romantic getaway. She deserved to know, though; this type of news couldn't wait two days. Ronnie is her best friend, too.

Ronnie *was* her best friend, too. I still can't believe she's gone.

That night, the coroner removed Ronnie's body from my bathroom, where Craig had found her. However, I eventually discovered the coroner isn't responsible for anything else. To put it bluntly, they don't clean after removing a deceased body from a private residence. And, honestly, neither Jill nor I were emotionally prepared to face this aftermath.

Brett was the first person to venture into our apartment after that night. He simply told Jill and me that he'd handle it. He and I may have had our differences in the past, but I'll never forget what he did for us that day. He found a local death cleanup service that promised to be compassionate and discreet. He took it upon himself to hire and schedule them to clean our apartment as soon as possible, refusing to let us repay him. I still have no clue how much it cost.

Even though I'm a hospice nurse, dealing with death every day, I never knew services like this existed. I guess it's one of those things you hope you never need to know.

Even after the apartment was cleaned, it still took two more days for Jill, Archie, and I to go back to the apartment. Today is our first day back. I hate being here, now. It no longer feels like our apartment—this place isn't our home anymore. The only thing that lives here now is sadness.

I'm engulfed in sadness, yet I'm also angry. I'm so angry with her. How could she do this to us? How could she be so selfish? Then, I feel guilty for being angry with someone who's gone—someone who felt this was their only way out.

I'm begging for someone to just tell me how I'm supposed to feel.

*It's like I'm going crazy.*

Although I can barely remember the night of her death, I still feel the pain vividly. It hurts so fucking bad.

Yesterday, the day of Ronnie's funeral, I bought a bottle of vodka. Over the last few months, I'd been trying to limit my liquor intake, but that day I was desperate. I needed something—anything—to numb my pain. To end this suffering and torment.

Jill's wild theory is that I have dissociative amnesia. Basically, it's when someone blocks out information or memories, often due to trauma. The more I've read up on it, the more I think Jill's wrong, but I don't have the energy to argue with her about it. Maybe it's better that I don't remember.

The day before the funeral, Zach and Sarah flew back to Bristol. My dad, stepmom, and half-sister attended the funeral, as well. Even my mother, Caroline, came. Although I didn't speak to her; just another thing I didn't have the energy for.

Jill and I both spoke at the funeral. We stood behind the podium together, holding each other, tears streaming down our faces as we fumbled through the eulogies we'd written. In the middle of her eulogy,

Jill broke into an uncontrollable sob. She ended up handing me her speech, so I could finish reading her words as she composed herself.

The last person to speak at the funeral was Craig, right after both of Ronnie's parents spoke. Craig paused briefly in front of Ronnie's casket before taking his place at the podium at the front of the small funeral home. Obviously, due to the nature of her death, the funeral was closed casket.

Months ago, Ronnie mentioned to me in passing once that when she died, she wanted to be cremated and have her cremains turned into a living tree. Unfortunately, she never put anything in writing, specifying her wish. It's not something you usually think about at twenty-six years old. As such, the decision about her funeral arrangements was left to her parents. I'm still unsure if Ronnie ever told her parents she wanted to be cremated.

Craig stood before his girlfriend's casket in silence, gently resting the acoustic guitar he'd brought against the steps leading up to the podium. I watched as he shoved his shaking hand into the front pocket of his jeans and pulled out a small, black box. When he opened that box, I felt like the wind had been knocked out of me. It was a diamond ring...an engagement ring.

"I should be putting this ring on your finger, not on your casket," he whispered, carefully setting the open box onto Ronnie's casket.

Beside me, Jill gasped. I immediately turned to console her, but Max had already wrapped his arms around her to do the same. That's when I lost it. No longer able to stifle my sobs, I openly wept. I felt Miles squeeze my hand, then turned to meet his gaze, his eyes red and swollen. He gently pulled me to him, kissing my forehead. He held me like that, his lips to my forehead, until my sobs quieted.

Craig picked his guitar up off the steps, then turned to address us all. "I wrote a song for my girlfriend. I hadn't wanted to sing it for her until it was perfect. But now I wish I would've just sung to her."

Then, his voice cracking, "I'd like to sing it for all of you if that's alright."

"You've got this, buddy," Brett called up to him.

Craig gave Brett a small nod in acknowledgment, then seated himself at the top of the podium steps. Before adjusting his guitar on his knee, he removed his cowboy hat from his head and placed it on the step, beside him. There was once a time when Craig thought the worst thing he could have was a cold, lonely head. But that's before his heart truly knew loneliness—knew the bitter desolation a life without her would bring.

Craig let out a long sigh. "This is Veronica's song." He began strumming his guitar.

"She can hear you, honey. She can hear you," Margo whispered from the row behind me.

Yesterday was one of the hardest days of my life. Never did I think I'd attend one of my best friend's funerals. At least, not at this age.

There are moments when I think this is all just a bad dream. That I'll wake up and find Ronnie lounging on our sectional. I'll hear her laugh again. I'll be able to wrap my arms around her.

But this isn't a bad dream—*this is my new reality*.

Now, I need to get a grip on my emotions. In a little less than two hours, I have to go back to work. I've already called out the last two nights. Luckily, my manager has been extremely understanding. She even offered to take me off the schedule for tonight, but it's time for me to get back to my normal routine. Work will help keep me busy, which should keep my mind off all the things that have consumed me over these past four days. Besides, I'm a hospice nurse. I deal with loss and grief for a living. If anyone should be able to handle this sort of thing, it's me.

An hour into my shift, I already want to go home. Tanya and Lucie have each asked me at least three times if I'm okay. Before their shifts yesterday, they both attended Ronnie's funeral in support of me. They know how deeply I've been hurting.

Even if they hadn't attended Ronnie's funeral, they would've eventually heard about her death. Bristol is a small town. The news of Ronnie's suicide spread like wildfire.

"Our admission is late," Lucie remarks.

I look down at my watch, realizing she's right. Our admission is thirty minutes late. "Maybe the transport team is behind," I say. I attempt to make small-talk. "How's school going, Luce?"

"Pharmacology is tough," she chuckles. "My least favorite class is probably my Peds class, though."

"You don't like pediatrics?"

"I don't like sick kids. My heart can't handle it."

My mind immediately drifts to Matty. "Mine either."

Tanya calls to us from the other nursing station. "Admission's here," She directs the transporters to room 542.

In unison, Lucie and I stand from our seats. I grab my stethoscope and report sheet from the nurses' station counter, following Lucie down the hall to room 542. Her arms are filled with toiletries and other supplies to bathe our new patient.

The two transporters roll the gurney into the room. No family members are with them; I'm sure they'll start trickling in throughout the night. On the hospice and palliative care floor, we have no visiting hours. So, families can come and see their loved ones at all hours of the day or night.

Lucie enters the room before me, but I'm only a few strides behind her. She comes to an abrupt stop at the foot of the bed, making me nearly collide with her. The transporters have already transferred our patient from the gurney to the hospital bed, but I don't hear the whir of the oxygen concentrator.

"She's supposed to be on four liters of O2," I say, pointing at the concentrator.

One of the hospital transporters—Luke, a thin man, just a few years older than me, with jet-black hair and a ridiculous handlebar mustache—addresses me directly. "You know we can't make this call, but I'm pretty sure she's DOA."

DOA, or dead-on-arrival, means the patient died in transport. Most patients who are admitted to hospice have a DNR, or "do not resuscitate," order in place, meaning if they pass, even during transport, no life-saving measures are to be taken. In layman's terms, no CPR.

"Do you still want me to put her on oxygen?" Luke asks.

I realize I still haven't answered him. In hospice, we consider administering oxygen to be for comfort rather than as a life-saving measure. But, obviously, it's not necessary if you're no longer alive.

Stepping around Lucie, I stare at my patient. With just one look, I know Luke's right—she's gone. I'll still have to assess and pronounce her time of death, but as I've said before, sometimes you don't need a stethoscope to tell you these things.

Finally, I turn to Luke. "There's no need." I remove my report sheet from my pocket, quickly rereading the patient's information. Her hospice diagnosis is end-stage liver cirrhosis due to alcoholism. The sheet in my hand states she's only forty-two years old. "Do you know if her family is on their way?"

"There's no family. No next of kin listed in her chart," the other transporter, whose name I don't know, replies.

"What do you mean no next of kin? She's only forty-two."

"Pretty sad, ain't it?" Luke says, walking over to me. He places his hand lightly on my shoulder. "Seems like she lived a pretty tough life." His voice is full of sympathy. He must know about Ronnie. How could he not?

When I look from Luke's hand on my shoulder, back to my patient, my entire body stiffens. All I see is Ronnie—my friend lying lifeless in the hospital bed before me. It hits me like a ton of bricks.

**She's gone. Ronnie's really gone.**

"Anything else you need from us, Nurse Sam?" Luke asks.

I try reining in the terror I feel. I have to remain professional. I can't be weak. I have to stay strong. Forcing myself to take a deep breath, I look up at him. "We're good, Luke. Thanks." As I remove my stethoscope from around my neck, my hands are trembling. I hope no one notices.

The other transporter nods at me then pushes the gurney out of the hospital room. "Take care of yourself, Sam," Luke says before following his partner out of the room.

"Take care of myself," I mutter sarcastically under my breath, clutching my stethoscope. I don't know even how to take care of myself anymore. And if I can't take care of myself, how am I supposed to take care of others? How the hell am I supposed to be a nurse?

Choking back tears, I pronounce my patient deceased. My forty-two-year-old patient with no family on record. When hospice patients pass away without family or next of kin and no prior funeral arrangements, we contact the coroner's office. The coroner then directs us to which mortuary to contact for them to retrieve the patient's remains.

Then, they're gone. Gone—*just like Ronnie.*

I can feel my chest tightening. My breathing quickens, and I suddenly feel as if I'm trying to breathe through a straw. My vision blurs. I'm about to have an anxiety attack.

"Sam? Are you okay?" Lucie asks, still holding her bin of toiletries.

"I'm okay," I lie. I have to get out of here.

"I'm still going to bathe her," she says.

"She doesn't have any family. No one's coming, Luce."

Tears well in Lucie's eyes. "I know, but I can't leave her like this. Her hair is all matted. It just doesn't feel right."

I walk over to Lucie, placing my trembling hands on her shoulders. "You're going to be such an amazing nurse, one day," I whisper before storming out of the room, practically running towards the break room. I just need some water, then I'll feel better. Water fixes everything, right? Or was that coffee?

Who am I kidding? *The answer is vodka.*

When I reach the break room, I search frantically for my water bottle, since vodka isn't an option. I can't breathe. I think I'm hyperventilating.

"Are you okay?"

I turn around to see Tanya standing in the entryway to the break room, and I breakdown. "I can't do this, Tanya," I sob. Crouching down, I cradle my knees to my chest. "I don't know if I'll ever be okay."

"I knew it was too soon for you to come back," Tanya whispers, crouching down next to me. She wraps her arm around my hunched body. "Alice is on-call tonight. I know she won't mind coming in to cover your shift. I'm calling her, right now." She pulls her phone out of her pocket. "You need to go home, Sam."

"I can't do this," I repeat, my body now rocking back and forth.

"I know," Tanya whispers, trying to calm me.

"What if I can't do this anymore? What if I can't be a hospice nurse anymore? What if I never stop seeing her?"

I don't have to explain myself further. Tanya understands me. "Samantha," her voice, taking on a motherly tone, "I'm not going to lie to you. It's never going to stop hurting. This loss will be painful for the rest of your life. But eventually, the hurt will feel different. The pain will be less sharp, more bearable. Ronnie's memory won't always bring you grief."

Forcibly wiping the tears from my cheeks, I look up at her. "Thank you...even if I don't believe you, it was nice to hear."

Tanya sweetly smiles back at me. "Okay, now give me the Cliffs Notes version and get your butt out of here."

Before packing up my stuff and leaving the unit, I give Tanya a report on my patients and new admission. I wasn't able to say goodbye to Lucie; she was still bathing the patient in room 542 when I left.

I'm just so thankful to have such a great charge nurse and friend. Charge nurse Marilyn never would've been this understanding. She never liked me. I bet she's enjoying her retirement. And enjoying not having to see me thirty-six hours a week.

I'm seated outside Summit Valley Hospital on a freezing cement bench, waiting for Miles to pull up. I'm too upset to drive. The winter night air chills me to my core. Wrapping my coat tightly around my body, I continue to shiver. I can't help it when my tears begin to fall once more. I feel like all I'm good at these days is crying. One thing I'm definitely not good at right now is being a nurse. I wasn't strong—I was weak...so incredibly weak.

Tonight, I failed. I failed my patients and my coworkers. But most of all, I failed my friend. How did I not see how deeply she was suffering? How could I have left her alone that night?

*I'm sorry, Ronnie. I failed you.*

# CHAPTER FIFTY-FIVE

## (April 2016):

I was pleasantly surprised when I was canceled from work tonight. Our floor has had an abnormally low census of patients the last few days. I'm now on a mission not to let a Saturday night off go to waste.

This weekend, Miles went back to West Virginia to visit his dad and sister. I offered to put in a PTO request at work so I could go with him to finally meet his family. He shot me down, saying there'd be plenty of other opportunities for me to meet them.

When I first got the call from work about my shift being canceled, I texted Miles and offered once more to drive out to his dad's house. His dad lives in Charleston, West Virginia, where Miles grew up. It's only a little more than three hours' drive from Bristol. I didn't mind making the drive to Charleston alone; I just really wanted to meet my boyfriend's family.

But once again, Miles shot me down. He said that it'd be pointless for me to drive out tonight. I wouldn't get there until around 10:00 PM, and he was planning on coming back home early Monday morning. Effectively, I'd only be able to come out there for one full day. Personally, I didn't think it was pointless if I got to meet his dad and sister, but who was I to argue? Maybe I'm just being sensitive, but I'm starting to get the feeling he doesn't want me there.

I take a long sip from my vodka juice-box cocktail. We're out of cranberry and orange juice, so a juice-box was my last resort. I begin slowly scrolling through my contacts in search of someone to spend my Saturday night with.

*Honestly, I should've just drank the vodka straight.*

Jill isn't an option—she's having dinner with Max. These days, it seems if she isn't at work, she's with Max. Don't get me wrong, I really like Max. I love that he treats her like the queen she is, but I miss my friend. It feels really lonely in the apartment without her, and I don't like being here alone anymore.

I text Craig, seeing if he wants to hang out. He promptly texts me back. Apparently, he isn't an option either—he's working a late shift tonight at The Cinedome. The newest *Captain America* movie just came out, so I'm sure The Cinedome is packed tonight.

Maybe I should go to the movies? I don't really want to see a movie by myself, though.

I try Tony next, asking what his plans are for tonight. He also immediately texts back:

**At The Barn Door with Calvin and some guys from the academy. Aren't you at work?**

I almost forgot to mention, Anthony Hernandez has been officially accepted back into the Bristol County Fire Academy. I never doubted him for a second.

**My shift got canceled.**

**Get your butt down here then. Brett just got here. He's off tonight too.**

**I'll be there in 30.**

I've only had one drink, so I think I'm okay to drive. I jump off of the couch and skip into my room to change out of my pajamas. It's a last-minute decision, but I'm going to wear a dress tonight. For once, I'm off work on a Saturday. I'm dressing up!

Reaching into the back of my closet, I grab the dress I want. Slowly, I run my fingers over the black fabric. No longer do I have to borrow this dress; now, it's mine. God, I wish it was still borrowed. That'd mean she'd still be alive.

After Ronnie's death, Craig was too distraught to go through her belongings. Her parents didn't want to intrude on their daughter's privacy, either, even if she was no longer here. They asked Jill and me if we'd go through her things. Ronnie's parents had told us to keep what we wanted and donate the rest. I decided to keep this dress and a pretty silver necklace with a pendant depicting the tree of life.

I first slip on Ronnie's form-fitting, little black dress, then finish my look by placing her tree of life necklace around my neck. After chugging the rest of my juice-box cocktail, I stare at myself in the bathroom mirror.

"You always looked way better in this dress," I remark, aloud. Over the last few months, I often find myself talking to her. Sometimes, I wonder if I'm slowly going insane.

I decide to wear my contact lenses instead of my glasses tonight, and I quickly curl my hair. Sorry, Tony—I guess I'll be there in more like an hour. Rifling through my makeup bag, I search for a nude lipstick to complete my outfit. When I inadvertently grab a tube of red lipstick, I change my mind. Ronnie would want me to wear the red.

If Ronnie was a color, she definitely wasn't a neutral one. She'd been a bold, beautiful shade of red. I apply the deep red lipstick, then stare at my reflection in the mirror, watching as a lone tear rolls down my cheek.

"I miss you," I whisper.

The Barn Door's parking lot is packed. After having to park in the back of the lot, I begin the long trek to the bar entrance. There's no way I could force my poor feet into a pair of heels tonight. Instead, I wore my favorite black high-top Chucks to accompany Ronnie's little black dress.

Swinging open the heavy wooden door, I enter the bar. I don't think I've ever seen it this busy. There are people everywhere. Scanning the crowd in search of my friends, I manage to spot Tony at our usual table with a group of men. I smile when I see Calvin sitting beside him.

Calvin is such a delightful person. He's easily become the newest member of our pack. I've grown to absolutely love him over the last few months. I have a strong feeling Tony just might love him, too. As Veronica would have said, I'm totally "shipping" them. Tony deserves to be happy, and I've never seen him happier than he is when he's with Calvin.

Calvin notices me first, and he instantly waves me over. I point to the bar to indicate I'm going to grab a drink first. The bar is just as packed as the parking lot, but I'm eventually able to squeeze through the crowd and secure a spot at the bar between two men.

Van grins at me from across the bar. "I'll be over in a sec!"

"Take your time!" I yell back to him.

"Well, well, well. Look who it is," the man to my right remarks. I look up and realize it's Nathan—Brett's asshole co-worker. Gross.

Brett peeks his head around Nathan to see who he's talking to. His eyes widen when he sees me. "Sam. Why aren't you at work?"

"Hi, Brett." I purposefully don't acknowledge Nathan. "I was canceled."

"I'm surprised you didn't go to the wedding then," he replies.

I stare back at him. I'm sure the confusion is apparent on my face. "What wedding?"

Brett's face falls as he realizes he's probably just said something he shouldn't have. "Uh, never mind. Let me buy you a drink."

Pushing past Nathan, I stand directly in front of Brett. "Damn, Sam," Nathan mutters.

I continue ignoring his existence as I stare daggers at Brett. "What wedding?"

"I'm not sure why he didn't tell you," Brett murmurs. "Miles's sister is getting married tonight. That's why Miles went back to Charleston this weekend." Instantly, my stomach drops. Why wouldn't Miles want me to go to his sister's wedding with him?

"I can't believe he didn't tell me." I can't believe my boyfriend hid his sister's wedding from me. Locking eyes with Brett, his pale blue eyes stare back at me. "Why aren't you there?" Miles and Brett grew up together. It seems odd he wouldn't be invited to Miles's sister's wedding.

"Uh, well...Kylie and I used to date in high school. It didn't really end well."

"Who *hasn't* Brett dated?" Nathan laughs. "My man here pulls all the chicks!"

*Ew. I can't stand this guy.*

"I can't believe you dated Miles's sister," I say. I also can't believe I wasn't invited to her wedding. Now, there isn't a doubt in my mind that Miles doesn't want me to meet his family. What does this mean for our relationship?

"Hey, folks. Sorry about the wait. What can I get y'all?" Van drawls.

"Two Budweisers and a..." Brett hesitates when he glances at me before finishing his order, "...and a cranberry vodka."

"And a double shot of vodka," I add. Both Brett and Nathan turn to look at me.

"What?" I snip at them. Tonight, I'm taking shots because tonight I don't care.

"Someone's trying to have fun tonight," Nathan grins. "It's a shame your boyfriend left you behind. I can keep you company, though."

Nathan reaches over to hand me my double shot of vodka. "I'm good," I sneer, grabbing my shot and throwing it back.

Out of nowhere, Brett forcibly shoves Nathan into the bar. "What the hell, man?" Nathan yells, appearing just as shocked as I am.

"You do realize that's my best friend's girlfriend you're talking to like that?"

"Calm down, bro. She knows I'm joking."

Brett turns away from Nathan to lock eyes with me. His pale blue eyes have once again turned to ice. "Did you think Nathan's joke was funny?"

Snatching my vodka cranberry off the bar top, I smile sweetly at Brett. "Nathan's joke was about as pathetic as he is." Then, I turn and saunter off towards where Tony and Calvin are sitting. My response must've caught Brett off guard because I can hear him burst into laughter as I walk away.

I know I'm being petty, but I'll never like this man. Not after what he did to Ronnie.

As it gets later—and I get drunker—I contemplate texting Miles to confront him about not inviting me to the wedding. Technically, he didn't lie to me. But he wasn't completely honest either.

"I'll drive you home tonight," Calvin leans over and whispers to me as I down another shot.

"Thank you," I slur in response. I'm way past the point of being able to drive, now.

Nathan walks over to our group with two women beside him. One of the women sits down next to Brett. She lightly places her hand on his arm as she greets him. I wonder if this one is Brett's newest girlfriend. I watch in horror as Nathan grabs the other woman's ass, uttering something completely degrading at her.

I know hate is a strong word, but I hate this man. I'm visibly cringing at his actions. When I look back over to him, I'm shocked to see he's now glaring at me. He proceeds to stomp around the perimeter of our table to where I'm sitting. Towering over me, he continues glaring as he snarls at me, "Alright, Sam. It's obvious you've got a problem with me. I'm getting sick and tired of your dirty looks and bitchy little comments."

Everyone around the table falls silent. Tony immediately gets up from his seat, walking around the table to stand behind where I'm sitting. Nathan then turns his glare on Tony. Meanwhile, I remain seated—Nathan isn't worth standing for. I can confront him from the comfort of my chair.

Looking up at Nathan, I smile. "If you didn't act like such a chauvinistic pig, I wouldn't give you dirty looks." Glancing across the table at Nathan's date, I address her next. "I know I don't know you, but I know you deserve better than him."

That's when Nathan grabs me by my wrist, physically pulling me out of my chair and toward him until our faces are almost touching. "Is that what you're mad about? Or is it that your friend had sex with me then offed herself?"

Standing before him, I'm left stunned. I wrap my hand—the one Nathan isn't clutching—around the pendant of my necklace. Ronnie's necklace. "Don't you ever speak of her again."

Before Nathan can respond, Tony dives between us. He pushes Nathan away from me, standing in front of me defensively. "Get the hell out of here!"

Nathan laughs sarcastically. "Who's gonna make me?"

"ME!" Tony booms, anger emanating from his voice.

Calvin steps beside me now, whispering in my ear, "Are you okay?"

"I'm fine," I reply. Calvin slips his hand into mine, giving it a squeeze. Then, he and I step forward in unison to stand beside Tony. I slip my free hand into Tony's shaking one. "Correction. We will," I announce, throwing Tony a quick smile.

Nathan laughs even louder. "Do you actually think I'm scared? Scared of a bitch and two..." That's when Nathan hurls a homophobic slur at Tony and Calvin—you know the one. My jaw hits the floor. Gasps ring out around the bar in reaction to Nathan's indefensible outburst.

*Hate isn't even a strong enough word to describe how I feel about this man.*

Before either of us can respond, Brett calmly walks over to where Nathan is standing...and coldcocks him. Nathan falls to the ground with one punch. Mind you, it was one extremely hard punch, but still. Nathan struggles to lift himself off the floor, blood pouring from his possibly broken nose.

Brett moves to punch him again, fists clenched. Before he can, I release my grip on Tony's and Calvin's hands, hurling myself at him. I wrap my arms around his torso as I collide into his back. "You don't want to be that person," I tell him. Instantly, his body relaxes in my arms. Then he turns around to face me. "You don't want to be that person," I reiterate, as I think back on his and my conversation in his hotel room after Zach's wedding. "You're not that person anymore."

He sighs, staring into my eyes. "Remember when I said you have a way of bringing out the worst in me?"

"Um, yes," I reply, confused.

"Well, you also have this way of bringing out the best in me," he grins, before yelling over his shoulder, "Get the hell out of here, Nathan!"

"Are you really choosing *them*? Choosing these losers over *me*?" Nathan sputters, finally managing to bring himself to a stand.

Brett turns away from me to face Nathan. "I'll always choose them. One hundred percent. Over and over again. I'll choose them. They're my pack."

"I thought calling ourselves a pack was corny," I remind him.

He laughs. "Shut up, Sam."

"He loves us, he really loves us," Tony swoons exaggeratedly, at which point Brett turns back around to roll his eyes at the three of us.

Nathan takes one large step towards Brett, getting in his face. "You can't kick me out. This isn't your bar, asshole!"

Please don't fight, Brett. Please. Nathan isn't worth it.

"But I can!" Van announces. As he approaches us through the crowd with a baseball bat in hand, he points directly at Nathan. "Get the fuck out of here!"

"Seriously? *He's* the one who punched *me*!" Nathan yells, motioning to Brett.

"Yeah, and you deserved it." Van pats Brett respectfully on the shoulder.

"This is unbelievable! You better believe I'm going to tell every person I know not to come to this shithole anymore!" Nathan barks at Van.

"Well, if they think it's acceptable to talk to people like you just did...they're not welcome here either," Van says.

The bar erupts into a loud cheer which, by the sound of it, indicates to me that the occupants at The Barn Door agree with Van; we don't tolerate any form of discrimination here.

Nathan sneers at Brett and me before marching over to the woman he was with. He snaps at her, "Let's go, Candace!"

"I'm good," Candace retorts, confidently walking away from him, flipping her bleach-blonde hair.

Nathan is incensed, screaming, "Fuck you all!" As he finally storms out of The Barn Door, the bar erupts into cheers once more.

*Good riddance.*

Ding-Dong! The Asshole's Gone.

# CHAPTER FIFTY-SIX:

The night has become a lot more enjoyable since Nathan exited, stage right. I've almost managed to forget about the whole wedding debacle. I'm sure Miles has his reasons for not inviting me. For all I know, maybe it's just an extremely small wedding and no one could bring a plus one. I only wish he would've been honest with me, but that's something we'll talk about when he gets back.

"So, do you think things will be awkward at the firehouse now?" I casually ask Brett.

"Nah. If Nathan gives me shit, I'll just kick his ass." Brett takes a long sip from his bottle of beer.

"Brett! Fighting is not the answer," I scold. *Ugh, I just sounded like Margo. When did I become "the mom" of the pack?*

"Seems pretty ironic coming from someone who tackled me in the middle of a wedding reception," he chuckles.

"Are you still hung up on that? It was one time!"

Brett smirks at me and I snort with laughter. "Plus, Tony's about to be part of that firehouse," he says. "Nathan needs to understand that treating Tony the way he did tonight won't be tolerated at work.

Tony's one of the best people I know, and he's going to be an excellent firefighter. It doesn't matter who he loves."

I smile at him. "You're a good person, Brett. A lot better of a person than I initially gave you credit for."

He grins back at me. "Being your friend has made me a better person."

"Alright, alright. Don't get all sappy on me," I laugh, giving him a playful nudge.

"Hey, I literally knocked a guy out less than an hour ago! I'm not sappy!" Then, he leans over and steals my vodka cranberry off the table, taking a quick drink from it.

"Give me that!" I shriek, cackling with laughter.

He hands my drink back to me then stands from his chair. "I'm gonna get another beer. Want anything?" Brett asks.

I point to my half-empty glass. "Another one of these, please." Brett nods his understanding, then turns to walk towards the bar.

Taking another sip of my cocktail, I pull my phone out of my purse just as AC/DC's "Highway to Hell" starts playing throughout the bar. I smile at the memories this song brings me as I glance across the bar at Calvin and Tony playing pool.

While I wait for Brett to return with our drinks, I decide to mindlessly scroll through Facebook. I stare at my phone screen as I chug the remainder of my vodka cranberry. After I hit "like" on a picture of someone's adorable dog, I keep scrolling and see another person I went to high school with had a baby. How did we keep track of every single tiny detail of another person's life before social media? Oh yeah, we didn't.

Right before I close the app, I notice a tagged picture on Miles's timeline. Miles never really goes on Facebook, so it's not often that anything appears on his page. The picture is of a pretty, petite blonde woman sitting on Miles's lap, kissing his cheek. Then, I look down at the caption which reads, "My super hot wedding date tonight."

Gasping, I drop my phone onto the wooden table. *This mother-fucker is cheating on me!*

My heart starts to race, as I dramatically jump out of my chair. Clenching my fists at my sides, I scream across the bar to Tony and Calvin. "Miles is cheating on me!"

Instantly, Tony and Calvin turn to stare at me. Both their mouths fall open in shock, then they both begin sprinting over to me.

Brett reaches me before they do. "What's going on?" He sets our drinks down onto the table just as Tony and Calvin approach.

"Look!" I shriek, shoving my phone at the three of them. "How could he do this to me?" I start to cry. "That's why he didn't want me at the wedding!" Tony and Calvin both look stunned.

"Miles would never do that," Tony gasps.

Brett yanks the phone out of my hand, examining the Facebook photo more closely. "Tony's right. Miles would never cheat on you. I'm sure there's a reasonable explanation."

"How are you two defending him?" I shout, throwing my arms in the air. "The proof is literally in your hands!" I turn to glare at Brett. "Who is she? I thought you were my friend. How could you hide this from me?"

"Hold on a second." Now, Brett's yelling, too. "Why do you automatically think I know about this?" He thrusts my phone back at me.

"Because you're his best friend and his roommate. You know everything about him."

"I don't know anything about this," Brett responds, more calmly now. "I do know who she is, though. She's Kylie's best friend—her maid of honor—but Miles would never do that to you."

The tears are streaming down my face. "Have they ever dated?"

"No. Miles used to have a huge crush on her in high school, but she was never interested in him." Brett's answer may have been honest, but his words strike me like daggers.

I fall to my knees, covering my face with my hands. "Well, she sure seems interested now."

"Probably not the best time to mention that last detail," Calvin tells Brett.

"Yeah, no shit! I see that now!" Brett snaps before kneeling beside me. "He would never cheat on you, Sam. You're his entire world." He wraps his arm around me, trying in vain to comfort me.

"Can you hand me my cellphone?" Brett obliges, grabbing my phone from where I dropped it on the ground. He places it into my trembling hand.

Before anyone can stop me, I call Miles. He picks up on the second ring. I put my phone on speaker.

"Hey, honey," he answers. I can tell he's attempting to muffle the noise behind him.

"How's the wedding?" I hiss at him.

He's silent for a beat, then he replies. "Sam, I can explain."

"Have you checked your Facebook lately? Can you explain the woman sitting on your lap, kissing you?"

"Wh—what?"

"I thought you loved me!"

"I do love you," he responds. "You know I'd never cheat on you!"

"LIAR!" I screech. "I hate you!"

"Sam! STOP!" He's yelling now, too. "Are you drunk?"

"That's none of your business. I hope you have an amazing night, Miles!" I reply sarcastically. "You can do whatever—or whoever—you want now. Because WE ARE DONE!"

Brett turns to me in shock, scolding me. "Sam!"

The sound of his voice gets Miles's attention. "Is that Brett? Are you with Brett?"

"That's none of your business either," I shoot back.

"Let me talk to him!" Miles snaps.

"FUCK YOU!" I scream into the phone. As soon as I hang up the phone, I hurl it against the wall. "Fuck him." My shaking body collapses back to the ground. When I hear Brett's cellphone ring, I spit, "Don't you dare answer him!"

"Sam, come on," Brett pleads. I glare up at him and he reluctantly obliges. He shoves his vibrating phone back into his pocket.

I look at my friends, begging them, "Please, no one answer him."

Slowly, Tony walks back over to us with my cellphone in hand. "Your phone screen is broken," he tells me.

"Yeah, just like my heart." I know I'm being dramatic, but I don't care.

"Oh, baby girl," Tony consoles me as he kneels beside me. He wraps his arms around me, and I collapse into him, sobbing.

Brett mutters under his breath, "Dammit, Miles."

I go to stand up, wiping a tear from my cheek. "I need a shot."

"No, you don't," Brett replies. "What you need is to go home. Come on, Sam. I'm taking you home, now." He walks over to me, helping lift me the rest of the way off the floor, setting me on my feet.

"I don't want to go home," I whine. "I want to keep drinking."

"I don't care what you want. I'm taking you home."

I look to Tony and Calvin for help; neither of them will look at me.

"Are you okay to drive?" Tony asks Brett.

"I'm fine," he responds. "I've only had two beers." Brett motions for me to follow him. "Let's go, Sam."

"You need help?" Calvin offers.

"It's okay. I'll calm her down," Brett calls over his shoulder. As if I'm not standing right here.

I turn to Tony and Calvin. "Bye," I mutter. Then, I follow Brett, my head hung low. I don't want to go home. I don't want to be alone. Not in that apartment—not tonight.

When we reach Brett's truck, he opens the passenger door for me. I try not to let my dress ride up my thighs as I climb into his truck. I'm so glad I didn't wear heels tonight.

I watch as Brett saunters around the front of the truck, then climbs in through the driver's side. He's in the process of putting his key into the ignition when the words start tumbling out of my mouth. "Why did you kiss me?" I blurt.

Brett freezes. He turns to lock eyes with me. "What?"

"On my patio. Why did you kiss me?"

He blinks repeatedly, in what looks like an attempt to focus his vision on me. He sighs before responding. "Why are you asking me this?"

"Why are you answering my question with a question? It's annoying."

Brett laughs, tossing his keys onto the dashboard. He rotates his entire body to face me. He finally answers my question, straight-faced. "Because I wanted to. If you haven't noticed by now, I kind of just do what I want."

I inch my body closer to his, knowing this is wrong. I know I should stop...but I don't care. I'm hurt and I want the hurting to end. I want to feel wanted. I don't want to be alone. And maybe, subconsciously, I want Miles to hurt, too. I know there's no better way to hurt him than *this*. "And what is it you want to do to me right now?" I purr.

He takes a sharp inhale of breath, and I watch as his pupils dilate. Scooting myself further across the truck's bench seat, I don't stop until I'm almost touching him.

After a long moment of silence, he finally replies. "You don't know what you're doing, Sam. You're drunk." He sighs, swiping his keys from the dashboard and turning back towards the steering wheel.

"I know exactly what I'm doing. What? You don't want me?"

Brett forcefully throws his keys back onto the dash, making me jump at the sound. He whips his body back around to face me. "This isn't fair," he says, motioning to me. "You already made your decision, and you chose him. ...You chose *him*—he's my best friend, Sam."

"Yeah, but we broke up. We're done."

"The two of you break up then get back together once every six months," Brett groans. "It's exhausting." He grabs his keys off the dash once more, shoving the key into the ignition.

But before he can turn it, I do something that shocks even me. I climb onto his lap, straddling his waist. I run one of my hands through his cropped blonde hair. His breath catches as he stares at me, speechless. I lightly trace his bottom lip with the pad of my thumb. I then move my thumb to graze my own lip, all the while, my eyes never leaving his. He doesn't move; he just continues staring at me.

"I'm going to ask you this one last time—then, I'll never ask you again." He continues staring at me, silent. "Do you want me?"

His hands move to my waist. For a second, I think he's going to push me off him. Instead, one of his hands moves to my face. He then lightly traces my bottom lip with his own thumb, mimicking my gesture. My lips slightly part at his touch, while his pale blue eyes bore into me. "I've always wanted you, Sam," he finally responds. "Since the day I met you."

"Then answer my question, Brett. What do you want to do to me right now?"

"Everything," he breathes, wrapping his fingers around my loose curls. He pulls me down to him, and our mouths meet.

I know I'll regret this tomorrow. I know what I'm doing is wrong. But I don't care. I don't want to think anymore. I just want to feel...and all I can feel is him.

I pull Brett's shirt over his head, tossing it to the floor of the truck. I greedily run my fingers across his sculpted abdomen before resuming our kiss. That's when I hear a loud knock on the driver's side window. Audibly gasping, I quickly pull away from Brett. He and I stare at one another for a moment before we both turn to look out the window.

Tony is standing outside of Brett's truck, staring back at us in shock. Brett gently slides me off his lap, onto the bench seat. Wordlessly, he hops out of his truck, still shirtless, and slams the driver's side door closed behind him. I can hear him and Tony start to argue.

I slowly open the driver's side door, following Brett's lead, and slide out of the truck. That's when I hear Tony yell, "You sure as hell calmed her down, didn't you Brett?"

"Shut up, Tony!" Brett snaps.

Then, Tony looks at me. "You forgot your cellphone." He hands me my phone with its now-cracked screen. "Come on, Sam. Calvin and I will take you home." Behind him, I can see Calvin leaning against his SUV across the parking lot.

"I'm going with Brett," I say, looking up at Brett. He refuses to look back at me.

"I just got off the phone with Miles. He was in tears," Tony tells me.

"I don't care," I say, crossing my arms in front of my chest. He's the one who cheated on me. At least I had the decency to break up with him before I kissed someone else.

"I can see that," Tony mutters under his breath. I glare at him in response. Then, Tony walks over to me, putting both his hands on my shoulders before he lightly shakes me. "Earth to Samantha Carter," he says. "I'm trying to prevent you from doing something you'll probably regret for the rest of your life. Let's go."

I jerk away from Tony. "I'm going with Brett!" When I look towards Brett once again, he's still refusing to look back at me.

"Go with Tony," he eventually mumbles.

"But...but," I stammer. "What about the things you said in the truck?"

When Brett snaps his head back, finally looking at me, his vision has turned to ice. "I don't give a shit about what I said in the truck. Go with Tony!"

"I don't want to," I squeak, taking a step towards him.

Brett takes two steps backward, trying to avoid any contact with me. "I don't want you to come with me," he growls. "I don't want you, Sam! I DON'T WANT YOU!"

At first, his words bring tears to my eyes; then, I become angry. All I see is red. I throw myself towards him, slamming my trembling palms against his bare chest.

"SAM!" Tony yells my name.

I shove Brett's body into the side of his truck with all my might. He glares down at me, grabbing my wrists, removing my hands from his chest.

"Tell me what this is, Brett!" I scream at him.

He looks at me confused. "What the hell are you talking about, Sam?" He places both of my arms down at my sides. His hands slowly move from my wrists to encapsulate my now clenched fists, in what I can only assume is an attempt to prevent me from hitting him again.

"Is this the best of you? Or the worst?" I hiss in his face, wrenching my arms out of his grasp, before turning and running towards Calvin's SUV.

When I climb into Calvin's car, I keep my head down, remaining silent in the backseat. I can feel Calvin's eyes on me, but I refuse to look up. A few seconds later, I hear the front passenger door open, then slam shut.

"Sam." It's Tony. I force myself to meet his gaze, his dark brown eyes staring back at me. Eyes full of an understanding that I don't deserve. He hands me back my purse. "You left it in Brett's truck."

"Thanks," I mutter. Tony's body remains turned toward me from the passenger seat as he continues staring back at me. Calvin proceeds to cautiously pull his vehicle out of the space where we're currently parked. "You think I'm a horrible person, don't you?"

"I think you're a normal person who's learning how to cope with some pretty horrible things," Tony replies.

I can feel the tears beginning to pool in my eyes. "Stop being so nice to me, Tony. I don't deserve it."

That's when Tony swiftly unbuckles his seatbelt and throws himself into the backseat. He seats himself in the middle, directly next to me. I can't help but smile at my friend.

"Anthony!" Calvin scolds. "The car is in motion! Seatbelts for safety. Please, buckle up."

Tony and I both laugh at Calvin's apparent concern. Tony obliges, and I hear the click of the seatbelt as he buckles it. Then, he leans over, wrapping his arm around me and placing a kiss on my cheek.

"You know, you and I are a lot alike," he says. "I've done a lot of amazing things in my life, but I've also made my fair share of mistakes. It took me a long time to realize the common denominator of the majority of those mistakes was alcohol."

"Do you think I'm an alcoholic?" I nervously bite my lip, awaiting his response.

"I just want you to know that you're not alone, Sam." It's not lost on me that he didn't technically answer my question. "If you ever want to grab some coffee with me, Calvin, and a few other badass people, you have an open invite."

"Are you referring to your Sober Squad?"

Calvin laughs from the front seat. "We're a judgment-free group. We're even welcoming to people who don't do CrossFit."

"Just think of us as a group of superheroes who all have the same kryptonite—alcohol," Tony jokes, giving my shoulder a loving squeeze.

"This isn't fair!" I giggle. "You're using Superman references and enticing me with coffee."

"Oh, am I?" he smiles coyly at me. "Things have been pretty rough for us all since we lost her. I just want to make sure you know that you're not alone."

I rest my head on his shoulder. "I miss her every day," I murmur.

"Me too," Tony whispers, resting his own head against mine. We don't say her name—we don't have to.

*I wonder if she knows all the heartache she left behind. I wonder if she thought about us before she chose to leave. Sometimes I can't help but wonder why we weren't enough to convince her to stay.*

Calvin pulls into my apartment complex. I hate that I'm going home alone. Drunk and alone. I'm starting to realize that I feel even more alone when I'm drunk. Hopefully, Jill is home by now.

"I'll walk you up," Tony says, pulling me away from my thoughts.

"Not necessary." I force myself to smile at him.

"If you haven't noticed, I'm the most unnecessary person that's ever existed!" Tony exclaims, throwing his arm into the air and striking a pose.

I snort with laughter as Calvin looks over his shoulder, chiming in, "Who can say no to that?"

"I'm irresistible," Tony claims, shooting a quick glance at Calvin, before sliding out of the SUV. He runs around the back of the vehicle to open my door for me. "My lady," he grins as he offers me his hand.

"Thanks for driving me home, Calvin," I call up to the front seat before placing my hand in Tony's and hopping out of the SUV.

"Anytime," Calvin replies as I shut the door.

Once we reach my front door, I pull Tony into a hug. "Thank you," I whisper.

"You and Miles will work this out," he insists.

"This time...I'm not so sure. He betrayed me." I release Tony from my embrace before moving to unlock my front door.

"Don't get offended," Tony starts. I pause, looking back at him, my hand still on the door handle. "You're a bit of a reactionary person," he says. "Just talk to him. Well, first listen...then talk."

I sigh. "I'll call him tomorrow when I'm sober."

"Good girl." Tony smiles at me before turning around and jogging down the cement steps.

"You should talk to *him*, too," I yell down to Tony.

He stops mid-jog and looks back at me. "I've already talked to Miles tonight, remember?"

"I mean Calvin—tell him how you feel."

Tony slightly tilts his head, staring up at me before giving a quick chuckle. "That obvious, huh?"

"Sooo obvious," I smirk with a dramatic roll of my eyes.

"Night, Sam!" He turns back around and finishes his jog down the steps.

I watch as he gets into the passenger seat of Calvin's SUV before I finally enter my apartment. I flip on the light switch, then turn to lock the door behind me.

"Jill?" I call. No answer. I look down at my phone screen to check the time. Almost midnight. She's probably already asleep. I also note that I've missed seven calls, all from Miles.

Should I call him back tonight? We should really both be sober for this conversation. I know he's been drinking tonight, too; but probably nowhere near as much as me.

Maybe I'll wake up Jill to ask her opinion. Technically, this is an emergency. You're allowed to wake your best friend up in the middle of the night for relationship emergencies. And to help you kill giant spiders. You shouldn't have to handle either of these situations without your best friend.

I kick off my Chucks at the entryway to our apartment and pad sock-footed to Jill's bedroom door. Archie is hot on my heels—as usual—with his tightly-curled tail. Lightly tapping on Jill's door with my knuckle, I call out once more, "Jill?" Again, no answer.

I creak open the bedroom door and peek inside her pitch-black bedroom. I open the flashlight app on my phone to briefly illuminate her room. Jill's bed sits in the middle of the room, perfectly made and without her in it.

She must've stayed at Max's house tonight. Which is fine, I just wish she would've given me a heads-up. Not like she needs my permission to stay at her boyfriend's house, it just would've been nice if she texted me.

I know it's selfish to feel this way, but I can't help it. Sometimes I feel as if I'm losing her, too.

Quietly shutting Jill's door, I walk back into the living room. I collapse onto the sectional after grabbing the remote off the coffee table. Archie leaps onto the couch. He walks in three small circles before plopping down onto the cushion beside me, letting out a long sigh followed by a few grunts in the process.

"Same, Archie. Same," I chuckle as I flip on the television and start surfing through the channels. I stop on the Travel Channel when I see an episode of *Ghost Adventures* is playing. I don't know why I'm watching this—I usually only watch this show when Jill forces me to.

I'm about ten minutes into the episode when I hear a knock at the front door. Archie starts barking as he runs to the door. "Shit!" I scream, jumping off the couch. Did I forget something in Calvin's car?

I scurry over to the front door, timidly peering through the peephole. When I see who's standing at my door, I rapidly unlock it and swing it open. My hands fly to my hips. "Can I help you?"

This man has a lot of nerve coming here considering how he talked to me tonight.

"Why can't it be both?" Brett stands awkwardly on my patio. I'm not inviting him in.

"I see you found your shirt," I sneer, leaning against the doorway.

"Why can't we be both?" He takes a small step towards me. I glance down, noticing his boots are covered in mud. Where the hell did he go after we left him in the parking lot?

"Are you high?" I laugh. "You're saying some crazy shit."

I expect him to laugh, too. Or at least smile. But he doesn't. He remains stone-faced.

"What if you and I are both, Sam?" He takes another step towards me, now standing only a foot or so away from me. I move my body slightly so I'm standing straight, looking up at him.

"Both what?" I ask, confused.

"What if we're the worst and the best? What if I feel guilty for coming here tonight, but I know I'd always regret it if I didn't? What if you drive me absolutely insane, yet I can never stop thinking about you?" He rests his hand on the doorframe above my head as he gazes down at me. For some reason, I can't think straight. Not when he's looking at me like that. "You asked me earlier what I wanted to do to you, Sam. The answer's actually pretty simple..." He hesitates momentarily before continuing. "I want to be with you."

I gasp. It feels like the wind was just knocked out of me. I stand frozen, staring up at him. I can't find the right words—or any words, for that matter. I'm undeniably speechless. That's when Brett's palm finds the small of my back, and he gently pulls my body into his. His other hand comes up to softly cup my cheek. He tilts his head toward mine, our faces mere inches apart. "If we do this, you need to know it can't be undone. There's no going back." His voice is barely above a whisper. "I'm only going to ask you this once. What do you want, Sam?"

From the depths of my consciousness, I hear a voice. A voice that's neither mine nor Brett's. A voice from my past. Her voice. *He's your person, Sam. Don't let him go. Don't make my mistakes.*

Miles. I can't do this to Miles.

But the longer I stare into these pale blue eyes, the more her voice fades. The less I think of Miles. I feel the warmth of his breath on my lips, and that's when her voice vanishes completely. That's when all I can think of is him.

*No longer does anything in my life feel certain. These days, there isn't much that I'm sure of at all. That is—except for the words that I utter next.*

"I don't want to go back."

Sam's story isn't over and neither is yours. Please continue to write your story;

**National Suicide Prevention Lifeline**

800-273-8255

https://suicidepreventionlifeline.org